MW01101922

MARKET CRASH

3194-ISLA

MARKET CRASH

FRANCIS BLAKE

3194-ISLA

Copyright © 2000 by Francis Blake.

Library of Congress Number:		00-192838
ISBN #:	Hardcover	0-7388-7830-8
	Softcover	0-7388-7402-7

All rights reserved. No part of this book may be reproduced or
transmitted in any form or by any means, electronic or mechanical,
including photocopying, recording, or by any information storage and
retrieval system, without permission in writing from the copyright
owner.

This is a work of fiction. Names, characters, places and incidents
either are the product of the author's imagination or are used
fictitiously, and any resemblance to any actual persons, living or
dead, events, or locales is entirely coincidental.

This book was printed in the United States of America.

To order additional copies of this book, contact:
Xlibris Corporation
1-888-7-XLIBRIS
www.Xlibris.com
Orders@Xlibris.com

CONTENTS

DEDICATION

To my six adorable and beautiful children,
Dan, Olympia, Chloe, Clarissa, Tristan and Georgina.
You are the princes and princesses of my heart
and the love of my life.
May God's blessings be upon you forever.

3194-ISLA

The Worldly Hope men set their Hearts
upon
Turns Ashes–or it prospers; and
anon,
Like snow upon the Desert's dusty
face,
Lighting a little hour or two–is gone.

Omar Khayyam

PROLOGUE

It was very early in the morning in late July. The sleek blue Jaguar sped along at high speed on U.S. 684 heading towards Manhattan. The good-looking woman at the steering wheel, in the dark blue suit that had Givenchy written all over it, was Alexandra Middleton and she was driving from her weekend home in Bedford for a most important 7.30 A.M. breakfast meeting.

Middleton was at the top of her chosen profession—money management. Newspapers all over the United States quoted her constantly and she appeared frequently on television. She mingled with the rich and powerful and her clients included many of America's leading corporations. She was an ambitious and restless woman who was not content with what she had. She wanted more, much more, and so she was constantly on the move, trying to build her business and become wealthier in the process. Like countless Americans, in this land of opportunity, she was driven by money, secure in the knowledge that money made the world go round.

She pushed a button on the dashboard and within seconds the public radio station FM 96.3 came to life. It was the morning news that the station carried every day of the week.

11

Alexandra heard the announcer say, "Today the Dow will open at 17,278.26 following Friday's twenty two point gain." The voice continued, "It was the fifth straight day that the market has gone up." She knew from sources on the street that money was pouring into stocks in record amounts. Newspaper accounts confirmed the trend. The market had become a one-way street to a shining city on a hill. Stocks had gone up, with scarcely a down year since 1982, but with occasional corrections–some of them rocky–like the one this spring. It was the longest bull market in history. More and more people were giving up their regular jobs. It was so much easier to make money investing in stocks. And so much more fun!

She lowered the volume. The voice droned on. She was no longer really paying attention. Her mind wandered. The economy was humming along. Interest rates were low with hardly any up or down movements. That made bonds unattractive as investments. The returns were considerably less compared with stocks. Her expertise was in the fixed income area–all types of bonds and money market products that paid interest. The stock market was making her job more difficult. Very much more difficult, as more and more institutions and individual investors switched from bonds to equities. But her group, thank God, was hanging in there. She didn't know how long this would last. It wasn't easy to buck the market. Certainly not for long.

There was another problem she had run into. Tired old men, who refused to move off to the sunny golf links of Florida, blocked her road to the top two positions at the firm. And there was something else. Success, as everyone knows, fosters envy. That had happened to her friend Bill Gates a few years earlier and she knew that a few of her colleagues harbored similar ideas. So she was seeking a way out of the dilemma, determined one way or other to achieve her goal. That was the main purpose behind the early morning meeting.

The radio announcer's mention of oil prices turned Alexandra's attention to that commodity. Oil was in plentiful supply once again and the price was back at $10 a barrel. OPEC had become a paper tiger. Amazing how the group had once held the world hostage. Or it seemed then. It was such a distant memory now. Most Americans didn't even remember the cataclysmic events of 1973. And they either didn't care or were unaware of the deep resentment that had been building among the oil producers at America's high-handed actions back in the first year of the new millennium.

Her thoughts turned back to the economy. America had been written-off in the 1980's. Management gurus and other experts led by Peter Drucker had told us ad nauseum, in newspaper and magazine articles, that Japan would soon surpass America as the world's largest economy. They had harped on the superiority of its management system. But events had turned out differently. Very differently. Japan had been mired in recession throughout the 1990's, its economy in a deep coma since then. This was the first year of any significant growth. Both Japan and Europe had been totally inept in the new age of technology that was reshaping the world. It was the Americans who had come out on top. Her entrepreneurs and managers had made their companies the most efficient on earth. Freedom and opportunity obviously made a difference. A smile lit Alexandra's face as she thought how the dollars had kept flowing back to America. First from the Arabs in exchange for military toys and useless hardware. And then from the Japanese in return for real estate–office buildings and golf courses–that had lost much of their value since the 1980's.

Yes, she mused, the last half of the twentieth century had been America's. And the twenty-first century would also be the American century. And the twenty-second as well. Rome had ruled the world for five hundred years. The Brits had

13

done it for almost three hundred years. Now it was America's turn. And there was nothing in sight that could possibly change this preordained order of the universe. She smiled at the thought. God, it seemed, had finally become an American. The triumph of America was complete.

It was the best of times. A time of unprecedented prosperity. The American public believed these times would roll on forever. It was difficult to imagine otherwise. Yet, unknown to anyone, sinister forces were about to be let loose. Something truly awful was just around the corner.

She came closer to the city. The car veered to the left following a curve in the road. The rising sun temporarily blinded Alexandra as its fiery rays lit up the eastern sky. In one quick motion her left hand reached out and pulled the sun visor down. Yankee stadium whizzed by on the left. The skyscrapers of Manhattan were now visible in the distance, rising like giant phalluses to meet the sky. Alexandra loved Paris. London and Rome were beautiful too. But there was no city like New York. No other city gave you the same feeling of power, the same sense of opportunity. It was the city of money and wealth. The adrenalin pumped through her blood. She was ready for the morning meeting.

Just as Alexandra was arriving at the Palace Hotel in New York, a momentous meeting was taking place some six thousand miles away.

It was extremely hot in Riyadh. The shamal was swirling outside to the north of the city, enveloping it in a sandy haze much like the fog that often descends upon San Francisco. Inside the centrally air-conditioned Yamameh Palace conditions couldn't have been more different. The royal residence might just as well have been in Spain or Italy. Only the dress of the footmen and servants gave away its location.

In the ornate eighty-foot long living room King Fahd sat with his brother, Prince Sultan, the Defense Minister, and his half-brother, Crown Prince Abdullah. Each man had an identical list in his hands. It contained the names of all male Saudi princes over the age of twenty five. There were more than five hundred names. Five hundred and nine to be exact. The founder of Saudi Arabia, their father, had been prolific in the children department. And the sons and grandsons had done their duty too. As a result, the House of Saud now numbered some five thousand princes and princesses.

The three corpulent men went over the list carefully. The progeny of each of Saud's fifty five sons was duly examined. They then turned their attention to the grandsons. The meeting lasted several hours. Fahd did most of the talking, but the Crown Prince and Prince Sultan were by no means quiet. They spoke up when they felt it to be necessary.

By six o'clock they had narrowed the list to three names. It was time for the Asar prayers, considered by many Muslims to be the most important of the day's five prayers. The three men adjourned the meeting temporarily.

Fahd, king for twenty one years, had been in failing health for some time. Abdullah and Sultan had been in their positions even longer. Much had changed in the country during this period. Gleaming steel and glass buildings had replaced the mud houses in Riyadh and Jeddah and the other major towns. Cars, four million of them, had taken over from the ubiquitous camel. The country had come out of the dark ages. But beneath the surface there was growing turmoil and restlessness. The three senior members of the Saud family were tired, old men. Saudi Arabia, they agreed, needed a new man from the next generation to lead it in the new century. They were no longer capable of the task. The fate of the Shah of Iran reminded them of what would happen if they failed in their mission.

Fifteen minutes later, their prayers over, the three octogenarians resumed their discussions. Within minutes they arrived at a unanimous agreement. God had surely guided them in their deliberations. The man they selected was Prince

3194-ISLA

Tarik, the second son of their long deceased brother Prince Mishaal.

That's when the trouble started. That decision set into motion the process that would eventually unravel the greatest stock market in the world and spread destruction and financial ruin upon so many unsuspecting people. And untold riches upon others. It would also alter the fate of nations and change the shape of history for the foreseeable future.

CHAPTER 1

The second presidential campaign of the twenty first century was about to begin formally, as it always does, in the dog days of summer.

August 6 was a particularly hot and humid day in Washington D.C. President Bush sat in the centrally air-conditioned Oval Office, chatting with Vice President Dick Cheney. They were awaiting the momentary arrival of an important visitor.

A famous English aristocrat, the first Baron Acton, Regius Professor of Modern History at the University of Cambridge, and one of the most erudite men of his age, had remarked in his inaugural lecture at the great University, as the twentieth century began, that "All power corrupts, and absolute power corrupts absolutely." For almost a century no one had seriously questioned the dictum. But things had changed. In the last decade of the twentieth century events had finally disproved Lord Acton's words.

It was not power but money that corrupted.

The 1990's had been the golden years of the stock market. The equity investment craze had engulfed the whole nation. It had become an addiction like alcohol or cocaine that

17

Americans could no longer do without. The stock market had added twelve trillion dollars to the wealth of Americans. Such a large infusion of money was bound to change behavior.

And it did.

It was in the sizzling 1990's that America, that most idealistic of nations, lost the moral compass that once governed its values and ideals. In the past, Americans had held their Presidents to high standards of behavior. After all, the President was not only the country's chief executive but also its head of state. He was a role model for the nation. About twenty five years earlier, a President had been forced to resign, the first time in the nation's history, over a cover up involving a "third-rate burglary." But that was another era. Then the economy had been heading south. Americans were not so well-off. It was a time of stress and severe economic disparities. The stock market was in the doldrums. The Vietnam War had wounded the country's psyche.

But a new age had dawned in the last decade of the twentieth century, brought about by the enormous growth of wealth through the stock market. Main Street had finally merged with Wall Street. And so for the first time in the history of the republic, a substantial majority of Americans were willing to overlook repeated lying, perjury, adultery and serial sex practiced in the White House by the President so long as he delivered stock market growth. America had become a nation of convenience rather than a nation of conviction. Those who knew Bill Clinton didn't believe him, for he reminded them of the man in Oscar Wilde's play who proudly exclaimed, "I have added a new dimension to truth. I have introduced the element of fiction into it." The old rules were no longer applicable to this President. After all it was only sex and he was associated with the good times; he had done so much for the economy. For similar conduct any other fellow citizen working in corporate America would have been instantly fired. But that was different. They didn't create wealth for the whole nation like the President did.

William Bennett, a frequent critic of the President, lamented in a television interview. "Our economic well-being has now become the only important measure for judging presidential performance. The stock market has brought about the behavioral change. America has finally become a commercial republic. The Promised Land has at long last arrived."

And so the forty-second President of the United States had escaped the Monica Lewinsky affair, just as he had escaped Travel Gate, White Water Gate, File Gate, Paula Jones and several other tawdry scandals. The nation was not prepared to hold Bill Clinton accountable for his actions. But the Republican-controlled House of Representatives had persisted. On Saturday, December 19, 1998 William Jefferson Clinton became the second President in American history to be indicted by the House of Representatives. The Senate tried him. It did not last long. They quickly caved in. The polls showed the people wanted Clinton to stay. In the end it was the congressmen who fell on their swords. Bill Clinton lived to fight another day.

But it had not been a total escape. Clinton's image had been tarnished and he had limped along the remaining two years of his presidency talking a lot, doing little and accomplishing nothing. Concerned about his legacy, he had, in the final few months of his presidency, given all his attention to getting his Vice President, Al Gore, elected as his successor. This relationship, unlike so many others, had endured the test of time. The effort had failed by the narrowest of margins–a few hundred votes in Florida.

The past four years, while not marred by any new scandals, had neither been distinguished by any major achievements. It was a time of small, incremental changes rather than bold new directions. True, the national debt had shrunk by fifty billion dollars but there was nothing that differenti-

3194-ISLA

ated social security, health care or education from the earlier period. In 2001, the Fed had succeeded in slowing down the economy without pushing it into recession and the good times had rolled on. The American public, already contemptuous of the institutions of government, ignored the gridlock and the shenanigans in Washington. It was far too busy getting richer playing the money tree like stock market.

President Bush had easily won the Republican nomination, unopposed, for a second term. All that remained was the crowning at the convention in Atlanta later this month. The well-oiled and formidable Bush machine was ready for action but the presidential election was proving to be troublesome. A sincere but rather boring politician without much charm and who's handling of the English language often evoked general mirth and laughter, Bush was having difficulty keeping up with his Democrat opponent, Senator Bob Kerrey, who had convincingly won his party's nomination, on the first delegate roll call, a day earlier. The latest poll showed Bush just about even with Kerrey.

At exactly ten o'clock in the morning, Patrick Blackwell, acting chairman of the Federal Reserve Board was ushered into the Oval Office. The Fed Chairman usually briefed the president monthly and this was one of those meetings. The presence of the Vice President might have been considered unusual but with the presidential campaign starting, Blackwell was not surprised to see Cheney in the Oval Office.

The acting chairman took the seat opposite the President and began the briefing.

"The economy is in good condition. The latest figures, to be released next week, show that it grew at an annualized rate of 2 ¾ percent in the last quarter."

The President and Vice President nodded. Blackwell went on, "Consumer confidence remains high and inflation continues at the very low levels seen in recent years."

On the economic front the United States appeared to be

in excellent shape. This was the longest expansion in war or peacetime in the nation's history. Much of the credit for this was due to Alan Greenspan the former chairman of the Federal Reserve. The 78-year-old Greenspan, a saint and hero of the Wall Street crowd, had suddenly resigned in early July citing health reasons. Rumor had it that he was in the very first stages of Alzheimer's. He had served as head of the Federal Reserve Board for seventeen years during which period the country had witnessed unprecedented economic growth combined with low inflation and full employment.

Patrick Blackwell, a respected economist, had been appointed two years earlier by Bush as the Vice Chairman of the Fed. More than anything else, Blackwell wanted to be the Fed's next chairman. It was a worthy ambition. After all, most knowledgeable people considered the chairman to be the second most powerful person in the world, after the President of the United States. In fact it was the other way round. With the end of the cold war, the financial markets and the economy had overtaken military might as the twin engines of the world's well being. And in the economic arena the Fed chairman exerted an influence far greater than anyone else including the President. His words and deeds had a substantially larger impact on global markets than anything the president of the United States might say or do–short of declaring war. In the summer of 1997 the Dow Jones Industrial Average had plunged 557 points in a single day after Chairman Greenspan's testimony to Congress in which he had used the words "irrational exuberance" in a reference to the stock market.

"What's the Fed's forecast for the U.S. economy for next year. Or if there is no forecast give me your best guesstimate?" Bush asked.

"Our surveys show that some weakness is beginning to emerge. In fact it is likely to be reflected in next quarter's numbers. The economic expansion has been the longest ever

3194-ISLA

seen. It simply cannot go on forever," Blackwell responded confidently.

George Bush had his faults, but he understood better than most people that the condition of the stock market would be the single most important factor in the coming election. If the American people felt rich, they would vote to keep the Republican Party team that brought them the riches in the first place.

Bush held Blackwell in high regard and was well aware of his driving ambition to be the Fed's chairman. But he had purposely decided not to appoint him to that position at this juncture. Once appointed and confirmed by the Senate, the President usually had very little control over the Fed chairman. And at this late hour in his presidency, Bush knew that he would have none. So he had, very shrewdly, appointed Blackwell as the acting chairman. This suited the Democrats perfectly and they had gone along with the President's decision.

The briefing continued with Bush asking a series of questions. Blackwell confirmed that the market was not expecting any Fed action on interest rates. Yes, the economy had slowed down somewhat and there were signs of further cooling. It was at this point that Bush suggested, in his most forceful manner, that the Fed should lower interest rates by at least 50 basis points after the next meeting of the Federal Open Market Committee in late September. He argued that this would be a pre-emptive move to forestall any decline in the economy next year. The Fed's surveys were showing that such a downturn was in the cards.

Several thoughts raced through Blackwell's mind as the President spoke. Only a Republican victory would secure him the chairman's job. If the Democrats won they would almost certainly nominate their own candidate. And just as certainly it would not be Patrick Blackwell. He remembered that in 1994 Alan Greenspan had unexpectedly raised interest rates, catching the market by complete surprise, to attack incipient inflation. And it had worked. What the President was saying surely made sense. It was a logical argument. He had also been thinking of it. Patrick Blackwell knew that such a move would send the stock market soaring upward to new heights. And that would in all likelihood seal the elections. It would also raise howls from the Democrats. But it was worth the prize. Apart from being a first-class economist, Blackwell was also a history buff. He recalled how the Protestant champion, Henry of Navarre, in another century, under similar circumstances, had converted to Catholicism to win the French throne, justifying his action with the words, "Paris is well worth a mass."

Blackwell came to a decision. He signaled his agreement to the President. The rate cut would be announced, as was the usual practice, immediately after the meeting of the Federal Open Market Committee on Thursday, September 30.

For the first time Vice President Cheney entered the conversation. "We shall never forget this brave move by the Federal Reserve," he assured Blackwell.

President Bush deadpanned, with biting lip sincerity, as Dick Cheney smiled, that Blackwell would undoubtedly have many opportunities, in the future, to put his stamp on the pages of history.

Bush felt elated with the morning's work. His spirits surged. Some one had said that a week was a long time in politics. Bush, who's whole career had been based on the unexpected, had just proven the point once again.

3194-ISLA

CHAPTER 2

On the same Friday, three hours prior to the White House meeting, Sidney Rosenberg stepped out of his apartment building and walked, as usual, the fifteen blocks to his Park Avenue office in midtown Manhattan. It was only seven in the morning and it was already hot. The walk took twenty five minutes and his mind usually meandered on an assortment of newsworthy matters. Today he reflected on the troubles at the firm.

Rosenberg entered his air-conditioned office on the twenty-sixth floor shortly before half past seven. He hung the weathered polyester jacket on a hook on the door, eased his gaunt, five feet eleven inch body onto a green leather chair and extracted a newspaper from a black Louis Vuitton briefcase.

Since joining Bernstein and Paulson–B&P–almost thirty years ago, Rosenberg had always come to the office at this time. Nobody was there this early, and it gave him time to read the newspapers and reflect on the market events of the previous day. He took a sip of the black coffee, purchased from the same sidewalk vendor on the northeast corner of 55th Street, and glanced at the paper. The front page of the

Wall Street Journal had three stories on yesterday's action in the stock market. The Dow–more correctly the Dow Jones Industrial Average or DJIA–was up 32 points. The index had just crossed the 17,400 mark. It was another new record. All the other major indices were up as well–NASDAQ, the S&P 500 and the Russell 2000. All were in record territory. The dollar was up against the yen, but slightly off versus the euro and the interest rate on the Treasury long bond–30-year Treasury bond–was down five basis points.

At seventy five, Rosenberg was a seasoned veteran of the equity market. He had seen it all–the ups, the downs and the sideways movements of the DJIA. But for the past twenty-two years it had been mostly a one-way trip, just up and up. As Rosenberg sipped the coffee and reflected upon the market another fascinating thought crossed his mind. A whole generation of equity portfolio managers had never seen a bear market. And the way things were going it was doubtful that they would see one. At least not in his lifetime.

The sudden ringing of the telephone startled him and brought him back to earth from his reverie. No one usually rang this early. He reached for the phone and automatically said "Sidney Rosenberg."

"Good morning, Sidney. It's Neal Johnson." A voice said at the other end.

Johnson was the Director of the Staff Pension Fund at Phillip Morris. The fund had ten billion dollars in assets, managed by twenty equity and fixed income managers. B&P had almost five hundred million dollars of this money. It was the largest equity account at the firm.

"Oh, hello Neal. What can I do for you?" Rosenberg asked in his most ingratiating voice.

Johnson ignored the question. "I tried to reach you yesterday but you had already left for the day." The voice had a hard edge to it.

This doesn't sound good Rosenberg thought as he casually

replied, "I'm sorry I missed you but I had a dinner engagement with one of our customers last night."

"I'm afraid I have to give you some bad news. Our Board met yesterday and decided to move our account from B&P."

"Neal, we've been together for sixteen years. It's one of our oldest relationships. I was personally involved in getting the account and I'll do whatever is necessary to keep it. Can you help?" Rosenberg pleaded.

"I wish I could. You know that, Sidney. Unfortunately my hands are tied. We have a new whiz kid heading the Personal Division and he's changing things around. The statistics he put together were just too compelling. The Board had no choice but to act on his recommendations."

"Listen Neal, it's true the numbers have not been good the past few years. I fired the last portfolio manager on the account. Our new man has done well. The performance has improved considerably in the latest six-month period. Give him a chance."

"I understand. But the weight of the overall evidence is just too overwhelming. Look Sidney, the Dow has gone up from 2,169 at the end of 1988 when we gave you the account to 16,950. That's a compound annual average return of 13.7 percent. At that rate our hundred million dollar portfolio with by you would be worth $780 million today. Do you know what we have with you right now?"

"I'll give you the latest number in a minute." He punched a few keys on the computer behind him and the amount flashed on the screen.

"It's four hundred and eighty million."

"Right. That's a 10.3 percent compound annual return after your 1 percent management fee. The difference between the market and your performance is a mind boggling three hundred million dollars. That's the simple math. Sidney believe me I tried. But there was nothing I could do against those numbers. If it's any consolation, it's not just you guys.

We're pulling the money from all the equity managers and putting it in an index fund."

The conversation lasted a few more minutes. They agreed to have dinner on the following Friday.

Rosenberg put the phone down, seething with rage. Anger marred the craggy features of his long and narrow face. A knot the size of a small marble bobbed on his right temple. "Damn it," he said aloud to himself. This was the third account that B&P had lost in the past two months. And just yesterday he had endured two painful conversations about performance from other dissatisfied corporate pension fund customers.

Something had to be done about the investment performance. The ten-year record was not bad but the five, three and two-year numbers were mediocre. B&P was in the sixtieth percentile. He had tried everything; juggled portfolio managers, fired some and even hired a few new ones, but the overall results had only improved very marginally though one or two of the new managers had done quite well. Maybe a team approach would work better but it was impractical under the existing set up. The firm needed a drastic overhaul. It was engulfed in the operating style and culture of its past and the powerful retail partners over whom he had no control wouldn't let go. It suited the bastards completely. They hated his guts anyway. He had given and then taken away institutional accounts from so many of them either for lack of performance, or to reward others. The moves were always temporary. He didn't have to assign a reason. But they hated each other just as much—for having more assets under management, for picking better stocks, for making more money, for almost anything you could think of. There was only one difference. They not only hated him, they also feared him because he knew how to manipulate them. And that dolt of a CEO, Peter Weisdick, didn't have the balls to take them on. No wonder the word on Wall Street was that B&P

27

was a collection of thirty warring feudal barons under one roof.

Rosenberg knew that the easiest and best way to solve the problem was to sell the firm. He could then persuade the new owners to give him the power–and the CEO job–to shake things up. There was no one else who could fix the place, except Alexandra Middleton perhaps. But, in his view, she lacked the political savvy to control most of the other partners who hated her. If he got the chance he would use the knife like a world-class surgeon and remove all the cancerous tissue, and maybe some benign tumors as well while he was at it. Besides, he felt it was the right time to sell. With the market at these levels and domestic and foreign investment and commercial banks rushing in to buy money management firms, he reckoned that B&P was worth in the neighborhood of two billion dollars. That price would make even the humblest partner wealthy.

"Thank God I've been thinking about this for some time," he said to himself. He had convinced the Management Committee, in mid-June, to appoint Goldman Sachs to investigate the possibility of a sale of the firm and find some potential buyers. The fools on the Committee had actually bought his story about several investment bankers phoning him to inquire if B&P would consider a sale. Everyone that is, except for Alexandra. So he had simply told her about the plan in advance. A number of potential buyers had surfaced and several meetings were scheduled in two weeks.

Just then his secretary, Erica Krauss, walked in with a fresh cup of coffee. Rosenberg requested her to ask Ronald Shapiro, who managed the Phillip Morris account, to come up to his office.

The hapless Shapiro arrived five minutes later. He was in his mid-forties, of average height and slightly over weight. Rosenberg immediately gave him the bad news.

"By the way, Johnson also let me know that we had cost

Phillip Morris $300 million in opportunity profits that they would have made had the fund been invested in an index account since its inception. He also implied that during this period we had collected millions of dollars in fees not to mention commissions on the sale and purchasetransactions. I suppose the god-damned ass was trying to suggest that we should have waived or refunded our fees."

The dazed Shapiro was speechless.

Rosenberg did not blame Shapiro for the fiasco. He had been at the firm for only three years and had managed the account for less than a year.

"It's not your fault, Ron." Rosenberg smiled. He actually liked Shapiro whose performance numbers were a lot better than that of most of the other institutional portfolio managers. "But it's going to cost both you and the firm a packet of money."

Rosenberg noticed the agitation on Shapiro's face. Beads of sweat lined his broad forehead. His right eye twitched nervously as he calculated the cost of this disaster. He would lose two million dollars in income because of this. It never occurred to him that Rosenberg had basically given him the portfolio as a favor and that he had played no role in winning the account sixteen years earlier. Rosenberg had done that. Where else could newly employed portfolio managers get paid on such a scale except at B&P? All because he was Rosenberg's current favorite.

"Now for some good news," he heard Rosenberg say. "I'm giving you two new accounts, Ford and IBM. They add up to $300 million."

Shapiro finally managed to collect himself. He thanked Rosenberg and shuffled out of the office.

Five minutes later Rosenberg took the stairs down to the twenty-fifth floor. It was time to lower the boom on two of his unsuspecting colleagues. After all he had just given the accounts they managed to Shapiro. He marched into the office of the bespectacled and rotund, Joseph Wechsler, fellow

3194-ISLA

member of the Management Committee and a senior retail partner. Without any preamble he proceeded to inform the surprised Wechsler that he was being removed from the management of the IBM account immediately.

"I don't have to tell you the reason but I will," Rosenberg said in a cold voice devoid of anger. "It's simple. Your numbers are lousy. They stink. That's why you lose two retail accounts for every new one that you get."

With that he walked out of the office, leaving a steaming Wechsler to work out his anger by himself. Which he did. With two big swigs from his hip flask.

Sarah Kaplan, another equity manager, was the next victim. A somewhat plain looking but elegantly dressed woman in her late fifties, Sarah had tried, two years earlier, to emulate the nouveau riche wife of a certain well-known Wall Street financier, in a bid to gain access to the wealthy jet set crowd in Paris. The attempt had failed miserably and Kaplan had given up all further ideas of becoming a part of the elite social circle of France. She was now devoting her attention to a narrow group of wealthy Jewish families in New York. Rosenberg, who had initially hired her many years earlier, had helped in establishing some of these contacts. As a result most people at the office thought that the two were close. Sara was also a friend of Alexandra Middleton and had often been invited to some of her exclusive social functions where she had succeeded in picking up some customers.

Rosenberg came to her office, located six doors away from that of Wechsler, a few minutes later. This time he was only a shade less abrupt. After a brief discussion on some specific stocks and the market's performance over the past week, he told her that she was losing the Ford account. He was impervious to all her pleas. "Don't worry. I'll try and introduce you to a few more wealthy families." Then glancing at his watch several times he left saying that he had to go to another meeting.

Fifteen minutes later, at exactly ten o'clock, a tall woman with auburn colored hair that fell just below her shoulders strode into Rosenberg's office. The meeting had been arranged last week. A cream-colored folder was held in a hand with perfectly manicured nails covered with shiny red nail polish. The slender body and the three-inch high heels accentuated the height and made her look taller than the five feet six inch she actually was. She displayed the bearing and easy manners of an eminently successful woman who was well used to competing in a man's world. Middleton was a partner and had been a member of B&P's Management Committee for the past four years, the only woman to have ever occupied that position in the firm's history.

She smiled and greeted Rosenberg warmly. His response was cooler but she apparently did not notice. Rosenberg's face betrayed no hint of his feelings. He had recruited her eighteen years earlier and knew that she was one of the indisputable stars of the firm, but he had recently concluded that the brilliance was, unfortunately, marred by some very serious flaws. He was awed by her knowledge, her intelligence and far ranging intellect and enjoyed discussing a variety of issues affecting the firm with her. She invariably came up with excellent ideas.

"Its been a lousy morning. We just lost the Phillip Morris account," Rosenberg told her. There was no point in holding back the information. She would find out about it anyway and then wonder why he hadn't told her. It was much better to let her know.

"That's just bad luck. The numbers were beginning to improve," she said in a sympathetic voice. "But Sidney, you have to start moving on the implementation of the ideas we discussed last month. We simply must get more new business."

She was referring to a number of proposals that she had made relating to new approaches in the areas of marketing,

FRANCIS BLAKE

compensation of the sales force and the rearrangement of the equity portfolio managers.

"Yes, yes. I'm working on it," he replied, his voice filled with impatience, which once again she failed to notice.

He then mentioned the removal of two portfolio managers earlier that morning.

"I know about Sarah. Who's the other one?"

"The news certainly travels fast here," Rosenberg replied. "Wechsler is the other one."

Alexandra was not on good terms with Wechsler who was one of several old fashioned, anti-women, male chauvinists at the firm with too much time on his hands and not enough work. She often saw him hanging in Jimmy Dolittle's office, which was next to hers, gossiping and ferreting information. He had a reputation for this. She refrained from making any comments about him to Rosenberg. But Sarah was a different matter. They were friends and she liked her.

"Sarah's numbers were not that bad. Not the ones I just saw. Besides you have known her for a long while. You should have given her at least a few more months."

"Yes, it's true that I've known her a long time. But remember that when it comes to business, personal relations don't mean a thing. The firm comes first. We were in danger of losing the account."

"I understand your rationale. I would have done the same thing under similar circumstances," she conceded with a smile, having decided there were other more important battles to fight. Sarah was not worth the effort.

Then pulling some papers from the folder she continued, "Let's go over some of this material for our meetings with the investment bankers and the prospective buyers."

"Okay, let's do that. But I also want to go over a few other items with you."

Alexandra was puzzled. "I'm making the presentation on

32

the fixed income business. Has something else come up since our last meeting?"

"Yes. You've been selected to make the overview presentation on the market and our business."

"That's great. Whom do I owe this honor to?"

"To our investment bankers," he replied.

Rosenberg disliked the arrangement. Weisdick was obviously not capable of making the pitch. The man was from another time, an era long since gone. Personally he would have preferred to make the presentation himself, but the investment bankers were adamant. In their view the firm had to put it's best foot forward. "You want to sell the firm. Don't you? Or are we mistaken?" Jay Goldberg, the Goldman banker, had finally asked. That had stopped the arguments.

"Ms. Middleton," he said in mock enthusiasm. "You apparently made quite an impression on the boys at Goldman Sachs."

They got down to business. The material was discussed at length. Various changes were made. By one o'clock they had covered every issue and were satisfied with the results.

As Alexandra got up to return to her office, Rosenberg turned to look at the computer screen on the sideboard behind his desk. While they were meeting the Dow was up forty points.

33

CHAPTER 3

In the Sulaymaniyah district in downtown Riyadh a hand
some man in Arab dress sat in the air-conditioned sixth-floor
office contemplating his next move.

So far everything had gone according to plan. He had
spent the better part of a year carefully and methodically
plotting out the details. It was all in his mind. The moves and
counter moves. Such secrets could not be put down on paper.
It was too dangerous. No one, absolutely no one, had any
idea of the scheme. Neither his adored wife, nor his three
lovely children. Not even his closest friends. To them it would
appear that an inscrutable and omnipotent God had destined
this course of events. Now the time had come to make the
final moves. The future he had been secretly working upon
was about to happen. He could almost see it in his mind's eye
as the excitement surged through his body.

Tarik Ibn Mishaal Ibn Abd al Aziz al Saud glanced at the
razor thin eighteen-carat gold Patek Philippe watch on his
left wrist. It was three thirty in the afternoon of July 28. That
meant seven thirty in the morning in New York. Maybe he
could catch Townsend before he left for the office. He picked

up the telephone and dialed a number. Within seconds a familiar voice was on the line.

"Michael Townsend speaking."

"Good morning, Michael. It's Tarik."

"Oh! Good morning, or rather good afternoon, Tarik."

"I was hoping to catch you before you left for the office."

"I was heading towards the door when the phone rang. Actually I have an appointment with a potential customer this morning. You know another one of those breakfast meetings." He seemed to be in a jovial mood.

They talked.

The matter he had mentioned last month had taken place. Yes he had been appointed to Saudi Arabia's Supreme Oil Council. He had also become a senior advisor to the king. The conversation lasted ten minutes. It was agreed that Townsend Associates would work on a special project for a three million dollar fee. Townsend was offered and accepted the job of chief executive of the Saudi National Bank owned by his friend Prince Tarik. They had discussed this subject several times earlier. The appointment was initially for a three-year period. Details of the compensation package would be worked out when Townsend arrived in Riyadh next week.

Tarik had met Michael Townsend, a fifty-nine-year-old Oxford-educated–he was a Rhodes scholar–American in 1982 when he had headed Citibank's subsidiary in Saudi Arabia. They had hit it off immediately. For the past twelve years Townsend had operated a very successful management consulting company that worked extensively with oil and defense industry firms, a segment not well covered by the bigger nationally known firms such as McKinsey and Boston Consulting Group. He was also well connected in the New York-Washington-Chicago-Los Angeles business and political network.

Three days later, on his way to Riyadh, Townsend came

3194-ISLA

to the firm's London office to brief his partner Timothy Wilkinson. An elegant looking man in his mid-fifties, Wilkinson was the product of Princeton and Harvard Business School. He had worked at McKinsey and later at Lockheed and his particular expertise was the defense industry. The two had met at a dinner party, some ten years earlier, at a mutual friend's house and had liked each other immediately. One thing led to another and soon thereafter Wilkinson had joined Townsend's company as a partner and was now responsible for the firm's European business.

The two men who had spoken on the phone a day earlier, met in Wilkinson's office overlooking Hyde Park. Townsend handed him a copy of the latest New York Times. "Here. Have you seen this?"

Wilkinson glanced at the article. It related to the recent unrest in Saudi Arabia. "To most people unfamiliar with the intricate details of world history," Wilkinson read, "the country of Saudi Arabia in the year 2004 AD is as much of an enigma as it was in 631 AD when the Prophet Mohammad united the whole country for the first time in its history."

He put the paper down. "You've lived there, Michael. Give me a quick run down. I can read this later." He smiled, "Of course I'll get more detailed information from our usual sources."

Townsend put his coffee cup down. "You know, it's a bleak and desolate land. But it has a beauty of its own." He sounded nostalgic, not having lived there for almost eighteen years. "There are two things that make the country vitally important to mankind..."

"Oil being one of them. What's the other?"

"First, it contains Mecca," Townsend continued, disregarding the interruption, "the holiest city of Islam, birthplace of the Prophet Mohammad and the site of the Kaa'ba, a shrine visited by over two million Muslim pilgrims each year from every corner of the earth. And of course even more importantly, the country sits on the largest sea of oil known to man. Oil, as we all know, is the life blood of the modern world."

"So as I see it," Wilkinson observed dryly, "God in his infinite wisdom created this hellhole and then, perhaps as a sign of his infinite mercy, endowed this worldly hell with the only thing that could possibly turn it into an earthly paradise."

"That's the gist of it," Townsend laughed. "And as the Times article points out, it's for this reason–the vast oil re-sources–that internal stability in Saudi Arabia is so important to the rest of the world."

"And what does it suggest?" From the tone of his voice it was clear that Wilkinson was not an admirer of this newspaper. It was too liberal for him.

"It expresses the earnest hope that the Saudi royal family will grasp the seriousness of the problem and undertake genuine reforms that would secure internal peace and stability."

"Which is where we come in?"

"That's right."

The two then discussed, for a few minutes, the consult-ing project that the firm would be working on. Townsend provided all the information he had. The full parameters of the assignment, which apparently related largely to economic development issues as far as he could tell, would be known by next week.

"Anyway, let me complete the history lesson." Townsend grinned. "It's quite interesting. Modern day Saudi Arabia is of more recent origin. Within thirty years of the Prophet's death, as Muslim armies marched across the continents of Asia and Africa conquering all before them, the capital of the empire was transferred from Mecca to Damascus by a new line of rulers, or Caliphs as they were called, from the Umayyad dynasty. Arabia quickly disappeared into oblivion for fourteen centuries, reduced to a ravaged land of constantly feuding Bedouin tribes."

37

"So when did it get united as a single country?"

Townsend sensed his friend's growing fascination. "Not until 1932 under the House of Saud. That's when it got its present name of Saudi Arabia."

"What's the origin of the Saud family? Is it like the family of the former Shah of Iran?" Wilkinson was curious.

"No, it's very different. The Shah came from peasant stock and his royal pretensions stretched back a grand total of fifty five years to his father who seized the throne. The Al Sauds are a more ancient family with a distinguished, if not great, heritage. They had been tribal chiefs since the fifteenth century in central Arabia. In the eighteenth century one of their ancestors forged an alliance with Abd al Wahab, founder of the puritan Muslim sect known as Wahabis."

"That sounds like Martin Luther's alliance with Phillip of Hesse," Wilkinson said, recalling one of his school history lectures.

"More or less," Townsend agreed. "In any event the alliance was a stroke of genius. The Sauds gradually captured most of Arabia, with occasional set backs, some more serious and longer lasting than others. Then in 1902, Abd al Aziz al Rahman al Faisal al Saud, known to the world as Ibn Saud, reconquered Riyadh. Ibn Saud was a determined man and over the next thirty years, by means fair or foul, through war and innumerable marriage alliances–he ended up with more than fifty wives–he managed to unite the country, becoming the first king of the newly-proclaimed Kingdom of Saudi Arabia in 1932."

"How is the present king related to him?"

"He's his son. In fact in the past fifty years four of the founder's sons have succeeded to the throne. Fahd, the present ruler, has been king since 1982."

The New York Times article that Townsend had read earlier, pleaded for a new generation, more attuned to the problems of Saudi Arabia, to take over. In the opinion of the writer, Saudi Arabia needed a younger version of the austere and remarkably successful Faisal who had been the country's third king.

"Tell me about your friend Tarik?"

"He's fifty years old and until recently had never been associated with the government though I'm told he's quite close to an uncle, the eighty-three-year-old Crown Prince Abdullah. Tarik is polished and urbane and has a fine agile mind. He's decisive and, unlike most of his countrymen, very hard working. In 1975 at the age of twenty one he returned to Saudi Arabia, just in time to see a great stream of money pouring into the Kingdom, thanks to a quadrupling of oil prices brought about by the Arabs under the leadership of his uncle Faisal."

"Yes, I remember that. We had long car lines trying to get gas." Wilkinson laughed, recalling his youthful escapades in those times at Harvard.

"Tarik proceeded to take full advantage of the situation. I understand that he took over his father's construction business. The company prospered as vast amounts of money were spent, or as some would say wasted, on infra structure projects ranging from roads, airports, bridges and office building complexes to schools, hospitals and factories."

"You mentioned yesterday that the man is fabulously wealthy," Wilkinson remarked. "Did he make it in the construction business?"

"No. Most of the money was made in the stock market," Townsend replied.

He then told Wilkinson about the banking venture. In 1980 the prince had bought a small bank known as the Saudi National Bank–SNB. Earlier than most bankers, he had recognized and understood the changes taking place in the world of finance. In 1982 Tarik had installed a quant group, consisting largely of Indian and Pakistani PhD's, at the bank's London office. This farsightedness had paid off handsomely. SNB had become one of the most profitable major players in the trillion dollar derivatives business.

Then in 1986 a friend by the name of Alexandra Middleton came up with an idea that solved the problem of interest-free deposits in Saudi Arabia. Islamic law forbade the payment of interest on deposits. It was considered usury. This of course suited the banks perfectly well; but even the most devout depositors, quite understandably, were not pleased. Funds increasingly began leaving the Kingdom for overseas destinations. Tarik and Alexandra's solution was both simple and brilliant. They began investing the customer's current account deposits in preferred shares in the United States. The funds in all the individual accounts were totaled and advised daily via computers to New York where the investments were made. Unlike bonds or certificates of deposit, preferred shares paid dividends. This was a legitimate investment under Islamic law. The prince was prepared to take the exchange risk, which in any event was negligible given the close linkage between the dollar and the Saudi currency, called the riyal. In the United States, the same Alexandra Middleton, who had originally conceived the idea, managed the funds. The deposits had grown rapidly since then, and according to Tarik, half a dozen American firms now invested the funds. In the intervening years SNB had emerged as the largest bank in the Kingdom with assets in excess of thirty five billion dollars.

Just then a good-looking secretary in her mid-thirties, with dark brown shoulder length hair, came into the room.

"Would either of you care for more coffee?" she asked.

"Yes, we'd love to have some more. Thanks, Betty," Wilkinson replied, looking up at her amiably.

She refilled their cups.

"Tell me about his stock market dealings since that's where he has made most of his money," Wilkinson said, as Betty Farnsworth walked out of the room.

"That story began in late 1987," Townsend began, warming up to the subject. "That's when Tarik directed his considerable energies to another business venture. It was startlingly successful. The timing was fortuitous. It was just after the October meltdown of the U.S. stock market that year."

He then mentioned how the desire for privacy had led Tarik to establish his company, Pegasus Investments, in Liechtenstein with the help of the worthy Herr Doktor Wolfgang Siefert with a half billion dollars in initial capital. The capital had come from the sale of the prince's construction company.

"What was his strategy in the stock market?" Wilkinson asked.

"He began with what we would call the value approach to investing. His initial foray was in the stocks of faltering American and European companies. In the late eighties that meant banks. And of course over time it led to switching to other sectors ranging from computers to automobiles. At the same time he made some big bets on technology companies like Cisco Systems, Intel and Microsoft as well as on some blue chips like Wal-Mart, Coca-Cola and Pfizer. But the thing that really helped him was his intuitive feel for future Federal Reserve policy at that point in time."

"What do you mean by that?"

Townsend described how Tarik had capitalized on the interest rate policy of the Federal Reserve, the central bank of the United States. It was of course well known that the Fed would not let the major American banks–Citibank, Chase, Bank of America, and Manufacturers Hanover to name just a few–go out of business. These banks were badly wounded giants as a result of the Latin American debt crises at that time.

The memory of what had happened brought a smile to Townsend's face. "The mechanics of helping a 'stricken' bank was well known: direct lending support from other major banks

41

and direct lending by the Fed through the discount window. What was not well known, even to any of us who had been in the business, was the strategy, if indeed there was one, that the Fed would use to help these banks rebuild their capital base."

"And Tarik figured it out?" Wilkinson asked in a surprised tone of voice.

"Yes. He sensed that the Fed would be forced to keep interest rates low for a considerable period. It was this rather than superior management skills that had saved the banks. You know, one doesn't have to be a genius to make a bundle borrowing at 3 percent from the discount window and lending to consumers at 22 percent, or for that matter even buying U.S treasuries paying 6 percent interest which were held in an investment portfolio and were thus not subject to being marked down in value in the event of a rise in interest rates. Only the banks have the luxury of putting their securities in either an investment portfolio or in a trading portfolio in which the asset price changes daily!"

This was precisely what had happened. The Fed had kept interest rates low, at three percent for over three years. Tarik's investments, bought near the bottom of the market, had gone up astronomically in value as company earnings skyrocketed. The Fed's policy helped all companies, and particularly the banks, to increase their net income sharply. He currently owned shares in Morgan Chase, Citigroup, American National, IBM, Cisco Systems, Oracle, Yahoo, Dell, Qualcomm, American Express, Coca-Cola, Wal-Mart, Ford, General Motors, Apple, Euro Disney and Lloyds Bank among others. The entrepreneurial prince had done well. In the process he had become a multi-billionaire. Last year Forbes magazine had considered him to be one of the savviest investors in the world and had estimated his fortune at around sixty billion dollars. Only Bill Gates, the founder of Microsoft and Larry Ellison, the chairman of Oracle, were ahead of him.

"Tarik's whole career has been a testament to boldness," an admiring Townsend observed. "He does not do things in dribs and drabs. That method never works. There is only one way to look at things. Careful analysis and then quick, bold and decisive action. This is the approach that has made him one of the richest men in the world."

The two men then discussed their financial arrangements during the next few years while Townsend was on a leave of absence from the firm.

"Tim, I propose that our present 60/40 arrangement be changed. You're going to be the senior partner in my absence."

"What would you suggest?" Wilkinson asked.

"My view is that until I return the new ratio should be 20/80. I think that would be fair."

"That's mighty generous of you. But I'll agree only on one condition."

"What's that?"

"That we exclude the Saudi contract from this arrangement. I absolutely insist on that." Wilkinson was adamant.

"All right friend. We have a deal." Townsend replied with a broad grin.

Back in Riyadh a few hours later on the same day, Tarik chuckled as he finished reading the article in his office. The New York Times, he mused, didn't know but its wish was about to be granted. Soon. Very soon. Just as the paper had hoped, a younger man in the Faisal mould, but even more dynamic and much better versed in western ways, would shortly be the new king of Saudi Arabia. Right now it was a closely guarded secret known only to four men. Riding down the elevator to the building's basement, the prince smiled as he recalled the words of his uncle Crown Prince Abdullah, pleading for family unity at a recent gathering of the huge clan. "A Saud has to rule the country," Abdullah had declared emphatically. "After all the financial security and welfare of five thousand Saudi princes and princesses depended on it."

43

To drive the point home the Crown Prince quoted the words of a well-known American industrialist who had said, "What is good for General Motors is good for America." Abdullah had drawn the right conclusion. He reminded his audience, "Surely what is good for the House of Saud is good for Saudi Arabia." In earlier times the message had invariably united them. This time the clan members refused to fall in line. Unity was secured only after their demands for fundamental changes in the family's power structure had been agreed to.

As he drove home Tarik thought about events of the past several months. The boredom gnawed at him. He had accumulated more wealth than either he or his family could possibly ever use. It had become a game, a testing of his skill. What he really hankered for was power. Real power. The power that no amount of money could buy. The power that only comes from ruling a country. And so he had plotted and planned secretly. The recent rioting and unrest had been fueled by money provided by him through a network of closed cells, which ensured that the origin of the funds could never be traced back to the source.

Tarik loved his country passionately. With all that wealth he could have lived any where in the world–London, Paris, Rome, New York. But he had chosen to live in this rugged desert, the land of his fathers. He felt that the old men in the family who formed the ruling elite were senile. They were weak. Too prone to compromise. Too dependent on America. Too backward and venal. And too willing to squander the Kingdom's wealth. The oil price decline and the recent riots had finally frightened these doddering old fools. Just as he had surmised. Yes really frightened the shit out of them. They had panicked and they had finally acted.

Things would be different under him. Very different. There was absolutely no doubt about that in his mind.

CHAPTER 4

A day after President Bush's get-together with the Fed chairman, another meeting was in progress six thousand miles away. It was held in the conference room adjacent to Prince Tarik's opulent office at the Saudi National Bank building in Riyadh. Three men attended the meeting in addition to the prince. Sitting on his left was Khalid Ashrawi, a fifty-one-year-old Syrian Christian, a former professor of economics at Harvard. On the other side of the long mahogany table was Doctor Ali Afridi–Bodger Afridi to his friends–a Pakistani, also fifty one, who had previously been the number three man at the International Monetary Fund in Washington D.C and prior to that, professor of mathematics at Princeton. Next to him sat the American, Michael Townsend, who had arrived the night before.

Anyone coming upon this scene would surely have wondered what this eclectic group of individuals was doing in the middle of the Arabian Desert and what the connection was between them. After all, Riyadh wasn't exactly on the circuit of the world's most frequently visited tourist resorts.

The explanation was actually quite simple. Tarik's mother was an Iranian from the Esfandiari family–yes the same one

45

that had produced the beautiful Queen Soraya, the second wife of the Shah of Iran. The stern Ibn Saud who was the king at the time, had felt humiliated by his son's marriage to an Iranian and one with a German mother to boot. So in a fit of anger he had banished the son, Prince Mishaal. As a result, Tarik had been educated mostly in England. First at Eton, that great preserve of the English aristocracy, an institution so intimately connected with English history that someone had actually claimed that the battle of Waterloo was won on its playing fields. Subsequently he had gone on to Cambridge, one of the world's most exclusive clubs that numbered among its graduates more presidents and prime ministers than any other university with the possible exception of its rival Oxford. Not surprisingly, the Syrian and the Pakistani had been at the University at the same time. Their friendship stretched back twenty nine years.

They were the prince's brain trust. He had recruited his two friends as his advisors in 1988. Together they had looked at American and European companies in financial difficulties. The combination of Tarik's boldness and judgment and their cold, calculating analysis had led to the investment decisions that had propelled the prince into the ranks of the infinitely wealthy. The advisors had also prospered. Money lubricated the arrangement. Their employer was the most generous of men.

Once the customary tea and coffee had been served, Tarik opened the meeting with the candor reserved only for his advisors.

"As you all know, two weeks ago I agreed to become the king's senior advisor. I felt obliged to accept the position. The kingdom is in very serious trouble. The very survival of the royal family is at stake."

He could tell from the puzzled expressions on their faces that their surprise was genuine. They knew of the recent riots, but this was something totally new.

"Is it really that serious?" Afridi inquired.

"I'm afraid so. We're in the throes of a crisis unknown to the world because of our ... I mean the government's penchant for secrecy."

Tarik put his cup down before continuing. "Let me quickly summarize the source of the trouble. Our legitimacy as a royal family is based on a compact rooted in desert tradition. In the old days," the prince explained, "the weaker tribes paid a tax to the more powerful tribe in return for protection. Our founder, Ibn Saud, extended this system to the government when he became the first king. Since then the population has accepted Saudi rule and the religious and political restrictions in exchange for subsidies."

He paused briefly and then added, "It's simply a form of bribery." A smile appeared on his handsome face highlighting the thin, slightly hooked nose and the shining dark brown eyes with the long silky lashes.

The men listened in silence, as the prince continued. "Unfortunately this compact is breaking down. The problem in a single word is money. The revenues are just not enough to cover the expenditures. The . . ."

"Yes," Ashrawi interrupted. "But this has been the case since at least 1991. I mean since the end of the Gulf War."

"That's right," Tarik replied, "but in the past the large reserves took care of the deficit. The Gulf War depleted the reserves. Very substantially. Our share of the war's cost was over seventy five billion dollars. Matters improved somewhat after that for a while but the sharp decline of oil prices during the past three years has exacerbated the situation almost to the breaking point."

"Not to mention the billions poured into poorly conceived projects like the King Fahd Medical City and the almost unused King Fahd International Airport in the Eastern province," Afridi reminded the audience.

"You're right," Tarik replied. "Those two projects alone

cost eight billion dollars. On top of that we have huge
expenditures on defense as well as enormous subsidies to
inefficient state-owned companies. Making the
predicament much worse is the greed and spendthrift
habits of the dynasty."

"If I understand you correctly," said the tall, powerfully
built man with the broad, muscular shoulders, "Falling oil
revenues combined with careless spending are undermining
the social and economic stability of the kingdom." It was the
American, Michael Townsend, speaking for the first time.

"Exactly," the prince acknowledged. "Now it has reached
panic proportions. So I have been asked to come up with a
plan. Why do you think I was selected?"

"Because you are a member of the family but still an
outsider," Afridi chimed in.

"There's something else." Ashrawi spoke up, "You've
never been associated with the government, and so you're
Mr. Clean. Besides, you must have some brains." They all
laughed at this as Ashrawi went on, "After all you didn't rely
on handouts like the rest of them. You made your wealth the
old-fashioned way. You earned it."

"Almost the very words King Fahd used at our meeting.
But I was also fortunate to have the assistance of people like
you. So gentlemen," he paused briefly for emphasis, "I need
your help now. We have to come up with a plan that will get
us out of this mess. Fast."

With that he walked over to the desk and lifted the phone.
"Sami, could you please bring us some refreshments."

Almost immediately a tall young man in Arab dress
appeared with coffee and soft drinks. Everyone opted for
coffee.

"Plans for reforming the system have been made many
times in the past," Afridi said, once the young Arab serving
the coffee had left. "But nothing came of it. Fahd is not capable
of taking strong measures. He's too weak and vacillating."

Tarik saw the same doubtful looks on the faces of the other two men. There were plenty of stories about Fahd's weak and conciliatory nature.

"That is true. But things are different this time."

"Why?" Ashrawi asked pointedly.

"Let me explain," Tarik answered. "It's extremely confidential. This time even some of the princes are in revolt. This has happened only once before. In the 1960's with Faisal and his older brother Saud. They're tired of the geriatrics at the head of the government. They are demanding changes. And they want them now." There was no need for them to know anything more. At some point later he would advise them. But not now.

While Tarik spoke, the rest of the group was silently absorbed in their own thoughts on the astonishing revelations of unrest in the Saud family.

"You probably don't know," Tarik interrupted their thoughts, "but in the 1960's Saud, the eldest son of Ibn Saud, was on the throne. He had two problems: he was weak and he was a spendthrift. As a result he almost bankrupted the country. So over his objections, the other princes imposed his half-brother Faisal as the head of the government. Faisal cleaned up the mess and eventually took over as king when Saud was deposed and packed off to Cairo. A similar arrangement might well occur this time. We will undoubtedly have major changes in the composition of the government in the next month or two."

The group then began reviewing the major issues facing the country. Oil accounted for practically all of the kingdom's revenues. It was the first item to be discussed.

Michael Townsend, having done consulting work for several oil companies in the past dozen years, was the first to speak. On his way to Riyadh he had spent several hours with Leo Drollas, deputy director of the London-based Center for Global Energy Studies, who was particularly

49

knowledgeable on the subject of oil. Townsend gave them a brief run down on the overall situation.

"World oil demand has picked up speed since the year 2000 with the recovery of the Asian and Latin American economies. Currently the daily demand for oil is around 85 million barrels. That's up from 83 million barrels in 2003. But for most of this time prices have, unfortunately, remained low except for a brief period from mid-1999 to the end of 2000 when they averaged around $25 a barrel–a big improvement on the number prevailing now.

Townsend opened the folder lying on the table in front of him and produced a chart that he handed to the others in the room. It traced the nominal price of oil from 1970 to the end of 2003. He then gave an abbreviated account of the history behind these price movements, the squabbling between the OPEC members and the role that Saudi Arabia had played. It had been a sordid one, by and large. All too often the country had done the bidding of the United States under the guise of protecting its own self-interest.

"As you can see," Townsend said pointing to the chart. "In early 1981 it was a shade higher than $35. For much of the 1990s the price averaged around fifteen dollars. For the past three years it has ranged between $11 and $14. Right now it's down to $10 a barrel."

"How does today's price compare in real terms with the seventies and early eighties?" The only economist in the group, the bespectacled Ashrawi asked.

"It's about a third of the 1981 prices."

Ashrawi made a quick calculation. "Based on a U.S. inflation rate of four percent, prices would have more than doubled in this period. On that basis the price should be around $90 per barrel. But that is clearly an unrealistic number."

Townsend then proceeded to recount the major problems that had bedeviled OPEC for almost twenty five years. The quota system was too complex; the group was too large. It was difficult to make them work together. Cooperation only existed when prices fell sharply. It vanished when prices increased as the temptation to cheat on the quotas became irresistible. It was also very difficult to persuade non-OPEC countries that accounted for over half of the total production to cooperate. They had been able to do this for a while five years ago.

"How?" Afridi asked.

"Venezuela, Mexico and Saudi Arabia signed the Riyadh Pact agreeing to substantial cuts in their oil production," Townsend said. "The very low prices prevailing at that time brought the other OPEC countries into line. We were able to slash supplies by five million barrels. That very quickly jacked up the price."

"And then what happened?" Afridi continued the questioning.

Townsend described how American pressure had led to the unraveling of the agreement. Oil production increased and prices tumbled as everyone began to cheat once again.

"I guess a lot of cheating goes on. But who are the major cheaters?" Tarik asked.

"Primarily Venezuela. Kuwait and the United Arab Emirates have been big but so have Iran and Saudi Arabia."

"I met Ali Naimi, the oil minister last week." Tarik told them of Saudi Arabia's current position. "Our daily oil production is 10 ½ million barrels. At the prevailing prices the annual oil revenue is thirty eight billion dollars. According to Naimi the kingdom's excess production capacity is slightly over 12 million barrels per day."

"I thought it was more like 4 million barrels." Townsend's demeanor reflected his surprise at the high number mentioned by the prince.

"Naimi said that's what most people think. But the information is outdated. Apparently we have been increasing our excess production capacity for several years unbeknown to the rest of the world."

Tarik broke the momentary silence that filled the room. "In my view," he went on, "we have two options. The first involves some loss of revenue, but it would probably give us a decisive voice in oil affairs for the foreseeable future."

He sensed that this had jolted the men. He got up and paced the room as he continued. "Under this option we would produce oil to our full capacity of 22 ½ million barrels daily. That will drive the price down sharply."

"To what level?" a stunned Afridi asked.

"Probably around $3 a barrel. Maybe $4 at best." Townsend and Ashrawi nodded in agreement.

"At that level Venezuela, Mexico, Russia, and even Iran would be wrecked economically. Britain and Norway would probably give up their North Sea operations!" Afridi exclaimed.

"Yes. That's precisely the point." Tarik smiled. "We would probably finish them off as oil producers if we maintained production at this level for three or four years. And then we can dictate price and quota terms. They will have learnt a lesson. The hard way. But that may well be the only way they'll ever understand."

"Yes. But at what cost?" Townsend wanted to know.

"I figure that, at those low prices, our revenues will decline to twenty five to thirty three billion dollars. Sure we'll hurt but not as badly as the others," Tarik observed.

"It won't be too severe if we can lop off some of the frightful waste in expenditures," Afridi commented bluntly.

"Yes, and that's one of the items we'll discuss later. But to continue with what I was saying earlier, do you know that in 1985 Sheikh Yamani pushed up our oil production in a big way to teach the OPEC members a lesson." Tarik added, "Oil prices collapsed and the producers were hurt severely. But so was Saudi Arabia. The Sheikh hadn't prepared the country for the shock of lower revenues."

"The Sheikh was a decent man, but he was overly concerned about western economic interests and not enough about Saudi Arabia's interests." Ashrawi observed tartly as the rest of them nodded in agreement.

"What's the other option that you had in mind?" Afridi asked, looking at Tarik.

"Work with the oil producers to cut production."

"But how? It hasn't worked in the past?" Townsend asked.

"I know. It's a more difficult task. We'll have to come up with a plan that appeals to every one's interest." He smiled as he spoke. "To paraphrase the words of Don Corleone we'll have to make them an offer they can't refuse."

"Such as?" Townsend retorted immediately.

"A completely new approach, Michael. A needs-based quota system perhaps. We would accept greater cuts than the others. Maybe a fund from which oil producers could temporarily borrow. But what ever option we select it must be credible or the markets will simply ignore it."

Everyone agreed that credibility was essential.

"Let's move on two tracks," Tarik proposed. "The carrot and the stick. The first option involves Saudi Arabia only. It's obviously easier to implement. And we would combine it with deep cuts in expenditures. I'll come to that later. But I would really like to go with the second option, if at all possible, provided we can come up with an acceptable plan. It won't be easy but let's give it a real good shot."

"By the way did you have a price target in mind under the second option," Townsend asked.

"Of course," Tarik grinned. "Gentlemen, the situation calls for boldness. I want to go for a $38 a barrel number."

That raised several eyebrows not to mention a muffled whistle or two from a few of the men. Their man Tarik was going for the jugular. Really playing hardball. But then you wouldn't have expected anything else from him.

3194-ISLA

"To get that price level you're talking of at least an eight percent cut in production. Probably closer to ten percent," Townsend warned.

"We have no choice. Let's go for it," an unfazed Tarik replied. "Before we go any further let me quickly mention a few things about expenditures. The first item is defense."

He enumerated the facts. Thirty percent of the kingdom's annual budget was devoted to defense. That worked out to about fifteen billion dollars. The country was the largest buyer of arms in the world. And it didn't help any way. During the Gulf War they were compelled to call the Americans. Educated Saudis were questioning the government's fondness for spending billions of dollars on weapons. Perhaps it was related to all those commissions that members of the royal family earned. In any event it was time to reexamine the issue. He wanted them to work on it in conjunction with the oil plan.

"We will concentrate on oil and defense," Tarik said to the men. "Revisions of the kingdom's industrial policy and the elimination of various subsidies including those to members of the royal family—its cost is around two billion dollars—are a lot more tricky. They require a little extra time. I have therefore asked Tim Wilkinson, that's Michael's partner at Townsend Associates, to work with Afridi on that project. They will come up with a new set of plans and priorities in the next forty five days."

Tarik then got up and returned to his office. The three men worked on the two topics for the rest of that day. By the following evening they had come up with a series of measures that completely satisfied the prince.

Over the course of the next several days the plans were flushed out and finalized and then bound in green, yellow and red folders. The green and yellow related to the two possible oil plans while the red folder outlined the new defense policy. The plans were duly presented and approved by the Senior Council consisting of King Fahd, Crown Prince Abdullah and Prince Sultan. It was further decided that Prince Tarik would be the Saudi representative and he would have complete freedom in the selection of advisors.

The Council also selected the Europeans for the initial discussions, to be followed by negotiations with the Venezuelans and the Mexicans. King Fahd personally made the arrangements for the meeting with the German Chancellor and the French President. Ali Naimi, the oil minister, was brought into the plan. He set up the meeting with his Mexican and Venezuelan counterparts.

It was to be in New York. On Friday, August 20 at the Carlyle Hotel.

3194-ISLA

CHAPTER 5

The magnificent château of King Fahd was situated in the Loire valley, a part of the country that had been the playground of the kings of France since ancient times. It was the land associated with the beautiful Diane de Poitier, mistress of two kings, and the martyred heroine and saint, Joan of Arc. Near by was the chateau of Chambord, one of the wonders of French renaissance architecture. Tours was a short distance away to the west. It was there, just a hundred and forty or so miles from Paris, that Charles Martel, grandfather of the Emperor Charlemagne, had defeated an Arab army in the year 732 AD in a desperate battle that saved Europe for Christian civilization. In the last quarter of the twentieth century Muslim money was accomplishing what Muslim armies had failed to achieve. Wealthy Arabs now owned great chunks of Europe.

As the records later showed, it was here, amidst the vineyards and the rolling fields in the heart of France, that on the eighteenth day of August 2004 at a meeting between the French President, Lionel Jospin, the Chancellor of the Federal Republic of Germany, Gerhard Schroeder and Prince Tarik al Saud, personal representative of the King of Saudi Arabia, an agreement was reached that changed the world's economic balance of power in the first decade of the twenty-first century. The French President and the German Chancellor arrived by helicopter from Paris, having just concluded their semi-annual meeting, which had become a regular feature of modern day Europe since Charles de Gaulle initiated this particular aspect of the Franco-German alliance way back in 1963 along with his pal Konrad Adenaur. During the short journey, Schroder handed to his colleague a brown folder containing information on their host. It had been put together by the Chancellor's office. Jospin put on his glasses and began reading the report:

> HIGHLY CONFIDENTIAL
> "Tarik ibn Mishaal ibn Abd al Aziz al Saud. Prince of Saudi Arabia. Born Mecca April 1954. Son of Prince Mishaal, a half-brother of King Fahd. Mother was Persian from Caspian Sea area. Maternal grandmother German. Educated in England at Eton and Trinity College, Cambridge. Reportedly a very charming, friendly and amusing individual who was very popular at both these institutions. Excellent student and sportsman. Married to a Lebanese for past twenty three years. Three children. Eldest son currently at Trinity College, Cambridge. Speaks five languages fluently—Arabic, Persian, English, French and Spanish. Austere habits. Does not smoke or drink. Fond of Savile Row suits made by Huntsman & Sons and Turnbull and Asser shirts. Not a member of the jet set crowd. Rarely seen on the social circuit. Frequent visitor to the United States. Vacations with family mostly in England, Italy and France. Not known to own any yachts, airplanes or real estate in either Europe or the United States. Generous, low-key, sociable and easy going. Well-read and knowledgeable with wide-

57

ranging interests. Not much known about personal
life or political views. Reputed to be one of the world's
richest people. Forbes magazine estimated fortune
of around $60 billion. 'A very shrewd investor'
according to Forbes. Extensive holdings of stocks in
US, German, French, British and Asian companies."

"Doesn't tell us too much," Jospin said, handing the file
back to Schroeder.

"Unfortunately not. But we'll find out in a few minutes."

A tall, slim man impeccably attired in a pin striped char-
coal gray double breasted suit with twin vents greeted the
two leaders as they alighted from the helicopter. The hand-
shake was firm and solid, quite unlike the limp, dead fish grip
of most Eastern leaders that they were accustomed to.

"Welcome to the Château As Salaam," he said in flawless
English. "I'm Tarik al Saud. It's a pleasure to meet you, Sir,"
he added in a deferential tone.

As they walked toward the house both Europeans had
the same thought: "This man bore as much resemblance to
an Arab as Luciano Pavarotti did to a Chinese. He could easily pass off as a European." The Chancellor ascribed that to
the German grandmother. The Frenchman gave the credit
to the Anglo Saxons. "You've got to hand it to the English,"
he mused to himself. "Their education system leaves its mark
on you for life."

They entered an opulent walnut-paneled library. Beautiful leather bound antique books lined the shelves. Jospin
being French had an ingrained sense of beauty. He noticed
that the ceiling, which was at least fourteen feet high, was
covered entirely by a superb fresco depicting one of the
countless legends of French mythology. A magnificent Van
Gogh painting hung above the mantle, and an antique
Aubusson carpet in muted shades of blue, gray and cream
graced the entire length of the beautiful parquet floor. The

furnishings were just as elegant in pale shades of cream and priceless antiques filled the room. Sunlight filtered in through the numerous windows giving the room a warm and cheerful glow.

The prince led them to a sofa on the far side of the room. The two visitors sat together on the comfortable couch in front of the wall, while Tarik sat on a chair opposite them. A liveried butler appeared and served coffee and then they got down to business.

"I suggest that we dispense with the formalities," the prince said in French. Jospin could detect no trace of an accent.

He continued, "In deference to Monsieur Jospin I propose that our discussions be in French, if that's agreeable to you, Herr Schroeder."

Jospin's language skills, like that of most of his countrymen, were almost completely limited to French. The prince was obviously well briefed.

"Monsieur, my complements," said a visibly relieved Jospin. "Your French is most certainly far superior than my English."

The Chancellor, whose language skills had been honed courtesy of the French occupation, after World War II, of Southern Germany where he had grown up, nodded his agreement.

Tarik immediately described with brutal frankness the situation of the OPEC member states. He spoke with a natural authority and assurance and without the aid of any notes.

"Unfortunately for the past several years the price of oil has been far too low. This has created serious problems for many states in the Middle East and in parts of Latin America. Economic development has come to a grinding halt. Our economies are at a standstill. There is a looming economic and social crisis. Things may soon reach the point of no return. Several states are threatened by revolution. My own government is most concerned. And worried."

3194-ISLA

He paused to let this sink in. The look on the faces of the two Europeans conveyed their understanding of the gravity of the situation. Revolution in one of the key Middle East nations could threaten the supply of oil to Europe. Both Germany and France were heavily dependent on oil from this area. This could have severe repercussions on their barely reviving economies. The Federal Chancellor had another concern. German banks had made huge bets on Eastern Europe, particularly in Russia and most of that country's foreign exchange earnings came from oil. Lower revenues would lead to more defaults. German banks were already beset with too many bad loans that were causing severe earnings problems. This could further damage the German economy.

"In the past decade," Tarik continued, "OPEC's efforts to increase oil prices have been unsuccessful by and large. You are well aware of the reasons so there's no point in dwelling on them. Moreover the policy of the British government has not been helpful. Unfortunately, the British have now become total lackeys of the United States. The Norwegians cooperated for a short while last year. The results of all this have been most unfortunate for us. Our imports of European products have declined. Relations with Europe have also suffered as the United States becomes increasingly dominant in world affairs. A counterweight is needed to the Americans. Europe is the natural answer."

These words made a powerful impression on both statesmen, particularly on the French President. The French had a love-hate relationship with the Americans going back decades and certainly since 1945 when Charles de Gaulle raised it to the level of high drama. They had been trying for a long time to make the Europeans play the role that Tarik had just finished asking them to assume.

So it was natural that Jospin was the one who responded to the prince's plea. "As you know, Europe has been trying to create a counterweight against the Americans for some time. In 1999 our common currency, the euro, was introduced as a part of this program. It was Germany and France that led the fight for the common currency. To our intense disappointment, and here I speak for both our countries."

He turned towards the Chancellor sitting next to him. The German nodded in agreement. Jospin continued, "Unfortunately the euro has not developed, as rapidly as we had hoped, as a reserve currency."

"I apologize," the affable prince said, "If I gave the impression that Europe has been passive. Indeed we are most grateful for the efforts that you have made to date to provide us with alternatives to the haughty Americans."

He leaned forward in his chair and spoke in a hushed voice, as if he was about to tell them something very confidential. "Saudi Arabia has come up with a new plan to solve the oil price problem. We believe that it will have great appeal to the Europeans."

The Saudi next proceeded to sketch the main features of the plan. As in the past, production would be cut back to reduce the supply of oil. This time however, the cuts would be limited to just a few key producers. There would be sufficient inducements in the form of fairer quotas, loans, subsidies and other measures to prevent these countries from backsliding. And a new alliance of oil producers would henceforth be responsible for oil policy. The OPEC Conference of Ministers had not really worked.

Tarik went on to brief the two leaders on Saudi Arabia's plans to cut its defense expenditures. He advised them that all domestic socio-economic development programs were under review. The objective was to bring the bloated expenditures down sharply. The cuts would also go a long way in appeasing the conservative elements in Saudi society and in reducing the country's dependence on imported laborers.

The prince then made his pitch. "I have come to you

3194-ISLA

today with a proposal." He noticed a keen sense of anticipation on the faces of the two Europeans as he continued, "Our policies can only be successful if they are perceived to be credible by the marketplace. So we want to create a massive amount of credibility from the start. We can only achieve this with your help." He paused briefly for emphasis. "My proposal is simple. We will switch the pricing of oil from US dollars to the euro. This will provide a big boost to the euro. In return we want an oil credit facility from your two countries that can be drawn upon by certain specified oil producers."

The proposal caught both the French President and the German Chancellor by total surprise. Then just as suddenly they were filled with a sense of elation as they began to understand the consequences of what was being proposed.

"Monsieur, will the other oil producers accept your proposal on the euro?" Jospin inquired.

"We have not specifically checked with them yet, but we are confident of getting their approval. Iran, Iraq, Libya, Algeria, Nigeria and Indonesia will go along with anything that damages American interests. The Venezuelans and the Russians are hardly likely to object. You'll have to tackle the Norwegians and the British. They are, after all part of the European Community. The others will simply fall in line. They'll have no choice."

That seemed to make sense to the two Europeans. In fact the more they thought about it the more the proposal appealed to them. Perhaps it was the answer to their problems.

For much of the past decade, most of Europe and particularly the two principal economies, those of Germany and France, had stagnated. Economic growth had been anemic and unemployment had remained high. Even as they met, eight percent of the labor force was unemployed in both France and Germany. The reasons for Europe's plight were well known to politicians and economists alike. Simply put, there was too much rigidity in the labor market. Overly generous unemployment benefits discouraged workers from seeking jobs. In Germany, unemployed workers were paid almost 60% of their last salary tax-free indefinitely. No wonder people didn't want to work. Who would?

High employment taxes reduced the incentive for firms to hire more workers. Strict job protection laws further discouraged companies from hiring because it was almost impossible to fire workers. And then there were the countless subsidies. German coal for god's sake cost $180 per ton compared with the open market price of $65. In both France and Germany employees worked considerably less hours per week than their American counterparts. France now had a 35-hour workweek! And the two countries had the highest average hourly compensation rates in the world. In fact German workers at $33 per hour cost almost twice as much as the average American worker. The consequences of all this had been predictable. So German and French companies expanded their operations overseas rather than in their home markets.

The politicians simply did not have the backbone to attack the problem. The population refused to support any move to dismantle the expensive cradle to grave welfare system. In sharp contrast to Britain where the people had sided with Margaret Thatcher when she took on the unions, the French and German electorate had backed the unions. Mass marches and road blockades had humbled several governments in France. The politicians were no longer in any mood to try. They had seen the light.

Fourteen years in age separated the two socialist leaders who were secretly conferring with the Saudi prince, but their views and approach to economics were very similar. They were long on image and short on ideas for tackling their countries' problems. In hindsight it was apparent that both had been elected on the flimsiest of promises: they claimed that

63

they could bring prosperity without pain. What the two countries needed was a Margaret Thatcher, the iron lady. Instead they had gotten Lionel Jospin and Gerhard Schroeder.

To the courtly Jospin–elected to the presidency in 2002–the appeal of the Saudi plan was first and foremost political. Economics took a backseat. It was a distant second. France, like Britain, was a third-rate economic and military power that continued to masquerade as a superpower. The charade had gone on since World War II. But then, France had always had an obsession with glory–La Gloire as they called it. Francis premier in the 16th century, Louis XIV in the 17th century and Napoleon in the 19th century had personified the ideal. Unlike Britain, however, France was consumed by an intense jealousy of the United States. Fearful of being marginalized, La Grande Nation had since the days of Charles de Gaulle, been the leading challenger of American diplomacy and economic ideas. Anything that reduced the prestige of the United States appealed to France.

Similar ideas were going through the mind of Gerhard Schroeder. But his focus was purely economic. The telegenic and youthful Schroeder had been reelected, by a narrow margin, as the sixth Chancellor of the Federal Republic of Germany in September 2002. Two years after his reelection the country remained in an economic quagmire. The bitter medicine was too painful to administer. His support was dwindling, as unemployment remained high. The Social Democrats had been humiliated in six state elections this year and had even lost in the Saarland–the heartland of the German labor movement. Here perhaps, the Chancellor thought, was a way out of the dilemma. Prosperity without pain.

There was another aspect of the Saudi proposal that the chancellor found most attractive. The principal shock of an increase in oil prices would be felt in the United States. The effect on Europe would be quite modest since it had insulated itself by imposing taxes that accounted for over seventy five percent of the price of gas. According to one estimate, European motorists were paying the equivalent of $200 a barrel for their gas! The idea going through the Chancellor's mind was this: If America got more involved in domestic economic problems it would, ipso facto, have less time to meddle in Europe. This would give Germany a chance to once again pursue its traditional Central European policy. The objective was a simple one. Increasing German trade and economic influence in that area, which in his mind included all the former Russian states including those in the Caspian Sea area.

It was apparent to both Schroeder and Jospin that this particular Arab who sat in front of them was no fool. He had done his homework carefully. Tarik and his advisors understood, as well as these two Europeans, that the special status of the dollar as the dominant reserve currency gave the United States many important advantages. America had not only been able to finance its huge budget deficits for years but also its huge trade deficits, currently running close to $300 billion annually, by simply printing the greenbacks or rather Treasury securities that were given to its creditors. This, in turn, increased investors' holdings of dollars and that inevitably turned the American financial market into the most liquid and diversified market in the world. And that, again, made it even more attractive to investors. And so it went on and on, each beneficial feature automatically creating the next.

These advantages were very much on the minds of the Europeans when they began their single currency project. The European Community–known in short as the EEC–had, after all, a much larger population than the United States. Its gross domestic product was also larger than that of America. Moreover the EEC was the largest trading block in the world. In total dollar terms its trading volume far exceeded that of any other country including the United States. And the combined bond market of the EEC was almost the same size as that of America. The cold numbers suggested that the euro would be a serious rival to the dollar. To a gambler the odds looked good that the United States would have to share its global reserve currency role, and the inherent advantages that went with this role, with the European Community.

But events had not exactly worked out this way. Since its advent five years back, the euro's share of world reserves had inched up to twenty percent. It remained a very junior partner of the dollar. What the Saudis were now proposing, if their assumptions were correct, was a complete change in the euro's position. At one stroke it would become, to the dismay of the Americans, an equal of the almighty dollar.

The liveried butler suddenly reappeared, as if on cue, with coffee. The cigar-loving Schroeder produced three Romeo y Juliettas. Jospin took one. To their surprise so did the prince. The information on him was not strictly accurate. It was true that he did not smoke, but he did occasionally indulge in an after dinner cigar. It was not exactly after dinner, but the moment seemed just right.

The Chancellor puffed on the cigar and then spoke to Tarik. "Yes. I believe you're right. Their economic success has made the Americans unbearable. They have become too arrogant. Envy and hatred will make the oil producers follow your lead."

"That's our assessment as well."

"All right," the pragmatic Chancellor now said, "tell us more about the loan facility."

"Actually its quite simple. It's essentially the usual plain vanilla facility, but suitably window dressed to appeal to the consortium banks, to investors and to the borrowers."

"How many banks did you have in mind for the consortium?" the German asked.

"We would like to limit it to a small number to maintain secrecy. That's crucial."

The conversation, at this stage, was between the German and the Saudi. It was too technical for Jospin. He was content to listen and occasionally nod his head in agreement.

"Would lending limits be a problem if the consortium is limited to a few banks?"

"It could be. I don't know what the exact requirements are in your countries. But the notes will be in marketable form and the banks can sell some or all to other investors," the prince responded.

Then exhaling the smoke from the excellent cigar he added, "By the way we want the notes to be guaranteed by the German and French governments to their respective banks. The oil revenues of the borrowers will in turn secure you. It will be a first lien."

"Why not secure the loans directly with the oil revenues?" the Chancellor asked.

"Because your guarantees will give the notes the highest possible credit ratings. That will lower the interest cost and also make it easier to sell to investors. Of course it will also be more attractive for the consortium banks."

Again the explanation seemed reasonable. The Europeans nodded in agreement.

"By the way, what amount did you have in mind?" the Chancellor asked, taking another puff on the cigar.

"Forty two billion dollars. At the current exchange rate that works out to a little over forty billion euros, to be provided equally by your two countries. By the way that represents four months of revenues at 20 euros a barrel of the nine oil producers we have in mind for the facility."

"Why the 20 euros?" Jospin asked, entering the conversation again after a long silence.

"That's the level the oil price must reach before any country can draw under the facility. And there will be a percentage limitation on the amounts of each draw. Its designed to make sure that each country sticks to the reduction quotas. For each subsequent draw the price level will be higher than the twenty euros. The exact numbers will be provided to the banks."

3194-ISLA

There was no question in their mind that the Saudis had thought through all the issues. The prince had come up with credible answers promptly. No humming or hawing. No hesitation. Just straight off the cuff.

"So," said Schroeder turning toward the Frenchman, "What do you think Lionel?"

"It's a big number but I don't see any problem." The Frenchman responded grandly.

"The Federal Republic," Schroeder said "also does not have any problem with the numbers. But we would like to add one condition."

Tarik leaned back in his chair, listening to the Chancellor.

"At least half the funds from the facility," Schroeder continued, "should be used solely for the purchase of European goods. That's good for our economies and it gives us political cover against the Americans."

The Saudi had no problem with that. After all money was fungible. He responded with well-disguised relief, "I agree. In fact it's the intention of my country to increase our investments in European companies. And our trade as well." Then turning to the French President he added, "We also intend to honor all our existing defense contracts with French suppliers."

The discussion continued for a further fifteen minutes. They agreed to proceed immediately with the necessary arrangements. It was also agreed that the Federal Chancellor would take the lead in this matter. The prince would make his representatives available for the meeting with the bankers in Bonn and Paris. He would also advise the two leaders once agreement in principal had been secured from the other key oil producers. While Jospin and Tarik exchanged pleasantries on the delightful beauty of the Loire countryside, Schroeder made two telephone calls from the adjacent room.

The first call was to Germany's Finance Minister, Graff Hans von Ansbach. The second call was to a Frau Ingrid Henkel.

CHAPTER 6

Like many politicians, both living and dead, the well built, sixty-year-old Gerhard Schroeder had a weakness. It was a serious but not a fatal flaw. At least in Europe. He was an enthusiastic devotee of the sport of kings. It was a hobby in which he had had considerable practice and had consequently attained a formidable expertise. No, it was not polo, though one could certainly classify that game as a princely activity. Nor was it big game hunting, another favorite of the monied class. The sixth Chancellor of the Federal Republic of Germany, like his very good friend Bill Clinton, the sixth Democrat to occupy the White House since 1950, simply found women irresistible. Especially women of a particular type–tall, statuesque, sexy brunettes with voluptuous lips.

No biographer or journalist had as yet noticed that these two men had another thing in common. They had the overwhelming support of women voters. Somehow women instinctively sensed the fondness of the two politicians for the opposite sex. They were also fervent disciples of the world's greatest philosopher of love, that remarkable Englishman, Lord Byron, who in an earlier century had summed it all up in two magnificent lines:

69

*"Philosophers have never doubted,
That ladies' lips were made for kisses."*

Now it was true that the Chancellor and the former President had great difficulty keeping their pants up. But once the pants were down they parted company. European tastes, alas, differed substantially from those prevailing in the uncivilized backwaters of America.

The Chancellor was on his fourth wife. But neither marriage nor high office had proven to be a deterrent to his extracurricular activities. In continental Europe what happened between consenting adults was no one else's business. You lived your life without worrying about all those prying journalists. And that the Chancellor certainly did.

Following the meeting with the Saudi prince, Schroeder returned to Paris with Jospin and then immediately took a plane to Cologne. From there he traveled by car to a secluded house on the outskirts of Siegburg, a pretty village some twenty kilometers south of that city.

The owner of the house, thirty-two-year-old Ingrid Henkel was expecting him. They had met at a dinner party in Bonn in the spring of that year. The attraction had been mutual and a liaison had rapidly developed. Ingrid ran a very successful Givenchy boutique on the Hohe Strasse, close to the Dom, as Cologne's magnificent Gothic cathedral was called. The early, and untimely, demise of her aged but wealthy husband had given Ingrid the means to live a life of leisure. With time on her hands she had indulged a desire, shared by so many of her countrymen and countrywomen, to travel to exotic places such as Phuket in Thailand, Bora Bora in the Pacific, Gilgit and the old silk route in Pakistani-held Kashmir, Outer Mongolia, the island of Seychelles in the Indian Ocean and other watering holes far off the beaten track of the average tourist. And of course to Majorca. Four million Germans visited the island last year, making its capital, Palma, the busiest airport in Europe during the peak summer months.

A chance encounter with an Indian aristocrat on the palm-fringed beaches of Goa had led to the completion of her sexual education in one very old culture. An ongoing affair with a virile Swiss had recently introduced her into the mysteries of the ancient Egyptian art of imsak. Another Swiss resident, the famous playboy, Prince Aly Aga Khan, had been the last great practitioner of this art form and he had left behind scores of women–in Hollywood, London, Paris, Monte Carlo, Rome and countless other spots–with the most delightful memories of his sexual prowess.

Schroeder enjoyed Ingrid's company. He found her relaxing. She was not only beautiful but also an excellent conversationalist. In other words she was a good listener on whom he could unburden all the problems that politicians faced in their ceaseless endeavors to improve the lot of mankind. Moreover the sex was absolutely unbelievable. Just simply unbelievable.

It had been a good day for Herr Schroeder. He was in an expansive mood. He talked about the meeting in the Loire and of the handsome Saudi who was apparently extremely wealthy but so modest and unpretentious. Ingrid listened attentively and urged him on. The wine loosened his tongue. He talked of the plan at length. It would be great for German industry and business. After four glasses of an excellent Bernkasteler wine Schroeder was ready. He could wait no more. Ingrid led him to the bedroom upstairs.

Within minutes their bodies were interlocked. The angles were quite incredible. She had introduced him to the different positions–with mysterious names like the Flower in Bloom, the Squeeze, the Mare's Touch–so lovingly illustrated in the Kama Sutra. A quick learner, Schroeder had already mastered three of these. There were thirty four more to go.

71

Luckily there were no neighbors to hear the groans and the shrieks that came from the house as they both found ecstasy in one mighty climax.

CHAPTER 7

At nine thirty the next morning Gerhard Schroeder walked briskly into the Finance Minister's office located in a complex of nondescript, contemporary white buildings along the west bank of Germany's greatest river, one mile south of downtown Bonn. The ministry had been transferred in 1999, along with other government offices, to Berlin, the Federal Republic's new capital, but a small office had been retained in the sleepy two thousand year old little university town on the Rhine River.

He was fifteen minutes late, having been held up by unavoidable personal business in a village near Cologne.

Inside the office three men, all in their early sixties, sat around a table at the far end of the large room chatting and drinking coffee as they waited for the Chancellor. They were Graff Hans von Ansbach, the Minister of Finance, Herr Doktor Walter Dietrich, Chairman of Germany's largest bank, Deutsche Bank and Herr Doktor Ulrich Buchner, Chairman of Bayerische Hypo-und Vereinsbank–HypoVereinsbank–the country's second largest financial institution. The bankers had flown in earlier that morning in company jets, from their respective headquarters in Frankfurt and Munich, at the urgent

3194-ISLA

request of the German aristocrat, also a banker by training, who now had the responsibility for the fatherland's financial and economic affairs.

Gatherings such as these occurred in countries all over the world but in the United States, however, they were quite rare, being held only in times of national emergency. Somehow they exuded an aura of collusion or something underhanded that would undoubtedly make them illegal under American law. But there was nothing unusual about it in Germany. Most Americans, including many who have lived there, were not well versed in German history and even fewer were aware of the close links that exist between the German government and the German banks. These links even predated the founding of the German state in 1870 and actually go back to the start of industrialization in the 1850's. The German government was about to use these links once again, as the record would later show, in the service of the state.

"Meine Herren," the Chancellor said once he had seated himself and managed to light one of his favorite Cuban cigars. "Yesterday, along with President Jospin, I met Prince Tarik al Saud who was representing the Government of Saudi Arabia. The meeting was arranged at the urgent request of King Fahd."

He paused to puff on his cigar. Then noticing the surprised expression on the faces of the two bankers he asked "Do you know the prince?"

"Yes I have met him on a number of occasions," the chairman of Deutsche Bank responded. "He is the chairman of Saudi National Bank. It's a major player in the global derivatives business. And he owns four percent of the shares of our bank."

"And six percent of our stock," said the chairman of HypoVereinsbank.

"I had no idea that he had any connection with the government," Dietrich indicated.

"Apparently this is a fairly recent development. In any

event at our meeting," the Chancellor continued, as he finished the fourth coffee of the morning, "The Saudis presented a detailed proposal."

There was complete silence in the room. The audience waited for Schroeder to continue. They had no idea about the proposal. Even the Finance Minister had not been briefed.

"The substance of the proposal," Schroeder went on, "is that the Saudis intend to take a series of actions aimed at raising the price of oil."

He then gave them a full account of the discussions that had taken place day earlier in France.

"I believe the Saudis are very serious this time," the heavyset Doktor Buchner exclaimed.

"What makes you come to that conclusion?" Von Ansbach inquired.

"Because this time they are using a first-class business-man who understands markets, and not some bureaucrat or political functionary."

"I agree with Buchner's assessment," said the Deutsche Bank chairman.

"So you gentlemen think that the plan might work?" Schroeder asked.

It was the gray haired, dapper chairman of Deutsche Bank who responded to the Chancellor's question.

"There's a very good chance that they will succeed this time. From what you have told us, it appears that the plan is carefully focused on just a few oil producers who can be more easily managed than the entire group of OPEC members. Moreover it seems that substantial inducements are also being offered to make these countries stay the course."

The chairman of HypoVereinsbank now spoke up. "The timing is also good. The oil producers have been hurt finan-cially for six years, except for a brief period from mid-1999 to the end of 2000. They cannot take it much longer."

3194-ISLA

"By the way, did they mention any particular price level?" Von Ansbach asked his leader.

"My recollection is that a ten percent cut and a thirty eight dollar price range was mentioned though I'm not sure. I do remember that both Jospin and I were impressed by the argument that even after this rise, real oil prices would be barely half their level in 1981 while the prices of Western goods had risen consistently in real terms."

A more general discussion ensued for the next twenty minutes. The Chancellor made it clear that he had agreed in principal and intended to keep his word. He then asked the assembled men the key question, "So gentlemen, do you see any major risks for Germany in this?"

As the senior business representative at the meeting, it was once again Doktor Dietrich who responded.

"For us, no. But for the Americans maybe."

"Please explain?"

"The Americans may not be averse to a price rise in the dollar twenty range," the Deutsche Bank chairman explained. "The low prices prevailing right now are putting pressure on their banks. More problem loans. But a much higher price level would not be welcomed."

"What level?" Schroeder asked.

"Dollar thirty five or thirty six a barrel. It could have, shall we say, a devastating impact on the stock market that would inevitable lead to a recession."

"Yes, but they know that. The chairman of the Federal Reserve has repeatedly said that the good times cannot go on forever," said the rotund Doktor Buchner who so far had been very much of a junior partner in the discussion.

"A recession is bound to occur. It's merely a question of time. From our perspective it's much better if we know the timing and can make use of the information," Dietrich responded.

"But the timing could be a problem," the Finance Minister interjected. "A presidential election is coming up in November. This would be a disaster for the Republican Party."

"Yes," the Chancellor shrugged. "But the two parties are more or less the same any way. Besides it's not our fault. It's no secret that the oil cartel has been trying, without much success, to raise prices. All countries have the right to protect their economic and political interests. The United States repeatedly intervenes against the EEC on behalf of its business interests. Just recently they raised customs excise taxes on a number of European goods."

"The Americans will certainly not like the switch in oil pricing from the dollar to the euro." Dietrich smiled with satisfaction at the expected discomfit of the United States.

"We can certainly expect that. But the euro part of the plan is of critical national importance. It will bring the euro to within striking range of the dollar as a reserve currency," Von Ansbach exclaimed with a thump on the table. "It will propel the European Community to the status of an economic superpower on a par with the Americans. And in a few more years with our larger population we will overtake them."

That America wanted to preserve its military and economic leadership position indefinitely could hardly come as a surprise to anyone. Only yesterday there had been articles in the New York Times and the Frankfurter Allgemeine on this very subject. With the collapse of the Soviet Union, no other power was capable of taking on the United States militarily. The Europeans had no interest in this area. After all there was no military threat to Europe. So why waste money on weapons? Let the Americans take on the petty and troublesome third world nations of Asia and Africa. If that gave them the thrills, so be it.

But on the economic front there were a very different set of calculations. The thirteen-member European Economic Community was an equal of the United States. It actually had a larger population and a larger economy. What it needed

3194-ISLA

was a reserve currency in the league of the dollar. The arrival of the euro in 1999 had finally set the stage for the confrontation. Now the Saudi plan would give the currency the boost that it desperately needed and in the process make Europe the dominant economic power in the world.

"This will make the European Community an economic superpower," the Chancellor exclaimed with relish. "And Germany is the dominant power within the Community."

The bankers and the Finance Minister nodded enthusiastically in agreement. This was the moment they had been waiting for.

It was almost 11 A.M. Schroeder had to catch a flight back to Berlin. Before leaving he extracted a piece of paper with a name written on it from his jacket and handed it to Von Ansbach. "This gentleman is an advisor to Prince Tarik. He will be joining you in fifteen minutes. The Saudis need an answer on the credit facility by ten o'clock tomorrow."

"That should not be a problem," Dietrich responded.

The olive-skinned man with the dark hair touched with white near the ears, who was shortly thereafter ushered into the presence of the three remaining men–the Chancellor having departed a few minutes earlier–was Dr. Ali Afridi. He had arrived in Bonn late last night. In addition to has native language, Afridi spoke excellent English and passable Spanish, but the language of Goethe and Schiller had proven to be too much for his linguistic abilities. A woman interpreter from the Foreign Ministry had, therefore, arrived to keep the conversation moving.

Afridi provided the necessary answers, through the interpreter, to the bankers' questions. They related to the security features, the note structure, the maturity period and other mundane matters that are part and parcel of such credit facilities. The banker's proposed an interest rate of 100 basis points above that paid by the German Government on comparable borrowings. Afridi agreed to this with suave dignity. "No point," he thought, "in arguing about the spread. The rate is better than anything the Latinos, Russians, Iranians or the Iraqis, who would be the principal borrowers anyway, could possibly get." That was another point in favor of the Saudi plan. He made a mental note of it. In the conversation later tonight he would mention it to Tarik.

The past fifteen years had not been a good one for the German banks. They had slipped badly, not in world rankings by assets, but in profitability. Intense domestic competition was the primary villain. It had forced them to go to foreign markets in search of loans. That had been a serious mistake. American banks had been the leaders in this type of lending in the 1970's and 1980's and it had almost castrated them. The Germans had presumably not read the innumerable books on the subject. So the Asian economic crises that began in 1997 had caught them, like every one else, by surprise. It hurt them badly. They were still hurting. This new oil facility was at least a move in the right direction. They stood to make almost half a billion dollars. And they didn't have to worry about borrower defaults. The Federal Republic was guaranteeing the facility. The tall, gaunt aristocrat who handled the Fatherland's financial affairs had reminded them yesterday, when he peremptorily summoned them to this meeting, that throughout German history what was good for Germany had also been good for its banks. Events were once again proving him right.

The two bankers made a total of eight telephone calls to their counterparts at Germany's other leading banks. These included familiar names such as Commerzbank and other unfamiliar ones such as Westdeutsche Landesbank and Bankgesellschaft Berlin that were unknown to the average American, or for that matter European, citizen. All had assets in excess of one hundred and fifty billion dollars. Within the hour they were able to arrange the twenty billion euro loan facility. Detailed information was faxed to the banks' chairmen immediately afterwards directly from the Finance Ministry. The signed agreements would arrive at the Deutsche Bank next morning. It was a mere formality.

A similar meeting was taking place at roughly the same time in Paris at the office of the Société Générale on the Boulevard Haussmann. The French Finance Minister, Laurent Fabius and Michael Townsend representing the Saudis, attended the meeting. At one thirty in the afternoon, Walter Dietrich, the senior German banker telephoned his good friend, Alain Deschamps, Chairman of the Banque Nationale de France. The conversation was brief. Everything was proceeding smoothly. They expected to conclude the arrangements no later than three o'clock.

Graff Hans Von Ansbach invited his guests to a late lunch at Halbedel's Gasthaus on the Rheinallee in nearby Bad Godesberg. The courtly owners greeted them at the turn of the century villa with its nostalgic souvenirs and antique furniture. Things were working out nicely–for the Germans, the French and the Saudis. It was time to celebrate.

And they did.

CHAPTER 8

New York, like the great cities of London and Paris has many fashionable and luxurious hotels, both old and new. The rich Asians favored the Peninsula on Fifth Avenue while the Latin jet set preferred the Hôtel Plaza Athénée on 64th Street. But for the old monied crowd, the Carlyle on upper Madison Avenue in the seventies, with its understated style, was still the hotel of choice.

It was at this famed hostelry that at precisely seven in the evening of August 20, Alexandra Middleton arrived at the Carlyle's equally famous restaurant. She came directly from office, after attending a meeting of B&P's negotiating team with the United Bank of France, one of the potential buyers of the firm. The get-together had lasted longer than expected and Alexandra had had to rush to reach the restaurant in time.

Archie Williams was escorted to the corner table just as Alexandra was being seated. Williams had visited B&P earlier in the day and the dinner had been arranged to give him a chance to get better acquainted with Middleton.

In the money management business–more correctly the investment advisory business–a key role was played by a group

3194-ISLA

of people called consultants. They were a kind of middle-
men between institutional and wealthy investors on the one
hand and the firms that managed the money on the other
hand. In the institutional market these consultants were known
as pension fund advisors. They assisted pension funds on asset allocation–a fancy word for describing how much of the
fund's money should be in equities, bonds, cash and alternative investments such as venture capital and hedge funds.
They also helped their pension fund clients select investment advisory firms to manage these different classes of assets. Usually three to five firms were selected to make presentations to the pension's board or trustees and one of these
was eventually selected. For each asset type there were nor-
mally several managers. Thus depending on the amount of
money to be invested, a pension fund might have four or five
firms managing equities and a similar number managing fixed
income. In some cases the actual number of firms was considerably larger. For these services the consultants were rewarded handsomely but not as well as the money managers.
The fancy cars, the huge estates, the vacations in exotic
places and the expensive lunches and dinners that the latter
types enjoyed made this fact abundantly clear.

Williams was a senior vice president at Oxbridge
Associates, a pension fund advisory firm located in Chicago.
There were several thousand such firms but, as is the common
condition in all economic activity, this industry like any other
had not escaped the concentration rule. Thus the top 75 firms
controlled eighty percent of the business. Oxbridge was in
the very top league with a handful of other firms like Frank
Russell, Callen Associates, William Mercer, Wiltshire
Associates and S&E Capital. Oxbridge had put B&P in a search
involving a large account. Some junior members of his firm
had visited B&P a few weeks earlier as part of the due
diligence process that all consultants needed to perform prior
to recommending a money manager for any business. Williams

visit was to get to know the firm and its principal fixed income portfolio managers first hand.

The evening began with the usual social chitchat that was common on such occasions: the weather, the theater, conditions in the Big Apple, the good movies seen recently, the sports events in town and so on. Ten minutes later the conversation switched to business, as was the case at most such functions.

"How did the market close today?" Williams asked.

The waiter appeared before Alexandra could respond.

They ordered drinks. A Campari soda with a twist of lemon for her; a vodka martini shaken but not stirred for him.

"The Dow was up 24 points."

The Dow Jones Industrial Average was an index of thirty blue chip stocks that currently represented about 15 percent of the value of all companies on the New York stock exchange but was generally used as a synonym for the overall market's performance.

"So the good times keep rolling on," he said with a smile.

She nodded, "It sure looks like it."

"It makes me feel pretty jittery. How do you see it?"

"Quite frankly, it scares me. It's a real crapshoot. The market is way too overpriced, certainly in historical terms. The Dow price-earnings ratio is now at 27 compared with 15 over the past seventy five years." She took a sip of her drink and then went on, "On the other hand, the economy is in good shape, it continues to grow. Inflation has picked up marginally but is still below three percent and interest rates remain at cyclical lows. The only negative is the slight slow down in the growth of corporate profits."

"You see any external threat that could knock the wind out of the market? Could the foreign investors suddenly withdraw their huge holdings of Treasuries?"

"I don't see that happening as interest rates in Europe

and Japan are lower than here. The political situation is quite stable. I mean there are neither wars nor anything threatening the world economic order. The only item of significance is the low prices of commodities, particularly oil."

"Yes but the oil price has ranged between $10 and $14 a barrel in the past three years and the oil cartel hasn't been able to do much."

"That's right," Alexandra replied. "Though after suffering three years of economic hardship one would imagine that these countries would make a greater effort at cooperation."

"Do you really think that's possible?"

"Everything is possible, but I wouldn't bet on it. Maybe a twenty percent chance that it will happen. On the other hand, the stock market is essentially driven by psychology, and as all of us know, market sentiment can change in a matter of minutes. In 1987 a few ill chosen words by the Treasury Secretary created a pandemonium. The market has been very volatile in the past few years. At these levels I'd forgo the chance for more gains and run for cover."

The waiter reappeared. "Are you ready to order?"

They were. He ordered a steak au poivre, medium rare. She chose a boiled vegetable platter. They also chose a "soufflé chaud aux framboises" for dessert instead of a first course. The wine waiter who was waiting nearby gave her the wine list and Alexandra ordered a bottle of Vosne-Romanée 1982.

He watched her order. She reminded him of some woman . . . yes, Ava Gardner. The same color eyes, the same dark hair and the same sleekly beautiful face. He had seen her on CNBC quite a few times. She was a more striking woman in real life. Her skin had the freshness of a spring day that wasn't apparent on television. There was a touch of class about her and she came across as a much friendlier and more engaging person than he had imagined. She looked young and he figured she was in her mid-forties.

"Have you followed your instincts in your personal portfolio?" the consultant asked, once the waiter having taken their order, had retreated towards the kitchen.

"But of course," she said smiling. "I've reduced the equity component from forty to fifteen percent and made a corresponding increase in municipal bonds with a duration of five years." She made this up on the spur of the moment, having always avoided equities for some irrational reason that had nothing to do with risks or returns.

"My firm has also turned cautious. We're now telling our pension fund clients to change their asset allocation and reduce the equity component to 50 percent. That's down from 65 percent."

She listened attentively, observing him carefully as he spoke. He was in his late-fifties, the sandy-colored hair was peppered white and he was beginning to put on a little weight around the waistline. The round spectacles gave him a professorial look. He reminded her of the children's orthodontist. Her thoughts turned for a minute to her husband, Phillip who was the same age but looked at least fifteen years younger. He was so handsome, so slim and so stylish. She loved him. A strong physical craving for Phillip suddenly engulfed her. She overcame the carnal desire with difficulty and refocused her attention. This was the time for business and not lewd thoughts.

"I assume you're advising your customers to increase their intermediate-term bond portfolios," she said cheerfully.

"He laughed. "That's right. How did you guess?"

It was her turn to laugh. "I just assumed that our inclusion in the competition next week was indicative of your new strategy."

As usual, the food at the restaurant was delicious. They talked as they ate and drank the superb Burgundy wine.

85

"By the way, I complement you on your superb taste. This wine is really excellent."

"Thank you. I've learnt about wines from my husband. He acquired the skills in his undergraduate days at Cambridge University."

The conversation turned back to business. "So tell me, which one of your B&P colleagues manages your equity portfolio?"

"None." She flashed a smile. "I actually use index accounts for all my equity investments. Particularly the Vanguard S&P 500 index fund."

"How come? I imagine there are some pretty savvy equity managers at your shop."

"You could put one or two in that category. But active equity management is very expensive and hardly anyone ever beats the market index consistently over time. You know they have a great year one year and the next they're in the dog-house. I was recently looking at some statistics. According to Lipper Analytical Services over the past five years the S&P 500 index has outperformed active managers by almost five percentage points a year. Over a longer period the number is not as large but it's still around three hundred basis points. And then for this lousy performance you're paying a fee of 1 ½ percent of the assets under management compared with 18 basis points that Vanguard charges on it's S&P 500 index fund. It just doesn't make any sense, does it?"

"You're right. It sure doesn't. And off the record I do the same. But," he smiled conspiratorially, "I can't tell that to my firm's clients. It would put us out of business. You don't expect me to do that, do you?"

"Of course not. But tell me how is the performance of most of the equity managers your firm has recommended?"

"Very similar to what you said. It's all over the place. Some do better than others, but the ranking changes every few years. None that I can think off has outperformed the indices consistently over the years."

"So how come your pension fund clients haven't switched?"

"There has been some switching but not much. You know how the business works. It's relationship driven. The job of the director of pension funds is a dead end position in most business corporations. The failures who have friends in high up places are shoved into these slots. These guys don't get big bucks but they like a good life. That is certainly available under the current circumstances. They visit New York, Los Angeles, San Francisco and other big cities calling on money managers, they get invited to lunches, dinners, sports events, theaters and other events; they go on junkets to exotic overseas cities. These perks are part of the job. And by using us, the consultants they buy a kind of insurance policy. If the performance of some money manager is lousy they can point the finger at the consultant. After all we did the recommending."

Alexandra was beginning to genuinely like the man. He didn't try to bullshit and he wasn't full of his own importance. There was a refreshing honesty and candor about him.

"Yes. You scratch my back and I'll scratch yours," she volunteered.

"Exactly. And if there's a performance problem it usually gets fixed quite easily. A new manager replaces an existing one. And the cycle of trips and visits then starts all over again."

They turned their attention to the marvelous looking soufflé that the waiter had just put before them. It tasted even better.

"By the way," she said after finishing the last of her dessert, "this is much less of a problem in the fixed income area?"

"What do you mean?"

"Well," she explained, "first the differentials in the returns between the index and the active managers are not as large. It's in the low teens instead of the 300 basis points that are prevalent in equities. And the fee differential between passive managers and active managers is also quite small, at least in absolute amounts. You know 35 basis points versus 15 basis points charged by indexers."

He nodded. "That's probably true."

As he was speaking, she suddenly noticed a very familiar face sitting at a table at the far end of the dimly lit room. It was Tarik al Saud. The faces of other two men were not visible from the angle where she was seated. She excused herself to go to the ladies room. On the way back to the table she quickly looked and recognized the two men sitting with Tarik. It was the Mexican and Venezuelan oil ministers. She had met them at a party at Gustavo Cisneros' house a month earlier. Gustavo was one of the wealthiest businessmen in South America and appeared to know practically everyone on that continent.

Alexandra rejoined Williams five minutes later. The conversation then drifted to their personal lives as they finished the last of the wine. He told her about his two sons who were both at college, one at Yale, and the other at Brown. She told him about Phillip and her four children. Her face lit up with pride as she talked about her family. The eldest, a girl of seventeen was in the eleventh grade at Horace Mann; the youngest was a ten-year-old boy. In between were two others, a boy aged fourteen and a twelve-year-old girl.

"I do hope that you will come and make the presentation next Wednesday. I believe you'll make a great impression on the Board," Williams declared. He was referring to the meeting of the Minnesota Teachers Retirement System for the selection of a new bond fund manager.

"I'll be there. And we're most grateful for our inclusion in the finals," she said sensing that he was favorably inclined towards B&P.

Williams looked at his watch as the waiter brought the bill.

It was almost 10.30 P.M. Alexandra paid, using a corporate American Express card. Shortly thereafter as they left the restaurant Alexandra noticed that the three men were still locked in earnest discussion. From the serious expressions on their face it was obvious that they were not exchanging views on the social scene in Acapulco. Something more serious was under consideration. Outside, Williams thanked her for the delightful evening and took a taxi tothe Grand Hyatt Hotel where he was staying. Alexandra, having declined the taxi ride walked the four blocks to her brownstone. Her thoughts were preoccupied with that scene back at the restaurant.

She was home fifteen minutes later. The children had already gone to sleep. Phillip was lying in bed watching television. She quickly changed into a white cotton nightgown and got into bed, snuggling close to her husband. Once again she felt a terrible urge to make love.

"I want you now. Make love to me," she whispered tremulously, kissing his neck and then locking her lips on his. He shifted side ways as her tongue went deeper into his mouth, moving, exploring. His hands felt her nipples. They were hard. He stroked them gently and then his hand traveled down to her vagina. She was so wet and soft and clamoring for him. He began to move his finger inside her in a circle. Her hands felt his erect penis. She suddenly sat up and began to lick the hard penis in her mouth. Then as he moved on top of her she guided it inside her. He began to move vigorously. Her body throbbed with excitement. She moaned, "ohhhh its sooo good. Give me more. Harder. Harder. Ohhhh I'm going to come. Ohhhh I'm coming," she yelled.

"How many times did you come?"

"Twice."

They turned sideways and he began moving his penis inside her slowly. Their tongues moved in each other's mouth as his hand began gently rubbing her in the area where the penis entered her body. She moaned softly, "slowly baby,

89

slowly . . . I'm very sensitive . . . Kiss my tits . . . ohhhh. More. Give me more."

"Do you like it?" he asked.

"Yes. I love it. Ohhhh I'm so excited. God I can't bear it. Ohhhh baby, I'm going to come." She let out a scream and arched her body. A huge fire raged inside her.

He continued to move his penis slowly and simultaneously rubbed the clitoris with his fingers. The wild screaming continued. He began to kiss her. Then as she lay softly panting he asked, "How many times did you come, this time."

"Oh many, many times. At least five or six," she whispered breathlessly.

"Darling I'm going to fuck you more," he said as he mounted her once again and began to move his penis rapidly and deep inside her. Wave upon wave of excitement coursed through her body. She felt like hot molten steel inside.

"Open your eyes and look at me." She half opened her green eyes.

"Ask me to fuck you." She looked up and asked, "Fuck me, Phillip, fuck me. Now. Give me more, give me more," she begged. An inarticulate cry escaped from her lips as she had another big orgasm.

"Darling, come in me now. I'm spent."

He lifted her legs and began to lick her feet beginning at the heels. She moaned as the excitement started to build inside her once again. Phillip then kissed the balls of her feet. It tasted of leather from her high-heeled shoes. Her excitement mounted. He began to suck her big toe with the red nail polish. She quivered as the powerful thrill rippled inside her. He started thrusting his penis vigorously inside her, at the same time putting all her toes in his mouth. Her excitement reached the breaking point. She let out a wild passionate cry as they both climaxed simultaneously and all their pent up desires were released in one final ecstasy.

They lay together panting for a few moments and then

he moved from on top of her to a side ways position, still holding her in his arms.

"Oh baby, I love you, I love you," she whispered. "You're the best fucker in the world."

"I love you too. And there's no one like you. Sweatheart. Absolutely no one."

A few minutes later he came out of her. They lay on their backs, holding hands.

"I saw Tarik at the restaurant," Alexandra said.

"I didn't know he was here."

"He was with the Mexican and Venezuelan oil ministers. They were having a very serious discussion. He didn't see me."

"May be he's going to make a major investment in some oil companies?"

"He doesn't need to talk to those two guys about that. Did you see that short announcement about him in the Wall Street Journal recently?"

"No. I must have missed it. What was it about?" Phillip asked.

"Tarik has been appointed a member of the Supreme Oil Council of Saudi Arabia."

"Oh yes. I now remember you told me about that."

"Phillip I think something is up. I talked with him on the phone last week. There was no mention of a New York trip. And then I see him having a very serious conversation with two oil ministers. Something is definitely cooking."

"Maybe, but I doubt if anything will come of it."

"I don't know Phillip. I wouldn't bet on it. I've known Tarik for almost thirty years. From Cambridge. You know, he's very charming and very thorough. And once he makes up his mind he always gets what he wants."

"It's late. Let's go to sleep. We'll talk about it in the morning."

He turned the bedside lamp off and kissed her lovingly on the cheek. "Goodnight darling."

———

91

"Goodnight, baby."

He was asleep almost instantly. Alexandra tossed and turned for a couple of hours. The picture of the three men in deep discussion kept her awake. She kept thinking about them until sleep finally overcame her a little after two o'clock.

CHAPTER 9

T he fabled Carlyle Hotel was the site of another conclave earlier that same Friday. Shortly after five o'clock Carlos
Rodriguez, the sixty-two-year-old Venezuelan oil minister and
his younger Mexican counterpart, Francisco Fuentes Carrera,
arrived at the hotel within minutes of each other. Tarik al
Saud met them in the beautiful lobby with the striking black
marble floor and the goblein tapestry covered walls.

All three men had arrived in the United States a day earlier. The prince had taken the Concorde from Paris. Rodriguez
had traveled via Miami, while Carrera had arrived on the regular Aero Mexico flight into JFK. They had gone through
Customs and Immigration Control without any hitch. No one
paid any particular attention to their passports, which in any
event made no mention of their ministerial rank or their link
to the oil industry.

They took the walnut-paneled elevator to the prince's
large suite on the thirty-fourth floor. Tarik opened the door
and led them to a seating area in front of a wide window with
fine views of Central Park and several landmark buildings on
Central Park West. As the two ministers sat down on one of
the two pale green velvet covered couches, Tarik walked

93

over to the bar at the other end of the large living room. He returned a few minutes later with two crystal glasses filled with Chivas Regal Scotch whisky and soda that he handed to his guests. Then sitting on the sofa opposite the two men, he resumed the conversation where it had been left off a few minutes earlier.

"Gentlemen, as you probably know my background is in finance. I am new to this business. Naimi, our oil minister is a technocrat with a technocrat's rigid approach to problems. So I was asked by my government to take a fresh look at the oil price situation."

The two Latinos drank their Scotch and listened.

Tarik continued, "The past three years have been devastating for all of us. Much worse than the nineties. For a brief period beginning in 1999 we were able to cooperate and oil prices rose to an acceptable level. But then the agreement broke down and the price is back at $10 again. It'll be heading down even further unless we do something."

He took a long sip of his drink. "It's time to correct the problem once and for all," he said emphatically.

The Venezuelan now spoke up. "I agree. But look, after twenty years of bickering we finally had an agreement that seemed to be working and then poof." He threw up his hands in a gesture of disgust.

Rodriguez was referring to the last agreement that had blown up in 2000 under American pressure. What happened was this. In 1998 Saudi Arabia, Venezuela and Mexico had signed the Riyadh pact to reduce daily oil production by 1 ½ million barrels and other OPEC members had later agreed to cut back their production as well by a further five hundred thousand barrels. Oil prices went up immediately, but within several weeks the market sensed that the production cuts would in fact not be met. The upshot was predictable. Sometime later another attempt was made at reviving the agreement. So in 1999 the three oil ministers met in Caracas. This time the results were better, at least for a while. By early 2000 the price of light crude had risen to $30 a barrel. It had even touched $37 at one point.

That's when the trouble started. The Americans got into action. Energy Secretary Richardson traveled to Mexico and the Persian Gulf countries. Shortly thereafter the agreement unraveled once again. It was the Mexicans who yanked the trigger first. They threatened to pull out. Then pressured by Saudi Arabia, OPEC agreed to an increase in oil quotas. After that Kuwait and the United Arab Emirates quietly increased their production beyond the approved limits. This led to matching actions by Venezuela and Saudi Arabia, anxious to preserve their market share in the United States. So the cycle once started had continued.

"We very much regret what happened. Unfortunately our previous administration was too subservient to the Americans," said the Mexican oil minister who had only recently taken over that portfolio.

Tarik smiled. "Regrettably that is a problem with many countries. Even my own." Then looking at Rodriguez he asked, "Going back to what you said earlier, what do you think is the reason for our inability to work together?"

"The answer is simple. There is too much distrust among the OPEC members."

Rodriguez had hit a raw nerve. There was a long history of distrust and conflict of interest between the oil producing nations and they were poles apart in their outlook. The South Americans did not believe that the oil producers could cooperate for long. They had different goals, different agendas. Besides in their view the reactionary primitive Arabs from the desert pumped far too much oil in relation to their population. The per capita income of Abu Dhabi and Kuwait was higher than that of most European countries while much of South America was going down the tubes. The Arabs really didn't need this much money. At least not right now. They could wait. Meanwhile the procreative activities of the macho Latino Catholics were adding massive numbers to an already bloated population. And this growing population had to be fed, clothed, educated and employed. So Venezuela and Mexico needed lots of money and they needed it now. These dumb Arabs just didn't get it.

The Arabs naturally had a very different opinion. To them all Latinos were greedy and corrupt. And immature as well. No wonder the Americans did not take them seriously. Or the Europeans for that matter. They were simple-minded peasants who kept over-producing children and oil thereby bankrupting themselves in the process and severely hurting other nations. Their behavior was so irrational. It was just pathetic. The stupid bastards couldn't even figure out the consequences of their actions. It was probably all because of the large quantities of Scotch whiskey that they consumed, something God-fearing Arabs never touched.

"I agree," Tarik said putting down his glass of iced tea on the table. "But surely we can overcome these differences. Others like the Germans and French have been able to do it."

"It's going to be very difficult. We've been too distrustful of each other for so long. Still as you said, perhaps with goodwill on all sides, a new beginning can be made," Rodriguez smiled, revealing a mouthful of crooked teeth in his clean shaven round face, whose shape was greatly accentuated by the oily dark hair that was slickly combed back.

"What would you suggest?" the prince asked, addressing the question to the Venezuelan.

"In our view, the present quota system is totally defective. Fundamental changes have to be made to take into account our population size and economic needs."

"We have a similar problem, but on a much bigger scale so we too need to produce more oil," Carrera, the Mexican oil minister said lending further weight to his colleague's assertion.

"What else?"

"We also need to come up with some firm understanding on our respective market share in the United States," Rodriguez observed as Carrera nodded his head in agreement.

Tarik noticed that their glasses were empty. "Gentlemen, let me get you another drink." He handed them the two tumblers filled with Chivas and spoke again as the ministers drank the golden elixir.

"We have been considering various courses of action on the oil front." Then changing the subject, he asked Carrera, "By the way what does Mexico spend on defense?"

"I don't know the exact amount but the figure is insignificant."

"Exactly. We too, are going to shrink our defense spending to the same level as Mexico. And we are also reviewing our domestic economic policies. The objective is to reduce overall government expenditures by forty percent."

"What is the point of all this?" The somewhat puzzled Rodriguez inquired.

"The point is actually quite simple," Tarik retorted. "I'm sure you both remember that back in 1986 Sheikh Yamani decided to teach the other oil producers a little lesson. So he doubled our production and the price tumbled within weeks from $30 to less than $10 per barrel."

Of course they remembered. That had almost wrecked the economies of both Mexico and Venezuela. That year was seared in the memories of many politicians in Latin America. And in the minds of many Americans as well. It had almost destroyed some of the largest U.S. banks.

Tarik continued. "Unfortunately Yamani had not prepared the Saudi economy for the shock either and so the experiment had to be discontinued. The results proved to be unfortunate for the Sheikh as well. He now lives mostly in London."

The message was finally beginning to register in the slowly

3194-ISLA

working brains of the two oil ministers. The same thought occurred to them simultaneously: "Good God, could it be possible that these dumb Arabs are going to repeat the 1986 experiment again?"

Just then Tarik got up and walked over to a nearby writing table. He opened a black leather briefcase, extracted two folders—one green and the other yellow—and returned, placing them on the oak coffee table around which they sat.

"Gentlemen," he said, resuming his place on the sofa. "I have come here with a proposal. Actually two proposals. My government intends to solve the oil price problem one way or the other. And it intends to do it now. Which plan we go with will ultimately depend upon you."

The voice was deceptively soft but the threat was unmistakable. The two men noticed the glint of steely determination in his dark eyes. It was obvious that the man was not to be trifled with.

"And what are the two plans?" the Mexican asked.

"Our first plan," Tarik responded, pointing to the yellow folder, "is actually quite simple. Saudi Arabia will immediately raise its oil production to its full capacity of twenty two and a half million barrels. With the current oil glut we estimate that the price will slide down to $4 per barrel. Maybe even lower. And we will enter into long-term contracts with the Europeans. We can implement this plan unilaterally. We do not need anyone's cooperation."

As he spoke the two South Americans felt a cold shiver run down their spine. The Venezuelan oil minister's hands became sweaty. The Mexican felt as though someone had kicked him in the stomach. Both men knew that if the Saudis pursued this strategy it would be all over. It was very doubtful that Mexico could survive financially if oil prices tumbled to these levels. And Venezuela would probably become a basket case in the same category as Bangladesh. There would be massive loan defaults, triggering economic shockwaves in many countries.

For the past six years Venezuela had gone down the abyss into the economic twilight zone, jumping swiftly from one calamity to the next with the practiced ease of an Olympic jumper. The financial firestorm that had first ravaged the East Asian Tiger economies finally reached the distant shores of South America in 1998. None of the countries escaped the havoc, but Venezuela was affected the most severely. It had suffered terribly. And the low oil prices made the suffering worse since a third of the nation's gross domestic product came from oil, which also provided practically all of the export earnings and most of the government's revenues. Structural inefficiencies, government mismanagement and rampant corruption further aggravated the economic plight. As a result, in the past three years its currency–the Bolivar–had lost more than half its value and the economy had shrunk by almost twenty percent, leaving millions unemployed.

The International Monetary Fund was back with its fifth bailout plan. The formula was always the same: harsh new austerity measures to reduce the budget deficit, higher interest rates to lure greedy foreign investors back. Another recession and more grinding poverty for the long-suffering majority of the population. The IMF loans were used to pay off Venezuela's debts to foreign lenders–banks, mutual funds, hedge funds and so on–in places like New York, London, Paris and Frankfurt. The trouble was that these damned programs never accomplished anything. The economy might improve eventually, but the poor remained destitute and the amount of debt continued to pile up. What Venezuela and the other emerging countries really needed was direct foreign investment by American and European companies and not hot money from mutual funds and other institutional investors. The free enterprise system was great for America. It

99

just did not work, without some adjustments and controls, in places like Venezuela and Mexico.

The economic crises in the emerging markets had created another even more devastating problem, one that might have far reaching implications for the future. The Latin American capitalists like their brethren in Asia had seen much of their wealth disappear. The slaughter in the stock market had been a blood bath of epic proportions. To be sure markets everywhere had done well recently with gains of forty to fifty percent, but the gains were not enough to wipe out the losses sustained earlier. The math was simple enough. To equalize, a fifty percent loss in one year required a hundred percent gain in the following year.

A large proportion of the dollars that remained in the hands of the wealthy had floated out rapidly, as a precautionary measure, into the hands of Swiss and American banks, for subsequent investments in overseas real estate or in the stock market. They were not likely to come back anytime soon. The foreigners had pulled their money out much earlier though lately greed had once again brought some of this money back, but the flows were no longer on the same level as in the past.

In December 1998 Hugo Chavez, a former army captain who had been cashiered for an unsuccessful coup attempt, was swept into power in Venezuela by a landslide. That's when he began knocking off the old elite from all its positions of power. In 1999, El Commandant, as he was known in the shantytowns and barrios, won a decisive victory, along with his allies, in the election for the new Constituent Assembly. Once in session the Assembly rapidly took control of the corrupt court system and then stripped Congress of its power to pass laws. Later that same year it came out with a new constitution allowing the president two six-year terms. The people of Venezuela overwhelmingly approved the changes in a referendum.

MARKET CRASH

Then Chavez was decisively reelected in November 2000. He also succeeded in solidifying his power over the powerful state-run oil company, Petroleos de Venezuela–known as PDVSA–which controlled the largest oil reserves outside the Middle East and which Chavez had called an "uncontrollable state within a state." Having installed an ally as its head and with his supporters constituting a majority of its board, Chavez slashed the sixty eight billion dollar investment program of the company and also cut its annual operating expenditures by three billion dollars. He also put an end to the privatization program started by the previous administration. Not that it mattered. No one was exactly rushing in to buy the state-owned enterprises.

But now what? The poor people who had helped Chavez win the election had not seen any improvement in their economic condition. Political changes would not satisfy or keep them in check forever. Chavez knew he had to do something. The old guard had resisted till the end at PDVSA. Lately he had talked of strengthening OPEC, seeking closer ties with its members and even production cuts to raise the price of oil. Chavez also needed the help of the industrialists and the upper middle class. It was they who invested and ran the businesses that provided jobs for the ordinary citizen.

But the wealthy were suffering even more than the lower classes of Venezuelan society. Not only had they seen a substantial amount of their wealth disappear like a ghost in the stock market gyrations but their lifestyle had also been severely disrupted by the greatly reduced foreign exchange earnings of the country. These Venezuelans were addicted to the liquid gold that had made Scotland famous all over the world. The country held the world record in per capita consumption of Scotch whisky, and was once the second largest importer, after the United States, of this precious commodity. Imports of whisky had had to be severely restricted. Now in these desperate times these macho men could no longer

101

3194-ISLA

drink their brains out in the evenings. Increasingly they were absent from Caracas for longer and longer periods, making frequent trips to Miami and New York.

The situation in Mexico was less severe and not as perilous. Its economy mercifully was not as dependent on oil even though that industry was still the largest employer.

Unlike most of the other Latin American countries, its gross domestic product had actually increased in the past two years. Membership in NAFTA had made this possible. These proud descendents of the great Aztec civilization were now dependent on their "Big Brother" across the Rio Grande River to keep their economy afloat. Every Mexican knew that in the mid-nineteenth century the Yankees had stolen almost a million square miles of Mexican territory–what now made up the states of Texas, New Mexico, Arizona, Nevada, Utah, California and even Colorado. It was larceny on a grand scale. Only pride now prevented them from giving away the rest of Mexico to the Americans. "What a pity," thoughtful Mexicans often joked to their American friends, "that the proponents of Manifest Destiny are no longer influential in the United States." Still the location of the country had been a great help. The annual flight of thousands of illegal Mexican immigrants to the United States provided an important safety valve that other countries in South America simply did not have.

The fear that ravaged Francisco Carrera's mind and sent cold shivers down his body, was not just from the Scotch, though that had helped considerably in at least numbing his brain. Its cause was different and was for a much more important reason. And the reason was this. For the first time in Mexican history since the revolution of 1910 an opposition party had won the presidential election. Vincente Fox, a former Coca-Cola executive and head of the country's largest opposition party–National Action Party–had been swept to power in July 2000 on a populist platform. Now if these fucking

Arabs did what this very non-Arab looking man in that exquisitely tailored Savile Row suit was telling them, the party would be over and whatever little had been accomplished would be destroyed. Hence the fear and the panic. And hence the need for more Scotch.

Tarik with his cold gambling instinct sensed that this was an opportune moment to ease the fears of his guests. He refilled their glasses with more Chivas. Then in his most soothing voice he said, "My government does not wish to create hardship for the oil-producing states. We realize that this plan would be harmful for your countries and we have no interest in doing that." Then in a conciliatory gesture he added, "We hope that a satisfactory solution can be worked out."

The South Americans were greatly relieved. Emboldened by the alcohol, the Mexican took the cue and asked about the second proposal that the Saudi had mentioned earlier. Once again, Tarik walked over to the writing table and brought back two typed sheets that he handed over to the two men. They began to read.

PLAN SUMMARY

1. Reduce daily oil production by 8.350 million barrels.
2. Limit production cuts to eight countries–6 OPEC and 2 non-OPEC.
3. Establish new five-member council to oversee oil policy.
4. Change existing oil quotas to better reflect economic needs of the oil producers.
5. Put into place a forty billion euro oil credit facility for use by the eight countries.
6. Switch to the euro for oil pricing and payments.
7. Members must guarantee adherence to Agreement for a minimum of three years.

They read the paper for the second time. Their countries could live with this. So what was the hidden

3194-ISLA

agenda? There must be some catch to it. It sounded too reasonable.

It was the Venezuelan who now spoke. "This looks reasonable. Tell us the details?"

Carrera nodded, signaling his agreement with Rodriguez's request.

Tarik filled in the details. The plan covered only eight countries. Which ones? Saudi Arabia, Venezuela, Iran, Iraq, Kuwait and the United Arab Emirates from OPEC and Mexico and Russia. Why only eight? Because this narrower approach permitted a more effective control over the whole process. Who would be in the new Oil Council? Saudi Arabia, Venezuela, Mexico, and Iran. Kuwait and Iraq would alternate as the fifth member every other year. Details of the credit facility were spelled out to the ministers. Both Townsend and Afridi had telephoned earlier in the day to advise that the negotiations with the Germans and the French had been successfully concluded. Carrera and Rodriguez were astonished to learn that the facility was already in place. The Saudis were really moving fast.

Tarik explained that the shift to the euro for oil pricing and settlement was connected to the credit facility, which was guaranteed by the two European governments. That accounted for the low interest rate. There was another ancillary benefit. Shifting their currency reserves to the euro would free Venezuela and Mexico of the ever-present threat of a freeze of their foreign currency assets. The United States would no longer have them by the balls. It would not be able to lay its hands on their euro-denominated assets. This in turn, he reminded them, gave the two countries greater financial flexibility in the future should they ever need to declare a debt moratorium on their loans from the American banks.

"There is one other thing that has an important bearing on the success of our plan," Tarik told them. "As you know there has been a change in the government in Iraq and the Gulf Region countries are working on a mutual defense alliance. That will reduce American influence and coercion in the region."

"Also in our case as well," Carrera assured the prince, as the man sitting next to him nodded in agreement.

The Venezuelan pointed out the irony of the move to the euro. "In 1978 Venezuela and some of the other OPEC price hawks wanted to shift the pricing of oil to a more stable currency than the dollar."

"I was not aware of that. What prevented it from happening?" Tarik asked.

Rodriguez smiled. "Saudi Arabia and Iran–the Shah was still on the throne–blocked the move."

The conversation then switched back to quotas and the production cuts Saudi Arabia had in mind.

"We recognize," the prince said in a conciliatory tone, "that quotas will only be willingly observed if they are fair and equitable. In my judgment they have to be linked not just to oil reserves and production capacity but also to economic issues such as population size and the economic pressures that are created as a result. We are therefore willing to increase the quotas of Venezuela, Iran and Iraq with compensating reductions in those of Saudi Arabia, Kuwait and the United Arab Emirates."

Was there a number that he had in mind? Yes, six hundred thousand barrels per day. The details could be worked out later. Had consideration been given to this in the production cuts that were envisaged for each country in his proposal, Rodriguez wanted to know? Yes, Tarik assured him pointing to the green folder. "The details are in here. You can read it later."

"You mentioned production cuts of 8.350 million barrels. What is that based on?" Carrera inquired.

"On the price level we're shooting for." Tarik responded.

3194-ISLA

"Let me explain. For the past twenty years oil prices have not kept pace with inflation. So while we have paid for our imports at the higher prevailing prices, our income has been coming to us at a much lower dollar value in real terms. Now I don't think we can make up for all our losses, but we have to get a substantially higher price for our oil. In my view a price of $38 a barrel looks quite reasonable. According to our calculations the cuts we are proposing will help us get there. And even at this number we are at less than half the price level that prevailed in 1981, adjusted for inflation. Or to put it another way, to match the price of $35 in 1981 we would have to be at $90 per barrel today! Yes my friends at $90."

That was a staggering figure. Surprise made the two South Americans totally speechless. If the production cuts that their countries had to make were not unreasonable, and the Saudi had assured them that they were not, then this price if it could be made to stick for several years, would put them back into business. Once again there would be plenty of money sloshing around. May be enough to loot without anyone noticing it. Scotch imports would resume. And yes, life would get back to normal.

"Incidentally, Saudi Arabia," Tarik informed his visitors, "will bear the brunt of the production cuts. If an agreement can be reached." He smiled "And I'm sure that it will, we will reduce our daily production by three and a half million barrels. In return we are asking that your countries cut their production by just eight hundred and fifty thousand barrels. That applies to each of you."

With that he handed them a copy of the green folder. "Please read this. For the time, we cannot release this material. It will be made available to you later."

The two men read the plan for the next thirty minutes while Tarik went into an adjoining room and made a telephone call to Townsend at the Helmsley Palace Hotel.

At eight they decided to continue the conversation over

dinner at the restaurant downstairs. Once they were seated and had ordered their drinks, Tarik brought up a subject that would be immensely helpful to them personally. He was looking for some real leverage and believed that any money the two could make on the side would prevent a reversion to cheating–in oil production that is. At least till the next election, which he figured was several years away. How these men could be bribed had been the subject of the telephone conversation a little earlier between the prince and Townsend.

In both Mexico and Venezuela, oil and corruption had always been closely linked like Siamese twins. Every six years–it had been four in the case of Venezuela until recently–a new group came into power and proceeded to plunder the country. In emerging markets everywhere the same principal was solidly enshrined in the ethics and workings of the State. Mobutu had done it in Zaire; Suharto in Indonesia had shown an expertise unmatched by any other ruler. In his day the late, unlamented Ferdinand Marcos had also shown an uncanny flair in this field. Even Benazir Bhutto was reputed to have chalked up two billion dollars in dirt-poor Pakistan!

Now our two oil ministers had been rather unfortunate. Circumstances had brought them to power at a time when the coffers of the state were literally empty. Not surprisingly the chance to plunder had all but disappeared. Tarik now offered them an opportunity to become part of the jet set crowd. He pointed out the large and immediate impact that an oil price rise of the magnitude that they had talked of might have on the financial markets. Not just in Caracas and Mexico City but also in New York. He suggested that they take advantage of the inside information. That is why it was imperative that these negotiations be kept strictly confidential and secret. What did they think, he asked? Yes they would like to very much. But there was a problem. They didn't have the money to make the investments. There was a simple

3194-ISLA

solution to that, Tarik assured them. Funds could be made available to them in the form of self-liquidating loans. In fact Saudi National Bank, which he owned, would lend them the money. Michael Townsend, the bank's chief executive, happened to be in town on business. He would ask him to visit them tomorrow and work out the details. They should check with Fox and Chavez later tonight. The bank would be more than willing to include them in the deal. He suggested loans of fifty million dollars apiece. The Mexican and the Venezuelan were ecstatic. It was an offer they simply couldn't refuse. They were beginning to really like this Arab. He was so different from the others that they had met.

The discussion went on for two more hours over an excellent dinner. All three men ordered steaks that were accompanied by a superb bottle of claret vintage 1982, which had been one of the greatest years for wine in both Bordeaux and Burgundy. The prince had declined the wine so the two men had enjoyed the bottle between themselves.

On the following morning Townsend visited Carrera and Rodriguez at their hotels. Arrangements were quickly finalized for four loans of fifty million dollars each. Forms and fiduciary agreements were faxed and duly returned within a few minutes with the signatures of Fox and Chavez. Townsend explained that the secret accounts would be opened in Liechtenstein–he would advise them the account numbers beginning with an alphabet followed by seven digits next week–and the money would be routed back and forth through a number of countries to prevent any trace back. The whole matter would be completely confidential and secret. There was absolutely no need to worry. He would personally take care of the investments. The loans would be automatically repaid from the investment gains. Townsend indicated to the jubilant individuals that the investments would be in hedge funds and he was confident that the gains would exceed one hundred percent.

The conversations were tape-recorded. Just in case they were needed to make sure that the oil agreement was honored. Tarik had carefully arranged that. It simply wouldn't do to have the King of Saudi Arabia bribing oil ministers and presidents. So Michael had done it. There would be no surprises down the road.

On Sunday, August 22, 2000 at a final meeting in Prince Tarik's suite at the Carlyle, agreement was reached on all points between Saudi Arabia, Venezuela and Mexico. Later on, much later, it would become known as the New York Pact.

3194-ISLA

CHAPTER 10

No financial institution that has any pretensions of becoming a global player can afford to stay away from the United States. The enormous scope and size of that country's financial market place had attracted banks, insurance companies and brokerage house from all over the world. They included large insurance companies like AXA from France and Zurich Re from Switzerland, banks such as Lloyds and Barclays from Britain, UBS and Credit Suisse from Switzerland, ABN Amro from the Netherlands, Deutsche and Commerzbank from Germany, brokerage firms like Nomura and of course all the large French and Japanese banks and investment houses.

When HypoVereinsbank decided to enter the U.S. market it turned to its investment bank, Credit Suisse First Boston, for assistance. David Fairfax, a senior banker at the firm, flew over from New York in July to meet the bank's chairman, Herr Doktor Ulrich Buchner.

"The commercial banking business is a dead end and you must avoid that market," Fairfax said emphatically in the chairman's wood-paneled office in Munich.

"Why?" Dr. Buchner asked.

"There is too much competition. We've gone through a decade of consolidation but there are still 8,000 banks. That's down from 15,000. They're all competing for the same business. It's almost completely consumer-oriented."

"What about lending to corporations?"

"Technology has changed that market," Fairfax explained. "Corporations are able to access the market directly. They no longer need bank intermediaries. The other problem is credit ratings."

"What do you mean?"

"Well in the old days most banks had triple-A ratings and this allowed them to borrow funds very cheaply and lend the money profitably to companies most of which had much lower credit ratings. Today there is no triple-A rated bank in the United States, so this particular game is over or almost over. Banks can only lend to lower rated and weaker companies. Most of them are not good at this."

"But there are so many foreign banks in the United States: the Japanese, the Swiss, the Germans, the French and the British."

"Yes, but none of them are doing well. The consumer market is very tough competition wise and the American banks are way ahead in technology and products. It's simply too costly to compete. Besides the foreign banks are much less qualified to lend to corporations."

The HypoVereinsbank chairman thought about this for a few minutes and then spoke.

"In my view," he declared bluntly, "we must either be one of the top three players in a business or not be in it at all. That's what you must keep in mind keep. I want you to analyze our opportunities on this basis."

"That's the right approach and that's precisely why you must avoid commercial banking."

"Okay. I understand. What about investment banking?" the chairman asked.

"The situation is no better there. There is even more competition in that business. Here also a great deal of consolidation has taken place, but in my view, we still have too much overcapacity."

There was considerable truth in what Fairfax said. In commercial banking some of the most venerable names such as Manufacturers Hanover, Chemical, Irving Trust and Security Pacific had disappeared into the dust heap of history. The condition was no different in investment banking. Old names such as Kuhn Loeb, Shearson, and E.F Hutton had been merged out of existence.

"But so many of our competitors are in that business in America," Buchner said. "Can we afford to ignore it?"

"Yes, because except for Credit Suisse which owns us," Fairfax said with great pride, "none of the others have been successful or profitable. Deutsche tried to start its own but it didn't work. It then bought Banker's Trust. That was a second-tier bank and the acquisition didn't help much. The British banks, NatWest and Barclays, failed at it miserably. So have the French and the Japanese."

"What about all the acquisitions made by the American commercial banks. How have they fared?"

"Not well. The problem is that the culture of the two businesses is very different. Commercial banking is hierarchical. The chairman has the highest compensation. Everyone else follows. Titles and perks are very important. Investment banking is the exact opposite. It's deal driven. Transactors make huge amounts of money based on measurable performance. No one has been able to fuse these two cultures successfully. Not Citigroup. Morgan Chase has come the closest but still not close enough."

"So what would you suggest?" Buchner inquired.

"The money management business," Fairfax replied without hesitation.

He then went on to explain that the business was like a

huge money machine. Unlike investment banking where deals had to be done constantly to generate earnings, the income stream of money managers was like an annuity. Once you got the business the revenues came in day after day, month after month. American and foreign financial institutions had already bought out most of the major firms in the industry. Only a handful of large companies were still available.

The debate between the two men went on for several hours. They examined all the possibilities. They went back and forth in their arguments and counter arguments. Finally Doktor Buchner came to a decision. The bank would go the money management route. He asked David Fairfax to come up with a suitable list of acquisition candidates. Fairfax promised to get back within the next few days.

Shortly thereafter the Board of HypoVereinsbank agreed, on Dr. Buchner's strong recommendation, to build a global money management business. They already owned a company in London and would now concentrate on acquiring a sizeable money management business in the United States. Board member Jurgen Pohl was given the task of overseeing the successful implementation of the bank's strategy in this area.

Three days later, Paul Erhard arrived in New York and on the following morning showed up at the office of Credit Suisse First Boston—or CSFB as it was known in the marketplace. The thirty-four-year-old Erhard, tall and muscular with flowing blond hair and blue eyes, was representative of the revolution now sweeping through German banking. A graduate of Harvard Business School and a former McKinsey consultant, Paul had joined HypoVereinsbank last year and was currently working as a special assistant to Jurgen Pohl.

At ten he met with Sam Price, a security analyst at CSFB. Sam covered the investment advisory business and had been on the Institutional Investor "All America Team" for the past five years. His credentials were perfect. Fairfax had arranged the meeting at Pohl's request. Its purpose was to provide broad as well as specific information on the money management industry to HypoVereinsbank.

Sam it turned out was also an alumnus of the famous business school and so the two men hit it off right from the start.

"The total size of the U.S. financial market," Price began, "is around thirty nine trillion dollars."

"I knew it was big but didn't realize that it was that big," Paul responded. "What's the breakdown?"

"Equities are the largest component at sixteen trillion, followed by fixed income at thirteen and the remainder is short-term money market instruments."

"What's the portion of this market that's in the hands of money managers?" Paul asked.

"Our estimate is nineteen trillion dollars. The top 250 managers have a shade over seventeen trillion of that number."

"How much of the nineteen trillion," Erhard asked, "is institutional money?"

"Tax exempt funds–that's pension funds, endowments and foundations–had eight and a half trillion dollars last year. The balance ten and a half is both domestic and foreign individuals as well as institutions. But it does not include any domestic corporate funds."

"Such as?"

"Well, for example insurance premium funds that are managed by insurance companies or trading accounts of investment and commercial banks."

"Would you have any information on the different type of money management firms that have the nineteen trillion?"

"Of course, I do," Sam said smiling. "Insurance companies manage eleven percent of the funds, banks and trust departments have thirty six percent and fifty three percent is in the hands of investment advisory firms such as B&P, Fidelity Investments, Alliance, Putnam and so on. Of the latter, some are independent, some are publicly-held and some are owned by banks and insurance companies."

He extracted a printout from his drawer and handed it to Erhard. "That's a listing of the top five hundred firms showing the total funds that they manage. It's published annually by one of the trade journals."

"And what's the product breakdown?"

"Equities is the biggest component with 58 percent; bonds account for 28 percent; Cash that's mostly short-term money market instruments are 10 percent and 4 percent is real estate and alternative investments."

"What are alternative investments?" Paul asked.

"Mostly hedge funds, private equity and venture capital."

"Is the business concentrated in the hands of a few players?" Paul enquired.

"Very much so. There are over 4,000 money management firms in the country. The top 100 account for almost 80 percent of the total business. In fact the top 50 have 60 percent of the assets. In the pension fund area, the top firm manages over $500 billion, while the tenth largest has $130 billion. After that the fall in asset size is even more precipitous. B&P, the 50th largest firm has $35 billion in institutional assets and the hundredth largest is down to only $15 billion."

"What about the fee structure?"

"It varies with the size. That is, percentages wise, you pay less the more you give in assets and there is also a differential between individuals and institutional customers. You can guess who pays more. In general, on the institutional side, the fee averages around 1.35 percent on the equity side and 30 basis points on the fixed income side."

"I would have thought the fee would be higher for the fixed income business. It's much more complex," Erhard said shaking his head in disbelief.

"It's certainly more complex but the equity side has the

115

higher returns. It also has more mystique. There is actually much less of a differential in mutual funds."

"I was reading about defined benefit and defined contribution plans. Can you explain what they are?"

"They are two different types of pension plans. In a defined benefit plan the employer guarantees a definite annual retirement benefit to each employee. To meet this future liability the employer invests funds in stocks and bonds. Annually a calculation has to be made to determine the net present value of the company's expected future pension obligations using a market rate of interest. The employer firm must put additional money in the pension fund if there is a shortfall between this calculation and the actual pension fund assets," Sam explained. Then he asked, "Do you understand this so far?"

"Yes. So in these plans the full market risk on the investments is borne by the employer."

"Exactly. Now in the defined contribution plans the situation is completely reversed. The employer contributes a specific amount of money for each employee who takes on the responsibility for making the investment decision. Changes in investment can usually be made monthly or quarterly and in some cases weekly. The future amount of pension benefits therefore depends entirely on the investment choices made by the employee."

"So in this case the investment risk has been transferred to the employee?"

"Yes. And the company has no unfunded liabilities since nothing is guaranteed. These plans were bound to grow once the employers discovered that the market risk could be transferred to employees. A fundamental shift has taken place. Practically all new plans are in this category and more and more of the existing defined benefit plans are being converted to defined contribution plans."

"What's the significance of this for the money managers?"

"The reporting requirements of the defined contribution plans are very onerous. They are tailor-made for the big mutual funds such as Fidelity and Vanguard. So it's not a good development for money managers who do not have very big mutual funds that can compete effectively with the majors. Incidentally in terms of assets, the old defined benefit plans still have roughly two thirds of pension plan assets."

Erhard nodded. Sam was impressed. He could tell that the man sitting opposite him had immediately grasped the long-term competitive significance of the changing market. That's what Harvard Business School was all about.

He continued, "Defined contribution plans have had one other major impact. It has made American workers–men and women–very comfortable with investing in stocks."

And so it had. It was borne out by the facts. In 1982 only six million Americans had mutual fund shares. Today the number was around seventy five million. So many different factors had coalesced at about the same time like a tightly furled umbrella. Corporate profits had zoomed, the economy had grown steadily, unemployment was low and inflation was nonexistent. Not surprisingly individual investors had poured record amounts into the stock market–on average almost $200 billion annually–through most of the nineties. Investor psychology had turned very bullish. The frenzy fed upon itself. It had created the greatest bull-run in Wall Street history.

"From my days at Harvard," Paul remarked, "I remember our discussions concerning the years since 1980. They've been absolutely spectacular for the United States. You're in the securities business. What do you think?"

"There's no doubt about that. You are too young to know, but Ronald Reagan's presidency was a turning point in American history."

Undeterred by Paul's smile at the mention of Reagan, Sam continued "Yes I know he acted as Bozo in a movie, but

3194-ISLA

his ever present optimism gave a sense of confidence to the people that had been missing since the catastrophe of the Vietnam War. And so the last twenty years have turned out to be a glorious period for the country. In fact the prosperity that was set in motion in 1982 has never been equaled in the two hundred and thirty year history of the republic."

"Yes, Yes. But in practical terms," Paul asked, "What does this mean for the market?"

Sam was quick with his response. "The stock market has captured the hearts and minds of the American people. It has become a national passion, a national pastime."

"You mean like the state lotteries."

"Oh, much more so. Look at the mutual funds. In 1982 there were about six hundred funds with assets totaling four hundred billion dollars. Now there are over nine thousand mutual funds with assets exceeding seven trillion dollars. You get an even better perspective of the dizzying upward propulsion of the stock market from the rise of the Dow. In 1982 the Dow stood at just over 1000. Today it's over 17,400. It took seventy seven years for the index to reach one thousand, which it did in November 1972. The next thousand had taken just over fourteen years. That number was reached in January 1987. The three thousand mark had taken only four years. Then the period was compressed dramatically. It took only four months for the Dow to go from six thousand to seven thousand. And it's been like that ever since."

The conversation then turned to money management firms. Investors were evidently attracted to the market by the high returns. In the past five years, the CSFB analyst noted, American investors had grown richer by seven trillion dollars. But the real beneficiaries of this unparalleled largesse, according to Sam Price, were the 4,000 odd firms–and the 32,000 professionals–that managed the funds of the investors. For their services they were paid a fee. On top of that, stock trading also generated commissions. All this added up to very big numbers that made the money management industry one of the premier businesses in America.

"Would you know what the gross revenues are?" Paul asked.

"So many of the firms are private and do not report their numbers, but we estimate that the amount is over two hundred billion dollars. It's a real cash cow."

The industry was doing better than the investors for whom it managed money for one very good reason. The firms got their fees and commission irrespective of performance. And performance was a real problem. In fact it had always been a problem.

Throughout the discussions Paul made notes on a yellow legal pad. He now looked up as he asked Price, "Tell me about investment performance. I read recently that this was a particularly vulnerable area for the industry."

"It's definitely a problem, but I'm not sure the industry is vulnerable. Take gambling. In the end the casino always wins. Or it would go out of business. The same thing is true in the stock market. Very few managers can beat the market. A friend of mine by the name of Bill Gross is considered the finest fixed income manager in the United States. Bill wrote a book in which he says that 'professional money management with a few exceptions is a gigantic rip-off because the product is not worth the fee you're asked to pay.' That says it all."

"What does he recommend?"

"Buying an index fund."

"Is it likely to happen. I mean most investors switching to index funds?"

"No. I think it's an extremely unlikely outcome."

"What makes you so confident?" Paul asked.

Sam smiled at his fellow alumnus. "For the same reason that the gambling industry is still there. More and more people are going to casinos. Ignorance, greed and stupidity, or a

119

combination of these, will keep the individual investor in managed funds."

The type and quality of people in the business was the final conversation topic that morning.

"Does the industry attract a lot of business graduates?" the German banker asked.

"I don't believe that's the case for some reason. It has people of very diverse background and a large number of portfolio managers have switched to the business midway through their career in some other profession. Very many haven't even been to college. Let me tell you something confidentially. Can you keep this between us Harvard boys?"

"Sure. You have my word on it."

Price had then told Erhard that all industries had their share of brilliant and mediocre people but the money management business was an exception to the general rule in two ways. First it had attracted more mediocre individuals than most other businesses.

Why?

For the simple reason that a lousy insurance salesman or journalist could do just as well at selecting stocks as a brilliant Harvard MBA or a first-class securities analyst. There was no correlation between brains and winning stock picks. It was all a question of luck and gutsy calls. Predicting future market behavior was a chancy venture. You needed balls to do something daring and out of the norm. And no one to the best of Price's knowledge had definitively proven that Harvard MBA's had better balls than a third-rate insurance salesman.

"What's the other exceptional thing about the business?" Erhard demanded.

The astronomical compensation level. A mediocre individual might have trouble making seventy-five grand in say the computer business. In money management, a mediocre portfolio manager had very little trouble making one or two million dollars annually. There were quite a few of these characters in literally every company. B&P had more than its fair share. The industry was simply awash in profits, which had risen year in and year out without break for twenty two years.

It was twelve o'clock. Paul Erhard had to leave for a luncheon appointment with David Fairfax. They agreed to have dinner that night. Paul was still a bachelor. Germans married much later than Americans. Price was between wives. In that respect he was American to the core.

The large income flows had attracted the attention of others. Commercial banks, investment banks, insurance companies and foreign financial institutions had all become enamored with the money management business. Its income was like an annuity stream and it was less volatile and seasonal than trading income or M&A fees. It was also very substantial and the risks were minimal. There were no loan write-offs or trading losses associated with the business. Consequently its capital requirements were minimal.

The result had been predictable. Over the past decade the M&A craze had overtaken the industry leaving very few large firms independent. Money management companies had been acquired at higher and higher multiples. Merrill paid five billion dollars for Mercury Asset Management; Allianz, the German insurer bought a controlling interest in Pimco; Mellon had acquired Dreyfus, Dresdner Bank had bought RCM over on the West coast, Montgomery Asset Management had been taken over by Commerzbank and Zurich Assurance had paid two billion for Scudder Stevens and Clark; Morgan Stanley had acquired Van Kampen Merit. The list went on and on.

These acquisitions had one other consequence. They made a lot of the portfolio managers who owned these firms extremely wealthy.

After a sumptuous dinner at the Cote Basque, accompa-

3194-ISLA

nied by a superb bottle of a 1983 Chateau Margaux, the two bachelors had retired to Club Macanudo, a fancy cigar joint on East 63rd Street before heading to party with the euro trash at the nearby Au Bar discotheque.

They sat quietly enjoying a Johnny Walker Black Label Scotch whisky and smoking a fine Partagas cigar.

Erhard finally broke the silence. "Give me your honest opinion. Is this the right time for us to buy a money management firm?"

Price was silent for a moment as he slowly exhaled the cigar smoke through his mouth and nose. "There are two answers. Yes and no," he finally said.

He took another puff from the cigar and then continued. "There are very few independent firms of large enough size that are still available. Getting a sufficiently large firm will help in building up the business quickly."

Erhard sipped his Scotch and nodded in agreement.

Price went on. "On the negative side it is rather late in the cycle. You'll have to pay a very high price-earnings multiple. There are risks in buying now, and there are risks in not buying now. In the end you guys have to weigh these factors and make your decision."

CHAPTER 11

The developments in the money management business had not gone unnoticed by the Machiavellian Sidney Rosenberg. He rapidly set into motion his plan to sell the company. The sale would not only enrich the partners but also give him the chance to reorganize the shop. More than half of the partners were over sixty five and at least six were in their late seventies. Anywhere else they would have been put to pasture long ago. But then things were very different at B&P.

The evolution and historical development of the firm, based on its original partnership agreement, had created a structure that set it apart from all other firms on the street. There was no retirement policy and these old geezers, with seven figure incomes, were unwilling to leave the firm voluntarily. When he had discussed the issue last year with Alexandra she had succinctly pointed out, "Since they barely do any work, they have retired for all practical purposes any way."

"That's why we need a retirement plan," Rosenberg had argued.

"We already have one. The compensation the older partners are getting is a form of retirement income in their view. They constitute a majority of the partners. It's unlikely we'll ever have the votes to change the system," Alexandra had responded petulantly.

Both Rosenberg and Alexandra understood the difficulty. It was an uphill battle. Most of these old partners were in excellent health and given the latest advances in medicine it was highly probable that they would continue to faithfully 'serve' the firm for years to come. There was a real danger that the place might become a geriatric ward in the not too distant future. To their credit they still came to the office regularly, drank interminable cups of coffee, gossiped, had two-hour-long three martini lunches and occasionally watched the ticker tape in the trading room. But the real reason for their daily trip to the office was to flirt and pursue the secretaries. They had great difficulty keeping their hands off women especially those in their organizational units. The assistants–several of whom were younger partners–did all the real work anyway.

Rosenberg had been excited about selling the firm. He had walked over to Alexandra's office at that time and announced without any preamble, "I have a brilliant new idea."

"What?"

"Sell the firm. At current rates it's worth two billion dollars."

"It certainly sounds good," Alexandra said. "But I'm not sure you can pull it off without making some of the changes we've talked of."

"No. You're wrong. We can make those changes any time. They are under my control. The beauty is that this will give us a chance to clean up the Augean stables in the retail business after the sale. I admit that it'll be much easier to do it in the newly reconstituted firm."

He was referring to the fact that in service industries people were considered the most important asset and any acquirer would undoubtedly want to keep many of the senior managers at least for a few years. His plan was to ease out the older partners after the sale by convincing the new owners that the younger partners were the ones who did the real work.

"You're going to have difficulty with the younger partners. Their share of the sale proceeds is not high enough since the bulk of the money will go to the old fogies for whom they work."

"I think I can fix that. Besides I've had discussions with Goldman Sachs and they are very excited at the prospect. They told me they had five or six prospective buyers right now scouring the marketplace."

To his surprise Rosenberg had succeeded without any difficulty in persuading the ageing Lotharios to sell the firm. Visions of enormous wealth made them an easy target for his scheme. They were effusive in their praise of Rosenberg and couldn't wait to lay their hands on this enormous pot of gold. As Alexandra had predicted the younger partners had opposed the idea but they had been quickly outvoted.

The result of all this maneuvering eventually led, in mid-July, to B&P's decision to put itself up for sale. The news had made headlines in the business section of the New York Times. It was also on the second page of the Wall Street Journal. Goldman Sachs was given the mandate to bring about this blessed event to a successful and happy fruition. Detailed information–much of it sensitive and either not known or scarcely understood by most partners–was put together for the potential buyers. After careful screening and canvassing Goldman came up with six potential candidates. The list included two foreign and four American financial institutions. The latter were all regional banks. Both Citigroup and American Banking Corporation had declined. In their view the price was too high.

Senior management of the Bank of Boston, Mellon Bank,

First Union, Bank One and the United Bank of France accompanied by their investment bankers met with the B&P negotiating group over a two-day period beginning on August 19. The sessions with each bank had lasted four hours. Presentations were made by a number of B&P partners. Questions were asked. Answers were given. As at most meetings some light banter had been mixed with serious discussions. The discussions had apparently gone well except in the case of First Union. At least that was the impression of all the members of the B&P members except for Alexandra Middleton. She was much less sanguine. The nature of some of the questions and the tone of voice of several key players led her to a very different set of conclusions. She mentioned these to Rosenberg but he dismissed them derisively.

Events had borne her out. The rejections had come swiftly, one after the other, on the following Monday to the dismay and consternation of Rosenberg. He had not expected this. And to add insult to injury the banks had made no counter offers. They had simply decided not to bid at all.

A tumultuous meeting of the management committee took place after these rejections, followed by an even more tumultuous meeting of the whole partnership. The initial shock gave way to anger. The older partners were particularly incensed. They had set their heart on this fabulous new wealth. Just when the fortune seemed within sight, it had gotten out of reach. They excoriated Rosenberg and Weisdick. They leveled charges that they had failed to build a viable institutional equity business or a saleable firm. There were rumblings about the need for management changes.

It was against this backdrop that the final meeting took place on Tuesday, August 24. At precisely nine in the morning a group of well dressed officials led by Board member Jurgen Pohl of HypoVereinsbank had trooped into the twenty-sixth-floor conference room at the B&P office in the Seagram

Building. David Fairfax, their investment banker from CSFB, accompanied them. Members of the B&P team had assembled in the room earlier along with their bankers from Goldman Sachs.

The meeting got underway after the usual round of hand-shakes and introductions. A butler in a white coat and black trousers served coffee.

Rosenberg started the meeting with an overview of the firm. "B&P Asset Management was established in 1945. For the next thirty years the firm managed money for wealthy individuals, mostly Jewish and entirely in equities."

The HypoVereinsbank group was listening attentively. He continued, "We expanded into the institutional business in 1975. In 1982 we began offering mutual funds and in 1986 we introduced fixed income products. Today we are the fifti-eth-largest money market firm with thirty partners and 450 employees. Despite our size, the firm still retains its entre-preneurial culture. Our focus is on profits and not on assets under management."

He paused for effect, and then went on, "Last year our net income before distribution to the partners was a shade over two hundred and twenty million dollars. This represents an increase of ten percent over the previous year."

The first question was asked at this point. It was from Pohl.

"How did the equity market do last year?"

"The Dow was up 21.6% and the S&P 500 index gained 20.3%. The Lehman Aggregate Bond index returned a negative 0.8%," Rosenberg responded.

Pohl made some notes as Rosenberg continued, "Our management philosophy is simple. We embrace change but avoid forecasting the future. In our view adherence to this philosophy has made the firm prosperous."

The senior German banker intervened again. "Can you please elaborate on this?"

3194-ISLA

"Certainly. What I mean is that we do not rush in with new products in anticipation of possible future demand. That's very costly. So we let others do the leading. We offer the product once we see that the idea has been accepted in the marketplace."

"And how long do you typically wait." Paul Erhard asked the question.

"There's no set time. It ranges from six months to several years," Rosenberg replied.

Alexandra Middleton's presentation was next. Copies of the material, bound in a blue folder, with color charts and bullet points were distributed to the group.

"We have three principal business arranged around specific customer categories–institutional equities, institutional fixed income and retail which is essentially focused on high-net-worth individuals," Alexandra began. "A fourth business, international equities and fixed income, was introduced three years ago. We have ten billion dollars in institutional equity funds, twenty five billion in fixed income and another twenty billion of wealthy customers funds."

"How many retail accounts do you have?" Pohl inquired.

"The retail group has 4,000 individually managed accounts. Then we have two hundred thousand customers in our fifteen mutual funds and another ten thousand in the WRAP product."

Alexandra then went on to explain that the firm had a full range of products and commented upon several of the most important ones. Finally she had described some of the firm's distribution channels and business dynamics. Accounts in the institutional area were specially tailored to customer requirements. Consultants who selected money management firms through an RFP process–known as request for proposal–dominated the business. Six institutional sales people covered 150 national pension fund consultants. The retail business was largely driven by referrals from existing relationships. There was also a ten person sales force covering five thousand financial consultants such as accountants and lawyers. Another five sales people focused on the WRAP programs offered by the major brokerage firms such as Merrill and Smith Barney.

"We have one major weakness," Alexandra then said. "International distribution." She smiled and continued, "That is why, in our view, HypoVereinsbank is such a great fit. We can leverage off your network to access the European, Asian and South American institutional markets."

Up to this point the presentations appeared to be going well. The audience was attentive. They listened without asking too many questions and they were deferential.

Now Jurgen Pohl intervened with some ideas of his own.

"As you know we are interested in building a global money management business. In fact I would say this is one of HypoVereinsbank's principal initiatives."

This elated the B&P representatives. Several had smiles on their faces. Both Alexandra and Rosenberg were in this group. The presentation was obviously going well.

"Last year we purchased Saturn Asset Management in the United Kingdom," Pohl said as Rosenberg and Middleton nodded their heads. They were aware of this. It had been reported in the newspapers at the time.

"We structured an ingenious deal with them," Pohl continued. He wanted to test their reaction. "It's performance-oriented. We bought fifty two percent of the shares at twelve times earnings. The remainder of the shares will be acquired at the end of five years. If the assets under management increased faster than the overall market the purchase of the remaining shares would be at eighteen times the earnings. If the asset growth lags the market the purchase will be at five to eight times earnings based on the pre-established ranges. Has B&P thought of such an approach?"

"It's an intriguing idea," Rosenberg quickly responded. "But we haven't given that any serious thought."

Nothing further was said on the subject.

The meeting resumed after a short coffee break. Alexandra then described in some detail the institutional fixed income business, the investment philosophy and the process used in the business. In response to questions she indicated that they had three hundred customers and that last year the group had won one billion dollars of new fixed income business. This year was shaping out just as well.

Ronald Shapiro made a similar presentation on the institutional equity business. He did a pretty creditable job. No questions were asked at this stage and it appeared that the Germans were satisfied. Rosenberg felt particularly pleased. It looked very encouraging and he was confident of hooking them.

From this point on it had been downhill all the way. The climax came, from the German point of view, during Hillary Schuster's–she was the head of the Marketing group–description of the institutional business development process.

"What was the size of your institutional equity assets under management at the end of 1993?" Pohl suddenly inquired during the presentation.

"We had five billion dollars."

"And where was the Dow at the end of 1993?

Hillary checked the papers in front of her. "It was at 3,754."

"At the end of 2003 the Dow was at . . ."

"16,441," replied Erhard.

Pohl pulled out his HP calculator and punched in some numbers. "So the market has grown at a 15.9 percent annual compound rate. At this rate you should have twenty two billion dollars under management."

"Unfortunately we had some unexpected personnel problems in the past four years. That hurt our performance. The situation has since been corrected," Schuster responded a little apologetically.

"Could you tell us what new institutional equity business you got last year?"

"Last year was the worst year for us. We did not get any new business. But the year before we got three hundred million," Hillary said trying to hide her embarrassment. She felt humiliated. It was all because of the lousy performance numbers of the portfolio managers. Only a few people in the firm were aware of the difficulties she faced trying to get new business. But now it was coming out in a formal meeting with potential acquirers. She saw a hint of a smile on Alexandra's face. The bitch would now use this damaging information even more effectively.

The Teutonic mind cannot comprehend illogical state of affairs. There was something odd in the American market that had bothered Pohl and raised some doubts in his mind on the future profitability of the U.S. money management business under certain assumptions. His assistant, Erhard, had come up with an explanation. Pohl decided to test the hypothesis on his hosts.

"What is the fee that you charge your institutional and retail equity customers?"

"On the institutional side it's around 1 ¼ percent. That's in line with the market. On the individual side we are at the upper end at 1 ¾ percent," Rosenberg replied since the question had been addressed at him.

"What does Vanguard charge on its S&P 500 index fund?" Pohl asked.

"I believe eighteen basis points."

"So what I don't understand is why all your customers haven't switched to Vanguard. From the evidence they would have obtained much better results at a fraction of the cost?"

Rosenberg smiled triumphantly as he spoke. He'd been on this wicket before. "Markets don't always act logically. Statistics, common sense and reason all support what you said. But that does not take into account the human side of the equation. When greed and self-interest come into play they make markets much less rational and a lot more interesting.

3194-ISLA

The switch will not take place for the same reasons that people still commit crime even though they know that punishment will be meted out. On the retail side its largely ignorance and greed. On the institutional side it's self-interest. We offer them access to the good life and the consultants provide the cover. All of us benefit. Of course the index business will grow but it will always be relatively small. It's less than ten percent of the total market." Rosenberg finished his short speech on a confident tone.

Two retail partners, both in their mid-sixties, came next on the show. They gave the Germans a picture of their market and their very different money management styles and business development approaches. The final presentation was on the mutual fund product. It had gone without incident but the Germans noted the very competitive nature of the business and the relatively small size of B&P in this market.

The meeting ended shortly after one o'clock. Pohl was as effusive as a German banker can be in thanking his hosts on the excellence of so many presentations. "Thank you for telling us so much about your firm," he said. "It's quite a money-making machine you have here. We'll be back next week."

Having declined a luncheon invitation from Weisdick on the grounds of a previous business engagement, the three Germans and Fairfax proceeded to the nearby Four Seasons restaurant, one of New York's most famous establishments. A waiter appeared as soon as they were comfortably seated on the leather banquettes at one of the corner tables in the rosewood-paneled, very masculine looking Grill Room. Everyone ordered Dortmunder Export beer. After ten minutes of ordinary chitchat and once the more important task of ordering lunch had been accomplished, the conversation finally turned to the morning's meeting.

Pohl had made up his mind. The session had confirmed what Alexandra had mentioned at their private luncheon on the preceding Saturday.

"I don't know about you gentlemen," Pohl said fixing his gaze on Fairfax, "but I was struck by several things."

He took a sip of the cold beer and continued, "The sense I got was of a lack of momentum, of tired old people in the driver's seat."

"You're right," Fairfax conceded the point, "but that can be easily changed once you acquire them. The firm makes a lot of money. The basics are sound."

"David, that's because a rising tide lifts all boats." The roly-poly, fifty-eight-year-old Pohl with his neatly brushed silver colored hair quickly responded. "Everyone in the business is making money. They have slipped ten places in rank in the past three years. They are losing market share."

"The company still makes a lot of money. Let's not over emphasize the market share aspect. Practically all companies in the business are suffering from that," Fairfax pointed out.

"Okay, I'll go along with that. But there's something else."

That's when the waiter arrived with the lunch. As they ate, Pohl was preoccupied with the point Alexandra had made about B&P's competitive situation last Saturday. His mind flashed back to that meeting.

He had first met Alexandra for breakfast in late July. He liked her immediately and got the impression that the feeling was mutual. She impressed him not only by her intelligence and cleverness but also by the way she wore her clothes with an aristocrat's casual elegance. They had spoken on the phone the previous week and agreed to meet for lunch on Saturday.

Paul Erhard had accompanied Pohl to the luncheon. Alexandra outlined her ideas on how they should proceed and he agreed to follow her recommendations. Their motivations and their goals were very different. The German wanted inside information that might give him a negotiating edge. Besides anything that created dissension in the firm was good. He figured that this would put pressure on them to

3194-ISLA

sell. And it would lower the price. Alexandra longed to be at the helm of the firm. That was one of her key aims at the July meeting with Pohl when she gave him the idea to buy B&P. But there were no signs of either Weisdick or Rosenberg being ready to trudge off into oblivion. This might nudge at least one of them into retirement. She was tired of waiting. Besides now she did not want to sell the firm. At least not yet. She had changed her mind since their earlier meeting. If her hunch on the stock market was right her partnership share would be greatly bolstered by the shrinkage in stock prices. And if this information made HypoVereinsbank less likely to buy, so much the better. The bank had access to management consultants who could put together a report in a few hours. Nothing would be linked to her. She didn't know anyone in that profession and couldn't even mention the idea to her husband. It was much too devious an approach for the straight-laced Phillip.

"What's your view of B&P's current condition?" Pohl asked her.

"You know over time all companies drift towards mediocrity. This has happened to corporations as diverse as IBM, Coca-Cola and Citigroup. Periodically they have to be re-energized and shaken up. Our institutional business is fundamentally sound. Of course there are problems that have to be fixed," Alexandra replied.

She then went on to provide a perspective that only an insider, with complete familiarity with the intricacies of the company can possibly have. She had the facts and the figures to back up her assertions. The entrepreneurial culture had been lost, the current structure prevented investments in new businesses. Why? Simple. There was no incentive for the old partners to invest in the future.

They wanted all the cash now. The partner's age and the quality of personnel were very worrisome. Management was out of touch with the rapid changes that were occurring in the market. It needed to be replaced. The declining competitive position was a cause for some concern.

Erhard with his management consulting background quickly put all of Alexandra's information into an excellent report on his Dell Inspiron 7000 laptop. Later that afternoon he took it to a nearby Kinko's outlet where the material was photocopied, collated and bound in 14 blue folders.

Alexandra supplied the names of the management committee members and a few other key partners. The latter were selected to provide the widest possible dissemination of the information within the firm. The mailing of the document was left to Pohl's discretion.

"You were about to tell us something when the waiter came," Fairfax tried to jog Pohl's memory.

"Ah yes. I am bothered by their competitive situation."

"I don't understand what you mean by that?" Fairfax asked worrying that the Germans might be trying to slip away from the acquisition. He had a great deal at stake. The fee for CSFB was around thirty million dollars.

"I mean that they have been responding to change instead of anticipating it. And it's been much too late. As a result they don't have the right products at the right time," Pohl replied.

Then looking at Erhard he asked, "What do you think Paul?"

"You're right. Their partnership structure interferes with that. There is no motivation for the older partners to fund the development of new businesses or incur expenses on new products that will benefit someone else in the future."

"I agree. But that's the past. You can change all of this. In my view you should reduce the price and go for it."

"What do you suggest?" Pohl asked, inwardly amused at the squirming of the investment banker.

"Perhaps an offer at fifteen times earnings instead of twenty. And we could also come up with adjusted earnings numbers justifying them on higher compensation payments to key staff members as an incentive to stay with the acquired firm."

Erhard now spoke up. "I'm not worried about the problems. We can fix those. But we'll need to buy another mutual fund company to get some momentum in that part of the business. B&P is relatively small in that area. However at the end of the day my sense is that the timing is wrong. I'm concerned that we have a stock market bubble here. I would recommend waiting three months."

That was very close to Pohl's view. But then he also had knowledge of the Saudi oil plan that none of these people had any notion of. He had always felt that Erhard was a very smart young man. This merely confirmed his judgment. The young man, he noted with satisfaction, was destined to go far in the bank.

"David lets work on the numbers for the next several months." Pohl said in his most authoritative voice, having decided upon HypoVereinsbank's strategy. "And let's also look at some mutual funds as Paul has suggested. Meanwhile I want you to tell B&P that for the time being we have decided not to bid."

They had one more round of beer. As they left the restaurant Pohl whispered something to Erhard.

Later that afternoon Paul visited the Post Office located at Rockefeller Center. He carried thirteen large envelopes in his hand that he gave to the postal clerk at window number five. Ten minutes later they were stamped and in the mailbox.

CHAPTER 12

It was still dark when Alexandra Middleton arrived at La Guardia airport on Wednesday to take an early morning American Airlines flight. At the airport she was joined by Andrew Ryder, one of her portfolio managers. They were heading for Minneapolis to make a presentation, later that morning, to the Board of the Minnesota Teachers Retirement System. At stake was a hundred million dollar intermediate-term bond account.

Alexandra headed B&P's bond portfolio management department, known as the Fixed Income Group. She had started the business back in 1986 and the group now managed slightly over twenty five billion dollars in fixed income assets. It was one of the great success stories of Wall Street. Along with Bill Gross of PIMCO, she was considered a legendary money manager and made frequent appearances on CNN, Fox and CNBC television stations. She had even been a guest on Louis Rukyser's Wall Street Week program. The growth of the business had led to Alexandra's rapid rise in the B&P partnership ranks and she was now the fourth-largest partner at the firm.

Asset managers like Alexandra, managed trillions of dol-

137

lars on behalf of both individual investors and institutional customers such as corporate pension funds, state and local pension funds, endowments, foundations and other non-profit organizations that included hospitals, universities and unions. The United States was by far the largest asset management market in the world. During the past decade the extraordinary returns in the stock market of sixteen percent compounded annually had greatly reduced investor interest in bonds where the return was considerably lower. As a result, institutional and individual investments in fixed income securities had declined from around forty percent to slightly less than thirty percent of the market. This in turn had intensified competition in the fixed income business particularly in the institutional area.

Now that the fixed income market was growing very slowly, one money manager's gain came at the expense of another, as pension fund accounts were moved between them usually for poor performance reasons. A hundred million dollar account was a big-ticket item. Just what money managers dreamed of. The best and the brightest from four or five firms, hand picked by a pension fund consultant, would be there competing for the business today. Alexandra was one of them.

Alexandra always took the early morning flights instead of going a day earlier and spending a night away from her husband and children whom she saw mostly in the evenings. Getting up very early was hard and she frequently felt a little tired; but it was well worth it since it gave her a chance to spend more time with her family. For most women, working and being a wife and mother was difficult. It caused too many emotional problems. Many simply could not cope with it and chose either not to work or not to have children. Alexandra had arranged her life in ways to come up with a balance. It had been easy when the children were toddlers and her business was still small. But it was much more difficult now that they were all at school and she was compelled to travel so often. On most days when she was in town she accompanied them to the bus stop in the morning on her way to the office and was home, not too late in the evenings to be with them. Fortunately Phillip had more time, now that she had persuaded him to take early retirement, so he helped them with the homework and arranged the play dates and whatever else needed to be taken care of. Each spring the family went to Jamaica during the children's school break and in the summers they spent a month in Europe. She loved the children and they adored her. Particularly since she was so generous with presents.

All faces turned in her direction as Alexandra, accompanied by Ryder, walked into the conference room in Minneapolis dressed in a superbly tailored navy blue Chanel suit. The plan administrator leaned towards Williams and whispered, "You said she was very smart but you didn't tell me she was beautiful as well."

Williams chuckled without saying anything. He saw that she was having a powerful effect on the audience. The board members vaguely remembered from their briefing that she managed a lot of money but the look on their faces showed that they were not prepared for this. Her youthfulness and good looks had taken them completely by surprise. They had felt tired and sleepy in the two earlier presentations. Now they were very attentive and fully awake. Their recovery had been nothing short of miraculous.

Alexandra introduced herself and Andrew and then informed them that Ryder would make the first part of the presentation.

"Our firm B&P was founded almost sixty years ago," Ryder began. "In accordance with our founders' ideals we have remained a partnership. This structure ensures that our thirty partners are intimately involved in the management of our clients' assets."

He continued, "We currently manage fifty five billion

3194-ISLA

dollars in assets of over four hundred institutional and thousands of individual clients. Our fixed income group manages twenty five billion dollars for a broad spectrum of customers."

More details on the company were provided. All had one objective. To demonstrate the firm's excellence and its suitability to manage the funds of the Minnesota Teachers Retirement System.

Five minutes later Alexandra began her presentation,

She explained the firm's philosophy in managing fixed income portfolios. "We add value to the portfolio," she said, "by integrating four elements: limited duration shifts, management of the yield curve, investing in all sectors of the bond marketing and optimizing security selection."

She then elaborated on the specific elements of these strategies. "If you look at page four of the document," she said in that engaging way she had with customers, "you will see how we manage the yield curve. As the chart shows you can get 95 percent of the yield of a thirty-year Treasury bond on a ten-year Treasury note with a third less risk."

The simple but colorful charts added further credence and weight to her story. Her friendly smile and the way she looked at them with those large green eyes conveyed genuine sincerity. They warmed to the presentation and with each passing minute became more and more impressed with her mastery of the facts.

"Chart two shows the spreads available in similar maturity securities of different credit quality over the benchmark Treasury equivalent. Right now the yield on ten-year corporate paper such as Ford and Coca-Cola is 7.25 percent versus 5.50 percent on ten-year Treasuries. This spread is unusually wide for several reasons." She explained the reasons in simple, easily understandable terms.

Alexandra then talked of the decision making process that they used at B&P.

"I chair a team of investment managers and product specialists to generate security ideas from all sectors of the fixed income market: Governments, Agencies, Corporates, Mortgages and Asset-Backed securities. We apply fundamental value criteria to determine deviations in sector weightings from a neutral position. Individual securities are selected after careful screening of issuer credit quality. I am responsible for the macro sector allocation decisions. Duration decisions are made by a small team under my direction."

She then quickly went over their performance statistics over the past one, three, five and ten-year periods. The firm had done well in most of these years but had slipped in 2000. This had hurt the five-year numbers, but the performance in the past three years had been very good. Overall B&P was in the top-tier of fixed income investment managers.

"A team of investment professionals works with each client. Of course this will also be the case with your account."

She looked at them again with that smile of hers and then continued. "The Minnesota Teachers account is an extremely prestigious one and we will feel very honored to be selected as one of your managers."

They nodded and smiled. There was something about Alexandra that created a remarkable rapport with most customers She had an instinctive ability to captivate an audience. Sensing this, she put in the final clincher. "If we are selected I assure you that I will personally meet with you at least semi-annually to review our performance."

It was now time for questions. The rotund figure with the large round glasses and heavily suntanned face was the first off the mark.

"Did you read Professor Siegel's new article in the Wall Street Journal yesterday?"

In the article Siegel had argued convincingly that stock

141

market returns would always out perform short-term government bonds in the long run.

"Yes, I did,"

"So what did you think of his thesis?" the man asked.

"That's an excellent question. I'm glad you asked," Alexandra replied, smiling sweetly at the trustee whose face beamed with pride.

"Professor Siegel says that stock returns have averaged around ten percent annually between 1946 and 2003 with a standard deviation of fifteen percent. That means that the returns on stocks in this period ranged between gains of twenty five percent and losses of five percent."

She looked at them and asked, "Are you following me?" They nodded.

"Short-term government bonds in the same period had an annual return of five percent but a standard deviation of only three percent. So bond returns ranged between a high of eight percent and a low of two percent. Their highest return is obviously much less than in the case of stocks, but at the lower range the bonds have done much better."

Once again she looked at them. They nodded their heads.

"Quite frankly I'm not at all surprised by the fact that the return on stocks is greater because the risk is also five times greater–a standard deviation of fifteen percent versus three percent for bonds. You obviously know that the greater the risk the greater is the potential for gain or loss. But Professor Siegel's comparison is absolutely meaningless. He's comparing a Mercedes with a Volkswagen."

She noticed the quizzical looks on their faces.

"Let me explain. We need to compare apples with apples. So we have to make some adjustments. The US government security is a triple-A credit while the S&P 500 stock index is single-A in credit quality. So to make the comparison meaningful we have to use bonds with single-A credit ratings. Now if we also factor in the same market risk–the fifteen percent standard deviation mentioned by Professor Siegel–and the same long-term maturity period, you will find that the returns on stocks and bonds are virtually identical over long periods of time. It's for this same reason that most of the comparisons made in newspapers are wrong. The returns become very similar between different types of securities once appropriate adjustments are made in the maturity, credit and price risk factors." She smiled and added, "Unfortunately there is no such thing as a free lunch."

The mention of free lunches brought grins to their faces. Free lunches were available all the time in this business. Obviously they were students of such matters. But she must have meant something different. They nodded in agreement, impressed by her ability to explain complex ideas in simple terms without appearing to be condescending.

The board member sitting on the right of Archie Williams decided to get some free advice on his investments.

"Can you tell us you views on the stock market and its likely impact on fixed income securities?"

"Personally I believe that the stock market is overpriced. The price-earnings ratio of the S&P 500 index stocks is now at an all time high of thirty times earnings compared with the historical average of around fifteen. What we are seeing is a type of hyperinflation with too much money chasing too few goods, in this case, stocks."

This was a very novel explanation that they had heard from no one else.

She continued, "On the one hand the supply of shares on the stock exchange is decreasing because of all the merger and acquisitions activity which has hit records for the past five years, and the stock buybacks by corporations. These have averaged two hundred billion dollars over each of the past five years. On the demand side over two hundred billion dollars has been pouring in annually into mutual funds since 1994. Additionally because of the much higher returns,

institutions and individuals have been transferring funds from
bonds to stocks. Clearly there is an imbalance. I don't believe
these price levels are sustainable. That's one of the reasons
we have so much volatility. At this point the market is more
emotional than rational. Anything could shift the sentiment
very quickly."

"What's the outlook in the next few months?" one of the
board members asked.

"I believe there will be a correction. It's difficult to predict the exact date with any degree of certainty but stock
returns will revert eventually to their much lower longer-term
historical norms. Of this there can be no doubt."

Alexandra's English accent had not entirely disappeared,
even after almost twenty years in the United States. It was
one of those intangibles that usually impressed customers
immensely. That morning it did not escape the attention of
the men in that conference room in Minneapolis. There was
something special about an English accent. It added a touch
of class. And people usually remembered that. As did the
three board members when they met later that week to pick
the winner.

"What's the implication for bonds and interest rates?" the
board member with the nicely tanned face asked?   .

"We believe that rates are likely to come down in the
next three months. If the stock market declines, investors
will seek the safety of Treasuries as they have done
historically. Inflation remains low and the Fed is unlikely to
change interest rates as the economy is growing at an
acceptable pace. So we have extended the duration of our
bond portfolio in line with this thinking."

The meeting lasted for almost an hour and a half instead
of the scheduled forty five minutes. It ended with the usual
exchange of pleasantries. Archie Williams escorted them out.
The last of the money managers, those from Neuberger &

Berman, were waiting for their turn. "I'll be with you in a minute," he said as they walked passed the seated group. "I believe the presentation went very well," Williams said encouragingly, once they were outside. "The rapport was good and I think you made a very good impression on them. I'll be in touch next week."

At exactly the same time as the presentation in Minneapolis was concluding, Peter Weisdick returned to his office in New York after meeting Sidney Rosenberg. They had discussed the day's bad news. At eleven fifteen that morning, Fairfax had telephoned from Credit Suisse First Boston to advise that HypoVereinsbank had decided to withdraw from the bidding. Weisdick was distraught. The partners would have to be told and most of them–especially the older men– would be furious and would vent their spleen on him and Rosenberg. In their frustration and anger they might even force management changes on the firm. He agreed with his strong willed colleague's suggestion that they delay passing on the news to the partners until the following week. "In the mean time," Rosenberg said, "I will meet Pohl and see if there is some way to revive the interest. The meeting has already been set up."

That had relieved Weisdick. Back in his office he began reading a report showing the performance of individual managers during the previous month. The results were much better than expected. Several managers had beaten the S&P index. He leaned back in his chair savoring this breakthrough. Suddenly he felt a searing pain in his chest. For a moment he thought it was just gas pains. That happened quite often. But the pain increased and became more excruciating. Everything in the room began to weave and look hazy as if a violent earthquake was shaking the building. The pain was unbelievable now. He gasped for air; breathing was becoming very difficult . . . impossible. He opened his mouth to scream for help. Nothing happened. No voice came out. He could

3194-ISLA

no longer see as he rapidly lost consciousness and the life went out of him.

Sometime later when his secretary walked in with coffee from the adjoining room, she saw his head resting on the desk. Peter Weisdick had been dead for twenty minutes. She screamed. The coffee cup fell on the floor staining the soft green carpet. A number of people rushed in from neighboring offices. Within ten minutes an ambulance had appeared. The medical workers tried mouth-to-mouth resuscitation. They thumped his chest. They even applied electric shock treatment. But it was all to no avail. There was no response. He was rushed to Lenox Hill Hospital. At 1:05 P.M. Peter Weisdick was declared dead.

Alexandra and Andrew walked to the American Airlines gate number six at Chicago's O'Hare airport to catch their flight back to New York, which was scheduled to leave in forty five minutes. Along the way Alexandra saw a gift shop. She walked into it with Andrew trailing along.

"I need to buy some gifts for the kids."

She checked the clothes and expertly picked a dress. Then she took two boy's shirts in different sizes and two bottles of perfume. It all took less than fifteen minutes.

Andrew was surprised by her behavior. Somehow he did not expect this from her. The explanation was not long in coming.

"With twenty five billion in assets there's too much traveling," she explained to Andrew as she paid for the goods. "I'm out at least three or four days a week. There's not enough time to spend with the children. I feel so guilty. This is one way of making it up. They enjoy receiving presents. And they feel their mom's thinking of them."

"You're not the stay home type," Andrew laughed. He knew that guilt made her use this form of bribery but he did not tell her this.

"That's true. I just couldn't possibly stay home."

As they approached the gate, Alexandra noticed a bank of telephones.

"Andrew, I'll phone the office while you check us in at the counter."

She handed him her ticket and walked over to the telephones.

"B&P. Ms. Middleton's office," said the voice at the other end that she immediately recognized as that of her secretary, Colleen Murphy.

"Hi. Colleen. We're back in Chicago . . ."

"Oh, Alexandra," the secretary interrupted hoarsely, "we've been trying to get hold of you, but you had already left the meeting. Something dreadful has happened."

Alexandra was very frightened. She thought it was Phillip or one of the children. Perhaps they were involved in an accident.

"What is it? I hope it's not my family?"

"No. No. It's Peter Weisdick. He had a heart attack and died instantaneously."

"When?" a shocked Alexandra asked.

"This afternoon around twelve thirty. They found him slumped on the desk."

As Andrew Ryder walked to a nearby chair with the two boarding passes in his hand he could see Alexandra talking on the phone. Rays of sunlight from a nearby window highlighted her long silky auburn colored hair. She looked very elegant but her face was grim and serious. He immediately thought it had something to do with the market. Perhaps they got caught on the wrong side of price movements. These things happen. After all you can't really predict what's likely to occur. Luck played a big part in their business. And market psychology was a strange animal. For an hour bond prices may edge up and then suddenly before you know it, they've reversed course and are spiraling down. All for no apparent reason.

He glanced nervously at the clock. It was two forty. A

voice on the loudspeaker announced that flight 362 to New York was ready for boarding. Alexandra continued to talk on the phone. He waited anxiously. Finally she hung up and rushed to the gate. They were the last to board the plane.

CHAPTER 13

The aircraft, a Boeing 757, was only three quarters full. They walked to their assigned seats midway in the plane. Alexandra eased her long slender legs in the confined space of the economy class cabin. Andrew took the aisle space next to her. It was one of those lucky days at O'Hare airport. Unlike the usual delays, the plane quickly moved down the tarmac and was airborne within twenty minutes.

Alexandra seemed preoccupied in thought. Ryder noticed that she looked pale; the color had drained from her face. Something had obviously upset her. He didn't believe that whatever was disturbing her had anything to do with the market. She was a pro and was used to the market's ups and downs. Besides she would have told him by now. No, he concluded, it was connected with something that had happened at the office.

"Anything wrong?" he finally asked, unable to keep quiet any longer.

Rider liked her. It was not often that people with limited money management experience got a chance to manage money. Alexandra had taken a risk on him and given him an opportunity. At the firm she had the reputation of being hard

149

on people. Some of the portfolio managers were genuinely scared of her. He didn't know the reason for this. She had been helpful and supportive of him.

"Yes. I'll tell you in a minute. As soon as I can compose myself a little more."

She closed her eyes.

The flight attendant arrived with the drink trolley. They both ordered vodka tonics. She gulped half of it almost immediately and followed with the rest in short order.

"Now I feel a little better. It's Peter Weisdick. He died early this afternoon."

"What?"

"Apparently he had a heart attack and died almost instantly."

They gestured for another round of drinks from the flight attendant who was just two seats behind them. This time Alexandra sipped the drink slowly. She appeared to be in a contemplative mood, wrapped in her own thoughts.

Several events of the past fourteen years went through her mind. She had not been personally close to Weisdick, and did not feel any particular sorrow at his death, but after her inclusion in the management committee four years ago, he had provided crucial support at different times on several important issues. She recalled with pleasure the note he had sent her after her appearance on the Louis Rukyser show 'Wall Street Week' on public television WNET. "Alexandra you were absolutely brilliant," the note had said, "You're a great ambassador for B&P and the partnership is very grateful for the many contributions you have made to the firm." This was the stuff that Weisdick was really good at. He spent a lot of times writing notes.

There was something else on her mind. That document she had collaborated on with Jurgen Pohl of HypoVereinsbank. Hopefully it had not been mailed as yet. She had not anticipated Weisdick's death, which complicated the timing drastically. She had to reach Pohl and have the project put on temporary hold. It was too late today. She would get hold of him in Munich early in the morning.

But the most important thought that passed through her mind related to the prospects that Weisdick's unfortunate death had opened up for her. Now it was up to Sidney to get her the president's job that he had promised her.

Ryder interrupted her thoughts, "Do you think there'll be many changes at the firm?"

"That will depend on who replaces Sidney as president."

"Many of us have been hoping it will be you."

She smiled diffidently, "Quite frankly so do I."

"What are your chances?"

"You know office politics is the one thing I'm not good at. I just don't know how to play the game. A lot of the older partners don't like me. They think I'm too ambitious, too radical in my ideas. So it will really depend on Sidney."

She wondered if she hadn't made a mistake. She had linked herself too closely with Rosenberg. Phillip had often advised her to be friendlier with the retail partners. He had also suggested inviting Kramer, the firm's biggest partner to dinner. She didn't like him and so kept putting it off. Maybe she should have slept with Kramer. She was sure that he had made a pass at her twelve years ago but she had ignored it. At the time she had been involved with that important consultant on the West Coast who had helped her win several big accounts and didn't have the time or inclination for another quiet fling.

"Last month I went to the Waldorf Bar with several of the younger partners. They supported you. In fact they said that you were Sidney's protégé and that the two of you would make a great team. Everyone agreed that the place needed shaking up."

"They're absolutely right about the place needing a jolt."

Alexandra had hired Andrew, a strapping, well-built man in his early thirties from NatWest Asset Management, a foreign bank money management firm that he had joined after graduating from Wharton. He had been with B&P for two years. His low-key conversational style, and the southern accent went well with customers. They liked him. So did Alexandra and he had quickly become one of her favorites to the consternation of some of the other portfolio managers in the unit. Events had justified her confidence. In the past two years his performance had been better than all the other portfolio managers in her group.

"What changes do you think are needed?"

Sitting next to her he was conscious of her long thin fingers, the perfectly manicured red painted nails, the expensive Harry Winston bracelet on the left hand and of course the perfume that permeated the air around them. He knew it was Calèche. His wife loved it as well.

"Well there are really two category of changes. Short term and long term. In the short term the first two matters that need to be addressed are the marketing and institutional equity groups."

She paused to finish her drink and then continued.

"The marketing department is totally ineffective. It's been that way for three years. The markets have changed but they don't have a clue. Too many of the sales people are lightweight. Hillary's a nice person but she really hasn't done a good job."

Andrew nodded his head in agreement but he was surprised at the mention of Hillary Schuster. By all accounts she and Alexandra were good friends but behind the façade it was obviously different.

"We also need to get rid of most of the institutional equity portfolio managers. I've told Sidney that he must do what I've done in fixed income. Get rid of the non-performers and the deadwood. You have to do the weeding out constantly. Andrew always remember that in business you must cut your losses immediately. It has to be based on meritocracy not loyalty or friendship."

Andrew listened with rapt attention. So the stories circulating at the office about her being hardheaded and tough were true. Beneath that pleasant, beautiful exterior there was an element of ruthlessness. You had to be careful not to cross her. He pushed the call button on the seat arm. A flight attendant soon materialized.

"Care for another drink?" he asked Alexandra.

"Oh, what the hell. Why not."

Andrew ordered two more vodka tonics.

This was interesting. For the first time she had really opened up. Perhaps the alcohol, combined with the Weisdick tragedy, had loosened her tongue. He was learning a great deal. There may never be another opportunity like this. He decided to press his luck.

"What's Sidney Rosenberg's background?"

"That's a remarkable story. No one's had such luck. Sidney has been in this business for over fifty years. Until the age of forty eight he was a total failure in his chosen profession. He had been fired from three firms and had then set up his own shop. On the verge of bankruptcy he took a vacation." She paused to take a long sip of her drink. "By sheer coincidence he ran into Abe Rosenthal at Round Hill in Jamaica. By the way that's where we usually go each year and I'm taking the kids there later this week. That fortuitous meeting led to his being invited to set up the institutional equity business at B&P in 1975."

Rider shook his head in disbelief "That's absolutely amazing."

"But that's not all," she said, as she stretched her long legs in the tight space. "Luck intervened again. The timing was right. The ERISA Act had been passed by Congress in 1974 establishing new standards for coverage, vesting, funding, investment supervision and so on. The pension fund consulting business took off. Sidney cashed in on this and by 1977 he had managed to raise over a billion dollars. It had taken the retail partners thirty years to get that much money. So he was made a partner in 1978 and a member of the management committee in the following year."

The institutional equity and fixed income business now had thirty five billion in assets under management and contributed more than half of the firm's revenues. In recognition of this feat the partners had bestowed upon Rosenberg the newly-created title of president in 1994.

Just then the conversation was interrupted by a woman's voice announcing on the loudspeaker that they were approaching La Guardia and passengers needed to buckle their seat belts.

Alexandra's thoughts slipped back to the opportunity created for her by Weisdick's sudden death.

The plane was making its final approach. It was flying quite low over the sea. She could see boats. Ryder once again interrupted her thoughts.

"I thought the presentation went very well today," he said.

"Yes. I think so too. And you did an excellent job. By the way you're going to manage the portfolio if we get selected."

Andrew acknowledged the complement silently with a smile.

Five minutes later they were on the ground. The plane taxied to its assigned gate. They hurried out to the terminal exit. Alexandra took the first taxi. She was home by seven. Phillip and the children were just sitting down to dinner in the family room. The two younger ones squealed with delight as Alexandra entered the room and took her place at the table between them.

CHAPTER 14

While Alexandra and Andrew were flying back from Chicago, Sidney Rosenberg sat in the living room of his large Park Avenue apartment reviewing the principal event of the day. The place was furnished in minimalist modern style by a not yet in fashion interior decorator who had been recommended by one of his fellow partners at B&P. Wall-to-wall carpeting in pale sand and green covered all the floors. The walls were painted in matching colors and the furniture was modern, nondescript and utilitarian. A large quantity of twentieth century abstract paintings graced the walls. There was none of any artistic significance or value.

As a young man Rosenberg had been passionately in love with a woman; she was not much to look at but had a certain degree of charm. He had wanted to marry her, but she had abandoned him and literally disappeared from his life. So he had remained a bachelor but had frequently lived with women. The last time was ten years ago. At that point he opted for variety and a parade of women, mostly young and some even attractive, passed through his life and kept him satisfied. A half dozen were from the firm, including at least one portfolio manager. After that for several years his urges had turned

155

towards kinkier sex. The dozens of escort services listed in the Manhattan Yellow Pages had responded to this need. It had all been very discreet. Now in the seventh decade of his life he was involved once again with someone at the office. She was married and therefore had not moved in. Once a week, every Tuesday or Thursday she came over and spent the night. Thank God it was Wednesday today. He just wanted to be alone.

He was being helped in his ruminations by a chilled and excellent bottle of Chevalier-Montrachet 1993. He tasted the wine. It was delightful. "Yes," he thought, "it was superb. Parker rates it a 92 and it lives up to his flowery description." Rosenberg was a connoisseur of wines and in his view no other white wine from anywhere in the world could equal a fine Burgundy. Now, as he sat on the coffee colored velvet sofa savoring the wine, he recalled the dreadful scene at the office earlier in the afternoon.

Peter Weisdick's death came at a most inopportune time for Rosenberg. The poor man had been putty in his hands and had become a useful ally in his almost ceaseless battle with some of the independent minded retail partners. He'd barely begun the task and needed more time to groom Ronald Shapiro. Another year, he reckoned, would be sufficient. By then he would be able to ease him in as his successor. Shapiro had turned out to be a good portfolio manager. Besides he was considered harmless by most of the other partners at the firm and as a result not only did he get along agreeably with them but was also well liked. Unlike Alexandra he was low-key, not particularly knowledgeable about the overall business and did not have a strategic mindset. This too added to his attractiveness; he was unlikely to rush in to make sweeping changes at the firm.

Rosenberg was unhappy about the sudden turn of events. Weisdick's death deprived him of the time that he needed to put his plan into action. He knew there just wasn't any way he could postpone naming a successor for more than a few months at most, so he would have to come up with an alternative strategy. He shook his head as he took another sip of the wine and said out aloud, "Why did the stupid man have to kick the bucket now?" He had never respected or liked Weisdick while the man was alive; now in death he liked him even less.

His thoughts now turned in another direction. He remembered very clearly, the day just four weeks earlier. The events were etched in his memory. It was a Wednesday. At around eleven o'clock he had just returned to his office from a meeting with Alexandra when the secretary had poked her head through the open door.

"There's a lady on the phone; she wants to speak to you."

"Who is it?"

"I don't know. She will not give her name but she's very insistent about speaking to you."

He nodded to the secretary and picked up the phone

"May I speak to Sidney Rosenberg?" The voice had a very slight foreign accent; it was European but he could not place it.

"This is Sidney." Rosenberg had no idea who this woman was. He did not know anyone with that accent or voice. For a moment he thought it might be one of the women from the escort services that he had once used. No, that couldn't be possible; no European woman was part of that group.

"It's Lillian. Do you remember me?"

"No. I'm afraid not."

"Sidney, it's been over . . ."

That's when it struck him like a clap of thunder. He had a sudden memory flash.

"Oh yes, of course I remember now. Lillian, how are you?" It was Lillian Schlechman. She had once been the love of his life. He hadn't heard from her or known of her whereabouts in almost 45 years. Since that July day in 1959 when she

3194-ISLA

suddenly vanished, leaving a short and mysterious note behind which he found on returning from the office to the small apartment that they shared in Brooklyn Heights. He remembered the note mentioned that she was pregnant and what she was doing was best for both of them. A few years later a postcard had arrived. It had been mailed from Los Angeles and simply said, "All is well. It was a boy." He had made a half-hearted attempt to find her but there had been no further leads.

"Sidney, I'm very sick. I'm dying. It's the last stages of cancer. I just have a few days, maybe a few weeks left."

"Can I do anything? Can I help in any way?"

"No, Sidney, it's too late for that. I have everything. I just wanted to tell you about the boy, your son."

"How is he? Where does he live?" Rosenberg asked like any anxious parent.

"He lives in New York. Take care of him Sidney. Promise me you will?"

"I promise you that I will. What's his . . ."

"His name is Ronald," she said interrupting him. "Ronald Shapiro. And he works at your office. He has no idea of his relationship to you. I have mentioned it in my will."

She continued without giving him a chance to speak, "Thank you Sidney. Goodbye."

And with that she had hung up leaving Rosenberg in a state of agitation tinged with excitement.

The information had jolted him. Since that postcard he had given the matter occasional thought. After all, the boy was his flesh and blood. He would be his ultimate legacy to the world. But all the investigations had yielded no results. And now the news had come so unexpectedly. He had closed the door to the office and sat back on the green leather chair to recover from the shock. That's when he became conscious of a serious potential problem. A really big problem if the relationship was ever discovered. Since its founding, B&P

had had a strict policy forbidding the children of partners from working at the office at the same time as one of their parents. Yet here was Ronald, his son, who was one of the younger partners at the firm. But then, he had no idea of the relationship when he had hired him and he figured that, since no one knew about it, he was safe. He would not mention it to anyone including Ronald for the time being.

Since that moment his mind had been occupied with a variety of schemes all of which had one aim: getting Ronald first to replace him on the institutional side and then eventually to take over the firm. This objective collided with his promises to Alexandra. What promises? That he would back her as his eventual successor. Weisdick's death made the issue more urgent and much more delicate. Right now Alexandra was the only person with the qualifications to take over that post and he was aware that even the partners who disliked her admitted that. Somehow or other he would now have to finesse her. He knew that if she became the firm's president there would be no stopping her and all his current plans for Ronald would be dashed forever. That is why the next move required careful thinking.

The wine put him in an expansive frame of mind. His thoughts turned to Alexandra. He remembered the first meeting and the day he hired her. Within the firm it was well known that she was his protégé. Over the years, a close friendship had also developed and he'd been a frequent guest at her homes in Manhattan and in Bedford. He was even fond of the children and enjoyed the political arguments with her delightful husband, Phillip. But the relationship was not fated to continue. A series of quite unforeseen and unrelated events that occurred in the past year had changed his feelings irretrievably. Then there were all those anonymous letters about her poor management skills and domineering ways with the staff. The failure to sell the firm finally brought the conflict to a head. Suddenly, from that moment, she had changed from

159

protégé to threat. Yes a threat to his survival, his very existence at the firm. He had felt that, with a little time, he would be able to take care of the problem. Now Weisdick's death left him no choice but to make his move.

In the next several days he would have to figure out how to proceed. Time was running out.

CHAPTER 15

I t had all begun rather unexpectedly nine months earlier.

Sidney Rosenberg did not travel much these days on official business, but he agreed to go that week to Salt Lake City with Hillary Schuster. They were making a pitch for an equity account to American General Stores. For the past several years B&P had experienced great difficulty in getting new institutional equity business and their asset growth came entirely from the increased market value of the portfolios of existing customers as the stock market continued its relentless upward move that had started, in the opinion of most experts, in 1982 and further accelerated in 1995 and only slowed somewhat in the first two years of the new century. Even here the firm's performance had not kept pace with the market. As a result their market share had actually slipped.

Now it must be stressed that B&P was not the only firm facing such problems. The vast majority of money management firms were in a similar situation; not only were they having a tough time getting new institutional business but they also found it very hard to beat or even equal the benchmark S&P 500 index. It was the difficulty in getting new

161

business that was acutely embarrassing for Rosenberg, especially when compared with the results of Alexandra Middleton's fixed income group. That group had started eleven years later but had very rapidly overtaken the equity group's numbers and now had two and a half times the assets under management. This had inevitably led, last year, to Middleton becoming a much larger partner than Rosenberg. He had not foreseen this development and it stirred a deep resentment in him.

The failure to get new business finally goaded Rosenberg into action and he ordered Hillary to take him along when B&P was next selected for an asset search by a pension fund consultant. He would personally make the presentation. There was a time when he was a master of this art. After all, had he not almost single-handedly created the institutional equity business at the firm and put a billion dollars on the books in a relatively short period?

It had taken some time to meet his wish. The firm was simply not getting into any searches.

The meeting was scheduled for a Friday morning and they had arranged to go skiing to nearby Deer Valley over the weekend. Sidney owned an apartment at the Stein Erickson Lodge that he used very infrequently now but which once, in years gone by, was overfilled with weekend guests from the New York and Boston metropolitan areas.

They arrived at the Lodge around two o'clock in the afternoon and had immediately taken to the slopes. It was a warm, sunny day. The snow was fresh and powdery. Hillary it turned out was a novice just as Sidney had suspected. He knew from past experience that she tended to over-exaggerate her expertise and skills at most sports and other hobbies such as playing the guitar and the violin.

Later that evening they had come down to the Lodge for drinks. Sidney wore a green blazer and gray slacks. He noticed Hillary's short, bright pink dress which revealed not only her generously proportioned bosom, but also substantial amounts of her shapely thighs and legs which were covered by black mesh stockings and matching pink suede shoes. He led her to a sofa in front of a very large and handsome fireplace where a roaring wood fire cast a warm glow that created a rather cheerful and tranquil atmosphere in the large room.

A waiter arrived immediately to take the drink order. Hillary ordered a rum punch, while Sidney requested a vodka martini.

"This is very pleasant," she murmured, admiring the room.

"Yes, the Lodge is very handsome. Isn't it?"

"Any idea how the market closed?" Hillary inquired. She took a considerable interest in the subject having invested most of her savings, like millions of other Americans, in stocks. Unlike the average American, however, she had several million at stake. Donald Kramer, the single largest partner at B&P, managed the portfolio.

"It was down a hundred and fifteen points."

That didn't bother either of them. The market had been very volatile for several years and they had gotten used to its daily gyrations.

Just then the waiter returned with the drinks.

"Cheers."

"Salud."

For several minutes they sat in silence enjoying the drinks.

"I thought the meeting went very well," Rosenberg finally observed breaking the silence.

"I thought so too. You really did a great job." She smiled and then added teasingly, "Almost as good as Alexandra."

Rosenberg decided to take the bait. "Yes, she's very good at this sort of thing. By the way, what's it like working for her?"

Six months earlier, at his insistence the institutional equity and fixed income marketing units had been combined into a

3194-ISLA

single marketing group. Now the department was organized on a geographic basis with each salesperson responsible for selling both equity and fixed income asset management products. Rosenberg felt that this structure would be more efficient because a single sales person could offer all of the firm's products to a pension fund consultant in Atlanta, or Chicago or any other city he happened to be visiting. Alexandra did not believe that one person could possibly have enough knowledge of so many complex equity and fixed income products. Failure, she had argued, was inevitable under this structure. Besides, she pointed out that consultants used different individuals for equity and fixed income products so the new organization was pointless. Rosenberg had had his way but as a compromise the unit reported to her. To many people the move had signaled Alexandra's growing power within the company and the increasing likelihood of her eventually succeeding Rosenberg.

Hillary Schuster was not pleased by this prospect. While she professed admiration for Alexandra Middleton she secretly resented her business success, her quick intelligence and her graceful stylishness. But there was more to it than just that. Hillary recalled their recent discussion on the changes that were occurring in the market.

"Tell me what you think is happening in the marketplace?" Alexandra asked.

"There is a lot more competition and it's getting more difficult to get the attention of the consultants," Hillary remembered replying.

That's when Alexandra proceeded to give her a little lecture on how technology was transforming the marketing function.

"In the old days," Alexandra informed her, "pension fund consultants relied on marketing people like you for information relating to money managers, such as performance statistics, investment style and so on. They then used this confidential information in their dealings with pension fund clients. Under that system the marketing staff got a firm into an asset management search and then it was up to the portfolio manager to actually win the account in the ensuing competition."

Alexandra then told her that the new technology was making the marketing staff irrelevant. All the information was now in data banks such as those run by Pensions and Investments, Nelson or Bloomberg. So all pension funds consultants now had easy and equal access to a firm's information. As a result they dealt directly with the portfolio managers in the investment manager selection process. The marketing people were becoming increasingly irrelevant. Their role was changing. It was switching more and more to servicing the firm's pension fund clients rather than getting new business from the consultants.

Alexandra was right and this is what worried Hillary Schuster. Her career was stalling. Failure was encroaching upon her slowly but inevitably. Without outside intervention there was no long term hope. If Alexandra Middleton replaced Rosenberg, the whole process would be accelerated. Not only would the role of the marketing staff diminish but the compensation structure would resemble that of the poor commercial bankers. Instead of her current seven-figure income she would be lucky to make a quarter million.

And Hillary Schuster was not going to take this lying down. She had thought about it for some time. In fact it had been the subject of a long discussion with her husband Ralph. They had both concluded that there was only one way to prevent this. Alexandra Middleton had to be stopped from succeeding Rosenberg.

"Tough. In fact very tough. We all know how relentlessly focused and driven she is. I'm now finding the true extent of it. And she's very demanding." She gave him an engaging smile.

Rosenberg's interest was piqued. He decided to probe

FRANCIS BLAKE

further. In business information was power and Rosenberg was adept at getting and using such information. This was what made him so powerful at B&P.

"I'm intrigued by what you say. Why do you find her more demanding?"

"Now that I'm working closely with her I'm seeing things in a very different perspective. She's constantly pressing for new business. She always finds fault with others. We're not doing enough or we're doing it incorrectly. She can be very tough on people. Because of her strong and dominating personality many of the staff members feel threatened and are afraid of her. They try to avoid her as much as possible."

Rosenberg was startled by what she said. "Is that really so? Tell me who's so afraid of her?"

"Art and Janet in my group are terrified of her. Two portfolio managers, Nick Daniels who handles investments in mortgage-backed securities and Pam Hopkins who manages short-term funds, told me that they try to stay away from her as much as possible."

"That's very surprising. Alexandra has such an outgoing and engaging personality. She comes across as a very sincere and pleasant person. You know I'm very friendly with her and Phillip and mix with them socially quite frequently. I must say I've never found her to be insincere."

"That's because she knows how to play up to you. You've been her Godfather at the firm. Believe me, Sidney, behind that façade of friendliness and warmth there's a very cold, calculating and devious person. She's a great actress who is superb at hiding her true feelings. She would have won countless Oscars if she had been in the movie business," Hillary said as she finished her drink.

Then she continued. "Two weeks ago at the firm's annual party she was so charming and effusive with Sarah Kaplan and then I overheard her joking with her husband Phillip about the poor woman. It was very cruel and mean spirited."

Just then the waiter brought them another round of drinks. There was a momentary silence and they appeared to be preoccupied with their own thoughts. Then the conversation turned to other topics.

"I've been thinking of an equity product," Hillary said, hoping to impress him as a fountain of new ideas. "A performance-based product," she continued. "No one else is offering this. I think we could get a lot of customers."

"How were you thinking of pricing it?"

"Well, I was thinking of a 30 basis point fee. That's higher than Vanguard but much lower than some of the other index managers. And than we would get a 4% performance fee if we do better than the index."

"It's an interesting thought. Almost like a hedge fund. I toyed with the idea last year but decided against it."

"Why?" Hillary asked, pleased that she had come up with the same idea.

"For two reasons. I did not think it would work. Despite what we tell customers it's very difficult to beat the market. We would have to become closet indexers. Put the bulk of the money in the stocks in our benchmark index and then with the remainder invest in some of the index stocks because they have the lowest price to earnings multiple, or because they are the stocks of the largest companies or for some such reason. But we'd have to be unbelievably lucky to beat the market consistently on this basis. So the net result is easy to guess. We would end up making only the 30 basis points most of the time."

"And the second reason?"

"Once you offered the product almost all of our existing customers would insist on switching to it. So we would exchange our current 1 ¼ percent fee for a 30 basis points fee. That's a great deal for the clients but a lousy one for us. The trade-off is simply terrible."

"Gosh, I thought I was being brilliant," Hillary laughed and finished her drink.

3194-ISLA

At that moment the waiter arrived with the dinner menu. They studied it for a few minutes and ordered the day's special.

"Enough of business. How do you feel after the afternoon's exercise?" he asked looking at her approvingly.

She was an attractive brunette in her early-forties, five feet three, with finely chiseled features and a tendency to wear flashy and rather provocative clothes that tended to reveal a bit too much of her sensual body. Her taste was a bit on the garish side. Too often it seemed that all the mistakes of Versace and Christian Dior some how ended up in Hillary's closet. She was wearing one of these now.

"Very relaxed and comfortable. I must say you look rather dashing in that blazer of yours."

He was pleased by the complement and a warm smile lit up the craggy features of his face emphasizing the aquiline nose.

"How is Ralph?"

Ralph Schuster was Hillary's husband. He was a management consultant at McKinsey and traveled constantly. This was the second marriage for both. They had been married for ten years and a three-year-old girl was the sole product of this union. Ralph had been severely wounded in the Vietnam War and still walked with a very slight limp.

"Oh, he's fine, but as usual he's on a trip. To London."

The waiter returned and escorted them to the dining room. Through the windows they could see the snow glistening in the moonlight. A fire was burning in the marble mantled fireplace. The candles on the tables that lit the room created an inviting and romantic ambiance. The food was equally good. After the smoked Norwegian salmon, they had rare lamb chops accompanied by a salad and followed by a perfectly baked Grand Marnier soufflé. An excellent 1982 Chateau Lafite-Rothschild made the dinner even more memorable.

After dinner they returned to the apartment. They sat on

the comfortable sofa drinking an old cognac and reading the Wall Street Journal. The tuner was turned on to one of the classical radio stations. Arthur Rubinstein was playing one of Chopin's ballads on a piano.

It was then that it happened. Hillary humming the tune got up and held her hands out to Sidney. "Oh I love this music. Let's dance."

As he got up he vaguely remembered a remark once made by George Barnard Shaw: "Dancing is a perpendicular expression of a horizontal desire." That became apparent moments thereafter when Hillary suddenly put her arms around his neck and kissed him passionately with her tongue moving hard and voraciously in his mouth. His hands groped and found her breasts. The erect nipples sent a tremor of excitement down his loins. He could feel the softness of her flesh and the warmth of her body. Her fragrance overpowered him. Her breathing quickened. "Take me now. Take me now," she gasped. Within minutes he had entered her. She was wet and ready for him. A few quick thrusts and it was all over.

Afterwards they lay in bed and talked. Forty five minutes later he made love to her again. This time long and lingeringly.

That weekend the skiing was limited to the afternoons. Most of the time was spent in bed and sex was the principal exercise. In between the sex, with ardent kisses and coquettish smiles, Hillary continued her campaign against Alexandra.

It was then that the first seeds of doubt were firmly planted in Sidney Rosenberg's mind.

169

CHAPTER 16

Swiss Air flight 493 from Moscow via Zurich landed at Cointrin Airport twenty minutes eleven in the morning on Thursday, August 26. Among the 150 passengers who disembarked from the MD 11 airplane was Grigory Yavlinsky, the newly-appointed Deputy Prime Minister of Russia.

Yavlinsky had come to Geneva on a mission of immense importance to Russia. He was meeting Tarik Al Saud the personal emissary of King Fahd of Saudi Arabia. This was the first meeting between a high-ranking Russian and a Saudi official in ten years.

The meeting took place over lunch at the Hôtel Beau Rivage on the Quai du Mont-Blanc. On his arrival at the hotel, Carl Mayer, whose family had owned the famed establishment since it opened its door in 1865, greeted Yavlinsky. Mayer immediately escorted him to the equally acclaimed Le Chat Botte restaurant where the prince was waiting for his guest. The two men shook hands and sat down. A wine waiter took their drink order. An ice-cold vodka for Yavlinsky and a Perrier for the prince. They admired the view from the hotel's flower-bedecked terrace restaurant overlooking Lac Léman as they waited for the drinks.

"For those of us who live in the desert, Switzerland is like paradise," Tarik said trying to make Yavlinsky comfortable. "Particularly on days like this."

"This is my first visit to Geneva. It is very pretty."

Clouds looking like giant cotton balls floated in the blue summer sky. Down below Lake Geneva shimmered in the sun. Sailboats raced around, their colorful spinnakers bloated by the wind like seven-month pregnant women. Beyond the lake, the lush green hills dotted with houses and the snow-covered Alps hovered in the distant horizon looking like an enchanting scene from a child's fairy tale book.

"Perhaps you can take a little drive around the countryside later on today. My car and chauffeur are at your disposal."

"Thank you. I would very much like to do that if there is any time," Yavlinsky responded, warming up to the prince's friendliness.

The drinks and the maitre d' arrived simultaneously. They sipped their drinks and ordered lunch. Both chose the house specialty, a crisp pan fried cod on a bed of peppers and eggplant. Tarik ordered a bottle of the 1995 Batard Montrachet white Burgundy for the Russian and an iced tea for himself. The conversation then took a more serious turn.

Tarik raised his glass. "Welcome to Geneva. And my congratulations on your appointment as the new economic czar of Russia."

"Thank you, your Excellency. It is a daunting job," Yavlinsky answered.

"We are in the process of introducing radical changes in our economic and governmental system," Tarik said in a low voice that seemed to suggest that he was sharing highly confidential information with the Russian. "Your country went through a similar process twelve years earlier. In fact if I recall you initiated many of the reforms."

Yavlinsky beamed with pleasure at the recognition of his

3194-ISLA

central role in the reform process, as Al Saud continued, "We do not want to repeat the same mistakes, so I am very interested in finding out first hand what went wrong."

Knowledgeable observers were well aware of what had gone wrong in Russia. It had been documented in numerous newspaper and magazine articles. So what was the purpose of these questions? The reason had more to do with strategy than with the pursuit of facts. Tarik knew that Yavlinsky had a big ego and this was a way to make him feel important. It would soften him up for the later, more important discussions. Yavlinsky unwittingly obliged.

"Russia is an example of what happens when change is too swift." Yavlinsky took a sip of his drink before continuing. "In my opinion the failure was due to two main reasons. First it was rooted in our past. For the past thousand years Russia was an autocratic, authoritarian state first under the Czars and then under the Bolsheviks. Unlike some of our neighbors we have no tradition or experience of free markets. So we had no idea how such markets work."

Yavlinsky noticed that Tarik was listening attentively, which pleased him immensely since the subject was close to his heart. "The second reason for the failure was that reforms were pushed too fast before we had the institutions, the customs, the mind set and the regulatory framework that make the free enterprise system work. You can write all the laws in the world, but they're just pieces of paper without an enforcement mechanism. That's what we lacked."

"That makes sense. We'll have to keep that in mind."

The vodka slowly got to Yavlinsky. He found his host to be a most charming and easygoing fellow. The man had no airs or pretensions at all. Exactly what the man from FSS– Federal Security Service, successor to the KGB–had told him in the briefing in Moscow yesterday.

"Tell me how you got into all that massive borrowing. That really hurt Russia."

"It sure did. And that was another mistake," Yavlinsky responded confidently. "Most people are not aware of this but for the first time in our history citizens and corporations were subjected to income taxes. It was the only way that the state could have sufficient revenues. Unfortunately we found it difficult, if not impossible, to collect much in taxes. So the government did what so many other states have done in the past."

"What's that?"

"It opened the printing presses. Hyperinflation soon set in and almost brought the government down. So under the guidance of the IMF the printing presses were shut down and Russia discovered another way to make up for the shortfall of revenues. We resorted to massive borrowings. And like alcoholics we were soon addicted to it. Unfortunately the borrowings were for day-to-day expenditures and not for productive investments."

Westerners had made the problem worse. Hedge funds, mutual funds, banks and brokerage houses all rushed in following the collapse of Communism in 1990 to do their bit for capitalism. Greed took over. But why Russia? For the simple reason that the returns were absolutely terrific and as far these investors were concerned, it was a one-way street since Russia was too big and too important to be allowed to fail. Political and strategic reasons would surely come into play. They found it impossible to resist a win-win situation. Billions of dollars soon found their way into government bonds and stocks in a country that lacked even basic accounting regulations. The markets were illiquid and the prices of most securities were derived on a best guess basis. But in the euphoria of the times no one seemed to care. After all the returns had exceeded a hundred plus percent for several years.

"So what brought about the change in investor attitudes?" Tarik asked.

"Sinking commodity prices, particularly of oil. As every-

173

one knows, oil and gold are our principal exchange earners. The gradual erosion of commodity prices eventually produced a devastating effect on investor psychology. Fear rapidly overtook greed. Western investors suddenly recognized what had been true all along: the reforms were just a great sham. It was all a mirage. A great illusion. They saw that the emperor had no clothes. So they bolted. But it was too late. The day of reckoning came six years earlier back in August 1998 when the dam burst with terrifying speed. Russia defaulted on its debts. Western institutions reportedly lost a hundred billion dollars in the fiasco and its worldwide aftermath."

"By the way, from what you've said, it appears that our countries have one thing in common." There was a twinkle in Tarik's eye, which did not escape Yavlinsky's attention.

At that moment the waiter returned with the lunch. The sommelier poured the wine. They sat in silence for a while as they ate the superb fish.

"How is the wine?" Tarik inquired solicitously of his Russian guest.

"It is excellent. You should try some." Yavlinsky enthused.

Tarik graciously declined the offer.

Yavlinsky was racking his mind at the earlier comment about the two countries having some thing in common. For the life of him he could not figure it out. Could it be that the prince was just pulling his leg?

"Is it oil?" Yavlinsky responded tentatively.

"That too. But something else. Like Russia, Saudi Arabia is also riddled with cronyism. In my view reforms can't work unless this problem is first resolved."

"I agree with you. And that is something we are tackling right now."

The International Monetary Fund had shoveled billions of dollars into Russia. It had all gone down a vast sewer. Most of it ended up in the vaults of the Swiss and American banks.

The Russian robber barons turned out to be the world's greatest experts in the art of looting–several cuts above the Venezuelans, the Mexicans, the Indonesians, the Pakistanis and the Nigerians.

"You also have to do something about the massive and pervasive corruption. We too have the same problem."

"Yes. But it's a very difficult problem and will take time to solve," Yavlinsky pointed out.

The new government had inherited a real mess from good old Boris Yeltsin. In the West he was considered a hero for engineering the collapse of the Soviet Union and the birth of a democratic Russia. But very soon thereafter the fault lines in his character had surfaced. His emotional and arbitrary behavior, the incompetence and the cronyism and the excessive drinking–not to mention his poor health–added momentum to the developing havoc. For much of the time during his second spell in office, Yeltsin looked more and more like a confused and bungling idiot. The springing of surprises was a characteristic feature of his presidency–the rapid and unexpected firing of numerous prime ministers attested to that idiosyncrasy–and he had lived up to that reputation till the end. On New Year's Eve the man had suddenly resigned, leaving the reigns of government in the hands of his not too recently installed Prime Minister.

That man was Vladimir Putin, a fifty-one-year-old former KGB apparatchik. He displayed a remarkable feel for the nationalistic yearnings of the average Russian and the invasion and subsequent victory of Russian forces in the war against the breakaway republic of Chechnya sent his popularity soaring. In March 2000, Putin easily won the presidential election. But four years later not much else had been accomplished. On the surface things appeared to be in better shape than before. But beneath the surface the story was different. That too was not surprising, for Putin, like his former boss, was also a creature of the oligarchs who had handpicked

175

him as Yeltsin's successor. Finally, pressured by parliament to reverse the continuing economic decline, Putin appointed Sergei Kiriyenko, a leading reformer, as the new Prime Minister earlier this year. Kiriyenko immediately turned to Grigory Yavlinsky, head of the Yabloko Party, to put Russia's economic house in order.

The irony was extraordinary. For all its enormous nuclear arsenal and former status as a super power, Russia was essentially a third-world country. Endowed with the richest natural resources in the world the country had an economy smaller than Switzerland or Belgium. In fact its economy was the same size as that of the state of Illinois!

By the year 2004 the economic disintegration was almost complete. Russia barely existed in name. Lawlessness was endemic, the economy was weak and corruption was rampant. Most of the institutions of government were feeble or incompetent. Regional provinces had gained power at the expense of the central government. The recent fall in the price of oil had once again brought Russia back to the financial abyss. The treasury was almost empty. In short the country was in one hell of a mess. It had been bumbling along for several years from one crisis to another. Something had to be done and soon.

So Yavlinsky was in Geneva searching for a way out.

After lunch, Tarik turned to the real purpose of the meeting. An American president had once remarked that two things usually came to mind when the name of Saudi Arabia was mentioned. The first item was oil. And the second? More oil. So not surprisingly, oil was the subject of the meeting between the two men. Or more precisely the price of oil.

"As we all know Russia is facing a serious economic and financial dilemma," Tarik smilingly pointed out.

The Russian nodded his head in agreement. The problem was too well known. There was no point in denying it.

"Do you expect renewed assistance from the IMF or the

Western powers now that Putin has taken over as the President?" Tarik asked.

"My government does not expect this to occur immediately. But over time, yes. There's been a lot of criticism in the press and in congress of IMF and the United States for their past assistance. So as you say 'once bitten, twice shy.' But we believe that aid will eventually resume once some progress is made in putting an appropriate infrastructure in place," Yavlinsky answered.

"Saudi Arabia may be in a position to assist you in the interim."

There was a flicker of relief on Yavlinsky's face as he waited to hear what the prince had in mind.

"Oil is the key to your financial solutions," Tarik smiled. "It could also be one of your major problems since it is Russia's principal export item."

Yavlinsky did not understand what the Saudi was driving at. He let him continue to talk.

"In early 1999 the price of oil touched a low of $10 per barrel. At that rate your costs to pump the oil were greater than the revenues. The following year we managed to get the price up as high as $37. That more than tripled your foreign exchange revenues and greatly eased the financial burden. But unfortunately the agreement did not hold, so now prices are down again to the $10 level."

He paused for an instant and looked at the Russian. "Unless we can get the cooperation of a few key states, the price of oil will collapse to around $4 a barrel."

"Why?" Yavlinsky asked unable to understand the logic of the argument.

"Because Saudi Arabia is determined to fix this problem once and for all. If we cannot get a solid, airtight, long-term agreement we intend to increase our production to twenty million barrels per day and inundate the market."

"And if you can get the agreement?" Yavlinsky asked.

3194-ISLA

"Then the price of oil will shoot up. In our opinion it will be in the $36 to $38 range."

"You have a plan to make this happen?"

"Of course," the prince smiled.

"Tell me the details. It may well be of interest to us," Yavlinsky said.

In the next half hour Tarik outlined the details of the plan. The credit facility was in place. As a quid pro quo future oil prices and settlement would be in euros. Both Mexico and Venezuela were on board. The Germans and the French would pressure the Norwegians to keep their production at current levels. He had not yet talked with the Iranians or the Kuwaitis but on the subject of oil prices both were solidly hawkish.

The Russian was truly surprised. He thought that the plan had not only been carefully thought through but it was also bold and imaginative. The FSS briefing had specifically mentioned that Tarik Al Saud was the tool of capitalists. But this man was no Western patsy. What he had just outlined would, in Yavlinsky's judgment, have grave consequences for the Americans. Yavlinsky was sure it would appeal strongly to his ultimate boss, the former KGB lieutenant-colonel who now presided over the destiny of Russia.

"What production cuts would you expect from us?"

"We want you to cut production by 500,000 barrels per day. That's a fifteen percent cut." Then to soften the blow he added, "Saudi Arabia will reduce its supplies by three and a half million barrels."

"And what is long term?"

"We want a three-year agreement."

"I believe we can live with that. Of course I will have to get my president's approval but I do not foresee any difficulty on that front. There is however a big problem. We need to borrow money. Now."

Over dessert they hammered out an agreement. Saudi Arabia would make Russia a three-year loan of four billion dollars. In return, the Russians would support the new Saudi oil plan. But in a departure from the unsecured investments of Western institutions, Saudi Arabia's loan would be fully collateralized by gold with a twenty percent margin. The gold would be stored in Zurich with the Commercial Bank of Switzerland.

While Tarik Al Saud was lunching with Yavlinsky on the terrace of the restaurant, a small burglary was taking place in his room three floors above.

Immediately on his return from the weekend tryst with Ingrid, Jacques Junot the chief foreign exchange trader of the Commercial Bank of Switzerland had walked into the office of his boss, Heinz Strecker, who was the head of the bank's global trading activities.

"Guten morgen, Jacques. How was Paris?" Strecker asked as he put some papers in the out tray on the desk.

"I need to talk to you about something very important," Jacques said, taking the chair opposite Strecker on the other side of the table.

"What is it?"

"I was in Paris to meet a German friend. I've been seeing her regularly for the past six months."

"So?"

"She is also a close friend of Herr Schroeder, the German Chancellor."

"Gruss Gott. Be careful Jacques."

"I found out that the Saudis are working secretly on something big. It has to do with oil."

"They've tried before. It was a flop." Strecker said.

"It's very different this time. According to my source Schroeder was very enthusiastic."

"Did she tell you why Schroeder thought that?"

"She mentioned two things. Have you heard of someone called Tarik Al Saud?"

"Yes, I've met him. He is a client of our private bank. He is fabulously wealthy and very clever."

179

"Well he's the mastermind of the plan. According to my friend the French and the Germans are backing the effort. He's now in America on business."

"Is there any way we can get more details?" Strecker asked.

"They had been drinking, so Ingrid didn't remember all the details but she did mention that this Tarik was coming to Geneva next week. Apparently he's a frequent visitor and usually stays at the Beau Rivage."

Maybe they could somehow get a copy of the plan. That's the thought that passed through the minds of both men. Jacques in fact had thought of nothing else since he first heard the story.

He broke the momentary silence. "Heinz this could really help our trading operations in a big way. A really big way."

"I know. But we have to be certain after what happened two years ago. This time we cannot afford to make any mistakes."

Strecker was referring to the trading debacle following the near collapse of a hedge fund managed by Horizon Capital Management. The United Bank of Switzerland had lost seven hundred million dollars. The number for Commercial Bank of Switzerland was equally bad. Its trading losses totaled five hundred million dollars.

The upshot of these discussions was the hiring of La Forge Consultants, A.G., a small Zurich-based firm that specialized in surveillance and security matters. Through the courtesy of the Swiss passport control at Geneva airport, Junot learned of Tarik Al Saud's arrival in that most cosmopolitan of Switzerland's cities. After that it had been a relatively simple matter to get what he wanted.

From the earliest days Swiss banks have been deeply enmeshed in the economic, political and social fabric of that mountainous country. Indeed the tight interlocking bonds between the Swiss banks, the government, business and society can be found in no other country on earth. This mutual embrace had paid off handsomely. Switzerland, a state with practically no natural resources except for cheap electric power, enjoyed the highest standard of living in the world. The primary source of this economic prosperity were the banks, which funneled vast amounts of money to industries at rates of interest unmatched anywhere else on the globe. They were also the largest employers of the local citizenry.

But this state of affairs could only continue so long as the banks' profits continued to grow. Unfortunately in the past decade all of Switzerland's main banks had come under severe pressure. Financial events in Russia, in Asia and in South America had been catastrophic for them. Like other Swiss banks, the Commercial Bank of Switzerland had suffered huge loan losses as a result of its international lending operations. The Russian default had cost the bank half a billion dollars in loan write-offs. Additionally there had been colossal losses in foreign exchange and securities trading.

The problem had been compounded by two further developments. First was the removal of exchange controls in the so-called emerging market countries. Thieving rulers, crooks and others in the same frame of mind apparently no longer needed the exclusive services of Swiss banks to hide their wealth. They were facing stiff competition from many other locations that had come to prominence as safe havens and American banks, in particular, were keenly eager to assist these individuals in their worthy and noble efforts. In fact, the Bank of New York had been involved in the largest money laundering scam in history. The source of the second trouble was America. Its booming stock markets and relatively high interest rates were sucking in huge amounts of money from Switzerland.

The Commercial Bank of Switzerland was desperate to increase its earnings. An appeal to patriotism combined with the payment of five thousand francs had secured the willing

3194-ISLA

cooperation of the housekeeping staff. Günter Bergdorf, the La Forge agent sitting casually in the lobby reading the La Tribune de Genève newspaper had been promptly informed the moment Tarik and Yavlinsky sat down at the terrace restaurant. Bergdorf took the elevator to the third floor and quickly entered the suite using a key provided by the maid. A methodical search revealed a green folder inside an expensive looking briefcase that was lying on top of a coffee table. Bergdorf calmly took out the folder and laid it on the table. He removed a small camera from his plastic bag and went to work. The eight-page document was photographed in less than five minutes. He replaced the folder in the briefcase, put it back on the coffee table and left the room.

Two copies of the plan were in Junot's hands on the following day.

Just around the time that the Swiss Air flight bearing Yavlinsky was taking off for Moscow, B&P partners and many of its staff members were filing into the Fifth Avenue Synagogue in New York for the funeral services of its deceased chairman. Several partners including Sidney Rosenberg and Alexandra Middleton eulogized the many contributions made by Peter Weisdick for the firm in his long and eventful career. But the principal event at the ceremony was the last minute arrival of Hillary Schuster. There was a rumbling buzz in the Synagogue when she appeared in a purple-colored mini skirt that barely reached halfway down her thighs, purple shoes with six inch stiletto heels and black stockings that had a seam at the back. Several partners snickered that she looked more like a tart than the head of the marketing department of a conservative and highly respected money management firm. Someone whispered that she was meeting an important customer after the funeral service.

Immediately afterwards Alexandra Middleton headed for the airport to catch the flight to Montego Bay. Her family had left earlier that morning.

Sidney Rosenberg returned to his residence with the document, which had appeared on his table that morning, to plan his next move at the management committee meeting that had been rescheduled for tomorrow. In the past several days he had tried, without success, to figure out what to do. Now quite unexpectedly, luck had given him the chance and he intended to make full use of it.

Ten minutes later Hillary Schuster joined him at the apartment.

3194-ISLA

CHAPTER 17

The weekly meeting of B&P's Management Committee usually took place in the chairman's conference room every Thursday. There was therefore something unusual about the meeting that convened at 4.00 P.M. on that last Friday in August. The date had been changed because of the sudden death of the firm's chairman earlier in the week.

In keeping with the company's origins, the retail partners dominated the committee, even though for the past ten years almost two thirds of the assets and over half the revenues were generated by the institutional business. The committee's structure had last changed following the stock market crash in October 1987 when B&P lost most of its sixty million dollar capital base in merger arbitrage speculation. At that point the group was expanded from five to seven members to include three representatives from the institutional side in addition to the four from the retail business.

Only five members were present at the meeting. Alexandra Middleton, the only woman in the group, was away on vacation. The other person missing was the chairman who had quite unexpectedly taken leave of the world, on a more or less permanent basis, but being one of the chosen race

184

was now undoubtedly in heaven, watching the proceedings with a kindly eye.

The fireworks began almost immediately.

For some strange reason the U.S. Postal Service was extraordinarily efficient that week. Perhaps it had something to do with the fact that the mail, from receipt to delivery, had to go only a few blocks. In any event the document secretly mailed by Paul Erhard duly arrived on the recipients desks on Thursday morning. Since that time it had preoccupied their attention to the exclusion of all else. That Friday, the rumor mill–that major source of information in any company–was more active than the New York Stock Exchange. Within the hour the workplace was abuzz with gossip, innuendo and misinformation. It was the principal topic of conversation among partners as well as the staff.

The graphic descriptions of the abilities and activities of many of the partners that were mentioned in explicit detail in the report elicited a great deal of laughter and ribald jokes. More thoughtful staff members, including a few of the younger partners, agreed that the firm's problems were serious and needed to be addressed. At the same time it was generally felt that nothing would be done. There simply wasn't any pressure to make changes since the firm's revenues were at an all time high. As one of the senior partners had recently said to an assistant, "Why rock the boat when profits are humming along? I don't see the point. Do you?"

The four grim looking committee members sat at the conference table talking about the report, copies of which were lying in front of them. Sidney Rosenberg arrived five minutes late and immediately took the empty chair that until recently had been occupied by Peter Weisdick. He saw from the expressions on their faces they were angry. That pleased him greatly. It would make his task of manipulating them to do his bidding that much easier.

"I see all of you have received copies of this mysterious report," he said, waiving the blue folder airily.

There were angry grunts around the table. Many of these men had figured prominently in the report. Their anger was understandable.

"Something must be done about this," Joseph Wechsler demanded in a sharp voice from across the table.

The weasel-faced Wechsler, a former reporter for the Village Voice, had been brought into the company thirty years ago by one of the original founders. The hunch had paid off. With the help of an underpaid assistant, the seventy-year-old Wechsler now managed a billion dollar equity portfolio, the third largest in the retail area. In his long investment career, which given his excellent health looked like continuing for many more decades, he had succeeded in attracting customers despite his mediocre performance. He was not bothered by the frequent turnover. Very early on he had linked up with a number of financial consultants who provided him with a steady stream of rich innocent victims.

"This damaging material is all over the firm. Our dirty laundry is being washed in public. We've become the butt of innumerable jokes all over the place. It's terrible."

The high-pitched voice belonged to fifty-six-year-old Franklin Strauss, an innocuous partner also from the retail group. This graduate of Wooster College was another long-term veteran of the firm. After 'inheriting' a half-billion dollar equity portfolio on the death of the partner for whom he worked, he was elevated to the partnership ranks two years ago. His lightweight intellectual qualities brought him to the attention of Rosenberg and Weisdick and made him an eminently suitable candidate for the management committee to which he was elected last year.

"I agree," Rosenberg said in a somber voice. Then glaring at them around the table he added, "This report has already turned out to be catastrophic."

He saw the blank look on their faces and realized they had no idea what he was talking about.

Rosenberg put on a grim expression on his face. "Just before I came here I received a phone call from David Fairfax at CSFB. He's the banker on the HypoVereinsbank deal." The conversation had actually taken place on Tuesday but he knew no one would find this out.

His fellow committee members looked at him anxiously. Rosenberg went on, "He informed me that HypoVereinsbank has decided not to make a bid."

It was a moment of high tension. The room exploded in anger.

"What do you mean?" Wechsler screamed his face flushed red as if he was about to have a stroke.

The man from Wooster was temporarily rendered speechless by the news.

"This is devastating. Absolutely devastating," a stunned Donald Kramer said in a voice choked with emotion. "I can't believe it. What happened?"

The owlish-looking Kramer with a chubby round face and matching round glasses had the air of a schoolmaster. With a fifteen percent stake he was, by a long shot, the single largest partner of B&P and was reputed to be worth over three hundred million dollars. Not bad for a poor boy from Queens! The sixty-two-year-old City College graduate had built up a solid reputation as a canny money manager. He managed a three billion dollar portfolio and although there were occasional rumors, spread by jealous partners, that he was somehow involved in insider trading, the charge had never been proven. His success could really be attributed to two aspects of his temperament that set him apart from his colleagues–he was perennially bullish and he had nerves of steel.

Not much was known of the secretive Kramer's private life. He was married to a muscular, well-endowed woman, a foot taller than him and had two grown-up children from a

3194-ISLA

previous marriage. No one at B&P had ever seen him with another woman, unlike so many of the other partners. His colleagues would have been greatly surprised–stunned is a better word–to learn that Kramer's greatest passion in life, apart from work, was sex. He simply loved to fuck and hardly a night passed without at least one shot at this delightful activity. They would have been even more surprised to find out about his weekly ritual. Each Thursday, following the management committee meetings, Kramer retired to an apartment on the West Side, not far from where he lived, where he proceeded to fuck the brains out of his secretary for the next four hours. This work, in the line of duty, earned a handsome reward for the pretty blue-eyed thirty-five-year-old woman with the long blond hair. She was the best-paid secretary in the United States earning two hundred and seventy five thousand dollars annually for her humanitarian services though the official records of the human resources department only showed a seventy five thousand dollar salary.

For the most part however, Kramer sought and found solace in the arms of his wife who apparently loved sexual congress even more than her husband and her nightly missions of mercy prepared him for the ensuing days nerve-racking task of picking winning stocks for lucky customers.

"This report happened," Rosenberg replied matter of factly.

"What does that mean?" an enraged Wechsler demanded.

"It means that the Germans are no longer interested in buying us because of this damned document."

"I hold you responsible for this mess," Kramer yelled in a menacing tone.

"It's your damned fault," Wechsler screamed again. "You have created the mess that has brought us to this."

"Yes, we all blame you for the problem." Franklin Strauss chimed in echoing the sentiments of his fellow committee members.

"I'm a little confused," Kramer said, recovering from his anger. "What exactly is the connection between this report and HypoVereinsbank?"

"Let me explain," Rosenberg said in a more solicitous tone. "The meeting with HypoVereinsbank last Tuesday had, in the opinion of most of us, gone exceedingly well. However by Wednesday there was a change in their attitude." He made up the story as he went along knowing that it would not be checked. "That evening I had drinks with Jurgen Pohl." Rosenberg again invented an event that he knew would not be verified. "He mentioned several things that are repeated here. I'm convinced that this document swayed them against the deal."

"But most of this information is not new. Some of it's been discussed at our meetings. The bank had access to much of this data," Kramer interjected.

"Don is right," Wechsler said picking up his fellow partner's theme. "HypoVereinsbank had access to our records in the due diligence process. And they probably dug up some additional details during their meetings and discussions with us."

"You're missing the point," Rosenberg retorted. "Yes, the material is available in bits and pieces. But not in this form. Here it has all been assembled together, it's been analyzed and conclusions have been drawn. A series of recommendations have been made. This is the kind of report that is prepared at management's request by corporate planning departments or by outside consultants such as McKinsey. It comes across very powerfully and that's why it's so damaging," Rosenberg explained patiently.

The explanation made sense to a number of the committee members who nodded their heads in agreement. Rosenberg noticed that both Wechsler and Kramer were moved by his story. He felt he was beginning to make some progress. The plan might yet work.

For a few minutes the room was silent. They seemed

189

preoccupied in thought at what Rosenberg had just told them.

"Who do you think did it?" Wechsler asked, breaking the silence.

"My guess is someone at the Bank of Boston. They have two individuals who once worked for us. They also have an excellent corporate planning group that can put together such a report. And they probably got the sensitive data from somebody here," Rosenberg answered.

"I still don't understand the inside involvement. The stuff, as mentioned earlier, was available to all the potential buyers," Wechsler shot back.

"No. I disagree," Rosenberg replied coolly. "There are too many instances where the items mentioned in the report could not have been picked up in the due diligence process. For example how you spend your time poking around gathering information on your fellow partners or how Richard Danser spends more time on the dance floor than at the office."

The dig had the desired effect. Both Wechsler and Kramer were infuriated.

"So who do you think collaborated from the inside?" an angry Wechsler demanded.

"I have given that considerable thought. I've checked out the operations and the accounting areas. I'm satisfied that no one there is involved." Rosenberg's face now assumed a sad expression. "I have tried to avoid coming to this conclusion but unfortunately there is no way of avoiding it. All the signs point towards one person. The culprit, I'm convinced after going through a careful process of elimination, is Alexandra."

This bombshell caught everyone in the room by total surprise. They all knew that Alexandra was Rosenberg's protégé. It was almost a father-daughter relationship and, from as long as they could remember, he had groomed her as his successor. Once again silence descended upon the room.

A shrill voice broke the stillness. "What made you come to this conclusion?" It was Kramer.

"Simple deduction," Rosenberg replied coolly. "Apart from myself, she is the only other partner with a comprehensive understanding of our company and the money management business. Many of the recommendations in the report are ideas that she has mentioned to me in the past. I should know since the two of us had many discussions on the subject. Besides she has contacts at the Bank of Boston."

This produced quizzical looks on the faces of the assembled men.

"The two individuals who previously worked in her group, I've found out, are now at that institution."

"But how do we know it's not you?" Wechsler retorted, unable to resist taking a shot at the man whom he despised.

"That's absolutely absurd," Rosenberg spat out, glaring venomously at Wechsler. "Why would I want to sabotage the sale? I'm the one who proposed it in the first place."

"What motive could she possibly have?" Kramer wanted to know.

Rosenberg sensed he was moving in the right direction. The meeting was starting to go his way. "She has several motives. The objective of the report is twofold. To sabotage the sale of the company and to put maximum pressure on us to make management changes. That can be the only explanation for the distribution of the report within the company." He paused for a minute before continuing. "Alexandra told me several times that she was not in favor of the sale. She is also increasingly tired of waiting in the wings and wants the chief executive's job."

"And how did HypoVereinsbank get hold of the document?" Wechsler asked, still smarting from Rosenberg's earlier rejoinder.

"Through Alexandra," Rosenberg replied. "She informed me shortly before the Tuesday meeting of having run into Pohl at a party over the weekend. And all of you know she's

big on the New York social circuit. I believe she delivered a
copy of the report to him."

That sounded plausible. In fact it sounded very plausible
to a number of the men.

"So what do you propose that we do?" Wechsler asked
Rosenberg.

"That we remove her," Rosenberg quickly replied.

"From consideration for the post of president?" Wechsler
asked. Both he and Kramer assumed that's what Rosenberg
meant.

"This is a very serious matter," Rosenberg declared
bluntly. "We have a traitor in our midst. It is a cancer in our
body that must be quickly and completely eradicated before
it destroys the firm. I therefore propose that we remove
Alexandra from the partnership at once."

For the second time the men at the meeting were taken
by complete surprise. In the ensuing silence the same thought
raced through the minds of three of the men there and they
came to a similar conclusion. If Rosenberg had turned so suddenly against his protégé she must be guilty. They were angry and bitterly disappointed at the failure to sell the firm,
which now appeared to have resulted from the actions of one
of their own partners. There could be no other explanation
for Rosenberg's anger against someone who was almost like
a daughter to him.

For the first time that evening, the handsome face of Simon
Klein came to life. The white-haired man, in a boldly striped
red and blue shirt, had remained silent through out the
proceedings. He had a young wife. For the past year he had
been busy donating his weak sperm for implantation in his
wife using the latest "in vitreous" techniques of modern
medicine. He had finally been rewarded, at age seventy two,
with a boy but, alas, all that constant masturbation had been
exhausting and he was still recovering from the Herculean
effort. That accounted, at least partly, for his silence so far.

The other reason was that he rather liked Alexandra. She reminded him of his much younger third wife who was also in the same business. But this was too much. He could not condone such treachery. He was compelled to speak up.

"I'm with you on this," Klein announced looking at Rosenberg.

"So am I." That from the balding whiz kid from Wooster College.

Rosenberg decided it was time to go for the kill. He would appeal to their self-interest. That he thought should do the trick. "For the time being the sale idea is dead. But we can do an IPO. That will require some changes in my area. We need to begin addressing those issues now."

The men sat there listening.

Rosenberg continued, "Alexandra is not a team player. I've been talking with a number of her subordinates. Many of them are afraid of her. She is too demanding and hard on people and that's reflected in the high turnover in her group. She..."

"She's too aggressive and self-centered. I agree with Sidney. Her staff management skills are very poor," Strauss interrupted Rosenberg.

"It's not good for the image of the firm," Klein interjected.

Rosenberg pursued the opening provided to him. "She's a threat to the partners and the very nature of this firm. If she gets her way she'll change the whole direction of the company. There'll be a retirement policy, before you know it, and many of the older partners including some of us will be forced out."

"The turnover is no worse than in your area, Sidney. Last week you removed Sarah and me from two accounts," Wechsler said in an unmistakable signal to Rosenberg that whatever the merits of the case against Alexandra he would have to pay a price to get his vote.

Rosenberg's words had a very different impact on Don

3194-ISLA

Kramer. He simply didn't believe him. The bastard had some hidden agenda. The problem was that he couldn't figure it out. The best thing to do, Kramer thought, was to drag this along and have a vote next week. He decided to speak up. "Sidney, We have never fired a partner so it's an extremely serious matter. We need to think this through very carefully. Very carefully."

"I agree. But Alexandra's behavior has been most egregious. It goes to the very heart of the partnership. It is the worst form of treachery. She has stabbed us in the back." Rosenberg said. Then turning around in his chair to look at Kramer directly, he continued, "You all know how much I like Alexandra. We have been friends for years. It hurts me deeply but there is no choice. In my view business comes before friendship. We cannot, I repeat cannot, condone her treacherous behavior. She has sabotaged the firm and her partners. Her actions are a personal attack on all of us and for what we stand. She has shown that she is not one of us. She is not a mensch."

"I agree it's serious, but we need to think of all the ramifications before we proceed. I don't want the firm to get involved in some gigantic lawsuit because of any hasty actions." Kramer was terrified of getting B&P involved in some major scandal. Clients did not like the bad publicity. They might take their funds elsewhere.

"There's absolutely no chance of a lawsuit," Rosenberg replied. "Our partnership agreement specifically allows the management committee to remove any partner at our sole discretion. Even without cause. We don't have to give a reason for our decision."

"How can you be so sure?" Wechsler took the opportunity to insert himself in the argument. He loved to hear his own voice.

"Because I have checked with our legal department. And to make doubly sure I asked our outside counsel as well. They have confirmed to me categorically that there would be no basis for a lawsuit." Rosenberg assured the men. He produced a paper from a file and put it on the table. "Here is the written opinion of our external counsel."

That impressed a number of them. It further confirmed their decision to support him. Rosenberg had done his homework.

"What about the newspapers?" Kramer demanded. "She could go to them and charge sexual harassment. That would create some very bad publicity. We could lose a lot of business."

"Again I don't believe that is likely. First it would be impossible to prove that charge. Not after she has been the first woman on the management committee. Her rise to partnership was also the fastest in the firm's history. Besides gentlemen I know her very well. She would never stoop to bring charges of sexual harassment. Its too demeaning for her," Rosenberg pointed out.

"What about the business. How much do we stand to lose? It could hurt us seriously if we consider an IPO," Kramer persisted.

"I think you are relying too much on your retail business experience," Rosenberg replied soothingly. "In your business the client's loyalty is primarily to you. It's very different in the institutional business. The principal loyalty is to the firm rather than to the portfolio manager. I've made a very careful analysis of the fixed income clients. I doubt if we would lose more than fifteen percent. Twenty maximum."

"But what if Alexandra joins a big rival firm. Customers would have the reassurance of solidity and her expertise. That could spell trouble for us business wise," Wechsler pointed out in an attempt to irritate Rosenberg.

"That won't happen," Rosenberg assured them.

"Why?" several of the men asked at the same time.

"Because I propose to fix it. You may not be aware of it but any major firm is bound to check with us before taking her on. I'll cast enough doubts to make sure she never gets hired."

"And you'll get us dragged into court," Kramer said.

"Not at all. The conversation could never be proven. It's done all the time," Rosenberg replied.

"What about the portfolio managers in her group. How many are we likely to lose?" Wechsler asked.

"One. Perhaps two. My plan is to double the compensation of the ones we want in return for a two-year contract. The money will keep them in place."

Wechsler had to admit that that was the most likely scenario. Money would buy them all. Including the partners who supported Alexandra. In the end no one would argue against the money. That's the way the world worked, anyway.

Kramer's mind was working furiously while the last argument was going on. He was not concerned about losing fixed income assets or portfolio managers, or for that matter about Alexandra. She was a smart cookie. There was no doubt of that. After all how often does someone build a twenty billion dollar business from scratch? And a woman to boot. On the surface their relationship had always been civil. She had directed at least a dozen customers to him over the years. But on the question of women Kramer had old-fashioned views. He felt that women were meant for fucking not working. But he had kept these opinions to himself. You don't want to be accused of being a male chauvinist. He would have liked to get inside Alexandra's panties but that was as likely as a trip to the moon. However that was not what colored his views of her. He had always considered her to be in Rosenberg's camp but now Rosenberg was proposing to change the landscape. The man had the scruples of Cesare Borgia. He could simply not to be trusted.

Kramer came to a decision. He did not like Rosenberg's idea. He did not trust the bastard's motives. Besides Alexandra had always been a restraining influence on him. He would become too powerful if he were allowed to get his way. Particularly now that he would be taking over as the CEO in place of Weisdick. "Sidney," he said, "the idea of removing a partner is very troublesome to me. I know you have leveled serious charges against Alexandra. It is possible she spoke with someone at HypoVereinsbank . . ."

"It's more than that," Rosenberg interrupted in an icy voice. "I mentioned earlier the need for changes in the institutional area. Getting rid of Alexandra is the first change. I am going to reorganize the group. There is no place for her in the firm. If we are serious about an IPO we must do this."

"I understand. The picture you have painted is very disturbing but don't you think she should get a chance to defend herself?" Kramer posed the question to the assembled men. It was going to be difficult but he was not prepared to let Rosenberg get away with it at least not until he had found out more about his motives in this whole affair. He was sure there was more to it than what they had heard.

"No. I'm afraid that won't work. She'll simply deny the whole thing and we have no way of proving it," Rosenberg said firmly.

Wechsler, Klein and Strauss nodded their heads in agreement. On this they were with Rosenberg.

"Okay. Why don't we think about it over the weekend and reconvene again on Monday," Strauss proposed as a peace gesture, hoping to win Rosenberg's gratitude.

The meeting ended shortly thereafter on the understanding that they would reconvene at the same time on Monday for a final vote.

Rosenberg stayed back in the conference room to chat briefly with Strauss. Ten minutes later he was back in his office and immediately telephoned Hillary. She was waiting for the call. They agreed to meet at his apartment in an hour.

3194-ISLA

CHAPTER 18

That evening Sidney Rosenberg returned home by taxi. It was the first time he had done this in almost a year. On the ride home he reflected on the deliberations at the management committee meeting. In his opinion they had, on the whole, gone rather well with one exception.

He leaned back in the taxi and closed his eyes for a few moments. The thought of his skillful deflection of their anger from himself to Alexandra brought a smile of satisfaction to his long thin face. He felt sure of the votes of Strauss and Klein. In the end, Wechsler too would be in their camp. The old fart was such a greedy bastard. He had actually insinuated during the meeting that his vote was available at a price.

It was Kramer's opposition that worried him. Kramer usually did not bother getting involved in any internal issue unless it restricted his freedom of action in the business. Yet in this case he had consistently sided with Alexandra and resisted all of Rosenberg's blandishments. This perplexed him, especially since he was aware that, while Alexandra and Kramer had a grudging respect for each other, the relationship was otherwise distant and cold. He also knew from the comments of one of the older partners–and Kramer held similar views–that their dislike of Alexandra stemmed partly from outdated values. These geezers believed women should be confined to their ancient role of child breeding and housework and found their presence hard to accept in the workplace. Well maybe as secretaries but certainly not as high-flying executives. And this deeply embedded attitude was highly unlikely to change anytime soon.

In fact the more Rosenberg thought of Kramer's reaction, the more disturbed he became. By the time the taxi arrived at its destination, Rosenberg was sure he had a serious problem on his hands.

Half an hour later Hillary Schuster sat on his green velvet sofa sipping claret, as Rosenberg gave her an account of the meeting.

"So we have four votes including myself."

"You are not worried about Wechsler? How are you going to get him on board?" Hillary asked.

"He's not a problem. I'm going to double the float that goes to the partnership from the fixed income group's revenues. That will give Wechsler a big chunk of money."

At B&P eighty five percent of the net revenues after payment of all expenses were allocated to the partners within the unit producing these revenues and the remainder was distributed to all the partners in the same ratio as their equity ownership of the firm. The equity ownership, in turn, was based on the revenues generated by the accounts managed by each partner. The fifteen percent that was shared by all the partners was known as the float. Rosenberg was proposing to increase this to thirty percent. You didn't have to be a genius to guess where these funds would come from. Hillary figured it out before Rosenberg finished speaking. They were obviously coming from the income currently earned by Alexandra.

"So how do we handle Kramer?"

"I still haven't been able to come up with an answer,"

3194-ISLA

Rosenberg replied taking a sip of the red wine. "Our whole scheme will collapse unless we can win him over. Do you have any ideas?"

"Why don't you give him some institutional accounts? We can say that the clients insisted on the switch. You know, play on his ego."

"No," Rosenberg said. "It won't work. The cunning fox will see through it straight away."

"Offer him the president's title," Hillary suggested. She was unaware that Rosenberg had someone else in mind for that office.

"Hillary, you don't understand. Kramer has no interest in administrative or management positions. We have to figure out a way to pressure him. Nail him down."

Then after a moments reflection, he added, "I wonder if he has any skeletons in the closet."

For a moment they just sat on the sofa wistfully, deep in their own thoughts. Hillary sensed that the plot's chances of success were slipping away. She wasn't going to let that happen. Not under any circumstances. Even if she had to use her darkest secrets. She figured that Ralph would understand and even encourage her to go ahead. Unfortunately there was no way to ask him as he was on one of his business trips. So she decided to take the plunge.

She broke the silence. "Sidney can I have some more wine." She held out her glass.

"Oh, excuse me."

Rosenberg fetched the bottle from the wet bar, poured her another drink and refilled his own glass at the same time.

She drank the wine and waited for Rosenberg to sit down on the sofa next to her.

"Let me tell you a little story," she began shyly. "I've never told it to anyone before."

She gave a coy glance to Rosenberg and went on, "Do you remember when we won our last big equity account?"

"Let me think. Yes, now I remember. It was General Motors. That was four years ago."

"Right. It was a big one, a hundred and twenty five million dollars. I can still remember the date. October 10, 2000. It was a beautiful Indian summer day. I felt elated and wanted to celebrate. Ralph as usual was traveling on business. I came down to your office but you had gone. I didn't feel like going home so I decided to go for a drink to the Waldorf Astoria. On the way to the hotel I ran into someone. We chatted and had a few drinks. Then we went to Onagiku for dinner. That's the Japanese restaurant at the hotel. It was all very amusing. We laughed and drank a lot of sake. One thing led to another and we ended up in bed."

She took another sip of her wine. Rosenberg listened to the story in a bemused sort of way. He was wondering what it had to do with the problem of Kramer.

"Sidney, I must say you have excellent taste? The wine is delicious." She smiled and continued. "Anyway the affair lasted three months. That last month, Ralph was away most of the time."

"What made you stop?"

"He said he was beginning to fall in love with me but couldn't afford to divorce his wife."

"Why not? More than half of all marriages end in divorce. It's almost the norm now."

"It had something to do with New York divorce law. He said it was an equitable distribution state and that his wife would take him to the cleaners."

"So you broke up?"

"Yes. It was time anyway. But there was something else."

"What?"

"I got pregnant."

"Did you have an abortion?" Sidney suddenly

3194-ISLA

remembered that she had a baby about three years ago. Was it possible that it was not Ralph's child?

"No. I wanted the baby. But I never told the man."

"What about Ralph. Did he find out?"

"Oh yes. I told him about it."

Rosenberg was both surprised and shocked by this revelation. Despite his affairs and dalliances, he was a very straight-laced man. He wasn't sure if he believed her. Most men wouldn't tolerate that. Ralph didn't look like someone who would. Something didn't seem to fit.

"You mean to say that Ralph didn't object?" Rosenberg asked without bothering to hide the skepticism from his face.

"That's another story."

"What do you mean?"

"Well now that you know this part, I might as well tell you the rest," she said after a moment's hesitation.

His interest was genuinely piqued. "Go ahead. I'm anxious to hear it."

"Did you know that Ralph was in Vietnam?"

"No. He has never mentioned it."

"He went there in 1967 straight out of school. He was seriously wounded in the groin in the Tet offensive that year."

Over the course of the next fifteen minutes she told him the full story. The wound had made him impotent. They met at a party and had a whirlwind romance that lasted all of thirty days before they got married. She only found out about the impotence on the honeymoon in Vermont. By then she was madly in love with him and gradually came to accept his sexual deficiency. Ralph satisfied her sexual desires in other ways. Then five years ago Ralph decided they should have a child so he urged her to have covert sex with other men. He did not want to go through a long drawn out adoption process. None of their friends had any idea of Ralph's condition. He was a big, strapping man so everyone assumed that he was very virile. A child would be helpful to his career. It conveyed the image of a solid family man, a good husband and father.

When she finished Rosenberg sat for a brief moment simply shaking his head. It was an incredible story. He would never have guessed, seeing the two of them together. "How deceiving appearances are," he said to himself.

Then he got up and picking up another bottle of wine from the wet bar, refilled their glasses. "We still need to find an answer to our problem."

Hillary looked at him quizzically. He obviously hadn't made the connection. "I just gave you the answer."

"What do you mean?"

"Sidney, the man I had the affair with was none other than Donald Kramer."

The revelation stunned him. His body jerked involuntarily into an upright position as he said, "What? Is that true?"

"Absolutely. I give you my word. Don's quite a lady-killer. He's very charming in private."

Rosenberg couldn't believe it. For the second time fate had smiled on him just as the situation was beginning to look hopeless. His mind worked furiously on the practicalities of applying the information. There were two problems in telling Kramer of his dirty little secret. It would be Hillary's word against his, at least until a DNA test could be done and there was no time for that. The meeting was on Monday. The other difficulty related to Hillary's position at the office. A straight confrontation was clearly not in her interest. She had to be made to look like a victim in this whole episode.

"Hillary, do you, by any chance, have any photographs of the two of you?

"No, I don't think so. The affair was conducted in great secrecy. Don was very careful. We only met at an apartment he owned or at my place when Ralph was away."

"That might be a problem."

3194-ISLA

He explained that blackmail would not work without hard evidence. Adultery was pretty common at the office. At least a dozen partners would make any list of world-class experts in this particular field. So if the news of the affair got out it was hardly likely to create a furor. It would be dismissed casually with "so what," or "so, what's new."

"Oh, I just remembered. I've seen photographs of Don coming into our apartment building."

"Where?"

"In Ralph's papers. There are also several VCR tapes but I don't know what's in them."

On the following day they reviewed the tapes at Rosenberg's apartment. Apparently Ralph knew more than he had let out. He had commissioned a private investigator and sophisticated video equipment had been surreptitiously installed in the bedroom. They walked over to one of the fast service photo shops on Lexington Avenue and ordered a half dozen eight by ten photographs as well as a copy of the tape. After lunch they spent the rest of the afternoon working on a plan.

Rosenberg was certain it would work.

Around the same time as the B&P Management Committee was meeting in New York, Alexandra Middleton was lying on a lounge chair on the wind-protected beach at Round Hill. There were 32 cottages on the 60 garden-filled acres of this world famous hotel–owned by the rich and famous–that were rented out to guests when the owners were not in residence. The family had holidayed at the hotel in Montego Bay for the past ten years. The children simply loved the place.

The long narrow crescent-shaped beach was dotted with blue umbrellas and white plastic beach chairs. Five large almond trees with their branches growing at a forty five degree angle to their gnarled trunks provided additional cover from the fiery afternoon sun. Alexandra lay there watching the clouds drift languorously by in the blue Caribbean sky. The waves rolled gently onto the beach. The pale blue sea stretched as far as the eye could see, bordered by numerous low hills cluttered with villas and large expanses of green lawns. Two wooden platforms floated in the water, thirty feet from the shore. A number of people were lying on the platforms sunning themselves while children swam back and forth.

Alexandra had arrived late yesterday night via Miami. As usual, the family was in cottage number twenty six which they had occupied for the past six years. It was built way out into the bay at the extreme end of the hotel property, and the rain forest almost jutted into it. The views of the setting sun were unforgettable from its verandah and at night the lights of Tryall Great House shimmered in the distant horizon like a light bedecked tourist ship out at sea. Babe Paley with her fine eye for location had built the cottage in the fifties. More recently Ralph Lauren had acquired it. He had insisted that Alexandra, an old friend–she also managed a portion of his billion dollar wealth–stay there during the family's vacation in Jamaica.

She was in a euphoric mood as she lay there drinking a rum punch. So what was the reason for this euphoria? The pleasant surroundings, the sun and the drinks all had an effect on her and contributed to the mellow feeling. But the real answer was much more straightforward and had less to do with the surroundings or the drinks than with recent events at the office. It was brought out by the knowledge that what she had wanted for so long was about to happen. She had chased her impossible dream and now she was on the verge of realizing it. What looked unattainable just a few days ago was now within her grasp. All because of Peter Weisdick's sudden death. How unpredictable life was she thought as she drank the 'rum punch.

Her mind meandered to the past. She remembered the Lakes School in Windemere, the small cottage and the rather

205

straitened circumstances in which her family lived. She was the first student from her school to go to Cambridge, and also the first from her family to earn that distinction. Just thinking of the long road she had traveled from the margins of poverty sent a shiver down her suntanned body. At school she couldn't have imagined the life she now led. She had no idea that anything like this even existed. It was at Cambridge that she had first understood the immense possibilities open to her. Two events had stuck in her memory and she lay there lazily reminiscing about them.

Phillip wandered over after playing tennis with Delphinia, their oldest girl who was now off sailing with her brother Julian. The two younger ones, Christian and Vanessa were building elaborate sandcastles nearby and simultaneously consuming vast quantities of Shirley Temples and banana daiquiris.

"Baby, be careful you don't get sun burnt," he said as he bent down and kissed Alexandra.

"I will. Can you rub some more of this sunscreen on my back?"

He opened the bottle and began to rub the liquid on her back.

"Darling, I was thinking of Cambridge just before you came."

Like his wife, Phillip too was a product of Cambridge. But he was a Trinity man, to be more precise, just as Alexandra was a Johnian. It was such a pity, Phillip felt, that most of his countrymen had either never heard of the place or knew next to nothing about it. There was no other educational institution quite like it except perhaps for Oxford. Unlike American universities, the University of Cambridge played a very limited role in a student's life which was centered around the twenty five independent colleges with hoary, ancient names like Kings, St. John's, Trinity, Clare, Magdalene and so on. It was the colleges that actually provided the education through the tutorial system. Once a week, students, usually alone, but often in groups of two, met for an hour with a don with whom they discussed the essays that they had written during the week. At the end of the session a new essay topic plus a huge number of relevant books were prescribed for the following week. There were eight tutorials each term and there were three two-month terms in the year. So essentially one's formal education consisted of seventy-two hours of tutorials! But the real work was done in the long hours spent at the library and the interminable socializing and discussions with the brightest and the best at pubs, coffee shops, restaurants and most of all at parties. The University, which boasted 70 Nobel Prize winners among its members, arranged the lectures but attendance was not compulsory–so few students ever came–and it set the annual exams. It was a remarkable educational system and for most students the experience was unforgettable.

"What were you thinking?" Phillip asked.

"How beautiful it is. We've seen so many towns over the years but none can match the beauty of the place."

"There's no doubt of that," Philip said. "You know it's almost forty years since I was a student there and I still miss it."

God it was so exquisite. For centuries the haunting splendor of its ancient colleges, the lovingly maintained lawns and the River Cam meandering along the backs had dazzled visitors. Cambridge was one of the loveliest medieval towns in Europe. No other place could rival its beauty on a sunny, spring day. Its open facades and ethereal vistas held residents and visitors alike in thrall, and the echoes of a distant age still lingered in its cloistered courts. The ancient buildings, mostly made of red colored bricks, mellowed by centuries of sunlight and rain, which had given them the softened tints and patina one sees in the little villages that dot the Tuscan landscape, left an indelible impression on the mind. And in the cobbled lanes and narrow streets students walked and went about their business as they had done since

Chaucer's days, their voices and laughter pervaded the air but was often drowned by the ever peeling bells of churches that littered the town.

While Phillip rubbed the sunscreen on her back, Alexandra reminisced about the day she had arrived at her college, St. John's.

She remembered entering the porter's lodge. Inside the fairly large office, the head porter in top hat and black coat was sorting the mail, while another gentleman in similar attire sat reading the evening newspaper.

"Good afternoon, miss. What's the name?" he inquired looking up from the newspaper.

"Middleton. Alexandra Middleton."

"Right. Just sign your name here, miss, if you please." He handed her a pen.

"Here's your key. You'll be in E4 Chapel Court. That's over to the right through the first doorway." He turned and pointed in that direction looking through the window at the back of the room.

Alexandra made her way to the staircase and saw her name printed in white letters along with four others on the wall at the foot of the stairs. She walked up four flights of stairs, opened the door and entered the room. The spaciousness of the suite surprised her. She was expecting a small room like the one at home. Instead there was a large kitchen with a window overlooking the courtyard, a slightly bigger living room with two gray covered armchairs, a gas fireplace with built in book shelves on either side and an old slightly battered desk with a straight-backed chair in front of the large window with views of the courtyard below and the chapel to the right. A slightly faded carpet covered the floor. At the back was a small bedroom with a single bed and a washbasin and built-in closets. The window opened onto the garden of the Master's lodge.

The rooms made a deep impression on her. So this was how the wealthy lived.

"You know sweet heart I was astonished by the size of my rooms at the College. I'd never seen anything like that before."

Phillip grinned. "I'm sure you were. So was I."

"I was even more amazed by the servant."

She was referring to the servants–known as gyps–who even today take care of the students. They were provided by the college and had been a part of Cambridge life since times immemorial. She recalled the scene vividly. She had been surprised when the door opened and a man walked in wearing a white cotton jacket.

"Good evening miss. I'm Tom White. Your gyp."

"Oh! Hello," she said still in shock.

"May I light the fire?"

"Please." She did not know how to address him.

He put her at ease, as he bent in front of the fireplace. "Gyps are addressed in different ways. You may call me by my Christian name, miss. If that's alright with you."

"Yes of course, Tom," she said hesitantly.

That was the first time she had ever had a servant take care of her.

"Oh by the way, Lady Annabelle telephoned while you were playing tennis."

"How is she?"

"She appears to be in great form. She wants us to visit her next month."

"Well, maybe we should. I'd like to show the place to Delphinia now that she's thinking of colleges."

Lady Annabelle was the other thing that had changed Alexandra's life. She was at Trinity and was the daughter of Lord Bixworth, a wealthy English aristocrat whose lineage went back three centuries when an ancestor had been given the vast estate for services rendered to the crown at the Battle

3194-ISLA

of Blenheim in 1704. Another ancestor had been with Wellington at Waterloo the following century. Alexandra ran into Annabelle early in the Michaelmas term on the 'backs' one evening. They hit it off immediately and the friendship blossomed. Annabel introduced Alexandra to her social circle and to a way of life that she had never known before, both at Cambridge and at her large and beautiful ancestral home in the Cotswold's. That lifestyle had left an indelible imprint on her mind.

Alexandra's brains and beauty had done the rest. She was always in great demand at Cambridge. The pick of the men were hers. She had combined an unusually active social life with hard work and had obtained a star first in the Economics Tripos. It was a rare achievement. Perhaps ten students out of 10,000 passed with such distinction.

Yes, there was no doubt about it in Alexandra's mind. It had all begun at Cambridge. It was there that she had first discovered that brains and beauty were an unbeatable combination. Cambridge had been the defining moment in her life. From then on money had become her principal goal. People could say what they liked but she knew it was money that made possible the good things in life. And she had never forgotten that wonderful remark of Oscar Wilde: "When I was young I thought that money was the most important thing in life. Now that I'm old, I know it." Everything else was a distant second. Her life was consumed by it. In her mind, money defined success and a person's worth.

Phillip lay down on the lounge chair next to her.

A waitress, in a brightly colored Jamaican dress, brought another round of rum punches. They both enjoyed having the drinks here and Alexandra maintained that no one in New York could make them quite like good old Zach at Round Hill.

"Did you read the document?" Alexandra asked, taking a long sip of her new drink.

"Yes. I thought it was quite damning. It pointed out all

the problems you've talked about. And the solutions were quite elegant. Very well conceived."

"I thought so too."

"Who do you think authored it?"

"I don't know who wrote it. But I think Sidney has a hand in it.

"What makes you think that?"

"He's the only one apart from me with such an extensive knowledge of the firm and the money management business. And it's a safe way of putting pressure on the partners to accept changes. Particularly now that the sale is unlikely to go through."

"What about HypoVereinsbank?" Phillip asked.

"I'll be surprised if they make an offer. It's not what they said but how they said it that made me conclude that they had no interest."

"I'm worried that people might think that you wrote the document."

"I know. But everyone knows I simply don't have the time to do any such thing."

"I hope you didn't discuss the report with Sidney."

"I couldn't resist it. Very briefly. He said it was garbage and threw it in the waste basket."

"I suppose that's the end of it. You know I've been think-ing of Peter's sudden death. It sure gives you a sense of the fragility of life. You're fine one minute and gone the next. Or on top of the world and in the next minute there is no mean-ing left to life. Fate, destiny call it what you will."

"Yes darling. But it has given me the chance to realize my dream."

"I know. When will it happen?"

"Probably next week at the management committee meeting. At least that's what Sidney led me to believe."

"Sweetheart I'm thrilled and I'm so proud of you. You deserve it."

_____

211

She moved over and gave him a kiss. They lay there holding hands as they talked.

"I'm counting on you to help me on the long-term strategy. That's your forte."

"You know I'll do absolutely anything for you."

She knew deep down that Phil loved and genuinely admired her. That had been the case since their first meeting. She found it very reassuring that he would always be there for her.

"Phil, I haven't forgotten the one page strategy paper you wrote that I used in my initial meeting with Sidney."

"So what's your agenda for the first hundred days?"

"Rescue the firm. Its been hijacked by the old partners."

"That's going to be difficult."

"Not if I can work out an alliance with Don Kramer. Did I tell you he has a 75-year-old partner in his unit? The man's taking home three million dollars. That's not small change, even for Kramer."

"From what I can gather the place is adrift," Phillip observed.

"It sure is. There's no cohesion. We have to restructure the equities business. It's a real mess. The performance stinks and they're getting no new accounts."

"Well, what can you expect from a cozy club of aging dinosaurs." Phillip's description made Alexandra laugh.

"We need more young partners," Alexandra replied. "They'll be more willing to invest in new products since they'll be there to reap the future rewards. At least ten percent of our income has to be invested in new businesses. We've become a second-tier outfit. All the petty quarrels and infighting has hampered our growth."

"That sounds exciting. You're so smart darling."

"We are all lucky people, Phil. Not smart," Alexandra remarked smilingly. "Rising markets and investor stupidity have made us wealthy. And the banks and brokerage houses that are buying the money management businesses will make us even richer."

For a while they lay there enjoying their drinks and watching the waves gently lapping at the shore. The children were engrossed in their sand castle project.

"Phil, I'm still thinking of Tarik and the two Latinos. I'm certain they're plotting. And it's not about reducing prices. You know OPEC hasn't worked for ages. He's creating a new alliance."

"You may be right. Who would be in it?" Phillip asked.

"My guess is that it will be Saudi Arabia, Mexico, Venezuela, and possibly Iran. Perhaps Kuwait. Iran and Kuwait are price hawks and all of them are really hurting from the lower oil price."

"That makes a lot of sense since these countries control much of the oil supply."

Can you imagine the bundle we could make in stocks and bonds by positioning correctly? Our performance statistics would improve dramatically and the business will take off again. Gosh I'm looking forward to it."

"You'll be in a position to do that soon. That calls for a celebration, darling. Let's go out for dinner tonight."

"That's a great idea. And we can take the two older children with us."

3194-ISLA

CHAPTER 19

The meeting with Joseph Wechsler on Monday morning lasted no more than ten minutes. Under the new arrangements proposed by Rosenberg, Wechsler figured that his income would increase by half a million dollars.

"Your arguments are very persuasive and you can count on my vote," he said piously.

They shook hands sealing the agreement.

A few minutes later Sidney Rosenberg walked into Don Kramer's office on the twenty-seventh floor. This meeting lasted considerably longer. They retraced all the arguments of the previous Friday. But they both held on to their previously stated positions.

"You have the right to organize the institutional business in any way you deem proper," Kramer conceded. "But I have a problem when it comes to sacking a partner, particularly one who has done such a terrific job."

"I agree that she's done an exceptional job building the fixed income business. But we need a different type of individual in that position now. Her management style is very disruptive and damaging to the morale of the staff. Even more, her recent actions have made the situation worse for all of us. So I reiterate my view that she really does not fit at our firm."

"I happen to think you are wrong. The actions you cite are not important enough to warrant the severe sanctions you propose," Kramer replied calmly.

Rosenberg let out a loud laugh. "That's crazy. It flies in the face of the facts."

The conversation, occasionally heated, continued for a while. It finally became evident that they would not be able to resolve their differences.

"I guess we agree to disagree," were Kramer's final words.

At that point Rosenberg calmly opened his briefcase, extracted a large brown envelope and slid it across the desk.

"What is this?" Kramer demanded.

"I suggest you take a look."

Kramer opened the envelope and took out the contents. There was a VCR tape and six large eight by ten photographs. He looked at the pictures.

"Recognize anyone?" Rosenberg asked nonchalantly.

Then while Kramer studied the photographs, he added, "By the way Don, you can view the tape at your leisure. Your wife would find it particularly amusing."

Kramer began to sweat profusely. Beads of perspiration lined his forehead. Rosenberg could see the fear in his eyes. He looked like a deer that's been cornered by a group of hunters with no prospect of escape.

"Oh, I forgot to mention. Apparently you're also the father of the lady's only child."

That was it. Kramer's economic well-being was at stake. With this sort of evidence his wife would demand an immediate divorce. He could not let that happen.

Within minutes, before Rosenberg's amused eyes, the man crumbled piteously. It was a pathetic sight.

It took an hour for Kramer to compose himself. He was really mad at Hillary. How could she be a party to this black-

3194-ISLA

mail? It was so unlike her. She had never mentioned any money or job-related problems to him. After all he was the largest partner at the firm and he could have helped her. He dialed her number. A secretary picked up the telephone. She was out of the office. When was she expected back? Not until later in the afternoon. Yes, she would give Mrs. Schuster the message.

The management committee meeting at 4:00 P.M. that Monday afternoon was unusual for the bonhomie among the five members.

At the outset, Kramer made a short speech: "I have given the unfortunate matter a great deal of thought over the weekend and have reluctantly come to the conclusion that Sidney is right. Such egregious and treacherous behavior is intolerable. There is no place in this firm for the guilty partner."

Wechsler also made a resounding little speech. He too agreed with Rosenberg.

The matter was then put to a vote.

All five members voted unanimously for the removal of Alexandra Middleton.

For the record, at Rosenberg's suggestion, a second vote was taken. The result was identical.

The committee accepted Rosenberg's recommendations and appointed James Dolittle and Hillary Schuster as co-heads of the Fixed Income Group in place of Alexandra Middleton.

Finally and again at Rosenberg's suggestion, they voted unanimously in favor of a new compensation package that would principally benefit the retail partners.

When Kramer returned to his office he found Hillary waiting for him.

Tears streaked her face. The makeup was all smudged.

"I got your message. Ralph telephoned me when I got back to the office. I came up here immediately but you had already gone to the meeting."

She told him the whole story about Ralph. Vietnam. The

terrible wounds. The impotence. Somehow Rosenberg had found out. The rest had been easy. He had blackmailed poor Ralph who had succumbed. She would never have betrayed him. After all she hadn't whispered a word about the affair to anyone in the past four years.

Was the story about the child true? Yes. Why hadn't she told him? I didn't want you to know. We wanted to show that it was our child. Ralph's and mine. She cried some more.

It all sounded so plausible. An hour later she left the office thinking that he believed her.

Back in Jamaica, Alexandra was unaware that she had been the sole topic of discussion at the management committee meeting on the previous Friday and again on Monday. Nor did she have any idea of what was being said about her.

All that changed at exactly eleven o'clock on Tuesday morning. The telephone rang. Alexandra went into the bedroom to answer it. Fifteen minutes later, Phillip found her when he walked into the room. She was sitting on the chair in the bedroom with a dazed look on her face.

"It was Sidney on the phone." Her voice was trembling. "They fired me from the partnership." Her eyes filled with tears.

Phillip looked at her, stunned, "What? I can't believe it. How can they?"

"He said that the management committee had voted unanimously. Twice."

"And why couldn't they wait to tell you in person. Just two more days."

"He claims that wasn't possible. The news has leaked. They have already sent a fax to all the clients."

Just then the hotel concierge wandered over with an envelope. The fax had arrived only moments ago. Phillip opened the envelope and read it.

3194-ISLA

WE REGRET TO ANNOUNCE THAT ALEXANDRA MIDDLETON HAS RESIGNED EFFECTIVE IMMEDIATELY FROM B&P TO PURSUE OTHER INTERESTS. WE TAKE THIS OPPORTUNITY TO THANK HER FOR CREATING THE FIXED INCOME BUSINESS AND FOR HER FOURTEEN YEARS OF EXTRAORDINARY CONTRIBUTIONS. SHE IS AN EXTREMELY TALENTED AND BRILLIANT MONEY MANAGER. WE WISH HER WELL IN HER FUTURE ENDEAVOURS. EFFECTIVE IMMEDIATELY, JAMES DOLITTLE AND HILLARY SCHUSTER HAVE BEEN PROMOTED TO RUN THE BUSINESS AS CO-HEADS OF THE FIXED INCOME GROUP. THEY HAVE OVER THIRTY YEARS OF COMBINED BUSINESS EXPERIENCE. WE WISH TO ASSURE ALL CLIENTS . . .

He pulled her up and took her in his arms.

"Don't worry. Everything will turn out alright," he said with a confidence he did not feel. But it was essential to keep her spirits up. He knew that confidence like virginity in twenty-first century America was a very fragile thing.

"Do you think so?" she asked plaintively.

"Yes. Absolutely. Be positive. Believe in yourself. Sweetheart you're the best in this business. Never forget that."

"Baby, promise me you'll never leave me. I need you so much."

"Darling," he assured her. "You know I love you more than anyone else in the world. You're my whole life. I'll never leave you. Never. I promise."

"Phil, I love you too. Hold me close. Never let me go."

CHAPTER 20

Three days later Victoria Spencer, wearing a light blue Chanel suit, walked into the first class section of British Airways flight 115 to New York with a confident stride. Her cool blue eyes quickly surveyed the few passengers in the cabin as the flight attendant guided her to a comfortable beige leather seat towards the front of the Boeing 747. She recognized no one. "Thank God," she sighed. "It'll give me time to think." She had always found airplanes very conducive to the thought process.

The plane took off on time. This was one of the many things she liked about European airports. They always managed to get the flights out at the appointed time. There were none of the interminable delays one encountered in America. Through the window she saw the vast panorama of London as the plane banked westwards cutting through the clouds. Ten minutes later it emerged in the sunlight as it climbed to its pre-arranged altitude.

Her vague musings were interrupted by a voice.

"May I offer you some champagne, madam?" It was the friendly looking flight attendant.

"I'll have coffee instead. Black, no sugar. Thanks."

3194-ISLA

"Right away, madam." She needed the coffee desperately. The caffeine would perk her up like a shot of adrenalin.

She went back to her rumination. It had been a long evening yesterday. First a cocktail party for the bank's wealthy customers and then the delightful time with Timothy Wilkinson at his opulent apartment in Mayfair. She had had much too much to drink and not enough sleep.

As an Executive Vice President of American Banking Corporation–known as Am Bank to friend and foe alike–Victoria was accustomed to traveling. It was, after all, one of the principal perks of executives in corporate America like the three-martini lunch that was back in fashion in these happier times. Commercial bankers, even the senior most, did not get–though this was changing as the wealth of several executives made clear–the very high compensation that investment bankers, particularly the M&A types, and the money managers took home. So the banks made up for it in perks. And why not? After all the expenses were tax-deductible and it was only reasonable that shareholders should foot the bill for all these hard working, tireless executives who toiled on their behalf. And so it was that senior executives jetted around the world–usually first class–living in glitzy hotels in London, Paris, Rome, Tokyo, Singapore, Buenos Aires and a host of other exciting cities, wining and dining in luxurious settings, all in the name of "Relationship Banking." The travel and entertainment endowed their plain work with glamour and gave them a lifestyle that was simply not affordable on their corporate incomes.

Like other senior Am Bank executives, Victoria enjoyed visiting the major centers of her far-flung empire that covered 70 countries around the globe. It filled an inner void and gave her a sense of power. All the bowing and scraping by the minions. It was also an antidote to the restless energy that propelled her like a giant Atlas rocket. But the past three months had been unusually hectic.

The explanation for that was simple enough. Victoria Spencer was, at that moment, engaged in a titanic struggle. It was the struggle for the top prize. She had dreamed of this prize for as long as she could remember. The second of two children, she grew up in an upper-middle class Jewish family in Scarsdale. Her parents had doted on an older brother. After finishing high school at Horace Mann, she had graduated summa cum laude from Yale and then spent two years, on a Fulbright scholarship, at Kings College, Cambridge. She joined Am Bank immediately afterwards, in late 1975, at the age of twenty four. An early marriage to her high school sweetheart had ended quickly and wounded her deeply. Steeled by this failure, she threw herself into work that became the elixir of her life. Ambition and energy combined with a sharp intelligence had led to uninterrupted success and a rapid rise up the ranks. Along the way she became politically adroit and well versed in the corporate game. In banking circles she developed a reputation for fresh, bold thinking and decisive action combined with an engaging personality that both peers and subordinates found attractive. One of her supervising officers had noted: "She has the ability to get other people to do what they don't want to do and still like it."

No one meeting Victoria Spencer confused her for a house-wife or a socialite. She exuded the air of a successful woman. Everything about her reflected authority, command and in-telligence. The five feet four inch tall Victoria sported shoul-der length blond hair and smiling blue eyes that softened the sharp Jewish features of her face giving it a decidedly softer look. For a woman of fifty three her body was remarkably attractive, though a shade on the plump side. She was not considered pretty but she was very well endowed in the breast department and men found her very desirable.

Am Bank, headquartered in New York, was the second largest bank in the nation, after Citigroup. Over the past ten

3194-ISLA

years the banking landscape had been transformed. Even before the repeal of Glass-Steagall, the banks had found a way around their expansion problems. As a result of consolidations their numbers had been reduced in half and some of the best-known names had disappeared into the dustbin of history. Am Bank itself was the result of the acquisition of five regional banks that had given it a presence from coast to coast and pushed it ahead of Morgan Chase and Bank of America leaving just Citigroup barely ahead in assets.

The author of this remarkable strategy, Henry Fielding, would reach the mandatory retirement age in a year's time. To meet this unfortunate contingency the bank was reorganized in June, setting up a four way horse race to succeed the soon to retire chairman. Four principal businesses were created and assigned to the leading contenders—Global Investment Banking, Global Trading, Global Consumer Banking and Global Wealth Management. Victoria had hoped to get the glamorous Global Investment Banking that accounted for twenty percent of Am Bank's eight billion dollar net income. She would have settled for Global Trading, another big money maker. Instead she found herself heading the Global Wealth Management Group.

Victoria felt bitterly disappointed. No woman had ever headed a major American bank. Perhaps the time was ripe. And yet the scales seemed tipped against her. At the time it had looked like the insidious working of what is commonly known as the old boys' network system. She recalled the meeting clearly. It had taken place four months earlier but was still vividly fresh in her mind like last night's party.

Henry Fielding had sensed the disappointment as he gave her the news of the new assignment in his football-field sized office on the twenty-second floor of the Am Bank Tower in midtown Manhattan. Victoria invariably kept her feelings under tight control and the change in her demeanor was barely perceptible as she listened to the chairman. An ordinary person would not have detected it. But Henry Fielding was no ordinary person. Nothing escaped the observant eye of America's most distinguished banker.

"Vicki," his voice boomed. "I know how you feel. You think you've been handicapped in the race. That's definitely not the case. You have my word on that."

Not knowing what the best response would be, Victoria decided that silence was the better part of wisdom and had kept quiet. She just looked blankly at him.

"The wealth management business," Fielding continued, "is a low-risk business that offers very high returns. Its capital requirements are minimal. In fact it's the most interesting business in terms of its risk/return profile. We need to increase our fee-based revenues. It's the only way to offset the income volatility in our investment banking and trading areas."

Victoria nodded in agreement. So far what Fielding said did make sense. This was, after all, the core strategy of the United Bank of Switzerland, the world's second largest bank, which had publicly announced it aimed to earn five billion dollars in private banking and investment management by 2005.

She remembered Fielding say in his most forthright and convincing manner, "The wealth management business is the key to our diversification efforts. Success will have a very significant impact on our share price as well."

He continued, "I personally selected you for this job because of your ability to take a bold, fresh approach. And by the way Bill Thompson is behind this one hundred percent."

Thompson was her mentor in the bank. The reference was presumably meant to give her comfort. She wasn't sure if she was being set up. And yet here was this old man giving her the impression that he had done her a big personal favor.

She had finally spoken. "Henry, I'll give it my best shot." It was said in a resolute voice to convey a confidence that she did not quite feel at the moment.

The old man had squeezed her right arm reassuringly.

3194-ISLA

"It'll be all right. I promise." And then he added somewhat enigmatically, "Remember Victoria, the race is not always won by the swiftest. Appearances can be very deceptive."

With that the meeting had ended and she accompanied Fielding to the auditorium where he announced the management changes to a hastily gathered assembly of Am Bank's senior executives.

Since then it had been a race against time. The words of a poem that she had read at school—and whose name and author she had long since forgotten—kept jogging her mind constantly: "The race is as long as recorded time yet as brief as the flash of an assassin's knife." There was no time to lose. And so she had been on the move ceaselessly. She visited Latin America in July. Twice. August took her to Asia and then Europe. And then in the past three weeks it was back to Asia and Europe again with a short break in the U.S. in between. This trip, in particular, had been very hectic. Paris, Geneva, Zurich, Milan, Monte Carlo, Madrid and finally London. The office meetings were long, sometimes productive but often tedious. The subject. Mostly the same: the plans and strategies of the Private Bank in the various geographic locations. The evenings were spent hobnobbing with the wealthy—the Rothchilds, Agnellis, Arnouts, Brandolinis, de Ravenals, Alexis de Ride, Lillian Betencourt, Pinaults, Von Siemens, Quandts, Berlusconis, Botin, Amalia Fortabat and countless others—at elegant parties arranged by the bank. Several of the parties were mentioned by Suzy, the well-known gossip columnist, in "W" and a number of other magazines had also carried stories.

Douglas Levine, a Vice President in the corporate planning department, briefed Victoria soon after she took over her new duties.

"The private banking business is one of the success stories of American banks in the past quarter century," Levine began. "They now count most of the world's wealthy individuals among their customers."

The thirty-four-year-old, six foot six inch tall Levine, was an up and coming executive at Am Bank. He was a graduate of Harvard Business School and had spent the past year in the corporate planning department working on the new organizational structure.

"How and when did we get into the business?" Victoria asked.

"All of us followed Citibank's lead as has so often been the case in American banking," Levine smiled. "We entered the foray in the mid-seventies. Prior to that, the Swiss had a virtual monopoly in this field. As the nationalistic Swiss like to say, they have been in this business 'Ab aeterno' which is Latin for 'from the beginning.'"

He then went into the details. That country's position as a money haven was bolstered by its long history of neutrality and political stability and its strong currency. Even the beauty and tranquility of the country had helped. The financial centers of Zurich and Geneva were wonderful places to visit and the ski resorts of Gstaad and St. Moritz–the playgrounds of the rich and famous–were nearby. Switzerland had actually invented the strict bank secrecy laws that protected the wealth of customers–or the loot depending on your point of view–from the greedy hands of foreign tax authorities. Or the hands of governments. As a result, the country had become the favorite place when it came to hiding money and this had been the basis for its remarkable economic development and the consequent high standard of living enjoyed by its citizens. So successful had the Swiss been at this game that they had actually charged customers, yes customers, interest for accepting their money in deposit accounts. But then, this was to be expected from a nation that had, in the name of national security, collaborated extensively with the Nazis during the dark days of World War II. Millions of dollars in cash and gold

3194-ISLA

belonging to holocaust victims had simply disappeared into the vaults of the Swiss banks.

"The game continued in the sixties and the early seventies," Levine said. "But then, the American banks caught on to it. They opened branches and incorporated local subsidiaries in Switzerland, Luxembourg, Liechtenstein and countless other little known and even less sparsely inhabited islands in the Caribbean. And they had managed to make big holes in the Swiss monopoly."

"Where did all the money come from?"

"A lot from businessmen and ordinary rich folk," Levine replied. "But also from corrupt government officials, dictators, gangsters, drug dealers and other crooks in Asia, Africa, Europe, Latin America and the United States. Lately Russia has been a major source. The customers objective, irrespective of their background, has always been the same: an attempt to escape from the clutches of the rapacious tax authorities and other prying eyes."

Some of the money was undoubtedly stolen, much of it was illegal and most of it had been quietly smuggled out. The Shah of Iran, the Sauds, Ferdinand Marcos, Mobutu Sese Seko, Salinas and countless other well-known names were all there. In numbered secret accounts. Their identity was known only to a very few select bank officials.

Victoria remembered the innumerable articles, in the mid and late eighties, in the pages of the New York Times, the Washington Post, the Daily News, the San Francisco Chronicler and even the Wall Street Journal descrying this massive theft and diversion of funds. The journalists accused US banks of lending vast amounts of money to developing countries and then getting most of it back in deposits from corrupt officials who simply stole large portions of these so-called development loans. Some of this had undoubtedly happened, but for God's sake money was fungible. The American banks didn't encourage the corruption. They were in the time-honored business of making loans and accepting deposits. It was too much to expect them to be the moral policemen of the world. American banks simply couldn't be expected to give up such lucrative business.

"The situation has changed dramatically in the past ten years," the lanky Levine continued in his easygoing manner. "What's happened?" Victoria asked. "Under American pressure or tutelage, exchange control laws were dismantled in country after country," the corporate strategist replied.

Levine went on, pausing briefly to let Victoria answer the telephone. "So money began to flow freely and openly across national frontiers and geographic zones. It no longer arrived at bank counters in suitcases. At least not that often," he smiled. "Of course the corruption and looting of countries has gone on at an astonishing pace. A notorious scandal occurred . . ."

"You mean at the Bank of New York."

"Yes."

Russian drug dealers and their collaborators had managed to steal and launder over ten billion dollars from that bankrupt nation.

"The freeing of currency controls combined with the worldwide rise in stock prices, have brought about a rapid rise in private banking assets," Douglas pointed out.

"Do we know the size of the market?" Victoria asked.

"Yes. The money of wealthy individuals now exceeds twenty seven trillion dollars. Two thirds comes from Europe and the United States and the balance from Asia, Africa and Latin America. Surprisingly the Middle East accounts for less than ten percent of the total."

What else was new? The world had become a relatively more secure place and Switzerland's position as a safe haven had suffered as a consequence. It now accounted for only twenty percent of this money. And these were held not just

227

by Swiss Banks, but also by the Swiss subsidiaries of American, German, French and British banks all competing vigorously for this huge pile of money.

"Anything else that I should know?" Victoria asked.

Yes, Levine had told her. Time had brought about one other change. A most important one. Customers, even the ones with the most to hide, had become more sophisticated. They were no longer prepared to accept low interest rates and they demanded much higher investment returns on their funds. And they were prepared to shop around. Banks were forced to invest these funds, on their client's behalf, in the stock and bond markets around the world, using their own investment management staff or often through outside money managers.

These were some of the thoughts passing through Victoria Spencer's mind as she languidly gazed through the window of the big jet. At 35,000 feet the dark blue sky stretched into the distant horizon. Victoria's thoughts turned to Timothy Wilkinson. She could see his handsome face with its masses of curly dark hair flecked with gray. She had been seeing him for the past two years whenever she was in London, which was often enough. At least once a month. Last night he had proposed marriage. She liked him. He was a charming man of very marked intelligence. Besides he was very amusing. It had been a long time, since her divorce really, that she had been so powerfully attracted by any man. But she had hedged her bets. She agreed to consider the proposal seriously once the monumental battle at the office, which was consuming all her time, was over. Anything else would not be fair. To Wilkinson or to her.

A man's voice startled her. She turned and looked. It was the chief flight attendant.

"What may I offer you to drink?" he enquired smiling down at her.

She looked at her watch. It was six o'clock. Time for a drink.

"I'll have a vodka tonic with lime, please."

She took the glass and stirred it gently. Quickly finishing the contents she signaled the flight attendant and ordered a second.

Her mind turned back to business. The drinks improved her mood. She felt much gayer and more optimistic suddenly. Last night Wilkinson had mentioned, very confidentially, the new Saudi oil plan. Its impact on the financial markets, particularly in the U.S., was obvious to any fool. This was an opportunity that could not be allowed to slip. She had to act fast. There was no time to lose. But what? Suddenly her face took on a more determined look. The idea came to her in a flash. She had finally figured out a course of action. A game plan began to emerge in the deepest recesses of her mind.

But first she had to talk with Bill Thompson, her friend and mentor, at Am Bank.

229

CHAPTER 21

On the same day, early in the morning, the three occupants of the Avis rental car stopped at the Mobil gas station on the Merritt Parkway. They went into the building and emerged five minutes later with some coffee in styrofoam cups. Shortly thereafter they were on Interstate 684 heading towards Bedford.

"Have either of you been to the place before?" Anne Nicholson sitting at the back of the car asked her two colleagues up front.

"No. I haven't," Charles Bradley answered.

The driver of the car, Brian Watson, kept his eyes on the road. "Neither have I, but I hear it's beautiful."

"So they say. And it's on 70 acres. Just 35 miles from New York." There was wonder in Anne's voice. She had been brought up in Staten Island and was unfamiliar with such grandiose places.

They took exit four and after driving through the village green on to Route 22, they turned at the first right on to Hook Road and arrived at the estate. The sign on the gate said "Belfield Hall" in small black letters. They drove down the long, winding dirt road lined on both sides with rolling grass fields, then past a pond on the right and then turning to the left arrived at a second gate. The driveway now became more formal, bordered by flowerbeds and huge flowering cherry trees.

As they took a sharp right turn, the house suddenly appeared before them in the distance.

It took their breath away.

"My God, it's spectacular!" Anne Nicholson exclaimed.

It was a visually stunning Georgian brick house, rectangular in shape and elegant in its simplicity and symmetry, with a hipped slate roof that made it look like an old French châteaux. The seven massive mullioned doors on the front of the house had huge casement windows positioned above them on the second floor. But the most distinctive feature of the house was the two massive chimneys that soared skyward from the flat roof.

"This is breathtaking," they gushed as Alexandra Middleton greeted them near the entrance to the house.

"Yes, isn't it lovely," she replied. Her love and pride in the house was evident from the look on her face.

"When was it built? It looks like its been here for at least two hundred years," Charles Bradley said.

"It was built for Phillip's grandfather in 1926 by an English architect called Edwin Lutyens. Have you heard of him?"

They shook their heads.

"Lutyens was an exact contemporary of Frank Lloyd Wright," Alexandra informed them. "In knowledgeable circles he is considered the greatest architect of the twentieth century. He only designed two houses in America, this and the British embassy in Washington D.C. But in England hundreds of his town and country houses are still around. His most famous work is the Viceroy's house in New Delhi, which is now occupied by the President of India."

"How tall are the chimneys? They're massive," Brian observed.

231

"They are sixteen feet wide and twenty feet high. Their position on the roof magnifies the symmetry of the house," Alexandra replied proudly.

As they walked towards the main entrance they saw the magnificent gardens that surrounded the building on all sides.

"The gardens look very large," Brian Watson said with a look of amazement on his face. He wondered how many gardeners were employed to maintain the place.

"There are thirty garden rooms featuring either gardens of a specific color or specific plant species. Lutyens, who collaborated with Gertrude Jekyll and is considered the creator of the twentieth century English garden, also laid out the structure of the garden," Alexandra said as they walked past one of the borders filled with blooming pink and blue flowers. "It's eight acres in size and do you know we have just one gardener taking care of it? In the summers we get a temporary laborer four days a week to help him weed and cut the grass. It's quite easy to maintain. Phillip and I have completely replanted the perennial gardens in the past three years. We both love to potter around."

They walked into the front hall and were astonished by its beauty. The room was enormous and it was two stories high. In the center was a magnificent T-shaped staircase with an intricately detailed wrought iron railing. The limestone floor looked ancient. Classical ornamentation and decorative trompe l'oeil paintwork, reminiscent of ancient Italian villas, covered the walls.

"That looks like the staircase in 'Gone with the Wind,'" Anne Nicholson exclaimed.

Alexandra smiled. "That's not surprising. Parts of the movie were actually filmed at the house."

They went up the wide stairs and entered the library. It was a magnificently furnished wood-paneled room with five windows that gave it a bright and airy touch. In the center of the near wall opposite the windows was a fireplace and the built in book cases were lined with old leather-bound volumes. The high ceiling had a frescoe painting that looked very old.

Alexandra saw them looking at the ceiling. "I had that done three years ago. It's a copy of that celestial map of the world," she said, pointing at an ancient looking globe that stood with another matching one on an antique table between two windows. "By the way, the different figures on the ceiling are the zodiacal signs of the children, Phillip and myself."

From the windows they could see the breathtaking formal gardens displaying an astonishing array of flower beds and borders, aged trees and rare shrubs that provided an ever changing tapestry of color through the different seasons. Numerous garden pools and fountains were visible and they gave the surrounding area a magical setting. The garden rooms were enclosed by tall green walls, which in this case were yew shrubs meticulously clipped to perfection.

Alexandra knew that her three colleagues were neophytes, despite the money they made, when it came to the social scene. For that matter, so were the B&P partners with all their wealth. She was also acutely conscious of the wrong image that the property might give them of her wealth and decided to quickly remove any misconceptions.

"This is all that is left of the Winchester wealth. Most of it was lost in the Great Depression in 1929. They managed to hold on to the house. Phillip's father spent years living abroad. You don't know but, like my husband, he was also with Citibank. Over the years the house fell into disrepair. We renovated it in the eighties when Phillip and I came back to the States. It now belongs to him and his sister who lives in Italy."

"So where did you meet Phillip?" Charles Bradley asked Alexandra. "Someone told me that both of you were at Cambridge at the same time."

"We were at Cambridge but not at the same time. Phillip

was there six years before me. He's the fourth generation of his family to have gone to Oxford or Cambridge. You've met him. He and his whole family are very anglicized." She laughed. "It was one of those chance encounters. I met him through my best friend. Her brother and Phillip were at the same college. One weekend she invited me to a party at her parent's country house. I was working very hard in those days and rarely went out. She told me she wanted to introduce me to one of her brother's dear friends who was visiting England. It was love at first sight. The rest as they say is history. We were married two months later."

"That's an incredible story. It doesn't sound like you," Anne Nicholson remarked with genuine surprise. Alexandra didn't look like the romantic type. At the office they saw the hard-edged businesswoman. Perhaps there was another side of her that they knew nothing about.

They helped themselves to coffee, biscuits and croissants that were laid out at one end of the long rectangular table and then sat down on the four chairs that stood on either side of the table and got down to work.

"Andrew Rider is driving over from Darien. He should be here shortly," Brian said.

"He's not coming," Alexandra informed them.

"What's happened?" It was Brian again. He had talked with Andrew last night. Something must have occurred at home.

"He telephoned this morning. Sidney has offered to double his compensation to a million in return for a two-year contract. He knows he's dealing with the devil but he said that the offer was too good to refuse."

The three former employees were shocked. There was no hint of this from Andrew who'd been in touch with each of them throughout the week.

It was Anne who expressed their collective sentiments. "That's really rotten. You were so close to him."

"One of the things I've found out from recent experience," Alexandra said wistfully, "is that people who you think are close to you are the ones who let you down. You live and learn. As someone once said, 'Heaven protect me from my friends. I can take care of my enemies.'"

The tone of voice left no one in doubt of her hurt and disappointment.

Alexandra now gave them a run down of events of the past two days.

"The meeting with Merrill yesterday went very well."

"Who did you meet?" Anne Nicholson asked. Anne a thirty-nine-year-old, hazel-eyed blonde with a svelte figure had worked with Alexandra for the past four years as one of the portfolio managers. Her forte was emerging market and international debt instruments. She was fired on Tuesday, the day after Alexandra's removal from the firm. Jimmy Dolittle, who was jealous of her intimacy with Alexandra, had taken a positive delight in handing her the pink slip.

"The first person I met was Michael Quinn. He seems to be in charge of the Institutional Asset Management group. And then I met his boss Carol Galley. She's from Mercury Asset Management in London but is responsible for the whole asset management business along with Stephen Zimmerman. They couldn't have been nicer."

"What did they ask?" Charles Brady inquired.

"You know, about the market, the fixed income business, my views on where the industry was headed, how we operated at B&P. Carol is very driven and wants to build the business rapidly but she's not too familiar with our market or the fixed income side. They were both very upbeat. Quinn said several times 'You're just the type of person we need.' It really was a great meeting."

"Did they ask what happened at B&P?" The question came from Brian.

"I just told them we had policy disagreements and it was a firm of tired old men."

3194-ISLA

"So you think there's a good chance of getting some kind of offer?"

"Yes. I'd say there's an excellent chance. I'm very excited about it. There's a place for all of you. We'll go in as a team. I've made that clear. Merrill has size and clout and as Phillip pointed out, it would give us a great platform for launching the business, particularly with regard to getting our B&P clients to switch."

"It sounds very promising," Anne remarked feeling very hopeful.

The others nodded their heads in agreement.

"By the way they want some material on our performance," Alexandra said looking at Charles across the table.

He opened his brief case and took out some papers that he passed over to Alexandra. For the next half-hour they wrote a cover note and played with the numbers in various ways. A few changes in the measurement period dates made the performance look even more creditable than it actually was. Bradley got up from his chair and walked over to the fax machine sitting unobtrusively in one corner of the room and faxed the information to Merrill.

"On Tuesday I have a meeting with Pegasus Asset Management in San Francisco." Alexandra told the group as she got up to get some more coffee. "It's been arranged by one of the directors of American Stores in Salt Lake City."

"What are they looking for?" Brian Watson asked. Alexandra had recruited the bespectacled chubby-faced slightly stocky Watson three years earlier from Fidelity. He specialized in corporate and high-grade bonds and his performance numbers were among the better ones in the group. He too had been fired the day after Alexandra's forced departure. Jimmy Dolittle felt he was too arrogant and did not like his attitude.

"They have about two billion dollars in fixed income mostly in a mutual fund. John Miller, who arranged the meeting, said that they were looking for someone to head the Fixed Income group and to beef up the business."

"I believe they're pretty big on the equity side. I seem to recall that they have twenty five billion in assets under management. I've occasionally run into them at presentations," Charlie Bradley observed.

"This too looks very promising. I told Miller that I wasn't too keen on moving to San Francisco but he didn't think that would be a deal breaker. Apparently the company wants to have a New York office."

Both Bradley and Nicholson were excited about going to San Francisco. The former had actually grown up in that area. But after seeing the country house they understood why Alexandra had qualms about moving to California.

"The other piece of good news is that I got a telephone call late yesterday evening." Alexandra paused to drink her coffee. "From the chairman of INVESCO."

The mention of INVESCO aroused their curiosity and they wanted to know more.

"So I'm going to Atlanta on Monday and will fly to San Francisco from there."

"I'd say that things are moving along quite nicely," Bradley observed with a chuckle.

"I would change that to very well," Nicholson said in an enthusiastic voice.

"Yes, when all is said and done it is very encouraging, but I think that we should move on two tracks. It's always wise to have a contingency plan," Alexandra reminded the group.

"Are you suggesting we also establish our own company?" Anne, who had immediately caught on to what Alexandra was driving at, asked.

"That's right. As a fall back position. Now I've spoken to over a hundred of our customers. The conversations were very encouraging. They aren't buying the 'Oh we had philosophical differences in our marketing approach' that B&P is dishing out. Most of the people I spoke with said that didn't make sense."

"Will they come with us?" Brian Watson asked the question.

"You know, they all say the same thing. Tell us once your plans have firmed and we'll talk again. Keep in touch. My sense is that it's a good sign. I'd be surprised if we didn't succeed in getting a very substantial number of these firms to come along with us. Charlie, how are you faring?"

"Not bad either. I've spoken to fifty of the customers who I've dealt with over the years. They're all very sympathetic. Again I think we'll get a good number of these clients to come with us."

Charles Bradley, a handsome and genial man in his early forties, had been in the marketing unit of B&P. Alexandra had hired him five years earlier from Fisher Francis, a competitor money management firm. He was easy going, articulate and very likeable and these qualities had helped him do well at B&P. In the past year things had begun to unravel. Hillary Schuster, who headed the combined institutional marketing group, did not like him. He had seen the handwriting on the wall and resigned from the firm following Alexandra's dismissal.

"So Anne what do you think?" Alexandra asked.

"My first choice is Merrill or one of the other big firms you mentioned but I like the idea of having a fall back position."

Alexandra turned to Brian who was sitting next to her. "What about you?"

"I agree."

"And you Charlie?" He was sitting across the table from her.

"I also think we should have a fall back position. What do you have in mind?"

Alexandra spelt out the details. She would retain fifty five percent of the shares and the other partners would have the balance. She made it clear that they would have to decide among themselves on the split of this forty five percent between them. She would accept their decision. She wanted majority control to make sure what happened to her at B&P never occurred again.

"I'm fifty and I'm having to start all over again," she reminded them firmly.

"What about capital? How much would we need?" Brian asked.

"We won't require much if we can get some big accounts straight away," Alexandra replied. "My guess is that at most we'll need around five hundred thousand. I could lend that to the company or we could get a bank loan that I would personally guarantee. Of course we'll all be liable for it."

"Would it help if we had some wealthy outside backers?" Chuck Bradley asked.

"Like who?" Anne countered with another question.

"The two that come to mind are Prince Tarik and Bill Gates. We managed substantial amounts of their money," Bradley replied.

"I'm not sure it helps us in any way. If we did get them to agree they would want a significant equity stake," Alexandra said, intervening to cut the debate. "And we could have a lot of disagreement in the future. That would put us back in the B&P situation. I think a better approach is to get their accounts immediately. For example if we could get the two accounts of Prince Tarik, which total a billion dollars, we would have a two million dollar fee income. That is the equivalent of a substantial amount of capital."

"Speaking of Tarik have you spoken to him yet?" Bradley asked.

"I haven't been able to get in touch with him on the phone. He's traveling. I've sent him a fax message."

"Let's go over the client list and segregate them into three categories: those most likely or definitely likely to switch

3194-ISLA

to us, those in the fifty/fifty group where we have a good chance and those unlikely to come with us," Alexandra suggested. "Brian will you put the list on the laptop and we can then have a print out and play with it further."

"In the first list," Charlie began, "I would include PPG Industries, the Denver Employees Retirement System, Oklahoma State Teachers Retirement System, Waterbury Retirement System, Amerada Hess, Kodak, Provident Mutual, Hitchcock Clinic, Exxon, Children's Aid Society and Deerfield Academy."

"Of the group I have talked with," Alexandra said confidently, "I'm quite sure of General Motors, Halliburton, Colgate Palmolive, Ford and the World Bank." Then after checking her notes, she added, "I'd also put Aetna, Brandeis, Ford Foundation, the New York Zoological Society, Reynolds Foundation, and Oklahoma Health Care in the same list."

For the next two hours they went over the entire client list. Each name was discussed from different viewpoints. How well did any of them, particularly Alexandra, know the pension fund officer? How was the performance? How solid was the relationship? How long had they had the account? At the end of the deliberations they had a hundred accounts in the first category, eighty were in the fifty/fifty group and the remaining one hundred and twenty were considered the least likely to switch.

Watson did the calculations on the computer. If the accounts materialized they would have four billion in assets under management in the first year and another two billion in the next year or two. These numbers only included switch over of existing accounts. In Alexandra's view, which was supported by Bradley, new customers would only start coming in after eighteen months to two years of operation.

Tasks were given out. Charlie would begin looking at premises. Alexandra would work with the lawyers to get the company registered with the SEC and also draw up a partnership agreement. Watson and Nicholson would investigate the cost of all equipment and databases such as Bloomberg that they would need and also come up with three-year income expense numbers based on their discussions.

The question of name came up. "What shall we call the firm?" Alexandra asked the group.

"How about Middleton Investment Management," Brian responded.

"That sounds pretty good," Anne observed.

Alexandra smiled. "I'm pleased but let's consider a few alternatives."

"How about Hercules Capital Management or Hercules Asset Management," Bradley proposed.

"I like Pericles Asset Management," Anne Nicholson suggested

They settled on Anne's choice. Smartness and wisdom and longevity were associated with the ancient ruler of Athens. Somehow it just seemed to be the most appropriate name.

Shortly thereafter the meeting ended. They agreed to meet early on Monday at Alexandra's New York townhouse. A temporary office had been set up there in the library until they moved to more permanent quarters. On the drive out they ran into Phillip coming in with the children. He had picked them up at school.

3194-ISLA

CHAPTER 22

At eight thirty in the morning on the following Monday, Victoria strode briskly through the thickly-carpeted hallway and entered the spacious corner office on the twenty-second floor overlooking Park Avenue. Sunlight filtered through the windows, filling the room with light.

A middle-aged man in a double breasted gray pin striped suit, blue shirt with a white collar and a red Hermès silk tie got up from his desk and greeted her warmly.

"Haven't seen you in a while," he said with a broad grin on his face. "Someone mentioned that you've been traveling."

"Yes I was in Europe. I got back last night," Victoria smiled warmly. She was pleased to see him.

"How is it going?"

"Good," she replied. "In fact much better than I expected."

As they sat down on the cream-colored sofa next to the corner window, a pleasant looking secretary in her mid-fifties came in with the coffee. Victoria's glance fell, as usual, on the large number of photographs on the glass table next to the sofa. Signed photographs of Presidents Reagan and Bush stood in the front. Behind were several photographs of Bill

Thompson with the Presidents and Finance Ministers of Brazil, Argentina, Venezuela and Mexico. There was even one with General Pinochet flanked by Victoria and Thompson. William Aubrey Thompson was Vice Chairman of American Banking Corporation. Friendly and urbane, he looked like the quintessential banker. The medium height, slightly stocky build and the thinning gray hairs combed slickly back completed the picture. He had come to the bank twenty years earlier from the International Monetary Fund in Washington D.C. For a few years he ran the bank's international division, before moving on to the even more important position overseeing Am Bank's large portfolio of global sovereign loans, most of which were either in default or on the verge of default. Thompson had played a major role in saving Am Bank–some would say the U.S. banking industry–in the darkest days of the global debt crises of the late eighties and early nineties. As a result, he was very well regarded in international financial circles and numbered among his friends many central bank governors, finance ministers and even a few presidents of various Asian, European and Latin American countries. Closer to home, Alan Greenspan, the former Chairman of the Federal Reserve, Robert Rubin, the former Treasury Secretary, James Wolfensohn, President of the World Bank and Horst Kohler, the newly-appointed head of the IMF were close personal friends, not to mention several key senators and congressman.

His work had earned the profound gratitude of Henry Fielding who had become the bank's chairman in the mid-eighties and whose tenure would have been one of the shortest in the history of modern American banking had it not been for William Thompson. A vice chairmanship had been his reward. Now just two years short of the mandatory retirement age, Thompson was the bank's elder statesman and goodwill ambassador wooing corporate customers and

3194-ISLA

governmental entities. The well-tanned face was a reminder of the substantial amount of time spent on golf courses around the world in the service of his bank.

Victoria had worked with Thompson on the debt crises. In fact she had been his deputy and it was whispered in the hallways and corridors of Am Bank that she was the real brain behind that effort. In any event, whatever the truth may have been, a close and friendly relationship had developed between the two and it was well known within the institution that Victoria was Thompson's protégé.

"So what do you make of it?" Thompson asked.

"I've come up with a number of ideas," Victoria smiled. "But I need your input and advice."

"I'll do anything to help," the vice chairman replied, pleased to be consulted.

"One of the more interesting things I've found out is that private banking is the fastest growing business in the financial area. Because the investments of the clients' funds are not on the bank's balance sheet, the capital requirements are modest and the return on equity is consequently very high."

"I imagine that's what makes the business so attractive for us."

"Unfortunately. The attractiveness has heightened the competition. As a result the margins are gradually eroding."

"Where is the competition greatest?"

"Right now in Europe and the United States where the customers are the most sophisticated. Here the regional banks like Wells Fargo and First Union are rushing into the business. The situation is actually getting worse in Europe. Not only have some of the smaller Swiss banks like Julius Baer and Vontobel become more active, but also the bigger ones like UBS and Credit Suisse are increasingly focusing on private banking as their principal business. They are the two largest players in the field. And the German, British and French banks are all moving in aggressively."

"That's because lending to corporations is going the same way it did in the United States–out of the window–and they are also failing to make much of a headway in investment banking," Thompson interjected.

"You're absolutely right. Now the Swiss are going one step further. They're emphasizing their ability to provide cradle to grave financial planning to cover every possible aspect of a wealthy individual's needs."

Victoria was referring to these banks' much greater willingness to provide the personal touch, whether of a financial or non-financial nature. Successful private banking, after all, required the careful cultivation of customers and long-term relationship building. More and more often this meant assistance in finding a suitable house, vacation home rentals, making travel arrangements, carrying briefcases, giving friendly family advice, going shopping for toys and jewelry and even meeting the needs of the flesh-call girls, escort services, parties and even arranging dates. This is what account officers meant when they talked of offering customized services to clients.

She drank the half-cold coffee and continued. "In absolute amounts our net income is increasing. Last year we made a billion two. That's a little over thirteen percent of the bank's income. But the percentage increase is slowing down."

"What's the explanation?"

"Two main reasons. One's the competition and the declining margins I've already mentioned. The other is a little more disturbing. Customers are not giving us more of their money. And we're having difficulty attracting new customers. More and more are going directly to the brokerage houses and the money managers. They are concerned about a perceived conflict of interest."

"What do you mean?" the vice chairman enquired.

"Well it seems that they are unhappy that we, and by that I mean banks in general, push our own products instead of

3194-ISLA

selecting the product that best meets their needs because we do not want to reduce our profits."

This was true of course. Banks had a vested interest in selling their own products–primarily investment management services–because it maximized their revenues. Unfortunately these services tended to be inferior to those available in the marketplace. What the wealthy really needed were asset allocators or 'fund-of-funds', which for a very small fee, would place the assets of the clients in the best investment vehicle, based on the risk parameters of each individual investor. Some of the smaller Swiss banks were moving in that direction but the industry as a whole was far removed from this ideal situation, which in any event was not likely to arrive anytime soon.

"Let me ask you a more fundamental question," Thompson said. "We keep reading in the papers that money manager can't beat the market because it is efficient. Presumably that means that no single person has any special information that's not available to other market participants."

He continued as she poured another cup of coffee. "I have to assume the wealthy are not stupid, or they wouldn't have made all the money. So the question is," Thompson paused to look at Victoria with a twinkle in his eye, "will these individuals shift their money to the index funds. It would be a lot cheaper."

"That's exactly what I first thought. So I pondered on the issue for a long time. I posed the question to our officers in London, Paris, Hong Kong and elsewhere. I think we all agree that while we may see an occasional switch to index funds, a mass movement is simply not in the cards. In fact I give it less than a five percent chance in the short or the long run."

"What makes you so confident?" the senior executive asked.

"A number of reasons. As you said, the wealthy are smart. But their smartness is limited to a fairly narrow business specialty–you know to the specific area in which they make money. They don't have the same aptitude in other areas. Let me give you an example. Take a baseball player like Derek Jeter. He's got an eighty or ninety million dollar contract but his specialty is baseball. That's what he's familiar with and that's what he concentrates on. He's out of his league in the world of high finance like the average American. So he hires financial consultants to do the investing. Now these financial consultants, or for that matter the family investment offices of some of the old wealthy families, have a vested interest. Their value is in finding the smart money managers."

"So how do these quirks of the wealthy prevent their shifting assets to low cost service providers?"

"Simple. Vanguard and the index funds are just not in a position to provide the one-on-one service that is a staple of the industry. Fortunately the rich are spoilt. The handholding and the ancillary services that we provide are just not available elsewhere."

"You mean there will always be suckers." They both laughed at the way he said it.

"Thank God for that," Victoria answered. "You know it's quite astonishing that even we bankers are prone to the same thing. And we are supposedly familiar with the markets, or at least that's what the average person believes."

"I guess we too get over involved in our limited area of expertise."

"That's right. And in the process we either do not know enough or simply find it much easier to rely on investment professionals to take care of our investments. I recently ran into your old friend, the vice chairman of Citigroup."

"George Farley?"

"Yes. He was with his financial consultant. The man looked like a snake oil salesman. Farley apparently has no clue about the market, so the consultant is taking care of his funds."

"That doesn't surprise me. By the way, have you any idea how Citigroup is doing in private banking?"

"They're the third largest in the industry after UBS and Credit Suisse. I heard that they made 1.4 billion dollars in the business last year."

"How does that compare with UBS?"

"UBS has more than four times the assets, but they only made three and a half billion. They have big problems in private banking and in asset management and have gone through a second reorganization in six months."

"Now that you have an excellent grasp of the business, how are you coming along on the strategy? Any progress? Remember we don't have too much time," Thompson remarked with evident sincerity.

"Bill, I'm working on it. I should have something definitive within two or three weeks at most. But there are a couple of things we need to initiate immediately. I want to expand your role as the senior statesman and goodwill ambassador to also cover wealthy individuals. Some really fancy entertainment at places we can rent like Bleinham Palace or the Brandolini Palazzo on the Grand Canal in Venice or St. Andrew's golf course would help us enormously in building long-lasting relationships. David Rockefeller did a great job over at Chase."

"I'd be delighted to help in any way possible," said a beaming Thompson, greatly relishing the idea of masked balls in Venice and hunting on the great estates in England. He made a mental note of getting formal clearance from Fielding at the lunch that afternoon.

"And I want to move aggressively in changing our investment strategy. I want to put more emphasis on alternative investments."

In late 1997 there was a huge scare in the market following a series of events that began in East Asia. The contagion had spread rapidly around the world like the influenza epidemic of 1917. It was followed in 1998 by the Russian debt default and the spectacular near collapse of Long Term Capital Management, a hedge fund that had attracted large amounts of money from institutions dazzled by the star attraction of its Nobel Prize-winning partners. Global markets spun in disarray as investors lost billions of dollars and pulled in much of what remained of their principal. Within a few months the situation changed completely. Memory in the financial market was very short. Analysts had gleefully predicted the demise of hedge funds. Within a year, institutions and individuals were pumping money into these vehicles completely oblivious of recent events. They had continued to do so ever since. Neither the crash of some emerging country stock markets nor the near bankruptcy of the HCM hedge fund in 2002 had slowed the process.

"What are alternative investments?" Thompson was unfamiliar with the language of the money management industry.

"Oh, I'm sorry. I just took it for granted that you knew the market buzzwords. I mean products like hedge funds, venture capital, real estate investments and private equity."

She continued, as he nodded to show he understood. "We've been too conservative in our approach. Wealthy investors don't need us to introduce them to KKR or Soros or Louis Marcus. They're household names. We have to find the next Soros, the next Forstmann Little before they're discovered by the rest of the market."

"That makes sense to me. How do you propose to find them?"

"Through research in the marketplace and systematic searching for new companies that specialize in these products but are still relatively small. And secondly by discovering individual money managers with great track records who are not currently involved in these particular products and then persuading them to switch over and start their own funds. By the way I've set up a two-person unit under Doug Levine,

249

reporting directly to me to engage full time in this effort. We're going to be more daring and we'll take more risks in selecting these managers many of whom may have great promise but not the three-year minimum record that consultants typically look for to protect their behind."

"I agree with you," the vice chairman said. "I'm not sure that the past record necessarily tells us much about future performance. Both the HCM and Tiger hedge funds had impressive track records and were highly recommended by all the experts. Yet they blew up."

"That's right. By the way part of the problem is the way the performance numbers are reported. They have little or no relationship to the amount of funds under management and the cumulative numbers are even less informative."

She realized from the blank look on his face that he was lost.

"Did you follow what I said?" she asked grinning.

"I'm afraid not," a somewhat sheepish Thompson confessed.

"Alright let me illustrate it for you. A fund manager begins with ten million dollars. He makes some aggressive and risky bets that work out. The first year returns are 40 percent. He is discovered and the money comes pouring in. It's a billion dollars in the second year. He no longer takes the same risks, plays it safer. The returns are no longer as good. In year two he's down ten percent. The cumulative return for the two year period is shown in the statistics as 26 percent and funds under management are reported as one billion."

"Okay I see your point about the lack of a relationship between the returns and the numbers as they are advertised or reported. What about the cumulative numbers?"

"Those are just as false. The twenty six percent number is quite meaningless. It applies only to the original first year investors whose two-year return is 26 percent. The second year investors have actually lost ten percent."

"Now I understand. You're right. The numbers obviously don't tell the whole story."

"Back to my views on the selection of portfolio managers. Instead of paying so much attention to past performance statistics we intend to focus more on whether their ideas are intellectually sound, whether the risks are defined and measurable and if we can philosophically relate to them."

"Victoria, the more I hear the more I like it. We have to differentiate ourselves from the rest of the pack." As usual he was impressed by her astonishingly single-minded focus and determined approach to problems.

"Bill, as I mentioned earlier the Swiss are giving more of their client's funds to outside managers in an attempt to improve investment performance and avoid conflict of interest–or at least show that they are avoiding it. I want to move in that direction too. That of course reduces our profitability. We have to share the revenue with the outside managers. When we manage it ourselves we keep it all."

"I guess we'll have to bite the bullet sometime."

"Yes but I'm hoping to balance this in two ways. First, increasing assets by attracting new customers and getting more funds from our existing customers through superior investment performance. And secondly by dramatically improving our in-house money management capabilities and broadening our product offerings. Unfortunately this is where we hit a brick wall."

She looked plaintively at Thompson and asked, "American banks dominated the money management business in the mid-twentieth century. What happened? What changed it?"

Bill Thompson knew some of this history. Alone among the bank's senior executives he had repeatedly stressed the importance of the business but no one paid any attention.

"You're right. In the 1950's and the 1960's the banks dominated the industry. They had entered the business through

251

their trust and estate management activities. The performance numbers were nothing to speak of but it didn't matter. No one really paid much attention to that in those days. Then in 1974 Congress passed the ERISA Act. It set new standards of coverage, vesting, funding and supervision of pension funds. The Act essentially revolutionized the industry and brought a great deal of professionalism into the business. Competition increased dramatically as new players entered the market. Pension fund customers began demanding performance. Pension fund consultants materialized to help the funds select money managers, do the asset allocation work and monitor performance."

"What did the banks do in the face of all this?"

"Not much. Or very little. Of course we added staff and became more professional but we were left far behind by the competition. Do you remember Walter Wriston?"

She nodded.

"Well, Wriston was probably the smartest banker of the century. He got Citibank into the consumer business, he revolutionized the back office and imbued them with the entrepreneurial 'can do' spirit that still pervades that institution twenty years after his retirement. Yet when it came to ERISA he completely misjudged it. As a result he missed out on two critical businesses. Money management, which has become one of America's most profitable industries, and mutual funds that today have a greater share of the financial assets of American households than all the banks combined. But then neither did David Rockefeller at Chase, or Clausen at Bank of America or McGullicuddy over at Manufacturers Hanover."

At this point the pleasant looking secretary brought in some fresh coffee. Victoria poured it in the cups for both of them.

She drank her coffee as the vice chairman continued. "The business was also not in the mainstream of banking—you know kind of a stepchild. It was isolated from our core activities by the proverbial Chinese wall. And of course the credit and lending officers in the so-called glamour businesses of the bank looked down upon it. So banks eventually ended up becoming secondary players in the money management industry."

"Why did we sell the business?" Victoria wanted to know.

"You remember, in the early 1990's," Thompson went on, "we desperately needed to boost our capital due to all those bad loans we had made in Latin America."

They both smiled at that. The memory of those times was still fresh in their minds. It had been the best and the worst of times.

"So we sold the business to St. Paul Insurance Company. Citibank sold theirs around the same time to USFG. Chase did the same. They sold out to the Union Bank of Switzerland."

Thompson took a sip of his coffee. "In retrospect it was a poor decision. The money that we raised was a pittance. The business did not require any capital under the Basel Accord."

He was referring to the agreement that governed the capital requirements of banks in the developed countries of the world. It had been in effect since 1988 and required banks to have capital of at least 8% of their risk assets that were defined in detail in the accompanying regulations.

"A few years later we recognized our mistake and re-entered the business along with Chase and Citibank."

Victoria cut in. "But the truth of the matter is that none of us have had much success. The retail business is dominated by the likes of Fidelity, Vanguard, Merrill and Dreyfus. It's the same story on the institutional side. We have five billion in assets, Citibank had about the same prior to their merger with Travelers while Chase claims to have ten billion. All in all not much to write home about," she concluded matter-of-factly.

"That's right," Thompson replied jovially. "And that's why I strongly urged Fielding to put you in charge of the business. It sure is a goldmine if the rebuilding effort succeeds."

She laughed. "Thanks for getting me into this mess. Anyway, I recall you were on some committee at the time we decided to get back into asset management."

"Yes. The Capital Investment Committee."

"I'm curious if you looked into buying a money management firm at that time? That would have jumpstarted our reentry into the business."

"My recollection is that we looked at several companies. Most of them were small with five billion or less in assets under management. The largest was B&P which had about forty or forty five billion."

"So why didn't we buy one of these firms?"

"We thought the small companies did not offer much value. B&P looked more promising until we examined their records and met the partners."

"And?"

"In a nut shell the price was too high. The business was slipping. They had not invested in new products so they were falling behind. There were too many old partners who we thought were basically trying to cash out. I don't think their portfolio managers impressed us. I recall a lady who was very capable and who really stood out. Unfortunately there weren't too many like her. Why? Are you thinking of acquiring some company?"

"No. I don't think that is the right approach," Victoria replied. "Besides most of the firms that are available are over priced. Allianz, the German insurance company paid $3.3 billion for seventy percent of Pimco Advisors. That gave it a valuation of $4.7 billion which was a steep twenty three times earnings, considering Pimco's net income was only $208 million."

"So what are the alternatives?"

"The first is to continue the present strategy and try to build the business from within."

"But can you make it work? It hasn't so far."

"Let me play devil's advocate and go over the issues first."

He smiled, as she went on with her explanation. "In this approach we run into two problems which are interlinked. We have difficulty attracting top-quality portfolio managers because of the culture issue."

"Is it similar to what we see in our investment bank?"

"Yes to some extent. But I'm talking of the industry and the nature of this particular beast. The asset management business is very entrepreneurial. There are few entry barriers and there are no regulatory capital requirements. In fact you need capital only to cover expenses until sufficient revenues are generated. Operating costs are low so it's relatively easy for a top quality money manager to set up shop with himself and one or two others, especially in the equity area where many clients tend to follow the individual portfolio manager rather than stay with his former employers."

"That probably accounts for the hundreds of boutiques in the industry."

"Precisely. And then our culture intervenes. We simply cannot pay enough. You mentioned investment banking earlier. The problem is similar but the magnitude is much greater."

"How did you come to that conclusion?"

"Because unlike investment banks which are largely public entities, the money management business is riddled with partnerships and private ownership. So not only do the first-class portfolio managers make five to fifteen million dollars in annual compensation, they also have an equity stake in the company. At the going price of twenty times earnings this is very valuable. Moreover these people have total control over their own destiny. No one asks them to make annual plans and quarterly forecasts or get involved in all the other paraphernalia that is part of our modern management culture."

"I understand," Thompson replied. "So in an effort to minimize the compensation gap between the private bank account officers and the portfolio managers we refuse to pay the latter what they can get in the marketplace."

"That's correct. So we tend to get lower quality individuals and we load them with our usual managerial perks. And they rapidly adapt to our bureaucratic, empire building ways."

"Right."

"Let me give you an example that illustrates some of the problems." Victoria checked some papers in a folder that she had brought along. "Citigroup has one hundred and seventy billion in assets under management, mostly from the private bank, and they have 220 portfolio managers. We have 190 managers for a hundred and fifty billion in assets. Fleet has 140 for fifty eight billion. On the other hand Pimco Advisors with two hundred and fifty six billion in assets has only 26 portfolio managers. Dreyfus runs eighty five billion with a team of 30."

"That's incredible. I assume you don't think this approach will work?"

"I've given it a great deal of thought. My conclusion is that there is absolutely no way to meld the culture into one. It just won't happen."

"So have you figured out a solution?" Thompson asked. It was obviously a daunting task for which there might be no solution. That would be a serious blow for Victoria's chances in the race to succeed Fielding. She was his candidate and he was worried.

"The sixty four thousand dollar question that we face," Victoria said, "is how do we create the same conditions in which money management firms operate and still have them as part of the bank in some shape or form."

"I assume," he replied, "you mean an environment where these people can operate without our interference and at the same time earn the high compensation and also have some kind of residual ownership in the business. That's quite a tall order, isn't it?" He did not see how that could be accomplished.

Victoria laughed. "Yes. But the solution suddenly occurred to me over cocktails in the airplane as we flew at thirty five thousand feet."

She gave him a summary of her idea. It would be a kind of hybrid joint venture with a small existing company or a group of top-quality money managers. The bank would have only a thirty percent ownership stake but the income distribution would be much larger, say around sixty five percent for the bank. She had the lawyers and her personal assistant working out the precise details. This company would eventually take over the investment of all assets currently managed in Am Bank's private banking group and the asset management division. What was lost in income would be more than made up in expense reduction. That covered not just the 190 portfolio managers, but also the research staff, the huge support staff, the premises expenses, the overhead expense allocations, the processing costs and so on. This structure gave the portfolio managers total control over their destiny, or almost total and at the same time assured them of a link with Am Bank's domestic and global reach and huge customer base. It had the added advantage of giving the bank a full array of products. It could add modules to this structure for the real estate investments, private equity and hedge funds that the private bank needed.

"That's a very interesting and novel approach," Thompson said with considerable enthusiasm. He thought it might just work. "By the way have you identified any company or group of individuals?"

3194-ISLA

She noted that Thompson had a more enlightened attitude on the compensation issue. The huge amount of money
that portfolio managers would make in this venture did not
faze him. Somewhere she had recently heard that his stock
options were worth seventy five million dollars. Not bad for
a commercial banker. Even Wriston had not retired with such
a pile of money. The industry was changing at least for the
top guys. That, she thought, probably accounted for the en-
lightenment. She didn't blame him for that. After all her own
stock options were worth twenty million and that had certainly changed her attitude.

"Yes. But I need to talk with them first. Meanwhile we'll
need the appropriate management approvals from the Capital Investment Committee."

He smiled. "That should not be a problem."

They discussed the strategy for a further fifteen minutes.
It was agreed that a formal proposal would be on his desk by
early next week. Thompson promised to get the necessary
approvals immediately thereafter.

CHAPTER 23

The Saudi military plane, a brand new Boeing 747, took off from Prince Sultan Air Base, sixty miles south east of Riyadh in the early morning hours of Monday, the sixth day of September for the two and a half hour flight to Isfahan. Prince Tarik along with Michael Townsend and Khalid Ashrawi were the only passengers on board. A crew of nineteen was also on the flight to take care of their needs.

Following the successful meetings with the Mexican, Venezuelan and Russian ministers, Prince Tarik and his advisers decided on a two-pronged strategy to win approval for the new Saudi policy. Iran was the critical factor in the equation and it was to be tackled first in bilateral negotiations. This would then be followed by a joint meeting with Kuwait, the UAE and Iraq. The Saudi Supreme Council approved the approach. Once again Fahd had personally telephoned the Iranian leaders and set up the meeting a week earlier. At his suggestion, the Kuwaitis invited the four nations to meet in their capital nine days later. It was the Kuwaiti Crown Prince, Sheikh Sabah al Sabah, responsible for the country's day-to-day affairs, who had actually made the arrangements.

3194-ISLA

The invitations to the four leaders had been duly conveyed. Personally by telephone.

Only eight people in Saudi Arabia were aware of the country's new policy. To ensure its continued secrecy all other members of the Saudi establishment, including its senior diplomats, had been left out of the loop. This explained Fahd's personal involvement in arranging the meetings as well as the early morning departure from the military air base instead of Riyadh, the site of the kingdom's principal international airport. In a final gesture, Fahd appointed Tarik as his personal envoy with plenipotentiary powers to negotiate and enter into agreements on behalf of the Kingdom of Saudi Arabia.

The 747 was Fahd's official airplane. It had been specially adapted for the monarch by Boeing. The fittings were not only luxurious but also comfortable. No expense had been spared. Mario Buatta, the famed American decorator designed the interior in pale hues of cream, green and blue. And the communications equipment, incorporating the latest technology, was several cuts above that of U.S. Air Force One, the aircraft used by the President of the United States.

The flight plan took the jet over the barren Nafud desert, then in a north-easterly direction over Dhahran, crossing the Persian Gulf at that point and then flying due north just east of Abadan and on to Isfahan.

The all-male crew served breakfast in the forward lounge of the plane, which was elaborately furnished with sofas and plush armchairs in silks and velvets. Antique oriental rugs covered the floor. The contrast between the barren, desolate desert down below and the heady luxury inside the aircraft couldn't have been more startling. Both Townsend and Ashrawi, flying in the plane for the first time, marveled at the miraculous power of money.

At a barely perceptible nod from the prince, the flight attendants cleared the remains of the breakfast, leaving the three occupants alone in the cabin. Townsend noticed the surreptitious glances of the crew at the prince. The man sitting casually on the sofa was a dazzling sight, for on this day the six feet tall Tarik, so completely westernized by years of long exposure to Europe, looked like an Arab Lawrence of Arabia with his slim, athletic body draped in the white robe of the Arabs known as the aba. A white cotton cloth called a ghutra, covered his head and was held in place by a round black cord. The short and portly Ashrawi was similarly dressed but the results were nowhere near as impressive. Townsend had not followed their example, having chosen wisely to stick with a navy blue double-breasted suit for the occasion.

The debonair prince was in a jovial mood.

"Khalid," his dark brown eyes twinkled mischievously, "I know what you're thinking. But even I can't persuade His Majesty to give up this expensive toy. So we might as well enjoy it."

An embarrassed Ashrawi lamely said "It's overly luxurious."

"I've never seen anything like this either," Michael added.

Tarik smiled. "You aren't the only ones."

He pressed a button on the wall next to the seat. A large screen instantly came to life. It was CNBC carrying the business news of the previous day. They watched the screen in silence. The news broadcaster reported that inflation remained mild as the U.S. economy continued to surge ahead. The Labor Department had announced earlier in the day that the CPI–or the consumer price index to the uninitiated–the principal inflation measure of the nation had risen 0.10 percent in August. For the past twelve months the CPI had risen a meager 2.5 percent.

It had been an uneventful day on the New York Stock Exchange. Following a four-day rally that had pushed the Dow up over two hundred and thirty two points, the market

3194-ISLA

had taken a breather. The index had slipped seventy two points to 17,638.46.

The big screen blanked out as Tarik, leaning sideways, depressed a small square shaped knob that looked like a telephone push button.

"So, Khalid what's your read on the market?" Tarik asked.

"I think it's overvalued now."

"Two weeks earlier you were still wavering. What changed your mind?"

"The earnings picture. It no longer justifies a price-earnings ratio of thirty five. It's too high by any historical measure."

The price-earnings ratio was one of the tools used by investment professionals. It was a way of calculating the market value of a company's share and in simple terms represented the present value of the firm's future earning stream.

Tarik turned slightly leftward to look at the American. "Well, Senor Townsend, what's your opinion?"

"I agree with Khalid."

Tarik looked out of the window for an instant, lost in his thoughts. Finally he spoke.

"I've been reflecting on the market for a while. I'm convinced that it's now treading into dangerous territory. It's dancing on the head of a pin. Sentiment could change instantly. And the news doesn't have to be particularly negative . . ."

"Like Jim Baker's remarks in October 1987," Ashrawi cut in.

He was referring to the polished Texan lawyer James Baker who had been the Treasury Secretary at the time. In the late eighties the U.S. trade gap with Japan had reached excessively high levels. The administration thought that this could be corrected via the exchange market by making U.S. exports more attractive. That meant a cheaper dollar versus the yen. The Treasury officials favored a lower exchange rate. The market was fully aware of the administration's policy. Yet when Secretary Baker repeated the administration's view a day earlier the stock market unexpectedly and quite suddenly took note. On Black Monday, October 19, 1987 it went into a tailspin. The Dow fell a bone crunching 508 points. That twenty three percent drop was the largest one-day loss in the market's history. Even the 1929 crash had not come anywhere close. After all on October 29, the so-called Black Tuesday, the Dow had lost a mere twelve percent of its value.

"That's right. And it can happen again. No let me change that to it will happen again," Tarik said forcefully.

"Could an oil price increase do it?" Michael asked.

"Yes," Tarik declared emphatically. "In the past the market has ignored the price rise. In 1995 and 1999 and then again in early 2000. But given its present highly volatile state, a rise could trigger a crash. Particularly if it catches the market by surprise."

"So it's time to bail out?" Ashrawi asked.

"Yes, but it's also a great opportunity to make money." He grinned. "We'll never time the market precisely. There's no way to predict the absolute top or the bottom. That's a fool's world. So it might as well be now. If we do this carefully and the change in our market posture remains a secret we'll have almost a month before the OPEC meeting. We'll begin the process later this month."

For Tarik the stakes were high. A twenty percent drop– generally considered a correction–which a handful of bearish investment strategists had been predicting for the past five years, would cost the prince close to eight billion dollars. Ashrawi and Bodger Afridi would also be hurt. Each man's fortune numbered two hundred and fifty million dollars. The munificent compensation provided by Tarik had started the wealth accumulation. The great bull market had done the rest.

3194-ISLA

Townsend was not in this league. His assets were a mere five million dollars. Just barely. It was the chance to make a fortune that had brought him to the barren desert for a second time. The management consulting business did not provide a big income because of the competitive pressures and the high overhead costs. That's what made working for Tarik so appealing. Unlike Citigroup, the prince was a most generous employer.

"How is the economic policy study coming along?" Ashrawi asked Tarik

"Very well," Tarik replied. "I had a long conversation with Tim and Bodger yesterday. The draft report will be available by month end. They're filling in the details. We agreed on some critical issues."

Not knowing the details, the two passengers made no comments. They just looked at Tarik.

He leaned back in the out size armchair, crossed his legs at the same time and then went on. "Let me back track a little and put the issue into the proper perspective. In the past twenty five years Saudi Arabia has spent almost a trillion dollars on social and economic development. We've had great successes and obvious failures. A lot of the money was wasted and corruption increased the losses. But much has also been accomplished. Roads, airports, factories, schools and hospitals have been built. The nation's infrastructure is now basically in place and the people have been transformed from Bedouin wanderers to urban dwellers. Modern towns have come into being in place of the mud dwellings of the past. The literacy rate is over eighty percent. We are the world's largest producers of desalinated water. But the price has been heavy."

The price Tarik referred to was not just money. Economic development required two ingredients: capital and labor. Saudi Arabia had plenty of capital. The problem was labor. This was true throughout the Arabian Peninsula. The same problem existed in Kuwait, the United Arab Emirates and Qatar. The local Arabs were few in number and were not interested in working as laborers or technicians. They wanted cushy sinecure jobs. So foreigners had to be imported in vast quantities. The result had been predictable. Throughout the Gulf states aliens now outnumbered the natives by a wide margin. More than half of Saudi Arabia's population consisted of foreigners.

"We just simply cannot continue on this road. Both the economic and the social costs are too high. Besides the goods that are manufactured or grown on the land are absolutely non-competitive on world markets. So we're coming up with an alternative plan."

The solution was daring in its simplicity. As described by the prince it had two key elements. First it envisioned the establishment of an investment fund. Like a social security or pension plan but with one major caveat. The contributions to the fund would be made entirely by the state. Fifteen percent of the annual oil revenues would go to the fund, which would in turn make investments in financial markets in America, Europe, Asia, Latin America and Africa. Secondly, instead of building factories in Saudi Arabia and importing laborers they would take the factories to where the laborers were available. In places like Egypt, Pakistan, Bangladesh, Syria, Jordan, the West Bank and other neighboring countries. Another fifteen percent of the oil revenues would be reserved for such investments."

"This makes a lot more sense than the earlier policy," Townsend said. "Industrialization is a means to an end and not an end in itself."

"By the way," Tarik added, "the investment results are very impressive. I had them work out the numbers. If we invested ten billion dollars a year for ten years and assumed a ten percent return, which has been the long-term return in the U.S. equity market, we would end up with one hundred and seventy six billion dollars in the tenth year. That's the

power of compounding. Over longer periods it becomes geo-
metric. The outcome is staggering. In thirty years we'll have
close to two trillion dollars."

Ashrawi and Townsend agreed. It was the right approach.
The numbers were just mind-boggling.

"Incidentally," Tarik informed his fellow passengers, "after tomorrow the planning phase will be over for the two of
you. The implementation process must start forthwith. We
have very little time."

"What do you have in mind?" Ashrawi asked.

"I will have less and less time to spend on the business.
The work advising King Fahd requires more attention."

His focus was changing from the single-minded fixation
on getting rich to a single-minded fixation on solving the
problems of Saudi Arabia.

He continued, "As of September 15, Townsend will take
over as chairman of the Saudi National Bank. Afridi upon his
return will, together with Townsend, share the responsibility
for Pegasus Investments. This may be the time for turning
over a portion of the portfolio, once the equity holdings we
talked about earlier have been liquidated, to outside portfolio
managers. We'll discuss the subject next week."

Then turning to Ashrawi he said, "As for you, my dear
Khalid, You'll be working with me on government matters.
Our oil and defense policy changes are only a beginning. Much
needs to be done in other areas. As an Arab you have the
right credentials."

There was a brief pause. His mind seemed to drift to
something else. Then he suddenly turned to Townsend and
asked.

"Tell me Michael. Is it true that the right wing hard-core
fundamentalists have hijacked the Republican Party?"

"That's certainly the view of a lot of people in America."

"Right," Tarik said with a broad grin on his face, "in Saudi
Arabia the religious zealots have hijacked the country to their

way of thinking. Did you know that the Koran says that there is no compulsion in religion?"

The question was addressed to both of them.

It was Ashrawi who responded. "Does it? I was not aware of it."

"Yes. Verse 256 of the second chapter. It's one of the most important verses of the Koran. Yet here in Saudi Arabia, where we implicitly follow the Koran, the religious police forces people to pray. Religion has become a cover for imposing outdated social policy on the population."

"Give me another example?" Townsend challenged him. It was a test to see if his employer would consider subjects regarded as too sensitive by most Saudis.

Tarik had no such qualms.

"I'll give you two," he said. "Take women. I'm not aware of the Koran forbidding women from driving. They drive in Kuwait, but not in Saudi Arabia. The second item is alcohol. The Koran forbids Muslims from drinking. But it has to be done of your own free will, not by force. None of us are completely pure. Some of us are sinners. We have to face temptation and overcome it. Banning the sale of alcohol won't make us into non-drinkers. It just drives the commerce underground. That's what happened in America during the Prohibition era."

"How do we do it? It's very difficult," Ashrawi said with weary resignation.

"Yes, Khalid. That's the challenge. The country has to be pushed into the twenty-first century. Fahd and the others are too timid to try. And the economic mismanagement has made it difficult to take on the conservative elements. We have to take the carrot and the stick approach. They can be bribed, you know. The whole system is based on it. On bribery I mean."

They nodded their heads. Perhaps it could be done. But by whom? Hadn't he just finished telling them that Fahd

267

couldn't? Nor could the king's half-brother, Crown Prince Abdullah. He was eighty three and like Fahd from another generation. So who would do it?

"You know there is another side to our new oil and defense policy that might prove useful," Tarik went on. "For years the conservatives have been hawkish on oil pricing and they've opposed the influx of the large number of Americans and the non-Muslim foreigners who maintain the military equipment and make the factories function. This will help to diminish their opposition."

"What about taxes?" Michael asked

No citizen in any state on the Arabian Peninsula had ever paid taxes. That was one of the carrots given to the population by rulers who wanted a free hand in government.

"No, that would be political suicide. It's not an option," Tarik replied.

Just then the pilot announced they were flying over Dhahran on the east coast. It was Saudi Arabia's oil center. Tarik flicked a button. The big screen lit up again. This time it showed the terrain over which the plane was flying. Powerful cameras in the underbelly of the aircraft filmed and instantly relayed the pictures to the TV screen. The city of Dhahran lay to the east. Oil rigs dotted the landscape as far as the eye could see. It was an awesome sight. Saudi Arabia's wealth and forty percent of the world's oil reserves lay down there in the barren desert.

Tarik turned toward Townsend, as the plane crossed the Persian Gulf and began its slow descent to Isfahan.

"Do you know the chairmen of Exxon and Texaco?" he asked.

"Yes."

"How well?"

"I'm quite friendly with both. You have something in mind?"

"Yes. I'm going to be in Paris on the twentieth. Perhaps

you can arrange a meeting. I have some ideas that would be of great interest to them."

He winked and smiled. Townsend got the message.

The American grinned, "I'll set it up."

3194-ISLA

CHAPTER 24

The big jet landed at Isfahan at 9.30 A.M. Iranian national time. It taxied toward a structure at the north end of the runway at a considerable distance from the main passenger terminal. This was the building used by the Iranian air force. The airport was one of its principal air bases. A large number of ageing F-4 Phantom jet fighters, F-14 interceptors and more recent Mirage 5 and MIG 25's lining the tarmac, confirmed this connection.

In keeping with the secret nature of the mission there were no ceremonies at the airport. Outside in the bright September sunlight a single Iranian waited to greet the Saudi delegation. It was Reza Khatami, the French-educated younger brother and close confidante of the Iranian President. Khatami solemnly shook hands with the three men and directed them to a black Mercedes 600 SEL parked nearby. They arrived at the hotel, twenty kilometers from the airport, half an hour later.

The Shah Abbas Hotel, in the heart of the city, had been a famed hostelry for decades until the 1979 revolution virtually ended all tourism to the country. Its faded elegance was a reminder of times past when the famous and the wealthy had visited the hotel and lived and dined in the splendor of its ancient rooms.

Isfahan was selected as the site of the meeting at the request of the Saudis. A provincial town, with superb architecture and a pleasant climate, it helped preserve secrecy that was simply not possible in noisy, gossipy Tehran. There was another reason for the choice. Tarik wanted to see the city. As a child he had often visited Isfahan, one of the most beautiful places in the world and one with the largest concentration of Islamic monuments in Iran. After all these years the prince still remembered the great square known as the Meidun-e-Emam. It had been laid out in 1612. At twenty acres in size, it was more than seven times larger than the Piazza San Marco in Venice and on all four sides it was surrounded by architectural masterpieces dating back to the seventeenth century. At the southern end stood the Masjed e Emam–completely covered with pale blue tiles–one of the most stunning buildings on earth. A beautifully proportioned old mosque, without the usual minarets, occupied the east side of the square. The west was taken over by a seven-story palace from where Shah Abbas, one of Persia's greatest kings, had watched polo games in days gone by. On the north was the bazaar lined with hundreds of shops selling local wares.

The Shah Abbas Hotel stood a short distance away.

Inside the hotel, waiting for the Saudis to arrive, were the two Iranian leaders. Both were clerics, only a few years apart in age, but they were a study in contrast in their backgrounds, personalities and beliefs. The sixty-four-year-old Ayatollah Khamenei, stern looking and bespectacled, had once been a disciple of the president's father. This had created a bond between the two men strong enough to survive their opposing viewpoints and beliefs. He succeeded Ayatollah Khomeni, the founder of the Iranian Republic, a modern-day Savonarola and scourge of the West, in 1989 as Iran's supreme spiritual leader. Cultured but rigid in his views, he was both

271

anti-American and a firm supporter of the restrictions imposed upon Iranian society by the Islamic Republic. Khatami, easier going and relaxed, had first won the presidential election by a landslide in September 1997, defeating the candidate of the conservative religious establishment. Unlike the Supreme Leader, his position had been achieved in a way more familiar to the West–through the ballot box. The soft spoken and charming Khatami was attempting to give greater freedom to the people in their daily lives. He also tried to reach out to the United States. Twenty five years had passed since the seizure of the American embassy. It was time for a change. Khatami had been exposed to western ideas first as a philosophy student at the University of Isfahan and subsequently as the head of the Iranian cultural center in Hamburg where he had also gained fluency in the German language.

Ahmad Maleki, an advisor to the Supreme Leader, met the Saudis at the hotel. He escorted them to an ornate reception room furnished in European style. As the men entered the room, President Khatami attired in an elegant gray pin striped robe and matching black cloak and turban, stepped forward. Khamenei in similar but less elegant garb, followed closely behind.

Tarik and the two clerics shook hands. The prince then introduced his two advisors to the Iranian leaders. Neither showed any sign of surprise at the presence of the American Townsend in the Saudi delegation.

Khatami led the group to chairs arranged in a semi circle at one end of the room and indicated that the prince should sit on his right. Ayatollah Khamenei sat on the president's left. Tarik's advisors took the chairs next to him while the two Iranian aides sat on the opposite side.

The fifty-nine-year-old president began the proceedings in English.

"Your Highness, we are pleased to welcome you to the Islamic Republic of Iran." Then in an obvious reference to the prince's mother, he went on, "we are even more delighted to welcome you back to the land of your mother."

"Your excellencies," Tarik replied, "We are most privileged to be received by you. And I am delighted to be back in Iran after so many years."

"Please convey our best wishes," Khatami said, "to His Majesty King Fahd and extend to him our warm invitation to visit Iran."

The conversation continued in this vein with the Saudis extending an invitation to the Iranians to visit Riyadh. Then Tarik smilingly quoted, in perfect Persian, a quatrain from Hafiz, the greatest lyrical poet of Persia:

"Full many a fair and fragrant rose
Within the garden freshly blows,
Yet not a bloom was ever torn
Without the wounding of the thorn."

That broke the ice. The atmosphere in the room was suddenly transformed. The Persians have a fondness for poetry unlike any other people. It was an integral part of their daily lives and verses were readily quoted in their ordinary conversation. A smile lit the stern visage of the Supreme Leader. Though lacking the charm of the Iranian President, he was well versed in literature. He now spoke for the first time, quoting several verses of Rumi and Saadi. Khatami joined in with verses from Omar Khayyam. For a while the conversation switched to Persian as the prince and the clerics delightedly traded verses.

Taking advantage of the more relaxed atmosphere, Tarik got down to the purpose of the meeting. He spoke in Persian since the Spiritual Leader was unfamiliar with any other language.

"In view of the close brotherly ties between our two countries," he said, looking at President Khatami who, under the

3194-ISLA

Iranian constitution, had the principal responsibility for economic and oil policy, "we have come to exchange ideas on the current situation with regard to oil."

"We believe that the price is too low," Khatami went on the offensive immediately.

He continued, "The United States and Europe have enjoyed unprecedented prosperity for years. At our expenses. We have borne the brunt of the burden. Our economic development has come to a standstill. Saudi Arabia's policy has been a major factor in keeping oil prices low. All too often you have bowed to American pressure."

"We tried in 1999. We signed the Riyadh Pact with Mexico and Venezuela and brought in the rest of OPEC. That raised prices to their highest level in seven years," Tarik reminded the Iranian cleric.

"That is true," Khatami conceded. "But that agreement collapsed because Saudi Arabia and its allies buckled under American pressure and agreed to production increases. We were the only ones to refuse to go along. And we all know what has happened since then. So once again the rich nations are benefiting but Iran is facing serious economic difficulties since our revenues have fallen sharply."

Most of Iran's difficulties were self-inflicted. For years it had resorted to the time tested method of printing money to balance the budget. As a result inflation was over fifty percent. Revenues covered only a third of the country's hundred and five billion dollar expenditures. The latest five-year development plan was a total mess with shortfalls of seventy percent or more in practically every sector of the economy. The riyal had fallen from 70 to the dollar at the onset of the revolution twenty five years ago to 9,400 now. Over twenty percent of the workforce was unemployed. That explained Khatami's concern. Overall responsibility for economic matters lay in his hands and matters had only become worse under his watch.

As in the case of the other OPEC nations, oil accounted for most of Iran's export earnings, in this case eighty percent. With a population of sixty five million–the largest among the states bordering the Gulf–Iran needed higher oil prices more than any other OPEC nation. The country was at the breaking point. Unless prices went up soon the days of the Islamic Republic were numbered. Western newspapers had carried several reports in recent days of internal unrest and large-scale demonstrations in Tehran.

"Your excellency," Tarik said in his most diplomatic manner, "we agree with your assessment. Last month we made a careful analysis of the situation with the help of these gentlemen." He nodded toward Ashrawi and Townsend. "My government is strongly of the view that we can no longer afford to have oil prices at this level. We are determined to do something about it. Now."

Surprise kept the Iranians silent. They had never heard such words from a senior Saudi official in a long time. For twenty-five years Saudi Arabia had been the leading dove in OPEC.

Tarik continued, "Saudi Arabia has decided to change its oil policy immediately. We intend to do everything possible to raise oil prices. But this can only be achieved through mutual cooperation. That is why we have come here today to seek your help."

Khatami, wary from past experience, smiled politely before speaking. "What has brought this shift in your policy? We worked together four years ago but Saudi Arabia then once again succumbed to American pressure and changed its policy. How do we know you won't do it again?"

"Your excellency is absolutely correct," Tarik conceded, smiling. "What was done then was ill conceived and Saudi Arabia too has paid a penalty." Then he leaned forward and added, "New members were appointed to our Supreme Council last month. There is now a nationalist majority that firmly believes that Saudi interests do not necessarily coincide with

275

those of America. That is what has brought about the changes in our policy."

There could be no other explanation for this turn around, the two Iranian leaders figured. Judging from his appearance, the man was probably telling the truth.

"What changes do you propose?" a much mollified Khatami asked.

"We have come up with a detailed plan." He signaled Townsend who produced a green folder from his brief case and handed it to Tarik.

"We do not believe," Tarik continued, "that OPEC is capable of handling the problem."

"Yes. That is now clear. Do you have an alternative strategy?"

"We want to put together a new group of eight major oil producers, five of who are from OPEC. Tight control over production will be maintained. A new oil council of six countries will be responsible for oil policy."

"What about cheating in production levels. How can you prevent that?" Khatami wanted to know. In the past Iran had been one of the cheaters but a long period of improper exploitation had severely damaged the oil reservoirs causing production to fall by a quarter. But there was still plenty of room for going around the prescribed quotas.

"By reducing the incentive for it," Tarik replied, smiling.

"How will you do that?"

"Through closer monitoring. But the best way for achieving that is through adjustments in oil quotas. We propose to increase the quotas of Venezuela, Iran and Iraq and reduce those of Saudi Arabia, Kuwait and UAE."

"What new quotas are you proposing for us?"

"An increase of a million barrels from the existing levels. The same for Iraq and six hundred thousand for Venezuela."

"Do you have a price level in mind?" Khatami asked.

"We are thinking on the lines of a $36 to $38 level."

276

"That's more than triple the current prices," Khatami observed. Iran had long pushed for such a price level and he was pleased that Saudi Arabia was now considering a similar number. "What production cuts will be needed to meet this target?"

"In our judgment it will require a ten percent cut in world oil production." Tarik replied.

"What's our share of the cuts?"

"Iran would cut its production by a million barrels." Then to ease the blow he informed them of Saudi Arabia's share of the burden. "I have been asked by King Fahd to advise you of our strong commitment to this plan. We intend to reduce our production by three and a half million barrels. We're prepared to make major sacrifices to make the plan work."

He then went over the main elements of the Saudi plan. The oil credit facility, the members of the new oil council and the future oil quotas. Mexico, Venezuela and Russia were already on board. Even the credit facility was in place. A consortium of German and French banks was providing it.

After this Townsend, at Tarik's request, explained the euro-pricing feature of the plan. He went over the details during the next fifteen minutes. Maleki acted as the interpreter.

Now the Iranians were even more astonished. The switch to the euro would hurt the Americans. First a large oil price rise and then this. It was a one-two knock out punch. And anything that hurt the Americans could only be good for Iran. For twenty-five years 'The Great Satan'–in Ayatollah Khomeni's memorable phrase–had tried to isolate Iran. The icy relationship had thawed recently from polar frigidity to a shade above freezing point. Still this opportunity to repay the Americans could not be missed. But why would the Saudis want to do this, the Iranians wondered? The United States was their patron. They were almost a client state.

Sensing the Iranian's thoughts, Tarik spoke up. "The

3194-ISLA

change in our oil policy does not change our old-standing friendship with the United States. As I mentioned earlier we have concluded that in the oil arena our interests do not coincide. I would also like to remind your Excellency that it was King Feisal who imposed oil sanctions against the Americans in 1973 and it was Feisal who nationalized ARAMCO. The change to euro pricing is necessitated by the need for the oil credit facility."

That satisfied the Iranians. The two sides reviewed the plan at length. For the first time, Ashrawi and the two Iranian aides joined the discussion. The Iranians were pleased and were all for it. Not that they needed much convincing. After all, they had been clamoring for a price increase. So they were hardly in a position to oppose the Saudi move. Khatami closed the session with a ringing declaration of support. "We welcome your proposals whole heartedly and will support the plan at the meeting in Kuwait."

Ayatollah Khamenei vigorously nodded his head in agreement.

The meeting then broke up for the obligatory afternoon prayers, which were held in an adjoining room. This was followed by a simple lunch consisting of mast va khiar (yogurt with cucumbers) and chelo kebab (rice with broiled lamb) washed down with several glasses of lemon tea. As he sat there eating the plain fare, Tarik wondered how different the conditions were compared to the ostentation and mindless pomposity that had once prevailed under the former Pahlavi dynasty. He agreed with many of the critics of the Iranian clerical leadership. They were often cruel, harsh and vindictive in dealing with their opponents, too intolerant of dissent. But their personal life was simple compared to the opulence of the Shah, or for that matter with the extravagance of the Arab rulers of the Gulf states including Saudi Arabia. And they were moving towards a more democratic system as the parliamentary elections held earlier in the year clearly demonstrated. He made a mental note to have Ashrawi take a good hard look at these developments. Perhaps they could learn something from the Iranian experience.

Defense and military spending was the topic after lunch.

Once again Tarik began the discussion, but this time he addressed Iran's Supreme Leader who, under the constitution, held responsibility for all security-related matters.

Tarik summarized the situation. For the past quarter century the two countries had spent vast amounts of money on armament. It was time to reverse the trend.

"His Majesty King Fahd has authorized me to inform you," Tarik said, "that Saudi Arabia has decided to unilaterally reduce its defense expenditures by fifty percent. We plan to cancel all our existing equipment purchase contracts."

"Iran welcome's Saudi Arabia's initiative. We wish to co-operate with you fully to reduce tensions in the region," Khamenei responded warmly.

For years Iran's attempts to export its militant Islamic revolution to its neighbors had terrified Saudi Arabia and the tiny Gulf states. The existence of a large number of Shia Muslims–the principal sect in Iran–in these countries had further heightened their fears. But nothing had come of it in the end. As happens in all revolutions, time had taken its toll. The Islamic Republic, having lost much of its revolutionary ardor, had been courting the neighboring Arabs for the past few years. Crown Prince Abdullah had visited the country on two occasions and as a result relations between the two states had warmed considerably to the great chagrin of the Americans.

"My government wishes to propose the creation of a Gulf Treaty Organization that would include all the states in the region," Tarik said, addressing his remarks to Ayatollah Khamenei.

Once again the Iranians were taken by surprise. What was the Saudi calculation behind this move? For that, one

3194-ISLA

had to go back thirteen years to the Gulf War. Tarik and his advisers learnt two things from that experience: first, the Americans assigned incalculable importance to the region and were unlikely to abandon Saudi Arabia to the wolves. Second, Saudi Arabia could never defend itself in any war. For the past decade neither Iran nor Iraq had posed any threat to the region. So the Saudis, recognizing the changes that had taken place in Iranian policy, were anxious to make them permanent. Hence the alliance proposal. The calculation behind the maneuver was simple. It would keep both Iran and Iraq in check. And the Saudis reasoned that this would be a lot easier within the confines of an alliance than outside it.

"What precisely does Saudi Arabia have in mind?" the Spiritual Leader asked.

Tarik smiled deferentially at the cleric. "We would like to create an alliance on the model of NATO."

"Have you discussed this with the other Gulf states?"

"Not as yet, Your Excellency. But as you know we already have a Gulf Cooperation Council. This represents an extension of that concept. His Majesty King Fahd wishes to approach Iran first. We sincerely hope that your great nation will join Saudi Arabia as a founder member of the new organization."

"We are honored by King Fahd's proposal and will give it serious consideration," Khamenei replied.

Details of the Saudi proposal were discussed for the next two hours. The alliance idea suited the Iranians. They were anxious to reduce the American presence in the region as much as possible and they wanted to be the principal regional power. The proposed pact promoted both of these objectives. Besides there was, the Iranians reasoned, one other advantage. Ever since the overthrow of the Shah, the Yankees had imposed economic sanctions on the country and while lately these had become increasingly irrelevant, the alliance would put the final nail in that particular coffin. So in the end Khamenei signaled his approval of the proposal in principal. Ashrawi and Maleki were charged with the responsibility for finalizing the agreement prior to the meeting in Kuwait. The Saudis undertook to obtain the endorsement of the other states.

Immediately following the meeting, Tarik drove around the Meidun-e-Emam. It brought back memories of those youthful days when he often visited the city with his parents.

At five that evening the Saudi delegation arrived back at the airport for the return flight to Riyadh.

3194-ISLA

CHAPTER 25

Alexandra caught the seven o'clock Delta flight 545 to Atlanta on the same Monday out of La Guardia. Twenty minutes into the flight, as she was reading an article on mutual funds in the Wall Street Journal, she heard a voice.

"That's a very beautiful ring."

She turned and saw the friendly looking man sitting next to her in the aisle seat.

"Thank you," she smiled. "It's a fifteenth wedding anniversary gift."

"May I see it?"

She moved her arm towards him and he held her hand lightly as he examined the ring. His touch sent a delicious sensation rippling through her body.

"Very pretty." He noticed the well-manicured long thin fingers and the red colored nails.

"By the way my name is Jack Carver."

"I'm Alexandra Middleton."

"So tell me Alexandra, do you have any children?"

"I have four, two girls and two boys."

"What a strange coincidence," he smiled. "I too have four children, but mine are all girls."

For the next several minutes the conversation turned to the children. His children were fairly similar in age to hers, a year more in two instances, two years less in the case of the younger ones. He had recently separated from his wife after a twenty-one-year marriage. She noticed his engaging sense of humor, the ready flow of complements and the friendly demeanor that made conversation so easy. He appeared to be in his mid-fifties, slightly shorter than her, with thinning silver-colored hair. He wore glasses and while he was not good looking, he certainly had a pleasant personality and she found him curiously attractive.

"You're originally from England?"

"Can you still tell?" she laughed.

"Yes. There's the slightest hint of an accent. So did you go to college here in the States?"

"No. Actually I was up at Cambridge," she replied.

"What another coincidence. I too was at Cambridge, on a Fulbright scholarship, at Sidney Sussex College."

During the ensuing conversation she discovered that he grew up in Iowa and had studied law at Yale prior to the two years at Cambridge. Their paths had not crossed simply because he was at the University five years prior to her time there.

"And what takes you to Atlanta? He asked.

"I'm in the money management business and I'm meeting some customers."

"You're the most beautiful money manager I've seen." He grinned sheepishly.

She smiled at the complement, "Thank you. And what about you?"

"I'm a lawyer at Sherman and Sterling and I'm heading to a meeting with the Chairman of Coca-Cola." He bent down to pick the pen that had slipped from his hand and found himself staring at her shapely long legs.

They talked during the rest of the flight. He had noticed

her the moment she came into the crowded passenger lounge in the stylish red suit. Now sitting next to her he observed the lovely creamy smooth complexion of her skin and the beautiful gold bracelet with the small gold encased ivory pendants of miniature Persian paintings on her left wrist. He was charmed by her sparkle. She was a very classy woman he thought. But something was bothering him and when he turned his head and glanced at her again he suddenly realized what it was. She looked familiar and he now remembered seeing her photographs in recent issues of W and Town and Country magazines.

Just before the plane landed in Atlanta they exchanged cards.

"Have a good day," he said warmly as they exited the plane. "Perhaps we'll meet again in New York."

"We've had great reports on you," Mark Raynor said to Alexandra when they met at his office at 1360 Peachtree Street in the Atlanta business district. He was the president of INVESCO Capital Management.

Alexandra smiled politely as he continued, "The people at Callan and Oxbridge think very highly of you."

"Thank you. That's very kind of them."

"Archie Williams gave me your name and suggested that I meet you. He gave me the bare details so I'd like you to tell me more about yourself and your business at B&P."

In the next forty five minutes Alexandra went over her career in considerable depth. She had started the fixed income business at B&P eighteen years ago. Did they have this business before? No, they were only in equities. In the succeeding years the assets grew rapidly and now totaled twenty five billion dollars. There were three hundred institutional customers and another 10,000 in the WRAP program that she had also managed. Last year they won a billion dollars in new assets and this year was shaping out just as well. She spent twenty minutes describing her portfolio management style and talked at some length of specific aspects of the process using charts and graphs that her group had put together.

"Why did you leave B&P so suddenly?" Raynor asked.

"My views increasingly diverged from those of Sidney Rosenberg to whom I reported."

"Is he the CEO?"

"No he's the president and the institutional business reported to him. He's the one who originally hired me?" Alexandra replied.

"So what happened?"

"I just got tired of the constant battling and decided it was time to move on. They're just a bunch of tired old men who won't let go."

After this Raynor spent twenty minutes telling her about his firm. They managed 48 billion dollars but practically all the money was in mutual funds. Of this amount only 8 billion was in bonds and short-term money market assets. They had experienced tremendous growth in their mutual fund business and the firm was well positioned to take advantage of this. So they were looking for someone to head the fixed income group and build the institutional side of that business.

"You certainly fit the bill." Raynor sounded enthusiastic. "And your experience, background and track record is absolutely spectacular. Just as Williams indicated. I have one other meeting scheduled for this week and then we'll make our decision. We might want you to come back for a second visit."

"Certainly. I don't see a problem with that." She smiled. Then glancing at her watch she added, "I'm afraid I have to leave for the airport or I'll miss my plane."

"Are you heading back to New York?" He asked as he escorted her out.

"No. I'm meeting some people in San Francisco." She volunteered the information to let him know that she was

3194-ISLA

having other interviews as well, hoping that this might put pressure on him to reach a decision quickly.

They shook hands and he said, "I'll be in touch later in the week."

The meeting in San Francisco did not go well. Pegasus Capital Management had about twenty five billion in equity funds but only five billion in bonds. They were losing customers because of their mediocre performance in the past two years. She met the acting head of the group and three other portfolio managers and quickly sensed the tension in a number of the men at the meeting. They were worried about their jobs and felt threatened by a new team coming in. She also got the impression that they preferred to operate without a formal group head as that allowed them total independence without any control over their investment performance.

It looked a lot like the independent chieftains she had spent eighteen years with at B&P. The experience had not been a pleasant one and she wasn't too anxious to repeat it.

On her return to New York on Wednesday, Alexandra found that the situation had gotten progressively worse. First there was a message from her lawyer. He had met several times with his counterparts at B&P and their external counsel.

"The partnership agreement," he explained, "gave the Management Committee the right to fire any partner without cause. And they do not have to give any explanation for their action."

"I understand Steve," Alexandra responded, controlling her anger with difficulty. "But it was never contemplated that this power would ever be used."

"That may be what they told you but it won't stand up in a court of law, unfortunately."

"Besides from a practical viewpoint there was no way any of us could refuse to sign the agreement at the time we became partners."

"I understand your frustration but . . ."

"So what are they proposing as a settlement?" she asked interrupting him.

"They initially mentioned a million dollars, but after my insistence that it was an absurd number they have come back with a counter offer of 2 ½ million dollars. They refuse to budge any further."

"Steve, they're stealing my business," she said bitterly. "My share is worth a hundred million if the firm sells at the existing multiples. Isn't there anything else we can do?"

"Not legally. We can threaten to go to the newspapers with the story. It's possible that reports of a highly successful woman being driven out from a partnership the way you were might infuriate a lot of customers and others out there. The resulting bad publicity might make them more conciliatory."

Phillip who was standing next to her shook his head. They had discussed this option last week and had agreed not to go in that direction. Both of them shrank from the publicity that she would receive. It could also hurt her future chances of landing a good job. She recalled how the bad publicity surrounding John Geutfreund's legal action after his dismissal by Salomon Brothers had ended up haunting him.

"I guess we'll have to accept the offer and I can then get on with my life," she told the lawyer in a dispirited voice filled with resignation.

Almost immediately the telephone rang again.

It was Michael Quinn from Merrill Lynch. Phillip saw her facial expression change as she talked. She looked deathly pale and tears welled up in the lovely large green eyes.

She put the phone down, turned and came into his outstretched arms.

"That was Merrill Lynch. They've decided not to pursue the matter further."

She was crying. "I'm no good. No one wants me."

3194-ISLA

He hugged her tightly. "Don't say that. I want you and love you. You know that. I'll always be there for you."

She continued to cry. "I'm well-known in the industry. The word's out on the street but there've been hardly any calls from the headhunters. There are hundreds of firms. No one wants me."

"That's just not true. Be patient." He kissed her on the head. "It'll work out. I know it will. You're the best in the business. Always, always remember that."

"Are you sure?" she asked plaintively.

"I'm certain darling. You must be confident. You've got to have the attitude of a winner. You've had it all your life. Don't lose it now," Phillip said, trying to comfort her.

After composing herself, Alexandra went downstairs to the library where Anne Nicholson, Charles Bradley and Brian Watson were busy working. Alexandra and Bradley spent the rest of the week and the following three business days making innumerable telephone calls to customers and consultants. They even visited a couple of the consultants in Connecticut and New Jersey. The results were not encouraging. The clients hedged their bets when they heard of a new start-up company.

Almost invariably it was the same response. "Alexandra, we admire you. We know your record. But our board is very concerned. There have been several unfortunate incidents recently with a number of small investment management firms. Now if you were at a large company the situation would be very different."

The unfortunate incident was a reference to the Common Fund, which lost two hundred million dollars of its funds because of fraudulent dealings by a small equity management shop that had falsified its accounting and investment records over a two-year period. It had made pension funds and endowments more cautious in their dealings with money managers.

It was the same story with the consultants. They were

full of advice. Start with smaller institutional pension funds. Build up your reputation. You know the way the SEC system works. Yes we understand it was your investment record but it belongs to B&P. This was the case a few years back, if you remember, when you were at the firm and some of your portfolio managers left. We'll do our best to help but you know we have a duty to our clients. We have to observe the due diligence rules. A lot of talk, a lot of advice, but nothing particularly helpful or useful as far as Alexandra or Charles Bradley were concerned.

At the usual Thursday meeting of the B&P Management Committee, Sidney Rosenberg apprised the members of the latest developments in the Middleton saga.

"We have reached agreement on the amount to be paid to our recently departed partner," he said trying to be amusing.

"So how much is it?" several of the committee members asked at the same time.

"The grand sum of two and a half million dollars," he said with a flourish.

"That's wonderful," Kramer cried. He had been the most worried of the members. "I thought we'd have to pay fifteen million at the very minimum."

"I must say Sidney, you've really done a splendid job," Joseph Wechsler, for once, sounded genuinely pleased.

"How many accounts have we lost?" Franklin Gross, the Wooster College star, asked.

Rosenberg replied nonchalantly, "I believe we have lost about a dozen accounts totaling two hundred and fifty million dollars. It doesn't amount to a hill of beans."

"Yes, so far so good. But for how long? It could become much worse if she ends up at one of those large, high-profile firms," Kramer said, turning towards Rosenberg.

"I've taken care of that also. At least with the ones she interviewed with," Rosenberg informed the group.

"How did you do that?" Kramer wanted to know.

"It only takes one phone call," Rosenberg smiled. "Off the record of course and suddenly you find you're no longer under consideration."

Matters had reached a low point by the morning of Monday, September 13. The head of Pegasus telephoned to tell Alexandra of their decision to continue with their present set up.

There was still no response from the INVESCO people in Atlanta.

"I have a meeting with my friend Victoria Spencer tomorrow. What do any of you know about Am Bank?" a subdued Alexandra asked her group as they all sat in the library of her New York townhouse.

"Someone told me once that they have a pretty big private banking business," Anne Nicholson said looking up from her laptop on which she was calculating different income expense scenarios with Brian.

"Most private banks use outside money managers. Maybe you can ask for some funds to manage," Brian wondered aloud.

"That's a good idea. What amount would you propose?"

"Fifty million," Anne suggested.

"I'd ask for a hundred," Brian interjected.

"They have an investment management group, but I've never run into them at any of the competitive presentations we were in," Charles Bradley observed. "Could it be that they're looking for a change of management?"

"I doubt it," Alexandra said. "Banks usually don't pay well. Instead they give large offices, the latest fancy gadgets, important sounding titles and similar perks. The problem is that you can't spend this. It's just an ego trip."

They all laughed.

That afternoon Alexandra felt utterly defeated and depressed. She sat in the living room of the master bedroom suite re-examining her life. It was falling apart both at the professional and personal level. Yes, this had been a terrible experience. At fifty, she was being forced to start all over again. And the recent events had further punctured her ego. For the past ten years she'd been the principal earner. Phillip's contribution was minimal. That thought filled her with resentment against her husband. He was a nice and decent man whom she had loved and until recently they'd had a great time together. But now, ever since her dismissal from B&P, she was beginning to see things in a new light. Phillip, having retired at her suggestion, was no longer in a position to contribute monetarily. But that was only part of the picture. Their financial situation also bothered her greatly. Money had once seemed to be in inexhaustible supply but between taxes, the New York house, the amounts spent redoing the Westchester estate, the private schools and their expensive lifestyle they had managed to spend most of it. Her insatiable mania for clothes and collecting household items like silk blankets, cushions, china, bed linen, antiques, and silver had further contributed to the excessive outflow of funds. And then there was the other problem that bothered her. Because of her dislike of her former partners she had avoided investing at all in stocks. The asset allocation of their savings had been terrible. Poor Phillip had tried to coax her into equities but she had resisted and in the end he had deferred to her judgment in the matter.

She was a woman devoid of faith and so faith could not sustain her. She could find no solace in anything spiritual since God did not exist in her vocabulary. Having once been poor she had sworn never to be in that position again. Mammon had been her guiding light. Money defined success. It defined a person's worth. She was under great stress, which was made worse by the menopause cycle from which there was no escape for women in her age group. That afternoon she decided to change her life. From her wallet she pulled out the card that Jack Carver had given her. She walked over to the telephone and dialed a number. They agreed to meet for lunch at the Four Seasons on Wednesday.

Earlier that morning Alexandra had checked him out. He was a senior partner and one of the highest paid lawyers at Sherman and Sterling. Her informant figured he was making around two million dollars.

And that had finally decided the issue as far as her future life was concerned.

CHAPTER 26

History records that the final arrangements that brought the greatest financial disaster to Wall Street were agreed upon at a secret meeting on the island state of Kuwait on Tuesday, September 14 at nine thirty in the morning. Two time zones away, most people in Western Europe were waking up with hangovers and at the same point large numbers of people in the United States, a further six time zones away, were engaged in acts that would undoubtedly ensure a hangover on the following morning.

There was no special reason for the selection of Kuwait as a venue for the meeting. It simply happened to be close by and convenient for all the participants. Adding to its attraction was the complete absence of journalists since none were stationed in Kuwait. None were expected as neither wars nor other grisly acts of violence that so fascinate American TV audiences were currently taking place in the region. At this moment the world simply had no idea what was afoot. The participants wanted to keep it that way. With the Middle East relatively calm, no alarm bells were set off in the United States, or for that matter anywhere else.

The representatives of the five oil-producing nations met

293

at the Seif Palace, the official residence of the Emir, over-looking the blue waters of the Persian Gulf. Seated around the circular table were the Emir of Kuwait, Sheikh Al Jabber and his cousin, Sheikh Saad al Sabah. President Khatami of Iran was at al Sabah's right and next to him sat the 87-year-old Sheikh Zayed of Abu Dhabi representing the United Arab Emirates. Iraq was represented by its new strong man, General Abdul Rashid. The Saudi delegation was headed jointly by Prince Tarik and Crown Prince Abdullah. Together these men were the most powerful group of individuals in the Middle East.

Much later it was argued that these nations had hatched a major conspiracy against the United States. Kuwait and Saudi Arabia were particularly reviled for joining the group. Hadn't the United States rescued these nations from the Iraqi on-slaught only a decade ago? Such was the logic of the losers. But not a shred of credible evidence was produced to sup-port the plot theory. The conspiracy buffs merely pointed a finger at the secret nature of the meeting as the basis for their conjecture.

True but so what?

Secret meetings were held all the time in Washington D.C., in New York and London and Paris and Tokyo. Both governments and corporations held such meetings. There was nothing special about such gatherings. How else could im-portant decisions be made? Just because a meeting was se-cret didn't mean that a conspiracy was being hatched. The theory wasn't worth a damn. At the Kuwait meeting there was no talk of assassinations or coups. No acts of violence or terrorism were contemplated or discussed.

The subject under discussion was mundane. Quite routine. What could these states do to raise the price of crude oil? Discussions with regard to this topic had been held thousands of times in the past quarter century. There was nothing new or conspiratorial about it. Except this time the Western media or the public had no inkling of this secret conclave.

Raising the price of oil was in fact no longer even considered a threat to Western economies. Hadn't the price gone up to the mid twenties dollar level and higher several times in the nineties? It had even touched the $37 number for a few days in 2000. And Western economies had continued to grow and prosper. So had those of Asia and Latin America. Even the stock markets had shrugged off the higher oil prices as the Dow, the S&P 500 and the Nasdaq indices moved relentlessly upward.

The only complaints had come from the spoilt motorists of the United States who were suddenly obliged to pay $1.60 per gallon of gas instead of $1.30. And this when car drivers all over Europe were paying three times that amount. So the Americans had put pressure on the Mexicans and the Saudis. They had forced an increase in oil production and within a few months the old established OPEC habits of what was politely known as non-compliance were back in fashion and oil prices were down once again in the low teens.

In late 2004 many responsible people, particularly the European and American Central Bankers and the IMF, were increasingly worried about low commodity prices, especially that of oil.

Why?

Because disinflation was raising its ugly head. Practically all raw material prices had fallen sharply over the past three years. The stock markets had as yet not sensed the seriousness of this situation because of the euphoric mood of the investors. Lower commodity prices were seen as antidotes for the inevitable inflationary pressures that build up in a full employment economy. But there was another side to the coin. Commodity producers were getting less and less for their exports. So to maintain their revenues they produced and sold more and more of their raw materials, which, in turn, further forced down prices. By late summer it had become a vicious circle. As a result the economies of a large number of emerging market nations were bearing an unbearable burden. Their people were sliding back into ever-deeper poverty.

Disinflation was worse than inflation. In inflation only the lenders and those with fixed incomes suffered. Disinflation affected every one. It had to be avoided at all costs. The world had not seen a serious disinflation since the 1930's. So it was hoped that oil the most used of all commodities would lead the way. It was argued that a price increase in oil would filter down to other areas of the economy and lead to eventual increases in the price of all commodities.

The problem was that no one had been able to successfully raise and maintain the price of oil for any appreciable period of time in the past quarter century. OPEC had tried repeatedly but had failed. In the late 1990's another approach had been used by Saudi Arabia, Mexico and Venezuela. For a while it worked but then it too had collapsed. And for a good reason. There was simply too much excess oil. Because the oil-producing nations didn't trust each other, they cheated. Massively. So they over produced. They could never agree on anything. And even when they did, the agreements lasted for a few months at best. All plans foundered on their rivalries. The big producers wanted to increase, or at the very minimum, maintain their market share.

So something completely new was needed. A different approach.

This is where the Saudis came in. For twenty five long years Saudi Arabia with its huge oil resources had been a force for price moderation. No longer. This complete switch in policy in less than a month was due to the exertions and views of one man. His name: Tarik bin Talal al Saud, a prince from the ruling family of Saudi Arabia. A man as yet unknown in the corridors of power. A man who would soon leave his mark on nations big and small all over the globe.

Two things distinguished the new approach from previous efforts to raise oil prices: timing and policy.

A series of events had occurred, many unrecognized at the time, during the past several years. The combination of these changes greatly facilitated the new approach and helped to make it a success.

Immediately following his meeting with the French and German leaders, Tarik met Colin Campbell in Paris. Campbell, who worked at the International Energy Agency of the United Nations, was considered a world authority on oil-related issues. He briefed the prince on his seminal work on the oil supply situation. It had been an instructive meeting for Tarik.

"The oil surplus is crumbling away even while the current market continues to show an excess of supply over demand." Campbell said.

"I don't understand how that's possible?" Tarik asked.

"Because new global discoveries of oil have already contracted sharply. A number of expert geologists have concluded that ninety percent of the world's oil fields have already been accessed and many are already depleted."

"And what are the estimates for the world's proven oil reserves?" Tarik enquired.

"Most experts have estimated these at a thousand billion barrels. Now at the present annual production rate of twenty four billion barrels the supplies would last another forty one years provided there was no growth in demand.

"I understand," Tarik said, "that you do not agree with these figures."

There were several question marks regarding the size of the current oil reserves. A number of OPEC countries including Venezuela, Algeria, Indonesia, Iran and Nigeria had vastly inflated their proven oil reserves.

"That is correct. My colleague Jean Laherrere and I have researched and analyzed this whole issue very carefully. We

3194-ISLA

have concluded that the actual proven oil reserves total only 850 billion barrels."

"So you believe that we will have a crisis much sooner?" Tarik asked.

"Yes. Our model indicates that a severe oil crisis is in the cards between 2010 and 2020."

More and more experts were veering to the Campbell-Laherrere view. For thirty years the IEA had said that oil discoveries were a function of price. In other words more oil would be discovered as the price moved higher. As a result of the research done by Campbell and Laherrere that agency now believed that this view was no longer valid.

This was where the difficulties came up. Oil was the economic lifeblood of the modern world accounting for forty percent of all energy used. The alternative energy sources that were frequently touted just didn't fit the bill. They required more energy to produce than they actually generated. Thus, for example, a gallon of ethanol required seventy percent more energy to produce than a gallon of the stuff actually generated. A barrel of oil, on the other hand, generated ten times more power than it took to pump it out of the ground.

Then there was the whole issue of oil demand, which could only continue to grow. Occasional economic downturns slowed this down a bit but could not depress it permanently. Since 1990 oil consumption had increased by fifty percent in Asia and by a third in Latin America. As more cars and other Western gadgets found there way into these countries demand could only go up.

The pumping of oil from mature oil fields presented another serious problem. Despite technological advances it was very difficult and costly to extract the remaining oil from mature oil fields such as Alaska and the North Sea. And in fact both British and Norwegian oil production had begun to decline in the previous six months.

A related event that further tilted the balance in favor of

the Arab oil producers were the dramatic changes occurring in the oil business, driven by rising costs and low prices. Several large mergers had created monolithic corporations that were bigger than many OPEC oil producers. AMOCO and BP had merged in 1998. In the following year Exxon and Mobil combined to create the world's largest corporation. They had quickly cancelled their costly exploration contracts in the Caspian Sea area and elsewhere. After all it cost around twelve dollars to produce and transport oil from these regions compared with the two dollar cost in the Persian Gulf region. The big companies were prepared to exert their power and work with the Gulf producers. Most had been friends and allies of the Saudis for half a century.

The arrival of Commandant Chavez in Venezuela and the new Mexican and Russian leaders also helped. Left leaning and populist they may have been in their economic ideas but they were more realistic when it came to oil. Unlike the corrupt politicians whom they replaced they understood the need to cut oil production. Chavez had only recently succeeded in gaining total control of Petroleos de Venezuela. The Mexican President had managed to stamp himself over the state oil monopoly immediately following his election in June of 2000. In Russia, Putin was finally beginning to make inroads in curbing the robber barons and the poorly performing state entities.

And the times had found their man. Tarik, recognizing this confluence of events, quickly seized the chance at hand. It was a propitious moment for concerted joint action.

All the countries represented at the Kuwait meeting were facing extreme economic hardship and they were dependent on oil for much of their revenues. Mexico, Venezuela and Russia faced a similar predicament. So they all had one common objective: an increase of their revenues. And from there the next step led to the logical question: What must be done to raise the price of oil?

299

Now when it came to oil the economic picture was clear. There were oil producers and oil consumers. When oil prices went down the oil consuming countries won and the producers lost. When oil prices went up the positions were reversed. It was like a seesaw. Sometimes one group gained. Sometimes the other. There was simply no way out of this cycle. Unfortunately the oil producers had been on the losing end of the wicket for far too long. So it was now their turn to be on the winning side. After all there had to be some measure of fairness. Tough luck if some countries like the United States lost for a while. That's the way the system worked. It wasn't the fault of the participants at the Kuwait meeting.

There was another more important reason for the urgency. Years of low prices had brought the Kuwait five and their three allies to their knees. Economically speaking that is. Even the Saudis had been compelled to borrow. Political stability in many of these countries was being rocked by shrinking budgets and massive unemployment. Unrest and rioting had occurred in Kuwait, Iran and Iraq. Violence was on the rise in Venezuela. In Mexico they had elected a populist as president. These countries could no longer afford to drift. Their rulers had finally been forced to come to terms with socio economic reality.

More than anything else the timing was driven by the Saudis. Or rather by events in Saudi Arabia. The massive riots in Jeddah, Riyadh, Dhahran and even in the holy city of Mecca, sparked by wide spread anger at the corruption and mismanagement of the kingdom's oil resources had done the trick. The Saudi royal family, finally grasping the nature of the internal opposition, took the steps necessary for its survival. It would be Tarik's job to institute economic and political reforms. The prince, not given to inaction, moved immediately to reverse the country's oil and defense policies. He wanted the changes to be the first act of the new administration. Old King Fahd had given him barely three weeks to draw the plans. The approach had been methodical, efficient and precise.

But why this need for joint action? Why the collaboration? The answer to that question was straightforward. Any of these countries acting independently or in concert with another could bring about a reduction in oil prices. Even a precipitous one in the case of Saudi Arabia. How? By simply revving up oil production. But not one of them, not even Saudi Arabia could raise oil prices single handedly. They needed each other like the tight embrace of long lost lovers. They had to act collectively or not at all. There was no other choice.

These were the circumstances that brought the five countries to Kuwait on that fateful September day. The conference had only two items on its agenda: oil and defense. After a short welcoming speech the host, Sheikh Jabber, turned the meeting over to the Saudis. Crown Prince Abdullah asked Tarik to take charge.

"For far too long," Tarik began, "we have mistrusted each other. For far too long we have paid the price for this. Our countries are making less from the sale of oil than they did ten years ago. We must make a new beginning. The time for action has come. We must seize this chance or future generations of our people will curse us."

"We agree," President Khatami of Iran spoke up in support.

The other five heads nodded in agreement.

"The times call for bold solutions. We have come here today," Tarik continued, "with a set of proposals. It represents a radical departure from the past."

"In which way?" the Kuwaitis wanted to know.

For almost a quarter century the Kuwaitis had been the leading doves, along with Saudi Arabia, in OPEC. They had also been one of the major over producers–the habitual cheats. In fact it was this stance that had infuriated Saddam Hussein

3194-ISLA

and had led to his subsequent decision to invade Kuwait. Both Kuwait and Saudi Arabia had cradle to grave social welfare systems that not even Sweden or Norway could match. Their citizens got the best deal in the world. Not only did they pay no taxes, but they also got free education and free health services. There was also free electricity, not to mention free telephone service and of course cushy, sinecure jobs. But the past few years had exacted a heavy toll on the finances of the two countries. Plummeting oil revenues and the growing welfare bill resulted in a radical shake up in Kuwaiti thinking. Growing deficits and shrinking assets had left the Sheikh no options. Since 2000, Kuwait had replaced Iran and Iraq as the leading hawk within OPEC. The Saudis had continued to muddle on. With that question the Kuwaitis were signaling the Saudis that only a radical plan would get their support.

"In several ways," the Saudi responded. "We are asking for big sacrifices now for future gain. We are proposing fundamental changes in the quota system and in the pricing methodology and in the policing of the quotas. I will give you details of all of these…"

"We would like to see a quota system that is more need-oriented," General Rashid interrupted. "It should take into account the size of a country's population. The present system is based largely on proven oil reserves and history."

"Iran also favors such an approach," Khatami joined in.

"That is indeed what we are proposing," Tarik replied. "Under our plan, Saudi Arabia, Kuwait and the United Arab Emirates will have reduced quotas while Venezuela, Iran and Iraq will have increases."

He then went over some of the details. No one objected. Not even the men from the UAE. After all the Saudis were saying that some of these changes would be put into effect gradually two years from now. Much could happen in that time frame. No point wasting time debating it now.

"We believe very strongly that our objective should be a

tripling of oil prices from its current level of $10 a barrel," Tarik informed the group.

The Kuwaitis wanted to shoot for a higher figure. They mentioned $40 as a more appropriate number. The Iranians pitched in with their support, but in the end all the leaders accepted the Saudi recommendation.

"This price level," Tarik went on, "will require fairly substantial production cuts from all our countries."

"What quantities?" the pragmatic ruler of the United Arab Emirates asked.

"Our experts estimate that world oil production will have to be reduced by about ten percent. That of course means more substantial cuts on our part."

No one disagreed. They were, of course, aware that sacrifices would have to made. It would be painful but the alternatives were even worse. Much worse.

Tarik continued. "In the past we have relied on all OPEC countries to cut production. That is too cumbersome. It has not worked. This time we will focus just on our five countries plus Venezuela, Mexico and Russia and we will have a mechanism to enforce the quotas."

He then went over the production reductions. "Iran has to reduce its production by 1,000,000 barrels, Kuwait by 550,000, UAE by 650,000 and Iraq by 450,000. The Venezuelans and the Mexicans have agreed to reduce their production by eight hundred and fifty thousand barrels each and the Russians by five hundred thousand."

His next words left them with no doubt that Saudi Arabia was deadly serious about the plan. They were prepared to use all their clout. To achieve their goal the Saudis were for the first time, abandoning all efforts to maintain market share and were even giving up on proportionality that had been the cornerstone of their policy for over twenty years.

"My country will reduce its production by three and a half million barrels."

3194-ISLA

"We are prepared to have our numbers increased to match those of our brothers from the UAE," Sheikh Sabah of Kuwait volunteered.

The Iranians made a half-hearted attempt to impose larger cuts on Iraq. The Saudis gave their rational for the lower number. "Under normal circumstances we would have agreed with you. But as you know, Iraq under the United Nations embargo has for many years produced oil well below its previous quota levels. Our numbers take this into account."

Support by the others of the Saudi position finally convinced the Iranians. They quickly acquiesced.

"We recognize that prices may not immediately rise to the levels that we want. To prevent severe dislocations in the initial phase when our production levels and our revenues go down, we have put into place a credit drawdown facility with a consortium of French and German banks," Tarik informed the gathering. Further details were provided. Then looking directly at General Rashid he added, "This facility will be particularly useful for Iraq."

Now all these countries stood to gain from an oil price increase, but Iraq due to its peculiar circumstances stood to gain the most. Not in absolute terms but relatively speaking. For over a decade it was viewed as the world's number one villain and the American-backed sanctions imposed by the United Nations had shoved its economy toward the dark ages. The country had been repeatedly bombed, almost on a daily basis, and yet no solution seemed to be in sight. The Americans, supported by their British lackeys, were determined to keep the sanctions in place.

All this had suddenly changed, eight months earlier, with the appearance of the dapper General Rashid. His accession to the leadership in Baghdad was one of those accidents that change the course of history. The Medina Division of the Republican Guards was responsible for the protection of the capital. When Saddam unexpectedly died–

Western intelligence sources claimed that he was poisoned–
Rashid who commanded the Medina Division quickly seized
power. The opposition, chiefly from Saddam's Takriti tribe,
rapidly evaporated as the rest of the army fell behind the
new leader. Like so many other Iraqis, Rashid was understandably anti-American; but he was also a pragmatist. Recognizing the inevitable, he immediately re-invited the United
Nations arms inspectors and gave them free access to all Iraqi
installations. At the same time he normalized relations with
Kuwait and Iran and negotiated an autonomy settlement with
the Kurds.

Iraq, like most oil producers, was a one product economy.
That product was oil. What happened to oil or more precisely
to the price of oil was of supreme importance to the country.
In the early eighties its oil revenue exceeded twenty six billion dollars. Now it was less than five billion. The oil fields
had been neglected for ages. Very large capital investments
were needed to bring these facilities to full production capacity. So Iraq had only one option. It desperately needed a
rise in oil prices.

The General smiled in agreement. "Yes. It would be most
helpful for us."

The Saudis then explained the critical element of the
plan relating to the euro. The sophisticated Kuwaitis and the
UAE ruler grasped its significance instantly. It would put
pressure on the dollar. There was money to be made.

Economics was not one of General Rashid's strong points.
"Please explain the importance of the euro pricing," he asked
the Saudis.

"The move will boost the euro's role as a reserve currency. It will also allow us to keep more of our reserves in
euros. That in turn does two things. First it keeps our assets
from the hands of the Americans since they will not be in
dollar-denominated bonds. And secondly it preserves their
long-term value because the Europeans, particularly the

3194-ISLA

Germans, have been more determined foes of inflation. It has also helped us secure the credit facility."

Rashid apparently understood this simple explanation for a smile appeared on his face. The general was elated by thoughts of revenge. Yes revenge. Throughout the 1990's the Americans had prospered like no other people on earth. During the same period the Iraqi population had been subjected to humiliating poverty by the economic sanctions imposed at America's insistence and enforced by its military might. Any action that damaged the American way of life was therefore very welcome and desirable. Similar thoughts had passed through the minds of the Iranians at the Isfahan meeting.

The Kuwaitis, the Saudis and the people from the United Arab Emirates had very different ideas. They were thinking of ways to take advantage of the economic consequences that might occur in the financial markets as a result of their actions.

By lunchtime the plan had been thoroughly discussed.

"Well gentlemen, are we in agreement?" Tarik finally asked. The relieved participants nodded their heads. Saudi Arabia's suggestion that OPEC ratify the plan at its October meeting was also accepted as was Kuwait's proposal that gradual production cuts should start at once.

After lunch it was the turn of defense. Once again the Saudis took the lead.

"Our countries are jointly spending eight billion dollars annually on the purchase of defense equipment," Tarik said. "Quite frankly this accomplishes nothing. We are just throwing the money away."

"Is there an alternative?" the ruler of the United Arab Emirates asked. In 2003 his tiny country with less than a million people had spent over two billion dollars on arms purchases. More recently it had entered into a six billion dollar contract with Lockheed for the delivery of seventy five of the most sophisticated fighter planes in the world.

"Yes there is. Saudi Arabia has a detailed proposal on the subject. But before we go into that I would like Crown Prince Abdullah to tell you about Saudi Arabia's unilateral actions in this field."

The aged Abdullah spoke for the first time. "We have decided to cancel all our equipment purchase contracts. At the present time these total twenty billion dollars."

"We too are reducing our expenditures in this area," General Rashid indicated. "Iraq has to concentrate on re-building its economy. We can no longer afford to have a large army so we have decided to reduce its size by one hundred and fifty thousand."

"As you all know," Khatami chimed in, "Iran has been reducing its expenditures on defense for the past several years. Most of it is from the reduction in the size of the armed forces. This was reported in the international press six months ago. We have to spend more on improving the lives of our people and finding productive employment for them."

"Our region now is at its most settled condition," Tarik spoke again. "Kuwait and Iraq have signed a peace agreement. Your two countries," he said looking at Khatami and Rashid, "are in the final stages of signing a similar agreement. We have no external threats. I don't think anyone believes that the Israelis are about to invade us."

The Saudis now put their plan on the table. "We propose a Gulf Treaty Organization on the lines of NATO."

Tarik then outlined the Saudi ideas in detail. For the next three hours the plan was discussed from every angle. It had great appeal for the small states of Kuwait and the UAE. What better way to control their larger neighbors? The big countries were beset by economic problems and were reducing their defense budgets anyway. To further solidify the support of the smaller states, he proposed that the Secretary General of the Organization should always be from either Kuwait or the United Arab Emirates. At Iran's suggestion it was agreed that the headquarters would be in Tehran. Each country would have permanent representatives in the secretariat. And yes, of course any country could still have bilateral agreements with the Americans or any one else. That did it.

It was Sheikh Jabber of Kuwait who finally sealed the deal with the comment, "We have an enormous amount to gain from such an arrangement."

By six o'clock that evening agreement was reached in principal on the new organization. The Saudis produced a document. All the countries signed it. Representatives were named by each of the states to a committee under the chairmanship of Crown Prince Abdullah. It would convene in Riyadh next week. Its task: to draw up the detailed Treaty document by month end.

The delegates kissed and embraced each other in the traditional Arab manner. Even the Iranians moved by the high drama of the occasion seized the opportunity to show their brotherly feelings. Half an hour later, as the setting sun illuminated the waters of the Persian Gulf one last time, the men left in their separate planes.

As the Saudi Air Force Boeing 747 sped towards Riyadh in the desert twilight, the two Saudis felt elated but for different reasons. Crown Prince Abdullah had been instrumental in Tarik's selection and was now filled with pride at the ease and charm with which his handsome nephew had handled the meeting. It boded well for the future.

Tarik's mind was occupied with other thoughts. He was concerned with history. It seemed entirely appropriate to him that Kuwait had been the setting for these two historic agreements. It was from Kuwait that his grandfather, the young Ibn Saud, known among the Arabs as the "Lion of the Nejd" had set out to conquer Arabia in 1902. Almost a hundred years later, he Tarik, was also setting out from Kuwait on an equally formidable task. This time to reshape Saudi Arabia.

3194-ISLA

CHAPTER 27

At the same time as the leaders of the four Gulf states were arriving at their respective capitals, eight time zones away in New York, Alexandra Middleton was entering an elevator at the Am Bank headquarters building on Park Avenue.

On the thirty-eight-floor lobby she walked to a desk where a gentleman wearing a dinner jacket was sitting.

"I have a lunch appointment with Mrs. Spencer," Alexandra said.

"You must be Ms. Alexandra Middleton."

"Yes."

"Please follow me. Mrs. Spencer is waiting for you."

He led her to a small oak-paneled dining room a short distance away.

Victoria was standing near a wall of windows at the far end of the room. Her face broke into a broad smile the moment she saw Alexandra. She walked up to her and greeted her warmly.

"My dear Alexandra. It's been ages since we met."

"Yes. The last time was at the Council on Foreign Relations."

A waiter arrived and took their drink order.

"I've been traveling for most of the past three months," Victoria smiled. "I tried to contact you when I got back two weeks ago. We had a very hard time getting hold of you."

"Yes. I've been traveling as well. I was in Atlanta and then on the West Coast."

The waiter returned and handed each of them a glass of white wine. They moved to the dining table and sat down in front of the two place settings that were laid out, Victoria sitting at the head of the table with Alexandra on her right. The waiter came back with the menu cards. They looked at it as they sipped the wine and both ordered the lentil soup and a vegetable platter.

"By the way, on my last trip to London I ran into your old friend, Lady Annabelle Bixworth, at a party. We had a most enjoyable conversation about the good old days," Victoria said, moving her chair slightly towards the right.

The good old days referred to their student days. The two had first met as undergraduates at Cambridge and had known each other for almost thirty years. Victoria had been at Clare, a neighboring college to the one that Alexandra attended. And while they had moved in different social circles their paths had frequently crossed, particularly since they both studied the same subject. As a result a relationship had developed, and though the friendship was not too close, it had been maintained over the years especially after Alexandra married and moved to New York.

"We'll be spending the next weekend with Annabelle at Cambridge. You know her husband Jeremy Pemberton? He's going to introduce me to some of his wealthy business associates."

"Speaking of business, I was quite surprised to read about your departure from B&P," Victoria said. "You never mentioned that you were contemplating such a move."

Alexandra took a sip of the wine. "I wasn't planning on leaving. Quite frankly I was quite surprised myself."

3194-ISLA

Ever since the meeting was arranged, Alexandra had thought about the handling of the questions that might come up. On this particular one she decided to throw caution to the wind and tell the truth. It could only win her sympathy. Her responses, seemingly so natural and spontaneous, were in fact carefully planned and rehearsed.

"You mean you had no idea this was coming?" Victoria face mirrored her surprise.

"Absolutely none. In fact, the week earlier our chairman died very suddenly..."

"Yes, I remember reading about it in the Wall Street Journal."

"My former boss, Sidney Rosenberg, was expected to take over as the new chairman. Just before I left for Jamaica, for a week's vacation with my family, he assured me that I would succeed him as president. Instead he telephoned to tell me of my dismissal."

"He actually did it over the phone? That's really low class and crass."

"Well he claimed they couldn't wait because the news had leaked. When I returned to New York, I didn't see any point in meeting him. So my lawyers met him instead."

"I remember meeting two women who were partners at the firm at one of your parties. Did they give you any information?" Victoria asked.

"They haven't been in touch with me. In fact they won't even return my calls." Alexandra said a little pensively. "It's in times like this that you find out who your friends really are."

"Did you have any problems at the firm?"

"None of any significance that I can think of. I had differences with Rosenberg on our marketing approach but nothing very important."

"Any idea why he would do such a thing? Victoria asked sympathetically.

"No, but I think it is related to the sale of the firm. We

tried to sell the company but couldn't. The partners were very upset with Rosenberg. There was even talk of removing him. That's when I think I became a threat to him. I was the only possible replacement. Then this anonymous report mysteriously appeared on the desk of the management committee members and a few other partners. It's like one of those management consultant-type reports."

She gave Victoria a detailed account of the document and its contents. They even laughed at some of the items.

"Who do you think is the author of the report?"

"I don't know but Sidney Rosenberg is probably behind it. I suspect he used someone at one of the management consulting firms to help him. In fact one of the ladies you met at my house, Hillary Schuster, heads the institutional marketing unit and her husband works for McKinsey. I wouldn't be surprised if she had a hand in it. She has replaced me in the fixed income group there." Alexandra figured no one would ever find out the truth. And she wasn't planning on committing financial suicide by telling anyone about her own intrigues.

"So you were framed. It's outrageous what greed makes people do. It's the Gordon Gekko mentality, you know. No principles, no scruples."

"Yes. But unfortunately there's no way to prove it."

"I really am sorry about this. You must have been very upset," Victoria spoke with genuine concern.

"I was for a few days. I built a twenty billion dollar business and they just stole it. But you know I'm an optimist so I began to focus on the future. I've always believed that things are shaped not only by what you do but also by luck and fate. Nothing is served by engaging in self pity."

To Victoria this was vintage Alexandra. Most individuals would have been crushed by such an arbitrary and capricious loss of all they had worked for. But here was Alexandra seemingly undaunted, determined, setting off on a new venture. She remembered the positive attitude and the tenacity and drive. It was apparent even then in their student days.

The waiter reappeared with the lunch. He refilled their empty wine glasses and left. For a few moments the room was silent as they ate the food.

Victoria broke the silence. "You know there's a saying 'when the going gets tough, the tough get going.' I'm sure you're going to do very well. After all you one of the best fixed income managers in the business. You have a great reputation."

"Thanks for the kind words," Alexandra said putting her wine glass on the table.

"You must be inundated by calls from headhunters and money managers."

"I am talking with a number of firms," Alexandra replied with an enigmatic smile that reminded Victoria of one of the many Madonna with Child paintings at the Uffizi.

In business, Alexandra operated on the principal that you colored the truth to serve your interests, particularly when outsiders were involved. You never put yourself at the mercy of someone else. Besides she was not on dangerous ground here since Victoria had no idea of the money managers she was having discussions with.

"What type of companies are you talking to?" Victoria realized she was unlikely to get the names but she figured that any information she could get would give her a better idea of Alexandra's thinking on the subject of the new job. She wanted to play it safe before making Alexandra any offers.

"I'm having discussions with two companies that have over two hundred billion dollars in assets under management. I guess you'd classify them as large. They're publicly owned. The other two are small-sized firms with assets in the twenty billion dollar range."

"Do you think the larger companies offer any advantages compared to the smaller ones?"

"Some advantages but there are disadvantages as well," Alexandra replied. "They have name recognition, so that helps with institutional customers. But on the other hand these firms have well-established retail and high-net-worth operations so we cannot access those markets. Unfortunately these are the areas with the greatest growth potential."

Victoria smiled regretfully. "Name recognition hasn't helped us."

"But that's because of some of the problems that banks and insurance companies typically face in this business. We discussed it some months ago."

"I know. By the way is compensation an issue?" Victoria asked.

"No. Carol Galley at Merrill made fifteen million dollars last year. On the other hand she doesn't have an equity stake in the company. That's an important consideration in my view."

Victoria made a mental note of the last comment and then said, "You can probably get that at the smaller-sized companies."

"Yes, but they don't have the same name recognition so it takes much longer to build the business. On the other hand we will have access to the high-net-worth individual market at these firms," Alexandra replied.

The waiter returned. This time with the desert menus. They both declined and ordered coffee instead.

"What's happened to all your portfolio managers at B&P?"

"Three of them resigned and have teamed up with me. I thought it made sense to move on two fronts. So we are simultaneously exploring the possibility of forming our own company. Of course the business would grow at a much slower pace but we would be our own masters."

"Oh yes. That certainly sounds like an interesting idea,"

315

Victoria said encouragingly. If they chose to go this route it would help Am Bank considerably. It supported her argument for the joint venture.

"We think so too. The responses we have gotten from the consultants and our previous clients have been most encouraging. In fact our counsel is in the process of registering the company with the SEC and we are looking at premises."

"Where?"

"On Madison Avenue. And I'm going to Paris next week to meet Prince Tarik. You remember he was with us at Cambridge," Alexandra said.

Victoria remembered that Alexandra had dated the prince when they were students. She also remembered that she managed a substantial amount of his money at her former employers.

"Speaking of him," Victoria grinned. "He is our largest shareholder. Or rather was."

"Why was? There's been nothing in the papers about his selling the shares," Alexandra pointed out.

"No. It's a private arrangement. He telephoned our chairman last week to advise that he planned to sell his shares. The call came at an opportune time. We were discussing a share buyback program so we worked out a deal with Prince Tarik."

To Alexandra this simply confirmed what she had suspected ever since she saw Tarik at the Carlyle. She was deeply disappointed and the feeling registered on her face. She didn't know if Victoria noticed it. It was such a great opportunity to make money. Really big money. But her prospects were so uncertain now. Fate had dealt her a very bad hand at the wrong time. She felt cheated.

"I was hoping that you would help us if we chose to go ahead with our own money management company," Alexandra said, looking at Victoria hopefully.

"What did you have in mind?"

"We know that Am Bank gives money from the private bank to outside managers. We were hoping that you would put us on your list."

"Definitely. I'll set up a meeting with our chief invest-ment officer. He is the gatekeeper. We get so many firms wanting to do business. But I don't think there should be any problem in your case." She smiled. "He's supposed to be independent but things can be arranged. How much were you looking for?"

"A hundred million?" This was the number that her group had come up with earlier.

"That is certainly in the ball park. We have given funds in that range to a number of firms."

"So tell me about yourself. How are you doing?" Alexandra asked.

"My plans are beginning to take shape. You know when I was given charge of the Global Wealth Management Group in June, I was quite disappointed. Since then I've come to appreciate the size and dimension of the business. It kind of grows upon you. So now I'm very excited about the possibili-ties. I don't know how much you know about Am Bank and my group?"

"Not too much," Alexandra confessed.

"In the private bank we have a hundred and fifty billion dollars of funds of wealthy individuals from around the world."

"I knew you were big but not that big."

"Among the American banks we're just behind Citigroup which has twenty billion more than us. But we are pygmies compared with the Swiss. UBS has seven hundred billion dollars in such funds and Credit Suisse has close to four hun-dred billion."

"That much. No wonder they have such large retail money management operations. They are quite small in the institutional pension fund business."

"Yes, like us," Victoria lamented. "And the issue I've been

grappling with for the last three months is how to close the gap. Private banking assets are growing at double digit rates annually and worldwide assets are around twenty five trillion dollars."

"The customers," Alexandra said, "are also becoming much more sophisticated. Which explains why Merrill and Goldman have been successful in invading the bank's turf."

"That's right. As I see it we have two opportunities. One is presented by the rapid growth of the market. The other comes from the relatively poor investment performance of the Swiss banks."

"I suppose the principal attraction of the Swiss is their banking secrecy laws," Alexandra opined trying to show that she did have some knowledge of the industry."

"Yes, but we can match that in Switzerland as well as elsewhere in places like Luxembourg, Liechtenstein, Bermuda, the Cayman Islands and so on. And in all fairness to the Swiss they are giving more of the money to outside managers. Some of this is reflected in their earnings numbers."

Middleton nodded and smiled in agreement.

The Am Bank executive continued. "We have two sets of issues. One relating to getting new customers and keeping existing ones and the other to investment performance."

"So one is connected to private banking and the other to investment management."

"Precisely. The two are of course inter-related." Victoria said.

"So have you worked out a strategy?" Middleton asked.

"Yes. The private banking side can be fixed fairly easily by expanding the number of our relationship officers, broadening our product offering, improved servicing and other similar moves. However the one that is most critical and has to be tackled first is a complete revamping of our investment management business. We cannot get more wealthy clients or retain the ones we have without better investment performance."

"Why don't you buy a money management firm?"

"We looked into that and decided that the multiples are much too high. It doesn't make sense. The price tag is enormous."

"So do what the Swiss are doing. Give more funds to outside money managers." Alexandra was hoping to strengthen her earlier request for managing some of Am Bank's business.

"We're already doing a fair amount of that. Approximately ten percent of the assets are managed this way. Unfortunately that approach reduces our income sharply. So it's not the most desirable."

"I can understand your dilemma."

"Actually I may have a solution to the problem. I'm going to tell you about it but first let me ask you something else. The problem of building the business is obviously a long-term proposition. But we have to put the appropriate institutional framework into place now." She looked inquiringly at Alexandra.

"I agree. It will take time."

"So put yourself into my position," the Am Bank executive said. "I'm in a four-way race for the top spot in the bank."

Victoria paused as the waiter came into the room and re-filled their coffee cups. She waited for him to leave and then got up and closed the dining room door.

She returned to the table. "I want that job more than anything else in the world. So what can I do to make a big impression on the chairman and our board?"

"Something that significantly increases your group's income in the short term," Alexandra replied.

"That's the conclusion I came to. The question then is what's the most likely source for such income?"

3194-ISLA

"A hedge fund."

"That's what I figured. Typically about ten percent of our clients' funds are allotted to alternative investments. So I've decided to change our asset allocation mix to match that number. That gives an additional five billion dollars for such investments. I was thinking of putting three billion in hedge funds and the remainder in venture capital and private equity."

Victoria understood the critical importance of the hedge fund and its relationship to short-term profits. If Wilkinson was right, and the evidence supported him, then the stock market would very soon be heading south in a very big way. The obstacles that Victoria faced were fairly straightforward. How could she go to one of the big hedge fund groups like Soros' Quantum Funds or Louis Bacon's Moore Group and tell them what Wilkinson had told her? That was using inside information and if it were ever found out it would be the end of her career. So that option was out. Moreover even if she went this route most of the income would be retained by the money managers so it didn't help anyway.

What about the bank? Couldn't it set up its own hedge fund? Again the answer was negative. Successful hedge funds were established around high profile money managers. It was like the movie business in some ways. Am Bank had no such stars on its payroll. It would be very difficult to justify putting three billion dollars with second-rate individuals. Besides there was still the other problem. She simply couldn't tell the portfolio managers how to run the fund. Nor could she have Wilkinson give them the inside scoop. It was much too dangerous.

That's where Alexandra came in. Victoria figured that she probably had an inside track to Tarik who, according to Wilkinson, was orchestrating Saudi Arabia's new oil policy. Alexandra would manage the fund the way she wanted without any overt involvement on Victoria's part. In this set up no one could point a finger at her. There was now absolutely no doubt in her mind. She needed the joint venture with

Alexandra Middleton desperately. Her career dreams were inextricably linked to that.

"By the way while we're on the subject of investments," Victoria asked, "what's your assessment of the stock market in the near term?"

Alexandra spent the next five minutes telling her why she thought the market was over-priced and a major correction would take place sooner rather than later.

Victoria was now more convinced than ever that Alexandra had the inside scoop on the Saudi move. She decided to take the plunge.

"I told you earlier that I had a solution to our money management problem."

"Yes. I'd like to hear about it," Alexandra said, putting her coffee cup on the table.

"I was thinking that you could work with us in our money management area," Victoria told her in a cool and calm voice.

Alexandra was startled by the offer. She assumed Victoria was offering her a job in the bank's investment management group. This was the one area she had absolutely no interest in, even in her present situation. She just couldn't take the mindless bureaucracy and besides the compensation was lousy.

"Thanks for the offer, but I don't think I could work..."

Victoria cut her off. "That's not what I had in mind. Let me explain my idea."

Alexandra was silent.

"I was thinking of a joint venture between the bank and your firm."

Victoria was worried. It would be a hard sell. She went over the details of her plan. The percentage ownership by each of them and the revenue split. The joint venture would be the investment management arm of Am Bank. She was planning to shut down the existing group in the bank. It was overstaffed and too costly. The new firm would immediately

321

take over the bank's institutional business. The private banking assets would be phased in over six months to a year though a higher percentage would also be given to other outside managers. The joint venture would also get five billion dollars of these assets as well initially. Alexandra would be the CEO and would manage the firm without any interference from the bank.

She finished with the words, "This structure gives you everything you told me you were looking for. It's very advantageous for you. I honestly think it's a much better deal than anything you can get in the market."

Alexandra was mentally calculating the numbers as Victoria spoke. She reckoned that with the Am Bank connection there was a very good possibility of getting at least a quarter to a third of her old business from B&P. She figured that the revenue on the assets transferred over immediately by Am Bank would be in the neighborhood of thirty million. Besides she had no offers from any firm on the street and the way it looked she wasn't likely to get any offer soon. Maybe God was on her side again after all.

"You can be very persuasive," Alexandra said with a chuckle. "But I'll have to check with my partners." She wanted to buy more time and create the impression of reluctance.

"There's one other thing," Victoria reminded her. It's the alternative investments in the hedge funds. We already have a billion and a half apiece with Marcus and Soros. Their performance for the past two years has been dreadful. My staff would object to giving them any more money. And we're not equipped to handle it internally. We don't have anyone who could do it in our shop."

"Why don't you look at some of the other hedge funds. I'm sure any of them would jump at the opportunity. They don't get a chance like this every day. I'd recommend Jeff Vinnick or Louis Bacon."

"I have someone on my staff checking into that. But I

have a much better idea. I'd like to have the new joint venture manage the hedge fund. You have the charisma and the professional standing to handle it. And if I remember one of your emerging market funds last year had returns in the mid-thirty percent range. What do you think?"

Alexandra's pulse was racing with excitement. This was simply unbelievable. But long years of practice had given her tremendous control over her emotions. It did not show on her face.

"I'm very grateful for this overwhelming vote of confidence in my group's abilities. Of course I am very intrigued by the idea." She smiled. "But we don't have any fund in place and it'll take at least two months to get one registered in Bermuda or the Cayman Islands. You might miss out on the action if there is a market correction in this period."

"There's no problem on that front. We identified a fund called the Falcon Fund. A money management group that subsequently decided not to pursue the idea registered it. We bought it from them last week and can get the changes made quite quickly. Within ten days at most."

Alexandra was astonished. This time she did not hide her surprise. She hadn't realized how consumed Victoria was with her dreams of power. She had obviously thought through and organized everything very carefully.

Victoria just sat there watching Alexandra. From the look on her friend's face she knew–Alexandra was hooked.

They traded opinions on the proposal for a further half hour.

"All right," Alexandra finally said. "I'm satisfied with the arrangements but I need to talk with my partners."

She promised to get in touch later that evening.

323

CHAPTER 28

Alexandra Middleton decided to walk home. She was tremendously excited and hoped that the fresh air and exercise would give her time to compose herself. The meeting with Victoria had gone beyond her wildest expectation. The hedge fund was uppermost in her thoughts and she mentally calculated the numbers as she walked. A return of fifty percent was not unheard of, particularly in this case where, if her instinct was right, a stock market crash did occur. A twenty percent performance fee, she figured, would bring in three hundred million in income and her group's share, at the proposed thirty/seventy split, worked out to ninety million dollars. "My compensation," she said to herself, "would be about half of that amount."

That thought made her heart pound. Her gait became more confident and purposeful as images of regained wealth floated through her mind. What she had just lost at B&P could perhaps be recouped in one fell swoop. And it had taken her fourteen years to get there. But in those days she hadn't operated in the rarified high-income world of hedge funds. And then she felt deflated when she realized that it all depended on her stock market hunch coming through. The outcome was not predestined. There was no guarantee that it would. She wondered what the future held in store for her.

That's when she arrived back at the townhouse.

When Alexandra walked into the library, Charles Bradley was having a conversation with someone on the telephone while Anne and Brian were working on the laptop. She sat down on one of the cream colored armchairs next to a coffee table. Once Bradley had finished they all joined her on the adjacent sofa and armchairs.

"So how did it go?" Anne broke the momentary silence.

"Pretty good," Alexandra smiled. "We had a very interesting conversation."

"You were there for quite a while," Anne observed.

"Well, you know how it is. We talked of the old days and then a lot of time was spent chatting about the events at B&P."

"Did you ask for some funds from the private bank?" Brian wanted to know.

"Yes. I asked for a hundred million. She didn't think that would be a problem."

Just then the butler walked in, clad in a white jacket and black trousers.

"My lady," he said looking at Alexandra. "Would you like some coffee?"

"Thank you, Ken."

He poured her a cup and then looked at the others who declined with a shake of their heads, except for Anne who requested tea.

"Did she offer to help get us some more business," Bradley inquired, speaking for the first time.

"Let me tell you of our conversation," Alexandra said, sipping her coffee. "They have a hundred and fifty billion dollars in the private bank . . ."

"But that's huge," Brian interrupted her.

"That's right. They're second to Citigroup among Ameri-

3194-ISLA

can financial institutions. Their investment management group manages most of the money in house. And as we guessed, the performance is nothing to write home about. There are a lot of unhappy customers."

"How big is their investment management group?" Anne asked.

"It's bigger than I imagined and very much more bureaucratic. They have 190 portfolio managers. Then there are dozens of assistants, research analysts, traders, marketers, back-office staff and so on. Overhead costs eat up a large chunk of the revenues. The institutional business is, if I remember correctly, quite small, about five or six billion dollars. That's why we never ran into them at any of the institutional competitive presentations."

"Sounds like a real mess," Anne commented.

Alexandra drank the coffee, before continuing. "Victoria's first priority is to fix this side of the business."

"That certainly makes a lot of sense," Bradley observed. "Unless that's done they'll be losing customers and getting new business will be that much more difficult."

"Are they buying a money management firm?" Brian asked. "And please don't tell me its B&P."

"No. She said it is too expensive buying one of those outfits. They looked at the idea carefully and rejected it. For the bank, ownership also brings with it other headaches relating to culture and compensation. Too much time is spent on these issues and in the end no one is wholly satisfied," Alexandra explained.

"So how are they proposing to fix the problem?" Anne asked.

Alexandra refilled her cup from the coffee pot that the butler had left on the table, before replying.

"Victoria has made a very interesting proposal. Let me explain."

For the next hour she went into the details. It would be a

joint venture. Am Bank would buy thirty percent of Pericles Investment Management for a nominal amount. An amount of a hundred million dollars would be separately put into the venture by the bank as equity and round tripped back so it was essentially a wash. But for the market it would look as if Pericles had a hundred million in capital. Under the arrangement, they and not the bank, Alexandra assured them, would have total management control. The company would be the investment management arm of Am Bank. The existing investment management group would be gradually dismantled over the next year. The institutional business would be transferred to the new entity immediately and it would also get five billion of the private bank's assets at the same time as well. Most of the remaining assets would be transferred over the course of the year.

"Operationally the bank will maintain direct day-to-day contact with its wealthy customers through its private bank account officers who in a way will be acting as our marketers," Alexandra explained. "That gives the joint venture worldwide entree to the fastest growing investor segment. And at no cost. We'll have direct and total access to institutional customers."

"I like that," Charles Bradley declared enthusiastically. He had always been on the institutional side of the business anyway.

"Leaving performance aside for the moment, I don't understand how this structure helps Am Bank," Watson looked puzzled.

"That's simple enough," Alexandra indicated. "First the way we run the business we would have fifteen to twenty portfolio managers and much fewer assistants and traders and secretaries. We'll use outside vendors for analytical support and much of the processing work. That reduces the size of the premises one needs. All this means huge cost savings running into the hundreds of millions."

The explanation made sense to them. According to

3194-ISLA

Alexandra the bank might have achieved its cost goals by simply spinning out the investment management group to the current employees. So why didn't they? The answer could be summarized in two words: investment performance. The bank felt that that group did not have enough talented individuals, so an improvement in results was highly unlikely.

"What are the revenue sharing arrangements?" Bradley asked Alexandra.

"It'll be the exact opposite of the ownership stakes. We'll get thirty percent and they'll get seventy percent."

"You don't like that?" Alexandra said, noticing the flicker of concern that appeared on Watson's face.

"It seems to be on the low side. The fee on the fixed income business is usually around fifty basis points so a thirty percent split gives us only fifteen basis points," Watson pointed out.

"That was my first reaction as well. But on reflection I realized that it's more than made up for by the enormous volume of their existing business," Alexandra reminded him.

"By the way what does Am Bank pay outside managers when they use them?" Bradley asked.

"Around eighty percent of the fee is paid out. That's one of the reasons why this joint venture is so attractive for them. To customers it looks as if their funds are being managed by an independent money manager and yet the bank doesn't lose most of the revenues as they do right now; though you have to remember that only a very small portion of the total assets are managed by outsiders."

"On the income front I doubt if we could have done better at Merrill or elsewhere. After all we would be employees," Anne said, agreeing with Alexandra's earlier remarks.

"So what do you think?" Alexandra addressed the question to Charles Bradley.

"I like it." The excitement was visible on his face. It

gives us a big platform to build the business on. We start with a bigger customer base and that helps with the consultants. Even more importantly I feel that our association with the bank will have tremendous appeal for them."

"And it will also appeal to our former clients." Brian too sounded enthusiastic.

"Anne what about you?"

"Now that I have a better idea of the whole picture, I'm thrilled," Anne exclaimed, putting her teacup on the table. "What about you?"

"Quite frankly, I'm very excited." Alexandra smiled. "In some ways it's even better than my deal at B&P. It's true the payout was much better there, but here we'll be masters of our own destiny. We run the show. No Sidney or Peter to battle with. And none of those damned old partners we had to contend with. We choose the people we want. Yes we would be better off having our own company, but it will take us years to get enough assets. That's now clear from what we've heard so far from our old clients and so-called consultant friends."

"What's the breakdown of the portfolio we'll get initially?" Anne asked.

"The institutional business is thirty percent bonds and seventy percent equities, while the private banking assets are equally divided between bonds and stocks."

"We'll need equity portfolio managers, won't we?" Brian said.

"For sure," Alexandra replied, smiling. I was thinking of Marvin Jensen at B&P. I always thought he was excellent. And Victoria mentioned the names of a few individuals who she thought were good."

"Jensen's very good," Brian volunteered his opinion.

"We can discuss the personnel stuff later," Alexandra said. There's one other thing I have to tell you guys. I saved the best for last." Her face broke into a grin.

3194-ISLA

She paused for a moment and saw their excitement mount as they waited with growing interest to hear the news. She got up from her chair and walked over to the window overlooking the garden at the back of the house that was now in full shade.

"Here's the situation at Am Bank. There's a four-way race going on for the chief executive's job. Victoria is the only woman in the group. Obviously all the candidates are trying to make an impact. Just as clearly this has to be something significant that can be achieved in the short term. All the things we have talked of will take time to produce results. So what offers Victoria the best chance of coming up with something meaningful quickly?"

She looked at them. They were stumped. No one came up with anything striking. Buy a company? That idea had already been discarded. Get a huge amount of assets? Not very likely. Increase the assets under management? But how? They racked their brains but couldn't come up with any workable solution.

So Alexandra gave them the answer.

"In Victoria's area the one business that would yield the highest income for the bank is hedge funds. Provided the managers come up with good performance numbers during the remaining quarter. Its been done before. Jeffrey Vinnik, for example did it in his first year."

It was obvious from the expressions on their faces that they had not grasped what she was driving at.

"Okay," Alexandra continued. "You know that hedge funds have a performance fee equal to twenty percent of the gains. That's a heck of a lot more than any of Victoria's other businesses. For equity management they get 1 ¼ percent only. The problem is that the outside hedge fund managers retain 70 percent of the performance fee and the bank currently has no hedge fund expertise."

"I'm beginning to understand it now," Bradley exclaimed.

"The bank has the asset allocation responsibility and presumably can move more of their client's funds into alternative investments such as hedge funds, private equity, venture capital and so on."

"Right. So what is she proposing," Watson asked finally catching on.

"A three billion dollar macro hedge fund that we would manage," Alexandra blurted out joyfully.

Anne Nicholson jumped up from the armchair unable to contain her excitement.

"My God, that's wonderful. It's the opportunity of a lifetime," she said, expressing their collective sentiments. "And you've kept us on edge for so long."

Alexandra laughed. "I just wanted to build up your excitement level."

"You said macro fund, but we don't have any expertise in equities," Brian wailed.

"Macro merely means that we can invest in any product anywhere. It doesn't have to be equities." Alexandra could see him calming down. "Do you remember Leon Cooperman?"

"Yes. He started the Omega Fund," Bradley replied. "And before that he was the chief equity strategist at Goldman Sachs."

"Right. And the best returns in Omega have come from bonds and currency gains in which Leon has no expertise. He simply hired people with experience in those areas," Alexandra pointed out.

"So we can do the same," Brian said with evident relief.

"I've already got two names. Both suggested by Victoria. She particularly wants us to take an Indian who is the chief investment officer in the Private Bank as a partner. According to her he's highly regarded within the bank and it would greatly facilitate the hedge fund effort. I've arranged to meet him tomorrow."

331

Half an hour later Alexandra telephoned Victoria Spencer and informed her of their decision. They talked for a few minutes and agreed that their lawyers should be briefed immediately. Moments later the lawyers had been contacted and the urgency of the task duly impressed upon them. Work on the agreements would commence in the morning.

"Our luck is finally beginning to change," Anne said, just before she left with Watson and Bradley.

Alexandra smiled warmly. "Let's hope that's the case."

CHAPTER 29

The story, written by staff reporter Matthew Walker, appeared on the second page of the main section of The Wall Street Journal on Friday, September 17.

AMERICAN BANKING CORPORATION IN JOINT VENTURE

"American Banking Corporation announced yesterday that it was acquiring a thirty percent interest in Pericles Asset Management, a recently-formed investment advisory firm. The bank's press spokesman, Richard Morris, said that under the terms of the agreement Pericles would be Am Bank's investment management vehicle. All existing institutional business will be transferred to this company according to the press spokesman. Sources at Pensions and Investments, an industry publication, indicate the amount of such business is quite small. It is expected that some of the staff in the bank's existing money management unit will be folded into the new vehicle.

"Commercial banks with the exception of a few, notably Morgan and Mellon, have not been too successful in competing against mutual fund giants like Fidelity or Vanguard

333

or against firms such as Alliance, Pimco and Merrill for asset management business. The lack of success has been attributed, by most analysts, to their failure to attract high quality portfolio managers for a variety of reasons, one of the more important being the low compensation levels relative to industry standards. The task has been made more difficult, according to knowledgeable observers, by the relative ease of entry in the money management business and the fairly small capital needs of the industry. Unlike commercial banks, there are no minimum capital requirements for money management firms.

"In recent years banks and brokerage houses have acquired many investment advisory firms. Mellon has been most prominent among the banks while Merrill paid five billion dollars for Mercury Asset Management. Additionally, the German insurance giant Allianz acquired Pimco in a transaction that valued the money management firm close to five billion dollars.

"Early this year Am Bank was reported to have seriously considered acquiring B&P, which has over fifty billion in assets under management. According to inside sources, the bank decided against the purchase after an in-depth review of that firm's business. Subsequently several other buyers also dropped out of the bidding. B&P continues to operate independently but there are rumors of an impending IPO.

"It is interesting to note that former B&P portfolio managers are the majority owners of Pericles Asset Management. Alexandra Middleton, the President of Pericles, was one of the principal partners at B&P where she ran the twenty billion dollar fixed income business until she suddenly resigned from the firm three weeks ago. She is considered one of the leading portfolio managers in the fixed income area.

"Banks and securities houses have found the money management business very attractive because it provides a stable and ongoing earnings stream unlike the more volatile income from trading and corporate finance activities. This has led to very high valuations of asset management firms currently estimated at twenty five times earnings. Sandra Flanagan, an analyst at Salomon Smith Barney, said "these high multiples, so late in the business cycle, pose considerable risks for the acquiring firm." In response to a question, Morris said that Am Bank considered the current price of investment advisory firms to be too high and unrealistic.

"Am Bank's strategy in this business appears to be very different from that of other banks many of whom have acquired investment advisory firms at considerable cost in the past few years. The bank appears to be pursuing the same formula that is often cited for the success of investment advisory businesses, without making an enormous monetary investment in an acquisition. By acquiring a minority stake in a firm it is betting that this structure will provide an entrepreneurial environment to a group of high-quality portfolio managers and enable them to create a large asset management business using the bank's extensive network and resources.

"It is not as yet clear whether the new affiliate will also be involved in managing assets generated by Am Bank's Private Banking Group. The bank spokesman declined to comment. Neither Victoria Spencer, Group Executive at Am Bank for the Global Wealth Management Group, nor Alexandra Middleton, the CEO of the affiliate were available. Under pressure from customers, banks have increasingly invested their private bank client funds with outside money managers in recent years. A banking industry analyst at Merrill, Jay Cohen, praised the deal. "In my view this is a very innovative approach."

"In New York stock exchange trading, Am Bank shares edged up $1.75 to $87.50 yesterday."

The announcement was delayed by a day because several crucial problems had to be resolved. The most important of these resulted from a suggestion made by William Th-

3194-ISLA

ompson. He had counseled Victoria to position the new hedge fund in ways that made it more attractive and desirable to the private bank's customers.

"I think we should have two more directors in the hedge fund," Thompson proposed.

"We already have two directors. They're pretty respectable," Victoria reminded him.

"Who are they?'

"The Right Honorable Jeremy Pemberton who is a very successful businessman and Iris Cantor a well-known socialite and philanthropist."

"They are certainly good choices but they were selected by Alexandra's group. We need to pick two directors as well."

Victoria laughed. "You have something in mind?"

"Yes, it's quite simple," Thompson said. "The credibility of the fund will be greatly enhanced by the addition of two really distinguished individuals to the board."

"You're right," she said admiring the man's flashes of insight.

"The public is very impressed–dazzled is a better word–by the reputation of well-known names. That's one of the things I have learnt over the years, my dear. Appearance counts. All too often it is much more important than the substance. The rich are no exception to this rule."

"You have any names in mind?" Victoria asked.

For the next twenty minutes they considered a handful of names. They finally settled on Jack Welch who had retired as chairman of General Electric and William Sharpe, a Noble prize-winning economist who had developed the capital asset pricing model that was extensively used in the money management business.

Alexandra agreed with the logic and the choices. It was left to Thomson to contact the two men. He spent most of Wednesday afternoon working the telephones. Finally both were located at mid morning on Thursday. He discussed the hedge fund with each of the men. There was some hesitation but his arguments were persuasive. In the end both men accepted the offer.

The lawyers worked through most of Wednesday to finalize the agreements. It involved complex classes of shares that gave Am Bank thirty percent of the voting stocks but a much larger share of the dividends. A confidential supplementary agreement spelt out the details of the revenue sharing arrangements.

At 8.30 A.M. the same Friday, the telephone rang in Victoria's office on the private line that bypassed the secretary. Victoria picked it up on the second ring.

"So I see from the Journal that we are going into a joint venture with an investment management firm," the amiable voice said at the other end.

Victoria recognized it immediately. It was Henry Fielding, the Chairman of American Banking Corporation. He was obviously joking since Bill Thompson had informed him earlier of the deal.

"That's right Henry. Do you approve?"

"Smart move, Spencer. Now make it work."

CHAPTER 30

Activity had picked up in other areas of Am Bank and was gradually building to a crescendo. In the past decade epic changes had occurred in the composition of senior management personnel at large American firms, many of which had become truly global in the scope and size of their operations and the make up of their staff. The leadership contest now taking place at American Banking Corporation epitomized the extent of these changes. Among the contestants for the top position at the bank were a woman, a German, an Englishman and an American.

In the business world, like in so many other fields, perceptions often counted as much, and maybe more, than reality. Fully conscious of the high stakes, these modern day gladiators were preparing for their own encounter with destiny. They were all coldly calculating individuals, relentlessly driven by ambition and single-minded in the pursuit of power that they craved for like a dipsomaniac's insatiable thirst for alcohol. Each had his or her own army of loyalist 'janissaries' throughout the institution. None of the contestants would admit failure until it was truly over. Scruples would not stand in the way. They had come a long way and the beckoning prize seemed to be almost within their grasp.

On the same day as the joint venture announcement, another meeting was taking place on the tenth floor of Am Bank's headquarters in a glass-walled office–known as the fish bowl–that overlooked the trading area, a gigantic room jammed with three hundred traders and salespeople occupying row upon row of desks crammed with computer screens, batteries of telephones and other electronic paraphernalia. On one wall six large digital clocks showed the prevailing time in New York, San Francisco, Tokyo, Singapore, Bahrain and London. On another wall a huge ticker tape flashed the latest financial information.

As the two men looked through the glass wall of the office, the trading floor appeared to be in total bedlam. Men and women were talking on telephones, sometimes on two simultaneously; some of the room's occupants were shouting and gesticulating wildly, while others sat like zombies staring at the computer screens. The telephones rang incessantly. It was difficult to imagine how anyone could possibly work in the midst of all that noise and commotion.

"It's not as wild as it looks," Karl Lutz, head of the Global Trading Group smilingly reassured the pleasant-looking visitor in the dark gray suit. "There is a method to this madness."

The man sitting next to Lutz was Ralph Schuster, a partner at McKinsey who had been retained jointly by Lutz and Christopher Taylor, who managed the Global Investment Bank. McKinsey was charged with the task of helping the two groups develop a strategy to reposition the two businesses in ways that would help them win more mandates from corporate customers for underwriting debt and equity issues. And any other income generating ideas the consultant could suggest.

"Yes. It's very similar to your London trading room," Schuster replied. He had just returned from a trip to that city where a McKinsey team was busy analyzing trading and investment banking activities.

"Let me give you a quick overview of our situation. You can get the details from the department managers when you meet them," Lutz said smoothly.

Schuster nodded. "That fits in well with our schedule. As you know a group of my staff will be here later this afternoon and we have appointments to interview all your key managers in the next several days."

Schuster shifted slightly to look at the man sitting next to him. He was of medium height with short dark brown hair. The face was smooth, and Schuster observed that it was remarkably unlined for someone involved in such a stressful job. He had done his homework prior to the meeting. He knew that Lutz, a native of Munich, had been a "wunderkind" in foreign exchange trading. His career had been meteoric. At an early age he had headed the bank's trading activities in Tokyo and London. Thereafter he had managed Am Bank's global foreign exchange business and finally this year, at age forty-two, he was named head of the newly-created Global Trading Group. Schuster had also found out that Lutz was a graduate of Chicago Business School and was the second highest paid executive at Am Bank. He lived in a big multi million-dollar house on Round Hill Road in Greenwich–that most favored bastion of the captains of American corporations–with a pretty wife, six years younger, and two young children.

"Last year our net income in Global Trading was two billion," Lutz began. "That's two hundred million more than in the previous year."

"Any particular reason for the increase?"

"Yes. In 2002 we got caught in the down draft of the HCM hedge fund crisis. The consolidated numbers don't tell the whole story. If you dig deeper you'll find that we did very well in foreign exchange trading two years ago while last year our fixed income trading numbers stand out."

"Is there any way to reduce the earnings volatility in your group?"

"Unfortunately not," Lutz responded. "It's the nature of the beast. Trading by definition will involve earnings volatility since we cannot always be on the winning side."

The proper way to offset volatility is to increase our fee-based income, particularly asset management, private banking, mergers and acquisition and other advisory business such as corporate finance. We still rely too much on trading. It accounts for twenty five percent of the bank's total income.

"How do your group's earnings compare with those of Am Bank's other businesses?"

"I just looked at those numbers yesterday," Lutz replied. "Last year as I mentioned earlier we made two point two billion dollars. The Consumer Group's number was three point seven billion, while the Wealth Management Group had earnings of one point two billion. The Investment Banking Group made one point nine billion dollars but seventy five percent of this was from lending activities primarily in emerging markets."

Schuster made a mental note of the point Lutz made about the last-named group's earnings. Most of the income was from commercial banking activities even though it was reflected in the investment banking numbers.

"How effective is the risk management system?"

"You can always tinker with the system to design a better mousetrap," Lutz smiled. "But it works pretty well. In general I'd say that American banks have done a much better job at this than the securities firms and the foreign banks. Of course one cannot always be on the winning side in trading but none of the American banks have sustained losses like some of the foreign banks and the brokerage companies."

He was referring to some of the huge trading losses that were reported in the press in the past. There was that fellow named Jett whose trading losses had resulted in the demise of Kidder Peabody. Then there was the bozo in Singapore whose billion dollar loss had led to the acquisition of Barings Brothers, the world's oldest private bank, by a Dutch company. Similar losses had brought about the forced sale of Bankers Trust to Deutsche Bank. These were not the only ones. The Swiss and the Japanese had produced some prize-winning losers as well.

"Tell me how you're organized?" Schuster asked.

Lutz walked over to his desk and opening the cabinet behind it, produced a chart, which he handed to the McKinsey man.

"As you can see we are organized globally around two functional businesses: market making and proprietary trading. Under this we have specific product lines such as foreign exchange, government bonds, corporate bonds, money market instruments, mortgage bonds, equity trading, derivatives, funding and so on."

Schuster nodded. "It's a very flat structure."

Lutz ignored the comment. "In our market making activities," he explained, "we deal with customers. Our proprietary trading is for our own account but the flow of information from our customer dealings is important. It gives us clues on the markets."

"And who are your principal customers?"

"Actually we have two very distinct set of customers," the German said. "On one side we have issuers who need funds. Typically these are corporations or state and local governments. On the other side of the equation are the investors. These are handled by our sales force and include money managers, pension funds, hedge funds, corporations, mutual funds, foreign governments and wealthy individuals."

"And which is your most consistently profitable business?"

"Foreign exchange without a doubt and then the fixed income area particularly U.S. Treasury securities and our funding operations..."

The jarring ringing of the telephone interrupted the conversation. Lutz walked up to his desk and lifted the receiver. He listened for a few seconds, rapidly gave his answer and then returned to his place on the couch next to Schuster.

He continued. "Let's talk markets because income opportunities are a function not just of our own effectiveness but also of the depth and breadth of the markets."

"I think that makes a lot of sense," the McKinsey man responded affably.

Schuster was a quintessential consultant, well versed in pleasing customers, coaxing out information from them and in general making them feel important. The management consulting business had grown exponentially since World War II. McKinsey was considered the best though it faced stiff competition from Boston Consulting Group, Bain and a host of accounting firms that had branched into this highly profitable industry. Consulting fees was one of the major expenditure items of American corporations and at any one point whole armies of consultants, from two or more companies may be working in different areas of a corporation such as Am Bank. In the eyes of detractor's, consultants were nothing more than magicians with words–bullshit artists if you really wanted to be truthful. Cynics noted that once an executive had decided on a course of action he usually brought in the consultants as independent experts to dish out the executive's pre-determined decisions in dressed up, glossy language. The result of the so-called recommendations of these independent experts invariably led to reorganizations and the firing of countless employees–now euphemistically referred to as downsizing.

"Let's go over the foreign exchange market," Lutz said.

343

"It's the largest and most liquid market in the world. The daily global trading volume is almost two trillion dollars. Yes, two trillion dollars."

"That's a staggering number," an impressed Schuster said. "Where does all of this trading occur?"

"London is the premier market. Its dominance has actually increased over the past three years. It now handles as much business as New York, Tokyo and Singapore combined."

Schuster made some notes on a yellow legal pad.

Lutz continued, "On a good day we might hit forty or fifty billion dollars in the four centers. So you can understand why foreign exchange dominates our activities. Incidentally all that newspaper talk of the gnomes of Zurich is just poppy cock."

"Really! I thought the Swiss were very big players in this market."

"No where near what they're credited with," Lutz responded. "It's a myth perpetrated by writers of fiction and poorly informed journalists but it plays well with readers. That way one can blame the bad foreigners for speculation whenever anything goes wrong in the financial markets as a result of currency swings. The truth of the matter is that American banks have dominated foreign exchange since the mid sixties. Citigroup is the leader. In fact its dominance was established by another German called Brutsche and his Pakistani sidekick." A smile of satisfaction covered his face at the mention of the role played by another German in another era.

Lutz then went on to talk about the fixed income market. The absolute size of the market in the United States was around thirteen trillion dollars.

"You know," Lutz said, "most people have no idea how much larger the daily trading volumes are in this market compared with equities. On television we frequently hear that a billion shares exchanged hands on the New York Stock Exchange. In dollar terms the daily trading volume is quite small. It's around thirty billion on the NYSE and about sixty billion for all the exchanges. By comparison in the fixed income market, the daily trading number is over one trillion dollars. Just in the United States.

The McKinsey partner made some more notes on the legal pad.

"What about Europe. Has the euro had any impact on volumes?" Schuster enquired.

"Yes, very definitely. The bond market is around ten trillion dollars and the conversion of all the debt from thirteen currencies to one currency has greatly increased outstanding bonds and therefore liquidity."

Lutz then explained that in the trading businesses most of the money was made in proprietary trading. This was true in the case of other banks and securities firms as well. They were all essentially speculating in the currency markets or in the fixed income markets and occasionally in equities.

"Let me give you a simple example. The differential between bid and offer prices on bonds is 2/32nds. So if we did a billion dollars worth of business in thirty year U.S. Treasuries we would make $625,000 provided we were on the right side, that is if we were able to buy at the lowest price and sell at the highest, which is an unlikely scenario. Certainly on an ongoing basis. On the other hand on a billion dollar proprietary trading 'long position' in the same product we would make ten million dollars if interest rates went down by ten basis points. Or an equivalent loss if rates went up by the same amount. The risks and opportunities are much greater in proprietary trading."

"So if you go long in a particular bond what are you speculating on?"

"Essentially it is one of two things that we may be doing. First we may be simply market timing that is, taking a rate bet. In this case we would be expecting rates to go down.

The other thing we might be doing is arbitraging. All fixed income securities are priced off treasuries unlike the equity market. For example Microsoft shares are not priced off some benchmark stocks. In the fixed income market U.S. government securities are the pricing benchmark. So a ten-year GE corporate bond is priced off the ten-year U.S. treasury security. These spreads typically widen or narrow at various times and we arbitrage between different securities betting that the spread will normalize through the action of arbitrageurs. That is, we go long in the security we think is going to increase in value and we short the instrument that is expected to decrease in value."

Lutz was referring to speculation on spread variations or what commodity traders called basis risk. In this case the speculation involved either changes in the usual spread relationship between two different securities such as treasuries and a double A-rated corporate bond, or changes in the spread relationship along the yield curve of the same security for instance a seven-year and a ten-year U.S. Government note. In street parlance this was often called yield curve arbitrage or convergence trades. Newspapers referred to all these strategies as "arcane" and "esoteric" but the reality was very different. This was the bread and butter business in the fixed income markets.

"The other very important money maker is our funding activities," the Am Bank executive continued. "Here we're also taking substantial interest rate positions based on our view of the market. It involves mostly time deposits and CD's in the Euro markets. For example in a positively sloping yield curve, which is usually the case, we may borrow say ten billion dollars from other dealers and clients for one month and lend a similar amount to other dealers for three months. The differential is considered interest income unlike the income we make in our securities positioning. That is reflected in the balance sheet as trading income."

Schuster was familiar with this. Commercial banks had done this interest rate gapping from times immemorial. It was the same thing as getting a demand deposit from one customer and lending it to another as a three-year automobile loan. He stopped taking notes and shifted his gaze back to Lutz. "Is there a difference in the quality and magnitude of trading operations between commercial banks and the investment banks?"

"Let me be a little more precise," Lutz responded. "In our proprietary trading operations we are probably better than the investment banks. Salomon used to be the best but they have discontinued this activity all together. But in market making we definitely have problems competing with them."

The general perception that investment banks were superior to commercial banks in the trading area was wide off the mark. Historically banks were the principal participants in the currency markets going back over a hundred years and had developed an expertise that investment banks were just beginning to match. The bank's trading function were extended in the early sixties of the last century to their funding operations, which involved buying and selling CD's, fed funds and time deposits. As a result a very entrepreneurial culture had developed in the trading areas of commercial banks that separated them from the slow moving, more deliberative and team oriented culture that prevailed in their lending operations. The long involvement in these activities had made commercial banks the dominant force in the foreign exchange and derivative markets and their proprietary trading expertise was the equal of any investment bank.

"What in your view is the problem on the market making side?" Schuster was trying to get all of Lutz's opinions and views on the subject.

"Our product offering is not broad enough. So investors don't want to deal with us. It's the classic what comes first, a chicken or egg problem. We need to have better distribution

347

capabilities. That means more investor customers. But we can't get more customers until we have a wider range of products to sell and that in turn requires more corporate bond and equity underwriting mandates."

Lutz explained that this had been a perennial problem for commercial banks. They had a very hard time originating corporate paper.

"If you don't have the product," Lutz elaborated, "You can't make a market in it. So if a customer wants that particular product he has to go elsewhere. Investors often swap between corporate and government bonds and if we can't offer quality execution they go to dealers who have a broader array of products. Unfortunately its not banks."

"Do you think Glass Steagall played a role in this?"

"Yes, very definitely, at least in the early years. Later on we figured out ways to go around the Act so it became more or less meaningless by the time Congress revoked it. But by then the damage had already been done. It essentially created a perception in the minds of senior corporate executives that investment bankers were smarter than commercial bankers. This has persisted to this day and has caused the difficulties banks have getting corporate bond and equity underwriting business."

"Is compensation or people quality an issue?"

"I don't think it's a problem in the trading area. We're pretty competitive with the market and we have as much talent as any other securities house. They say it's a major problem in the Investment Banking Group. They're probably right. As you know, back in the nineties Deutsche Bank tried to create an investment bank in the United States. They hired so-called stars from Merrill, Goldman, Salomon and other investment banks by giving them outrageous compensation packages. But in the end nothing came of it. The strategy didn't work. The Swiss at UBS tried a similar approach but again the effort was futile."

The conversation was interrupted by the appearance of a young man, in his mid twenties, outside the office. Lutz excused himself and went out to talk with the trader.

While Lutz was outside, Schuster's mind went back to the conversation with his wife last night.

"Did you read the announcement in the Wall Street Journal," Hillary had asked him.

"No, dear. What is it about?"

"Alexandra Middleton."

"What's happening?"

"She has formed a joint venture with Am Bank." She handed him the Journal.

"I don't like it," he said ten minutes later after reading the article.

"No. I'm very disturbed. This could hurt our business very badly." Hillary's voice trembled.

"What does Sidney think?"

"He's very worried also. In fact he joked about getting the Russian mafia involved in fixing the problem."

"Let's not get into that. That's much too dangerous. I'm sure Sidney will come up with a less violent solution."

"Just when it appeared that things were going our way, this joint venture occurs. I'm very concerned, Ralph. Will you also think what we can do to minimize the damage?" Hillary pleaded as tears welled up in her eyes.

"Don't worry darling. I will. I promise."

The problem had weighed on his mind ever since.

Just then Lutz returned to the office.

"Sorry. We had to decide about a few big positioning trades. The European Central Bank is in the market supporting the euro."

"By the way," Schuster asked, "what do you think about yesterday's joint venture announcement?"

"It's not on the grand scale that I associate with Victoria. I guess it helps the private banking business and it undoubtedly will improve our investment performance." He paused for a moment. Then he continued with a smile, "Anything would be an improvement over our present lot in the asset management group. But I don't see how this move helps us in the money management business."

"Why is that?"

"It will take forever to build a big enough institutional money management business using this approach. We don't have the luxury of time. It's a very competitive field."

"What would you do?" Schuster asked

"I think the asset management business is very important for us. We have to get off our butt and do what needs to be done. I would pay up and buy a large-sized firm and fold this new joint venture into it. That would give us the critical mass to rapidly build the assets in a major way. Otherwise we'll just be two bit players."

"Talking of mergers and acquisitions," Ralph asked, "Would it make sense for your group if the bank merged with or acquired an investment bank.

"Lutz smiled. "That's a familiar melody. It depends. The jury is still out on investment and commercial bank marriages. The smaller investment banks are too narrowly based to add any value. Lehman is basically a trading shop with reasonable corporate finance capability. So in this case we have two problems. The fit is not right and the price is too high. Travelers ignored both of these in its acquisition of Salomon and look what happened."

"I thought the merger was quite successful," Schuster volunteered.

"Yes, but at what price. They paid nine billion for Salomon, which was the best trading shop on the Street, and they ended up dismantling its primary business. Sandy is just too risk averse to accept that kind of income volatility. Deutsche Bank bought Bankers Trust. Again it was a big mistake. The same thing happened with ING's purchase of

Furman Selz. They bought small, third-class firms with very narrow businesses. Just a big waste of money."

"What about Merrill or Goldman?"

Lutz laughed. "That's a different story. Chase tried with Merrill but they weren't interested. I think the fit is much better in our case." He smiled again. "But that will have to wait for the next chairman. And even then not all of us would be willing to give up the CEO job and ride off into the sunset."

"Karl if you had to sum up what would you say is the single most important development that would help your business?" Schuster asked.

"It would take time but I would say without any doubt a first-class corporate finance business." Lutz replied.

"And in the short term?"

"Access to the Fed's Open Market Committee's discussions would help," he said with that easy laugh of his.

Later that afternoon, Lutz ran into the chief investment officer of the Private Banking Division in the senior officers' dining room. He was an affable Indian, in his mid-fifties, who had once been a rising star in the equity business and had been recruited by Am Bank five years earlier.

"What's happening in your area, Ravi?" Lutz asked.

"Well, you already know about the new joint venture," the CIO replied.

Lutz smiled. "Who doesn't? It's been in the news in all the papers."

"I'm moving over to the joint venture to work on a hedge fund."

"Is this a new fund?" Lutz had not heard of this.

"Yes. It's a global macro fund that the private bank is introducing. We came up with new asset allocation figures that permit three billion dollars in hedge fund investments."

"Are you giving out some money to Quantum or Marcus?"

"No. We have substantial amounts with them already and the performance has been sub par. Victoria and I agreed that we should manage this in the joint venture exclusively."

351

So there was more to it than just the joint venture. The hedge fund, Lutz realized, was Victoria's short-term response to the succession battle. He had heard about the secret revenue sharing arrangements between Am Bank and Pericles. So if the fund were successful, Victoria's group would make a fistful of money, greatly improving her chances. And if it failed it wouldn't matter. The losses would be for the account of the wealthy clients. They couldn't do that in his group. The losses went straight to the bank's income statement. He knew that he was facing a formidable opponent who happened to be a woman. She was playing her cards remarkably well. Walking back to his office Lutz thought the atmosphere in the bank was getting more and more tense as they got closer to 'D Day'. Right now he was beginning to feel what the gladiators must have felt at the pageants of ancient Rome. The thought sent a cold shiver down his spine.

CHAPTER 31

Hedge funds were back in their glamorous role as the Rolls Royce of the money management business. It was not so long ago–the autumn of 1998 to be precise–when, in the aftermath of the collapse of the East Asian "Tiger" economies and the Russian debt fiasco, they were blamed for all the ills affecting the global financial system. As usual Congress got into the act demanding broader regulatory oversight and a task force was set up to look into their operations.

Just when the situation looked desperate, it had reversed itself with unexpected speed. The world's equity markets once again resumed their rocket like ascent towards the stars, dashing to smithereens the dire forecasts of the pundits on the imminent demise of the hedge fund business, or at the very least of its complete emasculation.

Ever since, hedge funds had enjoyed their day in the sun, receiving increasing attention–and more importantly money–from the world's elite who were restlessly searching for higher returns on their funds.

This year the annual conference of hedge fund investors, sponsored by New Bridge Consulting Associates, was held at the Intercontinental Hotel in Geneva on Friday, Sep-

3194-ISLA

tember 17. As usual, the two-day conference was very well attended. The gathering naturally included a large number of hedge fund managers and a diverse collection of investors. The latter group consisted of private bankers, representatives of pension funds and foundations, fund-of-funds managers and of course large numbers of wealthy investors whose beaming faces often graced the pages of magazines and newspapers all over the world and who very naturally were accompanied by their financial consultants. Alexandra Middleton was attending her first such conference. She had arrived in Geneva the previous night accompanied by Jack Carver.

On the first day, the extra large conference room was jammed to capacity. Alexandra figured that there were at least two hundred participants in the room. They had assembled to hear George Soros, the renowned hedge fund operator, multi billionaire and large-scale benefactor of worthy and sometimes not so worthy causes.

The iconoclastic Soros was in fine form this morning. He gave the audience a wide-ranging dissertation on the state of the market and the industry, sprinkled with comments on the need for some form of controls on the international flow capital to developing countries, on the urgent need to rethink our views on the role of the state since market forces could not be counted on to take care of every problem despite what free marketers said and on the hot issue of moral hazard. The speech ended with an optimistic prognosis for the hedge fund industry.

"Contrary to expectations, the hedge fund business is thriving. Total assets exceed six hundred billion dollars managed by more than three thousand portfolio managers. The industry is thriving because it meets the basic needs of its customers."

Following the speech there was a question and answer session. The audience, which included many foreign journalists covering the conference, particularly enjoyed this feature as it gave free reign to the articulate Soros to enunciate his eclectic views.

"What's happening to the performance of the Quantum Funds?" someone in the audience asked.

"We have our ups and downs," Soros replied with a straight face. "That's life. We had many good years. Now we're experiencing the downside. It will change."

For years, the returns on Soros' Quantum Funds had been explosive, but in the past four years the performance had been less than stellar. The funds return last year was only 18 percent but that was much better than the negative return of the previous year, when Soros was caught, like so many others, by the sharp downturn in emerging market stocks.

"Can you give us your views on the Federal Reserve Chairman's recent statements that the regulators cannot micromanage bank lending activities?" The question was from one of the journalists, an older-looking man with a mane of silver-colored hair.

In the past few months a number of banks had announced losses relating to their lending activities in the United States as well as in emerging markets. Questions were raised in Congress on the efficacy of regulatory oversight.

"I agree with the chairman that it is neither possible nor indeed desirable to micromanage bank lending," Soros responded. "But surely when the government guarantees deposits, it also has an obligation to set reasonable standards for the use of those deposits. The regulators have a 1930's mindset. That's when the guarantee first came into being. At that time and continuing into the fifties, bank deposits were invested primarily in U.S. government securities and interest rates were not only low, they also barely fluctuated. So the asset side didn't matter. But since then the situation has changed completely. Bank assets are now invested in low credit quality loans and interest rates gyrate with a greater degree of frequency. Apparently the regulators haven't woken up to this fact. Regulatory oversight is lax and they are out of touch with reality. That is why we have repeated bank rescues."

"Speaking of rescues," an attractive woman asked. "Considering the excellent current condition of the global financial markets do you still consider that the Federal Reserve's intervention in the rescue of Horizon Capital Management was ill advised?"

Soros recognized his inquisitor. It was Alexandra Middleton. They had met frequently on the social circuit.

Horizon Capital Management, known in the market by its acronym of HCM, was a hedge fund run by PhD's and a couple of prize-winning economists, assembled by the legendary bond trader Mark Kravitz, that after a few spectacular years had faced total melt down in June 2002 when it lost over ninety percent of the value of its assets. In the aftermath one thing became clear. The fund with only five billion in equity–investments by the general partners and all the limited partners–somehow managed to borrow almost thirty times this amount from banks and securities firms who were too overawed by the reputation of the principals to bother asking for any collateral. The fiasco raised serious questions about the lending procedures of these institutions. It later developed that the big boys of the banking world had based their lending decisions on information so flimsy that an average businessman would have been kicked out of his bank for even suggesting borrowings on that basis. And the financial institutions included some of the biggest and the best–Morgan Chase, UBS, Credit Suisse, Bankers Trust, Merrill, Goldman Sachs, Bear Stearns, Lehman and Salomon Smith Barney. They were all there. These supposedly smart bankers had tried to make the public believe that it was all Kravitz's fault. He had made them lend his fund one hundred and fifty billion dollars with minimal collateral! They had done this before with John Merewether and his Long Term Capital Management Fund. They had also done this with Trump. He too had mesmerized them. Then too, it had been Trump's fault. And before that it was leveraged buyout loans and loans to Latin America much of which had had to be written off. You would have thought that the bankers had learnt their lesson by now. But these guys never did learn. It had taken a $4.5 billion package, engineered by the Fed, to save HCM. And who were the principal beneficiaries of the rescue. Yes, you guessed it right. It was the very fellows who had so recklessly advanced the funds that permitted HCM to build the huge leverage in the first place.

"I was opposed to it then and I still consider that it was ill advised," Soros said emphatically. "The danger to the financial system was blown out of all proportion. They were merely saving one of their own and the ignoble action was window dressed to show they were acting for the common good."

Then looking directly at Alexandra he went on, "How can the United States advise Japan and Venezuela and Korea and the other emerging market countries to allow their financial institutions to go into insolvency when the Fed is orchestrating precisely the kind of bail out that we are advising these countries against? We just do not have any credibility. It also reeks of hypocrisy and a double standard. When a select few are spared the ravages of the market you send the wrong message that says: 'Guys if your big bets work out you win. And if they go awry we'll rescue you.' All in the name of saving the financial system."

He paused for a few seconds to have a drink of water and then continued. "And by the way while we are on this subject let me say one more thing. The United States has been pressing developing nations to privatize their industries and public sector institutions. Yet we have the largest state-run educational system in the world. It's a mess. It's time that the United States followed its own advice for a change."

The next question also related to HCM. It was from a Swiss private banker.

"Prior to its rescue HCM approached you. Can you tell us why your organization turned down the request?"

Soros rejection of the bid was reported in the press at the time but the reasons for his negative response had never been revealed.

"For two reasons," Soros replied. "First in my view HCM was not really a hedge fund. It was more like the proprietary trading desk at Morgan Chase, Am Bank, Salomon, Merrill or Goldman. Its leverage was just like the leverage of these institutions ranging between twenty five to thirty five times the equity base. Most hedge funds have modest leverage, which rarely exceeds five times their investor funds base. I was not interested in acquiring a proprietary trading shop."

"Secondly there was too much of the rocket scientist superstar stuff that blind-sighted both the investors and the lenders. Now I don't have anything against legends." He paused for effect. Snickers were heard among the audience. "I understand that I too have a reputation of sorts." He paused once again as the audience laughed appreciatively. "That's why so many of you invest in my funds." There was some more laughter. "But in the case of HCM I believe it had gone to their heads. They became too smug, too arrogant. Besides I didn't need all those PhD's and Nobel Prize winners. They were in the wrong business. Their talents are needed by our universities."

This provoked some more laughter from the audience.

The final question was from a wealthy investor.

"Tell us what you think of the U.S. stock market?"

"I think it's very over-priced. The banks are over burdened by poor loans. Corporate defaults are at their highest level in years and consumers have borrowed more than ever before. We're living on borrowed time. Something's got to give. It can't go on forever."

He smiled and went on. "But then I've been saying this

for four years. And look what's happened to the performance of our funds."

Again the audience laughed.

Alexandra returned to her suite on the fourth floor of the hotel shortly after five o'clock. Jack Carver was sitting on the couch. He got up and went over to her. They kissed in the living room. She parted her lips and he pushed his tongue into her mouth. The kissing became more intense. She was very excited and could feel his erection. They quickly undressed and went into the bedroom. This was the first time they were having sex with each other. She noticed that his organ was small but thick. She lay down on her back and spread her legs. He got up on top of her. "Fuck me now," she whispered breathlessly. He entered and came almost immediately on the first thrust before she could reach her climax.

"I'm sorry. I just couldn't wait."

"It's all right," she said.

"I promise it will be better next time."

Five minutes later he went to the mini bar and brought back two gin tonics.

They lay on the bed drinking.

"So how was the conference?" Carver asked.

"Actually it was quite interesting. Soros was in top form. And I met a number of hedge fund managers as well as investors. A couple of Am Bank's private bankers were also there."

He turned on his side and kissed her lightly.

"By the way we're having cocktails and dinner with the Am Bank executives and some of their wealthy clients at seven. The bank car will pick us up."

"Are you sure I should come?"

"Absolutely, darling. I've told them you're a wealthy investor attending the conference. And you're investing five million in the hedge fund."

"In that case you better tell me something about these funds. I have no idea what they are."

She got up from the bed and talked as she dressed for the evening.

"Hedge funds have been in existence since the late 1940's. In their original form these private investment partnerships specialized in what is known as relative value or market neutral investment techniques."

"What is that?"

"All that means is that by buying some securities and selling others short, they "hedged" their bets and hoped to come out ahead whether the market went up or down."

"Okay. I understand that. Give me the details. How they are organized and what do they invest in?" Carver asked.

"All right. Since then much has changed in the character and composition of these funds," Alexandra replied. "As they are not registered in the United States, they are outside the regulatory jurisdiction of the Securities and Exchange Commission and are therefore not allowed to advertise or sell to the general public. Typically they are either limited liability corporations or limited partnerships and are usually incorporated offshore in places like Curaçao, the Cayman Islands, Bahamas, Bermuda and other similar island paradises. The investment manager is the general partner and each fund can, under the latest SEC regulations have up to 500 American investors who are limited partners provided they have assets of at least five million dollars."

"What about foreign nationals?" Carver wanted to know.

"There are no limits on the number of foreign non-U.S. tax-paying investors."

"So in a way the hedge funds are the mutual funds of the rich."

"Yes. They're not legally structured like mutual funds but the analogy is quite correct," she said with an affectionate smile.

"I'm familiar with mutual funds," he said. "Are there also different types of hedge funds?"

"Absolutely. Like mutual funds, hedge funds also come in different shapes and sizes and invest in a wide array of products and markets. Some specialize in U.S. equities, some in mortgages and fixed income securities, others invest in emerging market stocks, in health care or technology companies. The list is long enough to suit the needs of all investors. The offering memorandum of each fund describes the activities it can engage in. It describes the securities it can deal in–equities or fixed income or both, the extent of leverage the fund can employ, the use of derivatives and foreign currencies and a wide range of specific activities that the partnership can engage in."

"I see you mention leverage. That certainly differentiates them from mutual funds."

"You're catching on rapidly." Alexandra smiled and then took a long sip of her drink.

As she combed her hair, she continued, "Hedge funds are also different from mutual funds in their fee structure. In fact the only item common to all the various types of hedge funds is their fee structure. Usually they charge a one percent annual management fee and twenty percent of the gains as a performance fee. The largest hedge funds, like Quantum and Xenon, are macro funds that can invest in any currency, commodity or other financial instrument globally. Most hedge funds, however, are small shops managing less than fifty million dollars."

Carver smiled. "You said hedge funds have been there for a long time. Were they always this important or notorious?"

"Actually they really came into the public limelight in 1992 when George Soros made a billion dollars speculating against sterling and Louis Marcus made even more," Alexandra informed him. "So the money poured into the funds in 1993 and their assets more than doubled. Unfortunately

361

the timing was bad. The market was caught by surprise when the Federal Reserve unexpectedly raised interest rates in early 1994."

"What happened?" Carver was intrigued.

"The impact of the Fed's action was immediate. Rising rates decimated proprietary traders and money managers alike. I remember getting caught on the wrong side at B&P. It destroyed my performance numbers for several years. The gallant band of modern day buccaneers, I mean the hedge fund managers, didn't escape from the Fed's move either. Some old timers like Michael Steinhardt got out of the business. So did Odyssey Partners run by the legendary Leon Levy. Many others suffered big losses–not just the investors but also the hedge fund operators who, unlike mutual fund managers, invariably invest a substantial part of their own capital in the fund. It was rumored that George Soros' Quantum Funds lost six hundred million dollars, Omega Advisors were right behind with a five hundred million dollar deficit."

"Are you investing in the Falcon Fund?"

"Of course," Alexandra replied.

"Presumably a lot of money was withdrawn from the hedge funds after the 1994 fiasco?"

"Why do you assume that?" Alexandra asked Carver. "Do you know that throughout the bull market of the nineties the overwhelming majority of mutual funds under performed the market? Yet this did not, for some perverse reason, discourage the average middle class investor from pouring further billions into these actively managed but poorly performing mutual funds. But," she paused to have another sip of her drink. "The situation was very different in the case of hedge funds in the two years following 1994 when most of them limped behind the S&P 500 index. They lost billions of dollars in withdrawals. Why do you think this happened?"

"Don't make it difficult for me. I'm just a corporate lawyer."

She laughed. "Because my dear the wealthy are much

smarter than the average John Doe. That's why they're wealthier."

Jack finished his drink. "I'm fascinated by all this. What happened next?"

"All this changed abruptly in 1997 when wealthy investors again poured billions into the hedge funds. By now what had once been the exclusive preserve of the international moneyed class had been discovered by institutions that wanted to be part of the action. So foundations, endowments, colleges and universities rushed to become major hedge fund investors."

"And then we had the blow ups in the emerging markets. I remember reading that in the papers."

"That's right," Alexandra said. "Once again the timing turned out to be wrong. In late 1997 a large number of the funds were severely squeezed, many out of existence, as the crash of the Asian currencies and securities markets circumnavigated the globe. But it was not until the autumn of 1998 that the term hedge fund suddenly became a dirty word. In the American press at least. Soros lost two billion dollars in the Russian debt default. Not to be out done Julian Robertson's Tiger Group soon followed. It took a two billion dollar blood bath betting against the Japanese yen. But the world record for losses was the achievement of another brilliant group. That honor belonged to HCM, which managed to lose, despite its PhD's and Nobel laureates, four and a half billion dollars in the record time of a month."

"That's absolutely phenomenal."

This was a situation made in heaven for journalists who fanned the public frenzy with almost daily stories of big losses and the supposed speculative misdeeds of hedge funds who were depicted as the chief villains of the financial world. The papers ignored the six and a half trillion dollars mutual funds or the four and a half trillion dollars pension funds that were engaged in the same type of speculative investments in the fixed income and equity markets. Compared with them hedge funds, with just four hundred and eighty billion dollars, paled into insignificance. But the journalists didn't care for the facts. Fiction made better reading.

"Yes and the newspapers had a field day but their dire forecast turned out to be incorrect." Alexandra applied her lipstick and then went on. "Notwithstanding the hype and the bad publicity, hedge funds continued to thrive because wealthy investors needed to diversify their investments. They just moved their funds from poorly performing hedge funds to other hedge funds. There was simply nowhere else to go even when the hedge funds under performed the broad market in 2002. That year their returns averaged 14% compared with 20% for the Dow. The equity mutual funds did worse with returns of only 12%."

Just then the telephone rang. It was the front desk.

"Your car is here."

"Thank you. I'll be down in a minute."

She picked up her handbag and went down. Carver followed her five minutes later.

Louis Marcus took Lufthansa flight 4633 from terminal one at Heathrow airport at 9:15 A.M. on the same Friday. He was traveling light without any baggage, as he intended to return home later that evening. He had gone directly to the airport from his office on Queen Victoria Street, a few blocks away from those twin pillars of the British financial world: the Bank of England and the Stock Exchange. The traffic in London on this particular day was very heavy due to a cricket match that was being played at Lords and he had almost missed the flight.

Marcus was considered a powerful man in international financial circles. He was the bearer of one of the most famous names in the glamorous and highly secretive world of hedge funds, outshining even George Soros, Julian Robertson and Sterling Bridges. His record was better than theirs–in fact it was even better than that of Warren Buffet that other highly regarded guru of the investment world–and knowledgeable people considered him to be the world's greatest money manager. Someone had calculated that a hundred thousand dollars invested in his fund in 1970 would be worth one hundred and eighty five million dollars by 2000. He had first come into the public limelight in 1992 when he had made two billion dollars speculating against sterling. In 1994 Marcus had made another killing first by being on the right side when the Federal Reserve unexpectedly raised interest rates and then in Deutsche mark/dollar currency trading.

What was Louis Marcus doing on this flight heading for Frankfurt? A newspaper reporter would probably have connected it with his philanthropic activities in Eastern Europe. Marcus nowadays spent considerable time traveling on work relating to his charitable trusts. After all he gave away millions each year from his huge personal fortune.

But the reason for this trip was different. That big bet in 1992 had made Marcus a legend in the financial world. Myths had grown around him. People began to think that he was infallible. It had become a self-fulfilling fallacy. Until 1997. That year changed everything. He got caught in the East Asian financial upheaval. After that he recovered for a while but the past three years had been terrible and he longed to forget this period and put it behind him. Two billion dollars had rushed out of his twenty five billion dollar Xenon Fund in 2001. In 2002 and 2003 total withdrawals had gone up to six billion. The annual return last year was just a lousy three percent.

During the past eight months the seventeen billion dollar fund had picked up and out performed the market. Just when it looked like he had turned the corner, bad luck struck once again and the fund was clobbered, losing twenty percent of its value over a rotten five-day period, as a result of a bet against the yen that soured in August.

What mattered to Louis Marcus at this stage of his career was not money. It was his reputation that was at stake.

Now as he sat in the first class section, drinking a vodka martini, he reflected on the events of the previous week. The losses sustained by the fund worried him deeply. Maybe he was losing his touch. He knew he could not afford to have another down year. It would forever dim the luster of his name. He pondered how he could redress the problem. Unfortunately no solution seemed to be in sight. It was then that the telephone call had come. So he was heading for a lunch appointment in Frankfurt.

The memory of that moment re-ignited the old concerns. He ordered another vodka martini.

CHAPTER 32

In his office high up on the thirtieth floor of the Deutsche Bank building on Taunus-Gallus Strasse in Frankfurt's business district, the Spokesman of the Board of Managing Directors of the world's largest bank was having a bad day. It had started off well enough with an early morning meeting with the chairman of Daimler-Chrysler, Germany's largest industrial corporation. This was followed by an equally satisfactory lunch with the chief executive of Korea's Hyundai Corporation.

It was in the afternoon that the trouble had started.

Shortly after lunch Doktor Walter Dietrich received a transatlantic telephone call from a fellow chairman and banker. The conversation was brief. Henry Fielding, the soon to retire, chairman of American Banking Corporation brusquely rejected Deutsche Bank's secret amorous overture for a marriage between the two banks.

Just as the Herr Doktor was recovering from this blow, he received another transatlantic telephone call. This time it was from Rolf von Ackermann the head of all of Deutsche Bank's North American operations. He too was calling from New York.

3194-ISLA

"Walter. It's Rolf. Sorry to bother you . . ."

"Yes, Rolf what is it?" Dietrich interrupted him.

"I'm afraid I have a bit of bad news."

"Well, what is it?" von Ackermann detected the impatience in the chairman's voice.

There was a brief silence before von Ackermann came back on the line.

"I just found out that we have suffered heavy trading losses in our derivatives portfolio," he said defensively.

"Not again. We should get rid of the damned business."

Back in 1994 the derivatives group, which was the most profitable unit of Bankers Trust, had brought about the troubles that finally doomed that bank. In between there were a number of other incidents that had contributed to the demise, including Frank Newman's spendthrift ways and aloof demeanor. But it was the reports of the cavalier attitude of the derivatives traders and salesmen toward their customers and the lying and cheating of clients that began the unraveling. And now even Deutsche Bank was having difficulty controlling the business.

Von Ackermann deciding that wisdom dictated silence said nothing.

"What's the amount?" the chairman then asked, breaking the silence.

"It's two hundred and fifty million dollars," von Ackerman replied a little hesitantly.

"Mein Gott," Dietrich was angry. "I thought we had the right risk control systems in place now. What happened?"

"We do. These losses are within the limits assigned to the derivatives group. They think this is a temporary blip and the situation will correct itself in the coming weeks."

"Are they certain this will be the case?" Dietrich asked.

"They're very confident but they obviously can't guarantee a satisfactory outcome." Von Ackermann replied, hoping this would satisfy his superior.

368

"I have a number of other problems to contend with," Dietrich was trying to minimize any further damage. "Please reduce the traders' limits immediately to a hundred million dollars. And I don't expect any additional losses down the road."

Again there was a temporary silence on the phone.

"Ackermann. Are you still there?"

"Yes Walter. Okay, I will do as you say. But the traders won't like it."

"That's your problem. Solve it." Dietrich stared at his desk diary. It was the nineteenth of September. He continued in a firm voice. "Rolf, the third quarter ends in eleven days. Do you think the losses can be reversed by then? We simply cannot announce poor quarterly results again. The analysts will jump all over us."

"We'll try our best," the man in North America assured the chairman.

"Do that Ackermann."

The implied warning came through loud and clear. Rolf von Ackermann sensed that his career was on the line.

An hour later, Dr. Walter Dietrich sat behind his massive desk reviewing a "for your eyes only" preliminary flash report on the bank's third quarter results with Thomas Fischer, the chief financial officer. A scowl slowly spread over his face as he examined the computer printout.

"These numbers are awful."

"That's right," said the CFO.

"And they're likely to get worse. The New York office has a trading loss of two hundred and fifty million dollars." Dietrich informed Fischer who let out a low whistle.

"When did this happen?"

"I got a call from von Ackermann an hour ago."

Dietrich looked at the chief financial officer pleadingly but Fischer shook his head.

"Unfortunately Walter, we no longer have access to the special reserves."

Was there any thing else? Yes there was one other possibility. Since the time of Bismarck, the German capitalist system was based on a tightly linked association between banks and industrial corporations. At its heart was a structure of interlocking corporate ownership. German banks, historically, took equity stakes in German industries. Deutsche Bank had played a major role in German industrial development. Its destiny had been intertwined with that of Germany from the very beginning. Established in 1870, the same year a united Imperial Germany came into being at the Hall of Mirrors at Versailles, the bank had been the principal financial power behind the creation and development of the German electrical engineering industry. Over the years it had built up a massive equity portfolio carried at original book value on its balance sheet. So the scope for "milking" this under-priced portfolio was immense.

But unfortunately, here too, there was a problem. This avenue was no longer available. In a moment of reforming zeal, Dietrich had spun off the equity portfolio to the shareholders back in 1998.

"What about the investment portfolio?" Dietrich inquired.

"Yes. That was a possibility."

Dietrich nodded. "Perhaps we can get some income from the venture capital and private equity portfolios at Bankers Trust. Morgan Chase and Citigroup have been dipping into this source for years to improve their quarterly numbers."

"I'll speak to von Ackermann," Fischer replied.

Deutsche Bank had had a checkered existence since its foundation in 1870. By 1914 it had become the world's largest bank. In the years between the two world wars it was active in financing the industrial expansion of Germany. The Allied Occupying Forces, recognizing the crucial role the bank played in the German financial market, broke it into ten separate entities in 1947 and forbade the use of the Deutsche Bank name. Hermann Abs, perhaps the most brilliant of the

Spokesmen of the Board in the bank's history, regrouped the broken pieces after the establishment of the Federal Republic in 1951. In 1957 it had re-emerged as Deutsche Bank once again. And now forty-seven years later it was once more the largest bank in the world.

The two Germans examined the current situation that the bank found itself in.

"I'm afraid we're getting boxed in on all sides," Dietrich said.

"You're right. We have to take forceful action to correct this state of affairs," Fischer replied. The forty-five-year-old chief financial officer was a Board member and a close ally of the chairman.

"If only we hadn't been so complacent in the 1980's," Dietrich sighed.

"Yes. But now the competition is horrendous and no relief is in sight," Fischer said philosophically. "If only something could be done with all these state-owned cooperative and savings banks."

He was referring to the so-called regional Landesbanken and Sparkassen whose history went back even further than that of Deutsche Bank. Germany, as everyone knew, was over banked and over branched. There were more than three thousand banks in the country with twice as many branches per citizen compared with the United States.

"I don't think we can hope for much on that front in the near future," Dietrich responded. "But we must prepare ourselves for the inevitable changes that will occur in our corporate business."

The problem facing banks in much of the Western world were very similar though the phenomenon was most advanced in the United States. Technology was making the intermediary role of banks increasingly irrelevant. Their traditional business–accepting deposits and making loans–was in decline and had been in decline for over a quarter century.

371

The rise of the capital markets, particularly in the United States, had completely displaced the banks of that country in the corporate lending business except for companies with low quality credit. Big corporations such as IBM, Ford, General Motors, Microsoft, Intel and others directly accessed investors for their borrowing needs. Bank loans in America now accounted for only twenty percent of financial assets. In Germany the figure was still around seventy percent but the percentage share was declining steadily. It was astonishing but mutual fund assets in the United States now exceeded the total assets of all American banks put together. It was only a question of time before this happened in Europe as well.

"How do we do that?" Fischer asked.

"By continuing to build our investment banking capabilities worldwide but particularly in Europe and the United States," Dietrich observed.

"Walter a friend of mine at McKinsey recently pointed out that the problems that American and European banks face are essentially the same and so they are trying to meet the challenge in similar ways."

"Yes, But the results have been very different," the chairman interjected.

In America, banks attempted to race out of their difficulties in two ways: bank mergers and entry into new lines of business. Through repeated mergers and drastic staff reductions both money center and regional banks had succeeded in cutting their costs significantly. This provided short-term benefits but did not solve the long-term problem. The bank's entry into new businesses, such as investment banking and asset management, had as yet not paid off.

"How's that?" Fischer asked.

"Unlike the Americans, our situation is very different," Dietrich pointed out. "The unions and the existing labor laws prevent us and the French from shutting down branches or sharply trimming staff. Then there is the problem of our interlocking ownership structure that makes mergers and consolidations very difficult."

This failure to cut costs had eroded profitability. Costs gobbled up seventy percent of German bank revenues. The comparable number for American banks was only fifty eight percent!

With profits declining in their home markets and their efforts to merge blocked, German banks began to look elsewhere to go around their predicament. The destruction of the Berlin Wall and the subsequent reunification of Germany had presented the first big opportunity. German banks had collectively lent over thirty billion to Russia. Then the collapse of communism opened up their back yard. Eastern Europe became an important customer. Another thirty billion or thereabouts in loans. After that came East Asia. It was too good an opportunity to miss. American and European financial institutions rushed in to invest in the booming economies of Thailand, Indonesia, South Korea, the Philippines, Hong Kong, Singapore and Malaysia. The German banks with fifty billion dollars in loans had outstripped everyone including even the Americans.

For a while these moves looked very promising. As the economies of these countries grew rapidly in the early and mid nineties, the banks' revenues also surged. The unraveling had been both unexpected and sudden. The economic collapse of the Asian economies followed by the default of Russia in 1998 had turned good money into worthless paper. That put more pressure on earnings.

So Deutsche Bank had poor earnings and an armful of bad loans on its books. But Dr. Dietrich was a first-class thinker and he quickly came up with several new ideas.

"In the mid-nineties I tried to extend our investment banking initiative to the United States," the chairman reminded his colleague.

Fischer nodded. He knew all the details. The Board had

373

discussed the matter. America had the largest financial market in the world and Deutsche as a global financial intermediary had to penetrate that market. Herr Doktor's strategy had been audacious in its simplicity. People, he reasoned, were the primary assets of investment banks. So Deutsche Bank, he decided, would target the brightest and the best at various American investment houses and make them offers they simply couldn't refuse. So he did. The investment banks screamed. But they could do little. After all it's a free market and you either paid up or shut up. The Wall Street Journal had carried a couple of articles on this brilliant maneuver. For a while it appeared that the strategy might work. But in the end it came to nothing and a lot of money went down the drain.

"Walter, I still believe you were not that far off on that original idea of yours," Fischer said admiringly. "The investment banking business has remained a kind of oligopoly in America. Many firms have tried but very few have succeeded in getting into the inner sanctum. GE tried with Kidder Peabody. Then there was E.F Hutton. PaineWebber, Shearson and so many of the American banks have also made the attempt but only Morgan Chase has had any success. None of the European banks have made it either, except for Credit Suisse. We came close."

"Yes, Thomas," Dietrich smiled. "As the bible says, 'Many are called, but only a few are chosen.'"

At the same time as he was launching the investment banking initiative, Dietrich also attempted some cross-border acquisitions in Europe. With the European Economic Community proceeding toward a common currency, the move made a lot of sense. He had quickly zeroed in on Société Générale and Crédit Lyonnais. But such thinking was far too advanced for the Europeans. The French government quickly blocked the move. These were French national treasures that could not be in the hands of crass foreigners even though, in this case, the crass foreigners were close economic and political allies of France.

So in 1998 Deutsche Bank was stymied on all fronts. But Dr. Dietrich was not to be counted out. He was a resourceful fellow like a boxer who gets up repeatedly at the count of eight after being knocked down. If the Europeans wouldn't let him acquire banks he would go to that bastion of the free enterprise system. Deutsche had been in the United States for decades but its operations were relatively small. It now made a bold move to acquire a major investment bank.

Morgan was its first choice; Rolf Von Ackermann held confidential discussions with senior Morgan officials. The talks progressed. Both sides were interested. Then the negotiations began to make rapid progress. Only one issue remained to be resolved. The press got wind of the discussions. Word leaked out to the market. Morgan's stock price shot up as arbitrageurs bought large amounts of its stocks. Then suddenly the negotiations collapsed. The sides were too far apart on the composition of senior management of the new entity.

So Deutsche switched its attention to what was available. It turned out to be Bankers Trust, a second-tier institution that was reeling from huge trading losses in emerging market debt. The result of the negotiations was never in doubt once Frank Newman, the former Chairman of Bankers Trust, under whose wise leadership the bank had come close to bankruptcy, had secured a fifty five million dollar payment for himself under a five-year employment contract!

The transaction was approved by the regulators and consummated in early 1999. Financial analysts were, however, aghast at the move. And they turned out to be right. Bankers Trust, a minor player in the investment banking world, did nothing for Deutsche Bank's penetration of the American market. As a consequence investors pummeled its share price down.

3194-ISLA

In March 2000, Deutsche made its most daring strategic bet. It agreed to a merger with the stumbling Dresdner Bank, Germany's third largest, and pulled out of the retail banking business. In a huge gamble it bet its future on investment banking, a field in which its success had been modest at best. The merger fell through in early April as a result of management egos but Deutsche continued with the agreed upon policy.

Dietrich pushed this strategy with another bold move. He now informed Fischer of the results of this effort.

"Henry Fielding of American Banking Corporation phoned me this morning."

"And?"

"He did not see any benefits to either institution from a merger," Dietrich reported.

"I thought there were many advantages for both our banks," Fischer responded.

"Not according to Fielding. He said we added nothing to their corporate or consumer businesses and both of us were second rate in investment banking. The only strength we brought to them was in asset management. It was not sufficient to warrant a change in that bank's status."

Dietrich's move was not entirely bereft of logic. After all, Fielding was close to retirement. His ego would not stand in the way as it often does in mergers. Besides the transaction would add millions to his net worth. Dietrich reasoned that, like most heads of major American banks, Fielding owned a large amount of options on Am Bank shares that would become even more valuable if the merger talks succeeded. But Fielding had turned it down flat.

"Thomas, I have a grand scheme in mind that will catapult us to the very top," Dietrich confided to his ally. "But we have to fix our earnings problem. Only with improved earnings can our stock price go up. And we need to have a real improvement in our stock price to make this work."

"What do you have in mind?" Fischer asked.

"Between you and me, we'll go after Merrill."

His secretary buzzed him fifteen minutes after the chief financial officer left the office. She sounded a bit flushed. Prince Tarik was on the line. Dietrich picked up the receiver immediately.

"Prince Tarik. It's Walter Dietrich."

"Dr. Dietrich, I just had a conversation with Herr Schroeder."

"Yes."

"I advised the Chancellor that we now have all the approvals for our project. The formal announcement will be made after the next OPEC meeting."

"When is that?" Dietrich asked.

"On October 18. And by the way Dr. Dietrich until then it is imperative that strict secrecy be maintained."

"We understand completely."

"The plan will have maximum impact if it comes as a surprise. All of us stand to benefit. The oil producers, Germany, France and the banks."

"You can count on us," Dr. Dietrich assured the prince.

"One more thing," Tarik said, "we would like to have press announcements from Paris and Frankfurt on the credit facility the next morning following the OPEC news conference. Please coordinate this with Michael Townsend. I believe the two of you have met. He'll be in touch with you."

"Yes, we have. I look forward to hearing from him. May I ask if the euro-pricing proposal has also been approved?"

"Yes. In our view it's a package deal," the prince informed him. Then he asked, "Is your bank planning to take advantage of this privileged information?"

"We would certainly like to."

"I have no problem with that provided it is done very discreetly."

3194-ISLA

"I assure you that we will be extremely careful in our dealings," Dietrich assured the Saudi.

"Dr. Dietrich, we're hoping to see some improvement in your share price," Tarik said in a voice that left no doubt of the prince's concern in the mind of the bank's chairman. "It's languished for far too long."

"I assure you, we are working on it," Dietrich replied. Then he went on, "Prince Tarik if I may. For the sake of preserving confidentiality I would prefer not to check with my own people. I wonder if you could recommend a hedge fund manager?"

"Do you know Louis Marcus?"

"I've met him once. Very briefly."

"He's your man."

And with that the line went dead.

The hedge fund idea had been in his mind for a while. He had been thinking about it since the day they arranged the consortium financing. Ten minutes later he made two telephone calls. The first was to Herr Doktor Buchen at HypoVereinsbank. That conversation lasted fifteen minutes. The two chairmen agreed to pool their resources to take advantage of the opportunity that now presented itself.

The second telephone call was to Louis Marcus in London.

Louis Marcus arrived at Dr. Walter Dietrich's office shortly before 1:00 P.M. on the same Friday.

The two men talked over lunch in the private dining room next to the chairman's office. A large mahogany door connected the two rooms.

"Tell me, Mr. Marcus how is the hedge fund business these days?" Dr. Dietrich asked. He had been fully briefed by the Board member responsible for the private banking division. To muddy the water, the Board member had checked out Marcus with the head of Deutsche Bank's Swiss subsidiary in Geneva.

"Call me Louis, please, if you don't mind. Now to answer your question. The hedge fund business is doing very well. I wish I could say the same for my funds," Marcus responded without any equivocation.

"Oh! Are you having problems?" Dietrich looked quite surprised.

"Yes. Unfortunately we're experiencing some performance problems." He smiled ruefully. "It happens to all of us once in a while."

"I understand. What about your principal competitors? How are they faring?" the banker asked.

"Fortunately for us, all the big macro funds are in the same position. That includes Soros, Louis Bacon and the Omega Fund and some of the other big funds. It's the sort of losses that made Julian call it a day."

Marcus was referring to Tiger Management. Julian Robertson, one of the legendary investors of all times had closed his fund in March 2000 after twenty years in the business. At that point the fund, which at its height in 1998 had 22 billion under management, was down to six billion. Through its twenty year existence investors had earned a 26% compounded annual return. But bad bets in two successive years had done him in. His value investment style was not suited for the technology-crazed market. In an interview he said the market was crazy and he could take it no longer. Neither could his customers who had brought him to his knees by their fund withdrawals.

"Any particular reasons for the poor performance?" Dietrich inquired. He wondered if Marcus would tell him that his problems had gone on for three years.

"For thirty years my funds performed phenomenally well. The compounded annual return through 2000 was over twenty eight percent. Then in 2001 we hit a bad patch, and it has continued ever since. Just some incredibly bad calls. Mostly in foreign currencies but we also started late on the tech stocks

379

that are now driving the market. And as the demise of Tiger Management has shown, in this market neither smarts nor a great track record is enough."

The chairman of Deutsche Bank liked the man. He was honest and direct and made no attempt to hide the difficulties he had run into.

"How much money do you have in the funds now?"

"At its height we had twenty five billion in the five funds. Since then we have had some outflows."

"I have heard of an eight billion number." Dietrich decided to let the money manager know that he was well informed on the magnitude of the fund's outflows.

"I believe that is close to the mark."

"I also hear that this month you have experienced some fairly big losses?" Dietrich noticed the surprise that registered on Marcus's face at the mention of the losses.

"Where did you hear that?" the hedge fund manager asked. The information was not public. Perhaps the man was just bluffing.

"We have our sources," the bank chairman replied affably. "We actually did many of the currency trades with your fund and figured that you were on the losing side. But on a more positive note we may have a solution to your performance problems."

"What would that be?" Marcus asked, wondering what the banker had up his sleeve.

"Important inside information that no one else has."

"And why have you chosen us to share the information?" Marcus was wary.

"You come to us with very high recommendations from someone we have very great confidence in," the banker replied.

"And what is this confidential information that you have," Marcus asked in a tone that showed his skepticism.

Dietrich excused himself, got up and went to his office.

He returned with two folders and handed the green colored one to the hedge fund manager.

Marcus read the document in the next ten minutes. His face remained impassive.

"What makes you believe that this effort will succeed? It's been tried before and only worked for a brief period from the middle of last year till March of this year."

Dietrich now handed him the tan-colored folder. It contained the oil credit facility credit agreement. The hedge fund manager quickly read the material.

The banker spent the next half hour explaining the details. Yes, the French and German governments supported the plan. Their interest was in promoting the euro as a reserve currency. That would benefit Europe considerably. He explained some of the other reasons that made the Deutsche Bank confident of the plan's success, particularly the key role played by Prince Tarik. All the countries had now approved the plan. There was one other thing that made the situation very different. New leaders, Dietrich pointed out, had taken over in Venezuela, Mexico and Russia. Saudi Arabia's oil policy was now in the hands of a very astute businessman. Marcus knew Tarik well. It all sounded very plausible, very convincing.

"To show you our complete confidence in the plan," Dr. Dietrich went on, "we're prepared to put our money where our mouth is, as you Americans like to say."

"That's always a very persuasive argument," Marcus smiled. "What number did you have in mind?"

"Would three billion dollars help?"

The conversation lasted another forty-five minutes, some of it taking place in the back seat of Doktor Dietrich's Mercedes 600 SEL as they drove to the airport. By five thirty that evening Louis Marcus sat drinking another vodka martini on the Lufthansa flight heading back to London.

3194-ISLA

CHAPTER 33

At four o'clock on Monday, September 20, the two men wearing dark blue suits walked into the third-floor suite at the Ritz Hotel in Paris. A broadly smiling Michael Townsend, who had accompanied the executives from the foyer, introduced them to Tarik. They shook hands and the prince waived in the direction of the seating area near the window that offered a panoramic view of the Place Vendome. As the two sat down on the gray couch they saw the tall column with the statue of Napoleon in the center of the square, directly in front of the window.

Tarik noticed that the two men were a study in contrasts. George Mason, the chairman of Exxon Mobil, bore a striking resemblance to Senator Lott, the Republican leader in the Senate. A tall, heavyset man who wore big metal frame glasses, and whose fleshy round face was topped by a mass of meticulously combed dark brown hair, parted on the right. His colleague, Lee Perkins, the chief executive of Texaco, was a much shorter man with a hooked nose that resembled the beak of an eagle and a large egg shaped head bereft of any hair.

"Gentlemen, what may I offer you to drink?" Townsend asked.

Mason checked his watch and then asked for a Scotch.
"I'll have the same," Perkins replied.
Tarik smiled. "Thanks, but I already have a drink."
Townsend put the two glasses of Chivas in front of the
men, then going back to the bar he returned with another
Scotch and parked himself next to Tarik. The two American
businessmen sat opposite them.
"I understand you are flying back to Saudi Arabia later
tonight," Mason began.
"Yes. Unfortunately I received an urgent summons from
King Fahd earlier today."
"Under the circumstances," Townsend smiled, "I suggest
we get down to business immediately."
There was a murmur of assent.
Above it Tarik asked Mason, "George, your company
operates around the world so we're naturally interested in
hearing your views on the global economic situation."
Exxon Mobil was the largest corporation in the world. In
2003 its revenues totaled one hundred and sixty six billion
dollars. That number exceeded the gross domestic product
of every country in the Middle East. In fact, it put the company in the list of the top twenty-five countries in terms of
GDP. Exxon employed ninety thousand people and operated
refineries in fifty countries.
"The American economy is chugging along and the rest
of the world is picking is up speed," Mason began.
He took a sip of the Scotch and went on, "Last year the
U.S. economy grew by three percent but this year we expect
a three and a half percent increase. Europe is expanding but
only at around three percent. That's because Germany and
France are experiencing much slower growth. The Japanese
economy is finally moving in the right direction and, of course,
we are witnessing a remarkable turnaround in East Asia, which
is booming along at a five percent clip this year. In sharp

383

contrast, the economies of most of the oil producing countries are contracting for the second consecutive year."

"I agree with George's assessment," Perkins added.

"What's your forecast for world oil demand?"

"Last year it was eighty three million barrels per day. This year we'll end with eighty five million barrels. Our number for next year is eighty seven million. Global demand for oil is growing at a stronger than expected pace," Mason replied.

"Your overall assessment is similar to ours," Tarik observed looking at the two chairmen.

"What's the outlook on Exxon's earnings? The stock price is down twenty percent from its high in March?" Townsend asked.

"As you know our earnings are tied to the price of crude. In 2000 we made 14 billion dollars. That was the high point. Since then it's not been good. Last year we made slightly over eleven billion dollars. This year the number will be down to nine billion."

"That's an eighteen percent decline," Townsend said calculating the figure mentally.

Mason nodded.

"Our earnings show a similar trend but the numbers of course are much smaller," the Texaco man said.

"If I understand you correctly, the price of oil affects us all," Tarik said. Then looking steadily at the two men he continued, "So the question now is: what do we do about it?"

"I believe cooperation is in our mutual interest," the Exxon Mobil chairman intoned smoothly as his colleague nodded his head in agreement.

"Yes. We agree and that is why we are taking you into our confidence," Tarik said. "Gentlemen, in our view the situation is critical." He paused to take a long sip of the iced tea and then added, "We have, therefore, decided to break the impasses one way or the other."

The two oilmen drank their Scotch and listened attentively.

Tarik went on, "We have carefully examined the option of revving up our production to full throttle and flooding the market."

He noticed the flicker of concern on the faces of the two men sitting opposite him at the mention of lower prices. Talk of flooding the market made the oil executives think of 1986. That year Sheikh Yamani, then the Saudi oil minister, had done just that without any warning and oil prices had collapsed to barrel scraping lows. It had hurt the oil companies badly. Fortunately the Saudis weren't prepared for the loss of revenues either and the experiment was quickly terminated.

"In the spirit of Christian charity we decided not to pursue that strategy." Tarik grinned. "It's very damaging for many oil producers, not to mention our allies, the oil companies." His smile included the two men and by inference their companies.

They breathed an audible sigh of relief.

"Thank God. That's not what we had in mind. The last thing we need right now is lower oil prices," Perkins opined.

The expression on Mason's face reminded Tarik of that old truism, 'A picture is worth a thousand words.' The chairman of Exxon Mobil did not utter a word. He did not have to. The look on his face conveyed his feelings perfectly.

"An oil price rise would benefit all of us. The question is how do we achieve it?" Mason noted reflectively.

"We have a solution," Tarik replied. "We have come up with a plan to cut production."

"And what makes you think it will work this time?" Mason asked skeptically.

"For two reasons," the Saudi replied. "First the plan is grounded in a new quota system that takes away much of the incentive to cheat."

Tarik then turned to Townsend. "Michael, please give our friends the plan details, while I refresh their drinks."

He got up, went to the bar at the other end of the room and returned with three Scotches that he handed to the men.

———

385

Townsend explained the plan while Tarik was busy with the drinks. He mentioned the oil credit facility, the euro pricing that the French and Germans were hoping would jump start their economies, the smaller group of oil producers that were involved in the plan and the new oil monitoring council.

"What's your number for the reduction in production?" Mason asked.

"We're shooting for a ten percent cut," Tarik replied.

"In OPEC's production?" the Exxon chairman inquired.

"No in total world production."

"But that's over eight million barrels. It's almost double the five million figure of 1998-1999," Perkins gasped in astonishment. His background was in marketing and he had a Masters degree from Wharton Business School.

Mason thought, as he took another sip of the Chivas, that OPEC hadn't sprung a surprise in over twenty years. Maybe they had something up their sleeve this time. Either the man was a dreamer or he had real balls. The dreaming part didn't make sense considering the stories he had heard about his investment acumen and he knew of his immense wealth from the Forbes article. He decided to hear more before making up his mind.

"That's right," Tarik replied. "And we believe it can be done. Saudi Arabia is bearing the brunt of the cuts. We're planning to reduce our production by three and a half million barrel. None of the other seven members of the group have to cut their production by more than a million."

"What price level do you have in mind?" Perkins now asked.

"I'm shooting for a $38 per barrel price. Our economic experts advise that this level will not have a major impact on world economic growth or on inflation. The OECD countries have very low inflation rates right now and both Japan and Europe have plenty of excess economic capacity. Prices at the gas pumps will increase by twenty five or thirty cents but that will not stop American motorists from buying gas."

Mason's mind worked it out immediately. The exact number was not important. It was the level that counted and at that price the earnings number would be the highest in the company's history. Perkins had, almost simultaneously, come to the same conclusion. Apparently in the past fifteen years there had been a tremendous improvement in the intellectual quality of oil executives, which only went to show that given time, anything could change.

"But most manufacturers won't be able to pass off the increased costs to the consumers. Fortunately it won't be a problem in our case," Perkins pointed out.

"That's possible and in that case their profit margins will shrink somewhat. In turn that could conceivably impact the stock market. In my view the market is already substantially over priced so a correction is bound to occur one way or the other. The Fed will pump in liquidity to contain it within reasonable limits. They've done it repeatedly in the past."

"And what's the second reason you mentioned earlier that is special this time round?" Mason asked.

"The timing," Tarik replied confidently. "In life timing is everything and we believe that the time is right for the move. The plan has the strong support of Iran. Our relations with that country have been warm for the past several years and we are now moving to cement this with a formal alliance in the shape of a NATO-type organization. Kuwait and Iraq will be members. In Iraq the conditions have changed dramatically with the emergence of General Rashid. Venezuela now has a new constitution and Chavez is midway in his six-year term as president. In Mexico a populist is in power. For the first time in years the United States has very little influence in these two key Western Hemisphere countries. And there is also a similar nationalist in power in Russia. They are all under tremendous pressure to improve the economic situation in their countries. By sheer coincidence we have enormous leverage at the moment."

"So what do you think?" Townsend asked.

"Well," Mason admitted, "It certainly looks feasible . . ."

"Let there be no mistake about it," Tarik interrupted in a voice that left no doubt of his determination. "This is a battle we intend to win one way or the other."

Mason remembered that in 1979 Saudi Arabia, acting independently, cut its oil production drastically and the price had jumped by thirty six percent. He took a sip of the drink before speaking. "We're with you a hundred percent. Exxon will do whatever is necessary to make the plan work." It made sense to encourage the Saudis to work for a price increase. The man's determination was palpable. He had evidently, in Mason's judgment, thought through the whole strategy very carefully. And if it worked it could only help Exxon Mobil.

"You can count on us too. We'll do everything possible to help," the chairman of Texaco spoke equally forcefully.

"Now I have a proposal to make to you," Tarik said. "Our relationship with your companies goes way back to the past."

"That's right. Exxon has been closely connected with the Kingdom for over fifty years," Mason said. "In 1948 we bought a thirty percent share in the Arabian American Oil Company–ARAMCO. But we've been in the country much longer than that."

"Texaco as you know, discovered oil in the Eastern province in 1935 and we too were partners in ARAMCO. We also have a 50/50 joint venture with Saudi Refining Company. The joint venture refines and distributes oil-related products in the Eastern United States."

"You're referring to Star Enterprise?"

Perkins nodded.

"So how much oil do you buy from us," Tarik asked Mason.

"Right now we're lifting slightly over two and a half million barrels of oil."

"And Texaco?"

"We're buying one and a half million barrels."

"Good. Gentlemen," Tarik smiled. "This is our proposal. We're prepared to sell you crude in these quantities for the next five years at a dollar below the prevailing market price. That's a billion dollars in additional annual income for Exxon and over half a billion for Texaco."

"And what would Saudi Arabia want in return?" Mason inquired.

"We want an up-front payment of a billion and a half dollars."

The money would be the first installment in the fund he was planning to set up for the people of Saudi Arabia. Speculation in the commodities market would in all likelihood double the amount. In present value terms it would be far in excess of the concessions he was making to the two oil companies.

"Is this legal?" Mason asked. His background was in chemical engineering.

"Yes. Unless it can be proven that the three of us met and together planned the whole scheme. That collusion will be impossible to prove in this case. The transaction can be viewed in two ways both of which are perfectly legal. One way to look at it is as an up-front payment for an annuity stream. The other as payment for an option to buy specific quantities of oil at predetermined prices."

"That seems reasonable," Perkins observed. He was knowledgeable about this from the days, earlier in his career, when he had responsibility for worldwide purchases of crude oil and petroleum products.

"And by the way," Tarik assured the two executives, "You can check with your experts. Both your companies will come out way ahead in the transaction."

The two chairmen nodded. They had no doubts on that score. The prince obviously knew what he was talking about.

3194-ISLA

"Is there anything else in your proposal?" Mason asked.

"Yes. We would like to form a joint venture with Exxon and Texaco in Liechtenstein. The company will have five billion dollars in capital and the money is to be used exclusively for purchase of crude oil futures contracts," Tarik replied.

Both Exxon and Texaco operated extensively in the futures markets. There was only one difference this time. They would be privy to privileged inside information. Again both men reasoned that it would be impossible to prove such an allegation.

"What share split did you have in mind?" Perkins asked. The idea appealed to him.

"Saudi Arabia and Exxon would each contribute forty percent of the capital and Texaco would make up the balance. But we are prepared to consider any suggestions you may have."

They shook their heads.

"In addition the venture will have a billion dollars in credit lines from the three partners in the same proportion as our capital contribution. That's for use in an emergency only," Tarik informed them.

"That too makes a great deal of sense." This time it was the Exxon chairman who spoke.

"And by the way," Tarik assured the two chairmen, "We will come out ahead in the venture, because even in the worst case, Saudi Arabia's announcement of a three and a half million barrel production cut will result in a price change of a least five or six dollars per barrel."

"I'm for it in principal," the Exxon chairman announced emphatically. He was known for bold moves. In this case he figured there was no way they could lose. The plan looked like a license to print money.

"So is Texaco," Perkins indicated eagerly.

"Excellent. Gentlemen we have a mutuality of interest and we need each other," Tarik observed with satisfaction.

———

"What about the timing?"

"We have to move on this immediately, well before the next OPEC meeting. I suggest you work out the details tonight and tomorrow morning with Townsend. Most of the paper work has been completed," Tarik smiled. "In readiness of your agreement."

"Dr. Siefert, the Liechtenstein lawyer will join us in the morning," Townsend added.

"One other thing," the prince said helpfully. "You'll have difficulty with the SEC if you trade for your personal account on the stock exchange. I suggest you discuss the matter with Townsend and Siefert. They can fix you up. And believe me it will be impossible to trace back anything."

"That's most kind of you," Mason said.

They sat around having another round of Scotch and trading opinions on a variety of issues, all relating to oil. Half an hour later the two executives and Michael Townsend left for dinner at l'Ambroisie in the Place des Vosges.

Shortly thereafter Tarik headed for the airport for his flight to Riyadh.

Earlier that morning Tarik and Townsend started the gradual and orderly liquidation of the prince's investments in the United States. The six billion dollar equity position in Am Bank had been taken care of in a direct conversation last week between Tarik and Am Bank's Chairman, Henry Fielding. The bank was buying back the shares in two equal tranches, one in September and the second in early October. This approach, Fielding explained, permitted the bank to book the transactions in two different quarters.

That still left twenty billion dollars in equities. The investments were in fifty well-known corporations. Citigroup, Morgan Chase and AIG represented a few of the names in the financial sector; the technology group included companies such as Microsoft, Intel, IBM, Apple and Oracle. Among

---

391

the others were GE, Coca-Cola, Lucent Technologies, Home Depot, Pfizer, and General Motors. The list went on and on.

Townsend spoke with Andre Lamartine, the private bank account officer at the Commercial Bank of Switzerland and with Jean Pierre Laurent who worked in the same capacity at Credit Suisse. In the United States he contacted Angela Davis at Citigroup and Roger Moore at Morgan Chase. He also spoke with the account officers at Goldman Sachs, Merrill and six other brokerage houses and banks. Tarik spoke with Frank Harris, the account officer at Am Bank who had covered him for fifteen years. The water was muddied as much as possible. The shares were to be sold over a two-week period. The tasks and shares were divided in ways that made it impossible for any one of the banks or securities houses from knowing what the prince was up to. Besides all the shares were in nominee names and there was simply no way that any could be traced to Tarik. That explained why secrecy laws had such an appeal, particularly to the wealthy.

They next took on the bond portfolio. Unlike equities that were managed exclusively in-house, the fixed income portfolio was with outside managers. What was the reason for that? The explanation was simple. Tarik reckoned that the big payoff was in equities, so that's the market he had concentrated his attention on.

"I think we should extend the maturity of the portfolio," Townsend suggested.

"Why?"

"Because the Fed will pump in liquidity and reduce rates to stem the losses in the equities markets. And investors will rush for cover into Treasuries. Both of these actions will raise bond prices."

"Yes but much will depend on foreign investors. They hold a sizeable chunk of bonds and if they exit from the dollar the Fed's actions will be counterbalanced very considerably," Tarik retorted.

"That's possible but the Fed has unlimited dollar resources. It will have its way in the end," Townsend shot back.

"Perhaps. I'm inclined to liquify the portfolio, but I'll compromise, given your strong views on the matter. Let's increase the maturities on half the portfolio and liquidate the other half. We'll put the proceeds in a special money market account. I've already spoken to Harris about it. He's taking care of the account."

"Well, we have twenty managers. How do you want to deal with them?"

"Go over the list. Keep the portfolios with those who have done well this year and pull the assets from the ten worst performers. But don't do anything with the five hundred million at B&P. I'll take care of that."

Alexandra Middleton arrived at twelve noon. She was surprised to see another person in the suite.

Tarik greeted her with a kiss on both cheeks. "You look as beautiful as ever," he said with evident warmth. Then, he continued as Townsend walked up to them, "Alexandra this is Michael Townsend. I'm very busy in my new role as a Senior Advisor to King Fahd so Michael has taken over responsibility for the bank."

She bestowed an engaging smile upon him and said, "Michael, it's a real pleasure to meet you."

"I'm pleased to meet you too," Townsend said, admiring the pale lemon Givenchy suit she was wearing. He noticed that she was immaculately groomed and had very little makeup except for the glowing red lipstick and the matching nail polish. She had the class that came with money and there was an air of elegance and sophistication about her. But what impressed Townsend the most was not her beauty but the steely self-assurance that was evident in her confident manner.

"I've known Alexandra from our Cambridge days," Tarik said to Michael. "We were at neighboring colleges and moved in the same social circles."

393

He neglected to tell him that in his last year they had been lovers at Cambridge. He had loved her then and wanted to marry her. But the affair had foundered on his desire to return to Saudi Arabia. What would she do there? She couldn't work. And she was determined to have a career and make money. So he had gone off to Riyadh and she to London. They had kept in touch and over the years had remained friends. They met whenever he came to New York. But the relationship was strictly business now. The past was long since over. He was a good Muslim and a faithful husband who believed in the sanctity of marriage.

She was always so beautiful, Tarik mused as he watched her sitting besides him, and age had not dimmed its luster. He noticed once again as he often did, how with time she had blossomed into not only a very beautiful woman but also one with a commanding presence. That was fine in a friend or business associate but he wasn't sure he'd want that in his wife. There was the potential for too much conflict. He was aware of her past. She came from a humble background but had successfully managed to cultivate an aristocratic image that was so evident now. And of course he knew what very few of her fellow workers were aware of. That she was a divorcée. Her first marriage to Bruce Havelock lasted barely two years. Perhaps fate, Tarik thought, had been kind after all.

"That's right," Alexandra laughed. "It goes back thirty years."

"By the way Michael, this woman's absolutely brilliant. She got a star first in Economics."

"You didn't do badly either. After all you got a first in History," Alexandra shot back, blushing at the complement.

"And Michael isn't exactly dumb either," Tarik grinned. "He's an Oxford man. Actually a Rhodes scholar."

"So we have three overly smart people in the room. That's asking for trouble," Alexandra quipped.

394

They ordered room service.

Over lunch they talked of the problems Alexandra had encountered at B&P. She told them the same story she had mentioned to Victoria Spencer. Her voice betrayed no bitterness at the hand that fate had dealt her. She noticed that Townsend appeared to be preoccupied with something but Tarik listened with interest.

He was deeply moved. When she finished, he patted her reassuringly on the hand. "It's a setback. And it's devastating. They treated you very badly," he said with great feeling. "But knowing you, I'm sure you'll do well. In a few years it won't matter and you'll be thanking the bastards."

"Thanks for the kind words," Alexandra murmured sweetly.

"So tell me, what are you doing now. Can I be of any help?" Tarik asked. She felt genuine concern in his voice.

"I attended the hedge fund conference in Geneva and later today I'm meeting the private banking officers and their clients at Am Bank's Paris office."

She assumed that he was aware of her joint venture with the bank.

"Oh! Have you joined Am Bank?"

"In a way," Alexandra smiled. "We've formed a joint venture money management firm. There was an announcement in the Wall Street Journal last Friday."

"I must have missed it. That's excellent. It's a great bank," Tarik replied enthusiastically.

"Do you remember Victoria Spencer? She's an American who was at Cambridge at the same time as us?"

"Very vaguely."

"Anyway she heads Am Bank's Global Wealth Management group."

She filled him in on the details of the joint venture. Finally she touched on the delicate subject of the accounts at B&P.

"The two accounts that you have at B&P, your bond account and SNB's mutual fund account," she said hesitantly. "I'm hoping you'll continue to let me manage those."

Tarik laughed. "Of course. There's no question about that." Then he squeezed her right arm affectionately and said, "Did you really think I'd leave the accounts with those swine or give them to another manager?"

For the first time she relaxed. "No. Of course not," she smiled coyly. "I told my portfolio managers that you were the one client I was absolutely sure of."

"Good. I'm glad to hear you have such confidence in me," Tarik joked.

"One other thing. You mentioned help earlier. I'd really appreciate anything you can do for me particularly with wealthy Arabs."

She told him about the hedge fund.

"Definitely. But give me a little time to come up with some names. Michael will be in touch with you in the next two weeks. Now tell me how is Phillip?"

"Oh, he's fine. He took early retirement in January, so now he's spending more time with the children. You know, homework and going out with them. That sort of thing. As a result he has become very close to them."

"That's great. Your husband is a real gentleman and a first-class businessman. He should have come and worked for me at the bank in Riyadh." He laughed, "I had to get Michael instead."

Alexandra just smiled. Her mind was made up on Phillip. She wondered what Tarik would say when he found out. She dismissed the thought. There was no point in worrying about it. After all it was her personal life.

The mission on which she had come had been accomplished. She stayed till two o'clock and then took her leave.

"I hope we'll meet in New York soon. When are you coming there next?"

"I don't know," Tarik replied truthfully.

———

CHAPTER 34

Alexandra flew to London on Wednesday afternoon to meet Am Bank's private bank account officers and later to attend the cocktail party that the bank had arranged for fifty of its wealthy customers.

The four days in Paris with Carver had been heavenly. Except in the sex department. There he was no match for her husband. She would have to give him some lessons and bring him up to a more suitable performance level. But they had a wonderful time wandering around the city. Carver was very solicitous and was a most entertaining conversationalist. Earlier that morning, just before he left for the airport to catch his flight back to New York, he told her that his wife had moved out of his Manhattan apartment. He figured she would make a great trophy wife, so holding her adoringly in his arms he asked her to marry him. She had fallen in love and accepted eagerly.

Before leaving the City of Light, she contacted the lady lawyer recommended by Carver and had a lengthy conversation with her. On the telephone the lawyer sounded very professional and competent. Alexandra made an appointment to meet with her on the following Tuesday to

3194-ISLA

sign the attorney-client agreement. She would spring the surprise on Phillip next week.

Delphinia and Phillip were in the suite when she returned to Claridge's from the Am Bank function. They had arrived an hour earlier.

"How was the meeting with Tarik?" Phillip asked as they later lay in bed after dinner.

"It went very well. He was most gracious about the two accounts."

"I told you he would come through."

"I know, but I was getting a little paranoid after the bad experience with so many of my best clients. He has also promised to help me get some wealthy Arab customers."

"That's wonderful, darling." He turned and pulled her toward him.

She came into his arms readily, not only because she wanted to make love with him one last time but also because she did not want to give him any hint of what was going on inside her.

Her lips parted slightly and his tongue went inside her mouth as he kissed her with increasing passion. With his right hand he gently stroked her breasts and her nipples became hard. His hand moved to her vulva, which he rubbed gently. She was already wet. Her excitement mounted. In another minute he got up on top and entered her. He began to move inside her vagina. Within a few minutes she moaned, "I'm going to come."

He continued the thrusting as he asked, "How many times did you come?"

"Three," she replied hoarsely.

Phillip turned her sideways and now began to move in and out of her slowly. At the same time he massaged her clitoris lightly with his index finger.

"Darling, do it slowly. Very slowly," she cooed.

"Do you like it?"

"I love it. Give me more. I want more." Then she moaned, "Oh! I'm so excited. What are you doing to me?"

"I'm fucking you darling. And I'm going to make you come ten times."

"Oh, it's so good. Suck my breasts," she begged.

"Don't come yet," he said as he slowly sucked her erect nipples.

"I can't wait," she suddenly screamed. "I'm going to come." And then she kept screaming "coming, coming, coming, coming, coming. Okay, okay. No more, no more . . ."

"How many times did you come?" he asked.

"Many, many times, At least seven or eight."

He got on top of her again and began to thrust harder and harder.

"Alexandra open your eyes and look at me," he whispered.

They looked at each other as he thrust repeatedly into her. Then he began licking the heels of her feet and finally her toes.

She screamed again, "This excites me terribly. Oh, I'm coming again. Come in me now. Now. I'm spent."

He put her toes in his mouth, sucking them vigorously.

"I'm going to come, darling," he finally shouted.

"Yes, yes. Come inside me. Oh it's so good," she said as the semen shot inside her.

Afterwards lying next to him she knew this was the one thing she would miss. No one could fuck like Phillip. She wondered where he had acquired the skill.

They left early on the following day for Cambridge in the rented car that was waiting for them in front of the hotel. Delphinia wanted to visit the famous University and see some of the colleges. She had been there before as a child but the place had meant little to her then. Now as a teenager who would soon be graduating from school, she was beginning to visit colleges in an attempt to narrow the application list down to seven or eight. In the United States, this was an annual ritual observed by thousands of parents and their children.

Delphinia admired the narrow cobbled streets and the imposing architecture. The spires of the college buildings framed against the blue sky gave the place a very romantic touch. They visited St. John's where Alexandra had been a student. The college was built around a series of courts that surrounded velvety, bright green lawns that were usually divided into quadrants to allow for cobbled footpaths. Alexandra took her to Chapel Court and pointed out the rooms she lived in as an undergraduate.

"The poet Wordsworth lived in the room over there," Alexandra said looking in that direction as they walked through the Second Court.

They went over the Bridge of Sighs on to New Court and the famous 'backs'–large stretches of lawns along the banks of the river. Delphinia loved the broad sweeping openness and park like setting of this area with the River Cam meandering lazily past the colleges.

"I used to walk here often in the evenings. It was so peaceful and lovely," Phillip mused.

"Me too," Alexandra replied nostalgically.

They walked on the 'backs' over to neighboring Trinity, the biggest of the Cambridge colleges.

"This is the largest court at any college at Oxford or Cambridge," Phillip said with pride as they made their way into Great Court.

For a few moments they just stood there looking at the enormous court. It was almost the size of a large town square with a fountain in the middle.

As they walked towards the gate Phillip said, "Delphinia, do you remember that race in the film Chariots of Fire?"

"Yes dad."

"Well it actually took place here."

Then he pointed at one of the rooms and said, "Lord

Byron used to live there. He kept his pet bear chained outside."

"That's cool. But you're joking."

Phillip laughed. "No, Delphinia. It's true. You can read about it in his biography. And by the way those were my rooms as well when I was here."

"Oh, how exciting," Delpinia said breathlessly. "I'm going to tell all my friends."

They went punting in one of those flat-bottomed boats. Delphinia observed that her father was an excellent punter. They went past a number of colleges–John's, Trinity, and Clare–and as they drew in front of King's, Alexandra pointed out the great Gothic chapel in the distance that was one of the glories of Cambridge.

Later as they walked around the ancient town Alexandra declared, "Even after all these years I'm still awed by the place."

"I know exactly what you mean. I have the same feeling," Phillip acknowledged.

"So what do you think?" Alexandra asked, looking at Delphinia.

"Mom it's awesome. Absolutely awesome."

As they headed to the parking lot they saw a don crossing one of the courts at Trinity.

"That's what I wanted to be more than anything else," Phillip said wistfully.

"Why didn't you, dad?" Delphinia asked.

"Because I didn't think I was in their league as a scholar."

Alexandra heard his response and thought, "That's Phillip's real problem. He's always wanted the life of a Cambridge don. That's why he never had that burning desire to make money. He's too lost in intellectual pursuits and not focused enough on the things that count in life."

On the way out they drove to the village of Grantchester and had tea.

———

"Didn't some poet write about this place?" Delphinia asked.

"Yes," Phillip smiled. It was Rupert Brook. 'And is there honey still for tea?' was the famous line."

They arrived at Lady Annabel's house, a few miles outside Northampton, shortly after ten on Friday. Nicholas Hawkesmoor had built Darling Stone Park, one of the finest examples of English classical architecture, for the Farnsworth family in 1702. Lady Annabel and her husband the Right Honorable Jeremy Pemberton had acquired the large country house ten years ago. Nearby was Althorp, the ancestral home of Princess Diana. At the reception later that evening Alexandra and Phillip mingled with the two dozen wealthy and illustrious guests.

"We didn't see you this year in Venice," Count Arrivabeni said as he and his wife Princess Bianca d'Aosta cornered Alexandra. They were visiting London for a few days.

"We'll be there next summer," Alexandra smiled looking at Phillip who had joined them. "And we'll rent the villa again."

For several years the Winchesters had rented the Brandolini family villa that belonged to Count Arrivabeni–he was a Brandolini on his mother's side–some fifty kilometers north of Venice.

During cocktails Alexandra mentioned her new hedge fund to Rupert Hambro of the famous Hambros Bank and to Galen Weston the entrepreneur who owned the Canadian food giant Weston's.

Once the guests had imbibed sufficient alcohol, Jeremy Pemberton gave a short speech and then introduced Alexandra who made a brief presentation pitching her new hedge fund to the audience. She spoke with passion and knowledge in a highly polished manner and the presentation was well received. Several questions were asked by Sir Mark Weinberg, by Sir Rocco Forte and by Conrad Black of the newspaper empire. Alexandra responded with grace and humor.

"Isn't it amazing darling, that after eighteen years they still hold hands like new lovers," Lady Annabel remarked to her husband as she observed Alexandra and Phillip, hand in hand, chatting amiably with Amartya Sen and his wife Emma Rothschild. Professor Sen was Alexandra's Economics supervisor at college. He was now the Master of Trinity, the college that Phillip had attended.

Later after dinner, once the guests had departed, the hosts sat with Alexandra and Phillip in the library having a nightcap.

"I talked with a number of the men and I believe the presentation went very well," Pemberton observed.

"Thank you," Alexandra smiled.

"I'm reasonably confident that most of those who were present tonight will invest in your hedge fund," Pemberton continued. "And we'll repeat this evening the next time you come and hopefully get some more investors."

That same evening, Ralph Schuster was having drinks with Tim Wilkinson at the Bell and Whistle, a pub off Sloane Street in London.

"So what brings you to London, Ralph?" Wilkinson asked. They had known each other for many years and occasionally met to exchange opinions on topics of interest.

"We're doing some work for Am Bank in their Global Trading and Investment Banking Groups."

Wilkinson knew all about the project. Victoria had mentioned it when he spent a few days with her in New York last week.

"You told me of the two Saudi oil production plans."

"That's right. One with Saudi Arabia going alone and flooding the market. The other proposing severe production cuts," Wilkinson replied.

"I'd like to get the information in the first plan, the one about flooding the market to B&P," Victoria said.

"You think they'll use it if they found out?"

"Of course. Everyone wants inside information. The more

403

we can damage their performance record, the easier it will be to steal their clients."

"Do you think your friend Alexandra knows about the plan?" Wilkinson asked.

"That's my guess. She's friendly with Prince Tarik and manages money for him."

Then seeing the skeptical look on his face she continued, "Why? You don't think so?"

"He doesn't seem the type who would leak this kind of confidential information to anyone. But then I don't know him that well."

"You may be right, but this is very different. They used to date each other at Cambridge. Some of us knew they were lovers." Victoria smiled.

"Getting back to the original idea," Wilkinson asked, "How can we get the information to B&P?"

"I've already worked that out."

"You have?" Tim asked admiring her ingenuity.

"Yes. You know Ralph Schuster. McKinsey is doing a project at the bank."

She then gave him the details of the work that was being done.

"And you probably don't know but Ralph's wife works at B&P. I have met them both several times at parties."

"That I certainly didn't know," Tim grinned. "I'll have to make arrangements to meet Ralph. You want me to get a copy of the real plan to pass on to Alexandra?"

"No. That would be too dangerous. Eventually her staff members would find out. It'll backfire and I don't want to be linked to that. Besides I'm pretty confident she already knows."

Victoria had phoned earlier in the week to tell him of Schuster's visit to the bank's London branch. Later that same day Ralph Schuster called before Wilkinson could get hold of him. They agreed to meet the following day at the Bell and Whistle.

———

"And how's the project going?" Wilkinson asked as they sat at a corner table drinking scotch and soda.

"Reasonably well. It's a challenge but we'll eventually get there," Schuster replied putting his glass on the table.

"I'm sure you will," Wilkinson said with a smile.

"What about you old sport? What are you working on?" Schuster asked.

"We're doing some work for Saudi Arabia at the request of Prince Tarik. It's all very hush, hush."

"It must have something to do with oil," Schuster grinned. He knew that Townsend Associates had a large oil-related consulting business.

"That's right, but we're also working on economic policy issues aimed at radical reduction of government expenditures."

After three more rounds of drinks, Wilkinson appeared slightly inebriated.

They were discussing money.

"You know how it is. It never seems to be enough," Ralph said.

"Ralph old buddy. We've known each other for donkeys years." It seemed as is alcohol had loosened his tongue.

He picked the briefcase, put it on his lap, opened it and extracted a document with a yellow cover that he handed to Ralph.

"Here's an opportunity to make some real money," he said in a conspiratorial tone. "You're in no condition to read it now. But look at it tomorrow and then bring it back to my apartment."

Schuster also was at the office earlier that day. He put the folder in his briefcase.

They finished their drinks and went off for dinner to a neighborhood restaurant.

The National Day of Saudi Arabia was observed each

3194-ISLA

year on the twenty third of September. This year the day fell on a Thursday.

On the previous evening after dinner as they sat on a couch in the living room, Tarik had kissed his wife and told her that their lives would change forever on the following day. She was surprised at the news of Fahd's abdication but not at the fact that he had not told her about his selection as the new king. Samia Gamal was a Lebanese Arab and she knew that in the Arab world such business affairs were rarely discussed between husband and wife.

"Sweetheart," he said in his gentlest voice, "It will change nothing between us. We'll still do all the things we've always done and we'll travel the same way."

"Is that a promise?"

"Yes and you know I'll never lie to you. But we won't live in hotels that often. We'll now have to buy houses in Europe and the United States."

"I don't mind that," she sighed. "Besides it will keep me busy working with interior decorators."

That Thursday was like any other day in Riyadh–cloudless blue sky with the blazing sun scorching the desert air. At ten o'clock that morning Tarik arrived at Yamameh Palace in Riyadh. Fifteen minutes later King Fahd signed the Instrument of Abdication and Tarik was sworn in as the sixth king of the country and the first from a new generation. Earlier Crown Prince Abdullah had signed a similar document renouncing his right to the throne. The ailing Fahd had already recorded his farewell address to the nation. Immediately after the ceremony he flew with his wife in the Royal Saudi Boeing 747 to his villa outside Marbella on the southern coast of Spain.

Tarik returned to his house. He felt greatly relieved now that it was finally over. So his plan had eventually come to fruition. He was in a relaxed and cheerful mood when he met with his three advisors shortly before one o'clock.

"I have some very important news." He looked at them

and smiled affectionately. "King Fahd has abdicated. I was sworn in as the new king this morning."

Their astonishment left them momentarily speechless.

"It's alright." He laughed at their discomfort. "The announcement will be made at four this afternoon. Fahd has already left for Spain."

King Fahd spoke first.

"This is an auspicious day for the people of Saudi Arabia. Once again it is my pleasure to tell you of the progress that has been made by the kingdom in the past year."

He rattled off a few statistics.

"As some of you know," he continued, "I am in poor health. In the West a new century has arrived. I have ruled for eighteen years. It has been a long reign. The country needs new blood and a new generation of leaders. The time has come for me to take my leave. And so my fellow countrymen I abdicated as your king this morning. Crown Prince Abdullah and I have jointly selected my successor. The new king is my nephew Tarik Ibn Mishaal Ibn Abd al Aziz al Saud. Allah hu Akbar. God is Great."

And with that his image flashed off the screen.

It was Tarik's turn next.

"My fellow countrymen, by the will of God I have taken over as your new king. With the help of God I will do my best to serve you faithfully. Your well-being and welfare will be my one and only concern. The country has made great progress but much remains to be done. God willing, I will do my best to bring about the changes that are necessary to take the kingdom to new heights of prosperity."

Then he made a dramatic announcement.

"As a first step I have donated ten billion dollars of my personal fortune to the people of Saudi Arabia. A social security fund has been established. This will be augmented each year by the state . . ."

3194-ISLA

Like millions of readers throughout the world Alexandra was surprised to read the news in the Friday papers.

"My God," she said to Phillip, "I just met him last Monday and he didn't say a word about this."

"Yes, you know how secretive the Saudis are. Tarik's no exception," Phillip replied.

"And do you know what his last words were to me when I asked when he would come to New York?"

"No."

"He said 'I don't know.'"

At noon on Sunday Wilkinson telephoned Victoria.

She picked up the phone on the fourth ring.

"Did I wake you up?" Wilkinson asked in an apologetic voice.

"What time is it?"

"It's just past noon here."

"I went to a Private Bank function and didn't get back till very late," Victoria replied sleepily.

"Well, I had drinks with Ralph yesterday. He has a copy of the plan."

"Thanks Tim. I love you."

"And by the way, you haven't seen the papers yet. Our man Tarik has taken over in Riyadh."

The announcement caught Western governments by surprise as well.

Very little was known about the new king of Saudi Arabia.

CHAPTER 35

At the White House President Bush was awakened at 2.00 A.M. on Friday morning by a telephone call from Condoleezza Rice, his National Security Advisor.

"Sorry to wake you up this early Mr. President."

"That's all right."

"There's been a change of government in Saudi Arabia.

"What happened to Fahd?" He pronounced it as Fad. "Is he dead?"

"No. He abdicated."

"So that fellow Abdullah has taken over. We know him well . . ."

"But . . ."

Bush ignored the interruption. "He was here last year at the White House. We had a very good session. He's a good and solid friend of the United States."

"Mr. President, Crown Prince Abdullah did not succeed as king. Evidently he renounced his succession right at the time of Fahd's abdication."

"So who's the new man?" A note of urgency had finally crept into the voice.

"It's one of their nephews. A man by the name of Tarik," Rice replied.

"Who is he? What do we know about him?"

"That's the problem. We have very little information on him."

"Get the CIA on to it immediately," Bush demanded.

"They're already working on it. They are pursuing all possible leads. We expect to have a more detailed report very shortly."

The Saudi announcement received top billing in newspapers around the world. Typical was the headline in The New York Times, which screamed in bold headlines on the front page: "Major Upheaval in Saudi Arabia. New King Takes Over." The London Times was slightly more circumspect: "King Fahd of Saudi Arabia Abdicates. Nephew is New King."

Both the articles were long on inconsequential facts but short on hard crucial details that really mattered. The Times article noted: "King Tarik is a product of Eton and Trinity College, Cambridge. He is reportedly very anglicized and is said to order his suits from Huntsmans of Savile Row. In financial circles he is noted as a savvy investor and in his first act as king, he sent a highly symbolical message by donating a considerable portion of his personal fortune to the people of Saudi Arabia. While no one is aware of his political views, his background suggests a pro-Western orientation."

The announcement also set off a flurry of activity among Western intelligence agencies. There was a mad scramble to get more solid information on his political orientation and beliefs. None, not even the vaunted Mossad, had even remotely useful or significant knowledge of the man.

The State Department received a report from the U.S. ambassador on Sunday. He had just returned from a reception given by King Tarik for the diplomatic corps. For the first time the ambassadors and their spouses were together. The king and his beautiful wife mingled freely with the guests.

He had singled out the ambassador and talked warmly of the very close and special ties between the two countries and had reiterated his desire to continue this close relationship. The ambassador commented on the King's excellent command of the English language–"he has a very noticeable English accent"–and concluded by noting that his selection as the new ruler was dictated by the urgent need for wide ranging domestic reforms. The reception in his view symbolized a break from the past. So while domestic changes were definitely in the cards, few if any shifts were expected in the current foreign policy and the close alliance and reliance on the United States as the ultimate guardian of Saudi sovereignty. As a final note he added that the new king was a refreshing alternative to what the Saudis have had to date.

That same Friday Gerhard Schroeder, the German Chancellor telephoned his French counterpart, Lionel Jospin. The news came as a surprise but the man had impressed both of them. He was straightforward and direct and very western in his thought process. They were very pleased by this development for an even more important reason. In their view he would almost certainly press ahead with the oil plan and the deal made with the two European powers. They agreed that the German would send a confidential message to the king through Michael Townsend reiterating their strong support for his program.

The second presidential campaign of the twenty-first century was in full swing. The news was not good for the Republicans. George Bush was leading Senator Bob Kerrey, the Democrat candidate, by two points in the Gallup poll and by three points in the Marist poll. Given the margin of error in the two polls the race appeared to be even. Two other polls taken at the same time showed similar results.

Just as Alexandra, Phillip and Delphinia were boarding the plane on Sunday at Heathrow for the flight back to New York, Martin Shay, the campaign manager of George Bush was making a telephone call from one of the pay phones at the Hay Adams Hotel in Washington. It was to Sidney Rosenberg. He would be in New York tomorrow. His day was completely shot but there was something very important that he needed to discuss. Perhaps they could talk on the way to Rosenberg's office. They agreed to meet on the northwest corner of Park Avenue and 78th Street at seven on the following day.

Shay was there at the appointed hour. The two men exchanged compliments and shook hands.

"President Bush sends his greetings. He wants you to know that he is most appreciative of your support."

Rosenberg smiled. "Please convey my best wishes to the President. All of us are rooting for him."

"The race is very tight right now," Shay pointed out.

"Yes, we need one decisive break somehow," Rosenberg replied.

"I agree. And that is why I'm here. We require your support at this extremely critical juncture."

Rosenberg understood what Shay was driving at. He personally had always been from the conservative wing of the Republican Party and their friendship stretched back over forty years to the time when they had worked in the campaign of Richard Nixon.

"How much do you have to raise?" Rosenberg asked.

"Sidney, we need to make one final ad campaign push. It will be through the party as our finances are limited to the prescribed amount that each presidential candidate can spend. We're trying to raise fifteen million dollars. I'm hoping, in view of your past support, to get a million of that from you."

"I understand. You can count on me."

"Thanks pal. We really appreciate that. Hopefully you'll recoup it in the stock market in no time considering how prices are rising."

"I wish that were the case. The market has been very difficult for us," Rosenberg responded glumly.

"In that case let me give you a tip," Shay spoke in a confidential whisper. "Just between you and me. The Fed is going to reduce both the discount and the Fed funds rate by fifty basis points at its meeting on Thursday. We worked out a deal with the chairman."

"Thanks for the information." Rosenberg could not conceal the excitement from his voice.

"What are friends for," Shay smiled. "By the way send the check today. And thanks once again."

They parted company at the corner of fifty-seventh and Park.

Monday was a big day for Pericles Asset Management. It was the day the Falcon Hedge Fund became operational. The joint venture was operating temporarily from Am Bank's offices until the scheduled move to its recently rented premises on Madison Avenue in late October.

Early in the morning Alexandra met with a group of her portfolio managers. Investment decisions had to be made, so they exchanged opinions on the market.

"Let's begin with the fixed income market. Anne, what do think is likely on the interest rate front?" Alexandra asked.

"With inflation at an all time low and the economy growing at a sustainable rate, my sense is that the Fed will make no moves."

"What do you think?" The question was posed to Brian Watson.

"I agree. All the economic indices suggest that the Fed will maintain a neutral bias for the time being."

"Anyone have a different opinion?" Alexandra asked looking at the others.

No one did.

"I propose that we invest at least a quarter billion dollars, maybe more in East Asian country dollar bonds, particularly

413

Malaysia, the Philippines, Thailand and Indonesia. I expect
a narrowing of the interest differential between these bonds
and U.S. governments ranging between two to three percent,"
Anne Nicholson observed. "And of course by buying dollar-
denominated bonds we'll avoid any currency risk."

A detailed discussion followed, country by country, on
total outstanding debt, liquidity, available maturities and
coupons and other relevant considerations. There was some
talk on the maturity parameters that would be most suitable
for the portfolio. A capital allocation was agreed to but no
final decisions were made. It was further agreed that Anne
would keep in close touch with the dealers and gather further
information.

They next turned their attention to the equities area.

"What's your read on the stock market?" The question
was addressed to Ravi Shah who had recently joined the group
from Am Bank's private bank.

"As you know the market is very volatile and we are seeing big swings during the daily trading sessions. I think we're
at a point where we may see the market just drift for a while.
The consensus of opinion among analysts is that equities will
continue to rise. The Dow is up about 8 ½ percent to date
and the S&P 10 percent. Most estimates for year–end are at
the 20 percent mark, which in my view is too optimistic. But
there are some good opportunities in Mexico, Singapore,
Hong Kong and Japan."

"Which sectors are likely to do better domestically?" Brian
asked.

"I like some of the blue chips because they have remained
depressed in the past six months though earnings have been
strong."

Again a discussion followed with specific stocks being
mentioned as the best investment candidates.

Alexandra decided that the time had come to take the
group into her confidence and she now proceeded to do just

that. Throwing caution to the winds she gave them, for the first time, her views on the subject, "I'm certain that our major opportunity lies in the U.S. stock market." Then bestowing an engaging smile upon them, she continued, "I strongly believe we're going into a bear market. May be even a crash." A bear market was usually a drop of twenty percent or more over several weeks or months. However, declines of this magnitude in a single day or a few days were considered a crash. There had been only two crashes, one in 1929 and the other in 1987.

Their surprise was all too obvious. For several minutes the room was uneasily silent.

"How did you find that out?" Anne finally asked, grinning.

"I have my sources," Alexandra replied with a laugh.

Then she went on, in a more somber vein, to tell them how she had seen Tarik in serious discussions with the Mexican and Venezuelan oil ministers at a restaurant. Why would he be talking with the oil ministers? There was no mention in the papers about their presence in New York. He had also avoided contacting her, which was highly unusual. They were definitely planning something. Lastly, and most importantly, Prince Tarik had just become the king of Saudi Arabia. She pointed out her long association with the prince and her thorough familiarity with his thought process. He was not the type who took half measures. The meeting in Paris had confirmed her view.

"Why?" Ravi Shah asked.

"I saw some papers on the table that indicated that he was shortening the maturities on his bond portfolio," she replied.

"Why would he be doing that?" Anne asked.

"My guess is that he thinks that the Fed will pump liquidity as it did in 1987 and he believes that the yield curve will be steeper as foreign investors dump the long bond."

"So what do you think they're planning?" Watson asked.

"A massive cut in oil production. Believe me, every detail

will have been worked out meticulously. And in this jittery market investor psychology can change in minutes just as it did in 1987. By the way, in 1987 we also had a very similar situation. Oil prices were going up and our current account deficits were increasing. It just took a speech to trigger the market's collapse."

The speech she referred to was the one made by Treasury Secretary Baker attempting to jawbone the dollar down.

"In that case we'll see a rush into treasuries," Watson commented.

"That's right. But I wouldn't go beyond ten-year maturities. We don't know how the foreign debt and equity investors will react."

"What will be the timing of the move?" Ravi asked.

"Any restrictions in oil supplies will require OPEC's imprimatur. I checked and found the cartel will next meet in mid-October. So that's the most likely date," Alexandra pointed out.

She then told them of the sale of Tarik's huge holdings of Am Bank stocks in a buyback arrangement with the bank. That gave further credence to her belief that the Saudis intended to push the oil price up sharply. Then there was also the three billion dollars that the private bank had received in short-term deposits on behalf of the prince from various money managers.

They listened with growing interest. The interest soon gave way to conviction. All the indicators pointed in the same direction. A strategy was agreed upon. They would concentrate in the United States. Most of the money would be invested domestically. They would use two hundred and fifty million dollars to buy oil futures contracts and also short the S&P 500 index using options. After much debate they decided to invest up to seven hundred and fifty million dollars in equity put options. A billion dollars would be in treasuries as that was the most liquid security in the fixed income market. Nothing for the time being was to be invested in emerging markets. Five hundred million dollars of capital was earmarked for euro-denominated notes and bonds. They agreed to a three times leverage of the fixed income portfolio through bank borrowings. The rest of the funds would be invested in short-term paper.

At ten that morning Victoria spoke on the telephone to Alexandra.

"How were the meetings in Europe?"

"I think they went pretty well," Alexandra replied.

"I got glowing reports from everywhere," Victoria said. "By the way, congratulations are in order now that the Falcon fund is operational."

"Thanks. Our investment strategy is in place."

"Excellent. I'm expecting great results from you, Alexandra."

3194-ISLA

CHAPTER 36

Sidney Rosenberg arrived at his office that Monday morning a little later than usual and immediately got down to work. There was no time to lose. The Open Market Committee of the Federal Reserve was scheduled to meet on Thursday. His excitement was palpable. The information provided by Shay had quickened the flow of blood in his tired old body. He intended to take full advantage of the opportunity that had presented itself. A smile lit his heavily creased face as he mused on the outcome which, he had no doubt, would be the crowning achievement of his career.

He set into motion a series of actions aimed at achieving the goals established by his laser sharp mind. First, he telephoned Ronald Shapiro and arranged a meeting of the newly formed Investment Committee for later that afternoon. Here was a chance to improve the investment performance in the institutional equity portfolios that had lagged the market for years. They should now be able to do considerably better than the market indices by making appropriate adjustments in portfolio holdings into sectors that were likely to benefit most from an interest rate cut. The financial sector was an obvious choice. The manufacturing sector was another candidate, particularly those companies that borrowed heavily to finance their operations.

The Dow had hovered around the 17,800 level for the past two weeks. Analysts were increasingly talking of several months of volatile movement within a narrow range until a more definite pattern emerged with regard to the economy's future prospects and corporate profit growth. Rosenberg figured that the rate reduction would boost the Dow by at least seventeen hundred points. That would take the market to within striking distance of the 20,000 mark within the next three months. He realized that some portfolio managers might question the speed at which he thought the index would move. After all hadn't it taken the Dow twenty years to go from the 1,000 level to 2,000. That was true of course, but most people did not understand a simple fact: there was a big difference between absolute amounts and percentages. So that move from a thousand to two thousand represented a rise of one hundred percent while the thousand point move from 17,800 to 18,800 was less than a six percent increase. That was precisely why these thousand point increases at the higher absolute level that the Dow was now at were occurring so much faster now.

The failure to sell the firm irked him deeply and his mind had wrestled, for several weeks, with ways to redress the problem. So he could barely conceal his glee at the opportunity that was now available to rectify this problem as well. There was money to be made in the stock market by leveraging B&P's capital and Rosenberg smiled at the prospect of a billion dollar profit through such investments. It would represent a nice Christmas, or in this case a Hanukah, present for the partners. They would be eternally grateful to him. The thought that Alexandra would not benefit from these gains was a source of additional gratification for him.

With this in mind, he next telephoned the account officer at Am Bank shortly after nine o'clock that morning and arranged to draw down on the full two hundred and seventy

3194-ISLA

five million dollar credit line that his firm had with Am Bank and five other consortium members.

"When will you need the funds?" the account officer asked.

"Tomorrow."

"And where do you want us to send the funds?"

"Just credit our account at your bank," Rosenberg replied.

His final step was to telephone Jay Goldberg at Goldman Sachs.

"Jay, I want to let you know that we have decided to proceed with your IPO recommendation."

The management committee had not, as yet, voted on the plan but Rosenberg did not believe there would be any difficulty on that score.

"That's great news, Sidney," Goldberg gushed. "Your timing is excellent."

"We're thinking of coming to market in early December."

"That looks like the right time," the Goldman banker agreed. "As you know there are a number of matters that need to be taken care of."

"Yes and we're well on the way. Both of our institutional businesses have been re-organized and we have put an investment committee in place."

"What about the back-office and accounting areas?"

"The plan is rolling on that front as well," Rosenberg assured the Goldman banker. "We have contracted with Russell Reynolds to find a chief administrative officer and a chief financial officer and we should have these in place within the next month."

"That sounds great."

"And our accountants have come up with a satisfactory solution to the problem of double taxation. I mean on dividends."

"Excellent. Let's meet next week and get the ball rolling," Goldberg suggested.

———

"I think that should be okay. Just fix the date and time with my secretary."

Afterwards Rosenberg sat at his desk figuring the investments he'd make for the firm's own account. His thoughts were interrupted when Hillary walked into the office at eleven fifteen. She carried a file in her hand and her face was flushed with excitement.

"I have unbelievable information. Absolutely unbelievable." She declared radiantly.

"I can see it in your face. What is it?"

"You know Ralph was in London last week working on his Am Bank project."

"I remember you mentioning that," Sidney replied.

"Well on Friday he had drinks with Tim Wilkinson."

"Who is he?"

"He's a management consultant as well. Their firm is heavily involved in the oil industry and he and Ralph have known each other for a long time."

"So?" Rosenberg asked.

"Well they had a long conversation and plenty to drink. Wilkinson let Ralph on a secret. He told him they were working for the Saudi government. In fact they are working for Prince Tarik."

"You mean the man who just became king of Saudi Arabia?"

"Yes, yes. And he told Ralph that the Saudis were going to increase their oil production substantially in an attempt to take over the market and eventually impose some sort of discipline on it. Apparently they're fed up with OPEC and the other oil producers."

"What proof did he offer?"

"This," she said tapping the file. "It's a confidential memorandum signed by Tarik and King Fahd."

She passed the file to him.

Rosenberg spent the next fifteen minutes reading the details of the confidential memorandum.

3194-ISLA

"This is incredible information. You could get into very serious trouble if anyone found out."

"I know and that's why I brought it straight to you. But can we use it?" Hillary asked.

He smiled. "Of course we're going to use it. Did this Wilkinson mention when they would start on this project?"

"Yes. He said that the Saudis planned to make the announcement after the OPEC meeting in mid-October."

Rosenberg figured the Saudi move would boost the S&P by another five to six percent. That combined with the ten percent he expected from the discount rate reduction and the ten that the index had gained to date would make the fourth year of the millennium a banner year once again. The Dow would probably have comparable gains.

"So we have time to reposition the portfolios. But remember not a word to anyone not even to Jimmy Dolittle. By the way if he's here I'll tell him what to do?"

She nodded to indicate he was in the office.

Rosenberg picked up the telephone and dialed a number.

"Jimmy, this is Sidney. Tell me the maturity profile on your portfolios."

"Hi Sidney. In the short maturities we're around five months. In the intermediate maturities the portfolio duration is around two years."

Duration measured the sensitivity of a bond to interest rate changes. The higher the duration the more sensitive a bond's price was to rate fluctuations. So a bond with a duration of four would lose or gain four percent of its price on a one percent increase or decrease in the interest rate while a bond with a duration of fourteen would lose or gain fourteen percent of its value. The thirty-year Treasury bond maturing in 2025 had a duration of fourteen. Zero coupon bonds, on the other hand, had a duration equal to their maturity date and were the most volatile which was why they had the most appeal for speculators.

422

"What's the bias of the portfolio managers in terms of rates?" Rosenberg asked.

"We're not expecting any changes in the next several months."

"I want you to stretch the duration to the maximum that you're allowed."

One of the things that he liked about Dolittle was his willingness to accept orders from above without questions. A couple of the more perceptive partners had called him a peon to Sidney's great amusement in one of their periodic conversations recently.

"In the short-term portfolio we can go up to one year and the intermediate maturities we're allowed a maximum duration of five years. You want us to go up to these limits?"

Jimmy asked.

"Yes. And finish it by Wednesday at the latest," Rosenberg ordered.

"What's the likely impact of the Saudi plan on the market?" Hillary asked once Rosenberg was off the phone.

"My guess is that an oil price in the four dollar per barrel range would decrease inflation by at least half percent and that in turn, because of the resulting lower interest rates, will significantly improve corporate profitability across the board. Many sectors such as transportation would benefit even more. The oil industry would, of course, be a big loser."

"And what does this mean for equities?"

"It'll give a big boost to the stock market, both psychologically and economically," Rosenberg explained. "I would be most surprised if the Dow and the S&P don't move up by at least ten percent in the next two months."

"Then shouldn't we use the information for the investment of the firm's capital? It would be silly to leave the money in two-year Treasuries?" Hillary asked.

"Now you're getting smart. It makes a great deal of sense and I'm planning to take advantage of the information."

423

"Unlike our institutional portfolios you can use margin to increase the return on our capital, can't you?"

"Yes, but you're only allowed to borrow fifty percent. That helps, but not enough," he replied.

"So what's your thinking?"

"I'm going to use options."

"But isn't that very risky?" Hillary wanted to know. She had never used options and her knowledge of the product was therefore quite limited.

"In the normal course of events eighty percent of all contracts expire worthless so options are a high-risk strategy. But not when we have inside information and know for sure the direction in which the market is going to move. On top of that I intend to make it even safer," Rosenberg assured her.

"How do you do that?"

"Let me explain. Tell me what steps you would take in choosing an individual stock?"

"Let me see," Hillary said, "first you have to determine the outlook for stocks in general. Is the market likely to go up or down?"

Rosenberg nodded as Hillary continued, "The next step is to figure out which industry group will perform best. Is it going to be financials, or consumer durables, or electronics or some other sector? After that you have to figure out which companies in the chosen sector are most likely to do best."

"So it's a three-step process and to make money you have to be right on all three."

That's correct," Hillary agreed.

"Well I'm going to limit the guess work by using the S&P 500 index which is the most liquid and highly traded of the equity indices. And the beauty of this approach is that it's a one-step process. All we need to determine is the outlook for stocks in general," Rosenberg grinned. "And we have a good handle on that thanks to your friend."

He did not say a word about the information given to him

---

by Shay. There was no reason why anyone else should ever know about that.

"As usual Sidney you're way ahead of us," Hillary said admiringly.

Six blocks away on Park Avenue, Ralph Schuster was having lunch with Karl Lutz at Am Bank's headquarters. They were discussing the project that McKinsey was working on.

"I have a friend who is extensively involved in consulting work with oil companies," Ralph said to Lutz.

He continued, "I met him in London last Friday and to my surprise found that he's working on a very confidential project for Prince Tarik and the Saudis."

"Is that the new king?" Lutz asked.

"That's right," Schuster replied. "After we had a few drinks my friend showed me a copy of the plan."

"Why did he do that?" Lutz was curious.

"To help me make some money in the market."

Ralph opened his briefcase, took out a folder and handed it to Lutz.

"He gave me the plan to read at home. I surreptitiously made a copy of it."

Lutz quickly looked at the material, his interest mounting with every page.

"This is dynamite," he said when he finished reading the document.

"I want you to have it," Schuster said.

"Why me?"

"Because I admire you and hope this material will help in the epic contest you are involved in," Schuster said with considerable emotion.

"I'm genuinely grateful to you. By the way when do they propose to make this happen?"

"According to my friend the announcement will come next month after the OPEC meeting. The equipment and

425

facilities are all in place and they'll be able to pump the targeted volumes without any delays."

At the same time as Lutz and Schuster were having lunch, five time zones to the east Michael Townsend was meeting, for the first time, with George Soros in the catwalk-shaped promenade lounge of the famed Dorchester Hotel in London. Nothing of significance was discussed as they waited for their martinis. When they finally got the drinks and had ordered two more they got down to business.

"We have one thing in common," Townsend said as he sipped his martini.

"And what's that?" Soros asked.

Townsend smiled. "We both have degrees from Oxford."

"Ah, yes of course."

For a few minutes they talked of that ancient university town located in one of the most glorious regions of England–the Cotswolds.

"My investors are high stake players who are looking for the best money manager they can find. Your name was recommended by several sources," Townsend said turning to more serious matters.

"I'm pleased to hear that," Soros grinned.

"We are of course aware that you have one of the best performance records in the industry. A hundred thousand dollars invested with you in 1969 was worth a hundred and thirty million dollars thirty years later. It's very, very impressive," Townsend said in a voice oozing with admiration.

He paused to take another sip of the martini. "Unfortunately since then, the glory days are over. In three of the past four years," Townsend continued, "Your funds have run into performance problems."

"I see you have done your homework. What you say is true. We've made a shit load of poor investments in this period," Soros freely admitted.

"We have an idea that might greatly interest you," Townsend smiled mysteriously.

Soros was once considered the world's greatest investor–even better than his chief competitor Louis Marcus, though the record did not bear this out–and his Quantum hedge fund, which at its height had over twenty billion in assets, was now in third place with twelve billion dollars. Four years ago, after disastrous losses from wrong bets on technology stocks and the euro had led to the resignation of his two top lieutenants, Soros was forced to reorganize his huge Quantum Fund into a series of smaller funds. At the same time he lowered the risk profile–and the potential returns–which resulted in a significant pull out of funds by investors.

Quantum had started in the fifties as a macro fund that made leveraged bets on price movements of a wide variety of financial instruments all over the world such as stocks, bonds, options, derivatives, commodities and foreign currencies. For years, these funds were the best performers among all hedge funds and held the largest amount of investor funds, but recently their performance had gone south in a big way and last year they averaged a meager 12.6 percent return when the Dow had yielded over twenty two percent and the Nasdaq's gains had exceeded 30 percent. Not surprisingly, large withdrawals occurred but even after the huge drawdowns they remained the single largest type of hedge fund.

"What would that be?" Soros was intrigued. He had no idea of any connection between Townsend and the Saudis. The meeting was set up through friends who had merely informed him that Townsend represented some very wealthy investors looking for profitable investment opportunities.

"Information. Very valuable information that will give you the chance to rebuild your once great reputation. You'll make profits on a scale immensely greater than the success you achieved in sterling."

3194-ISLA

Townsend was referring to Soros' greatest financial coup, the one that had turned him into a legend. He was the man who broke the Bank of England. In 1992 Soros had made a billion dollars in a month on a bet against sterling!

"You don't look like the type of man who acts on the basis of charitable impulse," Soros deadpanned.

Townsend laughed.

"So what's the quid pro quo?"

"A simple business proposition that'll be mutually beneficial for you and me."

"I'm listening," Soros said.

"You're the investment guru who said and I quote, 'you have to be global in your thinking. You must know how an event here will cause an event there.' In return for the information, you will open an account on my behalf in a nominee name and fund it with ten million dollars. This represents a very small payment for the billions that your fund stands to make," Townsend paused for a moment as if he was in deep thought and then continued. "Come to think of it I'll make an even better offer, one that will make the deal infinitely more attractive from your perspective."

"And what is that?"

"In the event of gains I'll only take the profits on the ten million dollars and repay the principal back to you."

"And in the event of a loss?"

"You'll absorb it and keep whatever is left of the principal. However that situation is not likely to occur."

A week earlier Tarik had suggested this approach to Michael. They were discussing their investment strategy and had concluded that while the news of the oil plan and the other related arrangements were likely to have an effect on the extremely volatile U.S. stock market, which in both their judgments was grossly over valued, a hefty nudge would also be very desirable. That decision led to the choice of Soros and the name given to the German banker. These money managers wielded enormous influence over financial markets. Their every move was watched. Besides, hedge funds with their billions of dollars could be leveraged into a colossal attack on the exchanges. And that could only help to move the market in the direction that Tarik wanted.

"That's a most attractive offer . . ."

"Additionally we would place with you very substantial amounts of money," Townsend interrupted Soros. "You see George, we have great confidence that you can use our information to make a bundle and are prepared to risk our funds."

That caught Soros' attention. "What amount were you thinking of?"

Townsend hesitated before replying, "Three billion dollars."

"It's an offer I can't refuse," Soros said simply.

"Do you know a man called Prince Tarik?"

"Yes," said the grand master of the investment world.

"Good. You see it all began with him."

With that Townsend opened his briefcase and extracted a green folder that he handed to Soros.

By nine o'clock that night they had worked out all the details of the agreement.

The stage was set for the big assault on the market.

3194-ISLA

CHAPTER 37

Immediately after lunch, Rosenberg began his investment moves.

"Have you figured out how many options contracts you will need?" Hillary asked as she took the chair opposite him in his office.

"That depends on how much profit you want to make and the likely movement in the underlying index," Rosenberg replied.

"You told me earlier you expected at least a ten percent gain in the S&P 500."

He nodded in agreement as she continued, "So what's your profit target?"

"A billion dollars."

"But that's enormous," Hillary gasped in astonishment. Her surprise was clearly evident from the tone of her voice.

"Well, Hillary you have to think big. I chose the number because that's what we expected from the sale of fifty percent of the firm. This is another way of achieving the same economic result and," he smiled, "in this case, as a bonus, we'll also retain all our shares."

"So how many contracts do you have to buy?"

"Let me see. The S&P 500 index closed yesterday at 2,287.10."

He punched some buttons on the computer and the Chicago Board Options Exchange page came up on the screen showing the delayed quotes on the S&P index.

"The premium on the December at-the-money call options at a strike price of 2,285 is sixty points," he said staring at the screen. "A point equals one hundred dollars so each contract costs six thousand dollars. Are you with me so far?" He turned his head to look at her.

"Yes."

"Good. So ten thousand contracts will cost sixty million dollars."

"I'm with you so far," Hillary said.

"Okay. Now to figure the number of contracts we have to take into account an options delta. Do you know what that is?"

"Vaguely. Is it something to do with price movements?"

"Yes. It measures the change in the price of an option relative to the change in the price of the underlying security. An at-the-money option has a fifty/fifty chance of closing in the money, so its delta is fifty. That means that for every dollar movement in the price of the underlying security the price of the option changes by fifty cents. The delta of a deep in-the-money option is a hundred, so one dollar of price movement in the underlying security results in a one dollar change in the price of the option."

"That makes sense."

"So my assumption of a 230 point increase in the S&P 500 index translates to a 230 point profit on each option contract. That's twenty three thousand dollars. Now can you calculate how many contracts we will need?"

"Yes," Hillary smiled. "We divide the one billion dollar profit target by twenty three thousand dollars. That's 43,480

3194-ISLA

contracts," she said reading the number from her HP calculator.

"Okay, now calculate the cost."

She punched the numbers into the calculator. "That works out to 260,880,000 dollars."

"Yes, but the premium might go up. So if we assume a price of sixty five we will need around two hundred and eighty five million dollars for the transaction."

"But our capital is only seventy five million dollars," a puzzled Hillary said.

"I've arranged loans to cover all our needs," Rosenberg replied.

They began buying the call options shortly after two o'clock on Monday afternoon. Rosenberg placed the orders through Merrill Lynch, Morgan Stanley Dean Witter and Bear Stearns. Hillary went through Lehman, Goldman Sachs and Salomon Smith Barney. To avoid unwanted price movements they decided that each would buy seven thousand contracts daily in the next three days, placing the orders gradually throughout the day in close consultation with each other.

The first five thousand December 2,285 S&P 500 calls traded at 60. The next thousand were done at 62 but then the price started to inch up. On the following three thousand it was 65. By three thirty that afternoon they had bought the remaining five thousand contracts at an average premium of 67 points.

That day the S&P 500 index closed down 4.50 points to 2,282.60. The fourteen thousand contracts bought on Tuesday, in quantities ranging from three to six thousand, cost an average of 73 points.

The final fifteen thousand four hundred and eighty contracts were bought on Wednesday. By then the market had incorporated the substantially increased interest in calls and the premium was up to 78 points.

Six blocks away, the portfolio managers of Pericles Asset Management gathered in the conference room to begin making their investment moves. They had a lot of money to invest–a little over three billion dollars and with the leverage of a typical macro hedge fund this amount would balloon to several times the three billion number.

"Did you make the interest rate arrangements on our uninvested funds?" Alexandra asked Anne Nicholson.

"Yes. We'll get the overnight fed funds rate."

"We agreed to invest the equivalent of one and a half billion dollars in triple-A and double-A European corporations," Alexandra said as she flicked on the Reuters page on the screen. "The dollar/euro rate is 1.0425 so what does that work out to?"

"That's a shade over 1.4 billion euros." Brian Watson read the number on his pocket calculator.

The introduction of the euro, in January 1999, created a single large European bond market in place of the hodgepodge of eleven smaller national bond markets denominated in currencies like the Italian lira, the Belgian franc, the DM and so on. This gave it a depth and liquidity that big institutional investors wanted and as a result, in its very first year, the euro quickly replaced the U.S. dollar as the principal currency of international finance on global capital markets. Of the 1.4 trillion dollars of bonds issued by corporations, governments and international institutions on international markets, over forty five percent were denominated in the euro compared with forty two percent in the dollar. This year the number was even higher, surpassing fifty percent of the 1.5 trillion issued through the first eight months of the new millennium.

"Okay, Anne," Alexandra said looking up at her, "will you please make sure we buy the euro notes and bonds within the next two days. Do you have a copy of the companies on our approved list?"

3194-ISLA

"Yes. What duration did we agree on?" Anne asked.

"Four years. And please don't buy any bonds with maturities beyond ten years."

"You want me to buy the intermediate-term treasuries?" Brian Watson asked Alexandra.

"Yes," she replied. "We made a capital allocation of a billion dollars which with the agreed leverage gives an even three billion dollars. And by the way the duration is not to exceed five years and the maximum maturity of any issue must be under ten years."

Alexandra then turned to Colin Stewart. "Have you figured how many put option contracts we will need?"

"Based on our profit target of six billion dollars we will need 131,000 contracts."

"What's the cost?"

"Given our market correction estimates of at least twenty percent, I think it's best to use out-of-the money options," Stewart said.

"What do you think Ravi?" Alexandra asked her equity specialist.

"I agree with Colin."

"So what's the number on this basis?"

"The premium on the five percent out-of-the money December puts is 39 points. Using a more conservative 45 point number to accommodate any unexpected price rise, gives us a total cost of 590 million dollars."

"And if we use the full 750 million capital allocation?" Watson inquired.

"Then we could buy around 167,000 contracts."

"What's our risk on the higher number?" Alexandra asked.

"As you know the premium in both cases consists entirely of time value which will shrink with the passage of time. In the worst case we would obviously lose the full amount," Stewart replied. "But using our sophisticated computer model and plugging in a variety of scenarios my worst case guesstimate is that we would not exceed our five hundred million dollar loss limit in the next thirty days."

"Good. I can live with that. Let's go for the higher number," Alexandra said. "Unless any of you have other ideas."

"What about the market? Can it accommodate such a large order?" Anne inquired.

"There'll be no problem on that front but as in all markets we have to trade carefully to keep the supply/demand balance," Stewart assured the group. "Over the past several years the market has grown dramatically. Last year options contracts reached an unprecedented 952 million and this year so far it is over one billion. The average daily trading volume is around four point two million contracts."

"Okay, then it's decided. We're going with the higher number," Alexandra announced in a voice tinged with impatience.

"How much time do we have to complete the transactions?" Stewart asked.

"The OPEC meeting is scheduled for the eighteenth of October so we have fifteen business days to buy the contracts," Alexandra informed the group. "To be on the safe side lets make that fourteen. So we need to buy at least 12,000 contracts each day. More if the market permits without a large price appreciation. Ravi, Colin and I will concentrate on this."

"What about the oil futures?" Brian asked.

"I've worked out the numbers," Colin replied. "A contract is for a thousand barrels. The asked price for the December contract is 10 ½ points so each contract is worth ten thousand five hundred dollars. Assuming a 13 ⅛ point price tag, to be on the safe side, we can therefore buy 190,000 contracts based on a ten percent initial margin requirement with our 250 million dollar capital allocation."

"In that case let's start accumulating the contracts in the next three days." Alexandra looked at Colin who accepted the responsibility with a nod of the head.

435

"Let me see what's still left," Alexandra said, reading figures jotted on a paper. "We still have to buy three billion dollars worth of spot euros. Anne will take care of that as she invests the funds in euro fixed income securities. So that leaves us with eight hundred million dollars for short term investments which can be used tactically in any segment of the market as the situation develops."

"We should put five hundred million in fed funds," Ravi proposed.

"Agreed," several voices responded.

"And we can invest the remaining three hundred million in ninety day commercial paper," Watson suggested.

"Seems fine to me," Alexandra said. "Will you take care of that Brian?"

"Yes, I will."

In the next three hours Ravi Shah and Colin Stewart bought twenty thousand put contracts on the Chicago Board Options Exchange through five brokers. The first ten thousand December 2175 puts priced at 39 were acquired through Credit Suisse First Boston. Bear Stearns did the next five thousand at a price of 40 ¼. They ran into increasing difficulty after that as another major put buyer appeared on the scene. It was mostly a down day on the stock market with small declines being registered by all the indices. The last ten thousand contracts were bought through UBS and Merrill in two equal lots at a premium of 43 and finally at 43 ½.

The crude oil futures contracts trading on the Mercantile Exchange in New York began the day at 10.65. Within the hour the price started climbing as two major buyers entered the market bidding up demand. Stewart managed to buy 12,000 contracts for December delivery at a price of $10.75 per barrel.

Early that Monday morning the traders at Exxon Mobil's headquarters in Irving, Texas received orders to purchase three and a half million crude oil futures contracts with delivery dates ranging from December through April. The time frame: two weeks. Keith Barker, who was the head trader, ordered each of his five traders to buy at least 50,000 contracts daily on the International Petroleum Exchange in London and on New York's Mercantile Exchange focusing primarily on the cheaper far dated paper. The men knew how to go about doing this. They were seasoned operators in this market in which Exxon and the other oil companies were major players.

In New York at the Madison Avenue office of Townsend Associates, Michael Townsend and Bodger Afridi also began to implement the investment strategy on behalf of their employers, Pegasus Investments and Neptune Advisors, the latter being the Liechtenstein arm of the recently established Saudi Pension Fund. Between them they had eighteen billion dollars available in cash in the United States. King Tarik approved the strategy at a meeting in Riyadh on Saturday. The centerpiece of the plan was a three billion dollar investment in equity put options. Another quarter was earmarked for investments in euro government bonds, which would create a long position in the euro. Forty percent of the funds were slated for U.S. treasuries with the balance, excluding the amount invested with Soros, in short-term instruments primarily commercial paper and certificates of deposit.

Their approach differed from Alexandra and her group in one important respect. Townsend and Afridi directed all their investments through a group of private bank account officers who in turn placed the buy orders with brokers. This provided an extra layer of secrecy and privacy that marked Tarik's operations from the very beginning and fitted well with the natural Saudi penchant for secrecy.

"I propose we buy equity index options since they are the most liquid," Afridi said.

"I agree," Townsend replied.

"My suggestion is that we use two billion dollars to buy the S&P 500 index. That's the most traded and liquid option on the Chicago Exchange. And five hundred million dollars apiece on the S&P 100 and the Dow Jones Industrial indices which are the next most liquid."

"That seems reasonable. What strike prices do you have in mind?" Townsend asked.

"Well, at our last Riyadh meeting we unanimously forecast a stock market decline in the neighborhood of thirty five percent."

Townsend nodded as Afridi continued, "So I think that in the S&P 500 we should buy three series of out-of-the money options." He looked at the computer screen. "The S&P closed at 2,287.10." Then using a pocket calculator for a few minutes he jotted down some numbers on a sheet of paper.

"Let's buy five hundred million dollars worth of December puts at a strike price of 2060. That's roughly ten percent out-of-the money. The premium on these is 18 ¼. Assuming a twenty percent higher acquisition cost, we get 228,000 contracts. Another five hundred million dollars on five percent out-of-the money puts. The current strike price on these is 2175 and the premium is 39 points. On the same twenty percent higher cost assumption we will have 107,000,000 contracts. And finally we'll use the remaining one billion on two and a half percent out-of-the money puts with a current strike price of 2230 that are trading at 47 ³/₈. That gives us 176,000 contracts. Of course depending on what happens in the cash market we might have to change the strike price on all the three series each day."

"Sounds good to me. What about the S&P 100 and the Dow options?"

We'll have to buy those close to at-the-money level with November expiration dates so we can get the maximum liquidity," Afridi said.

"Let's do it. I'll speak with Lamartine at UBS, Laurent at

Credit Suisse, Angela Davis at Citigroup and Roger Moore at Morgan Chase. That leaves you to deal with Am Bank, Goldman and Merrill."

Five minutes later Afridi was on the telephone with Frank Harris at Am Bank.

"Frank, I want you to buy a total of 100,000 S&P 500 December 2175 puts in the next fourteen days. That's five percent out of the money. We'll tell you the strike price level each day. In the same period I also want you to buy 100,000 S&P 500 December 2230 puts. That's two and a half percent out of the money. Again we'll give you a new strike price number each day. At the market on both."

"Right. We follow the usual settlement procedures through Siefert in Liechtenstein?"

"Yes," Afridi replied.

Similar phone calls for different contract amounts were rapidly made to the private bank account officers at the other banks and in the next hour all the orders had been placed.

That day the brokers were able to buy only 30,000 of the 2060's at an average premium of 19 ½; 16,000 of the 2175's at an average price of 42 ¼ and 18,000 of the 2230's at 48 ½. They also bought 70,000 of the Dow and 15,000 S&P 100 contracts.

On Tuesday the market rallied following an early morning announcement of the merger between AT&T and Yahoo. By the end of the day the Dow was up 114 points while the S&P 500 advanced 26 points. Options volume increased substantially as more investors sold puts at the strike price levels wanted by Alexandra's group and the Saudis. To them it looked like a no lose strategy. They believed this bull market would never end and the put premium simply improved their investment performance numbers. Ravi and Colin succeeded in getting 25,000 additional put contracts at a premium of 43 ¼. In an effort to minimize costs, Afridi's bankers also actively traded puts on the exchange. By the close of

439

business they had bought another 12,000 of the 2175's and 48,000 of the other two series in addition to 15,000 S&P 100's and 80,000 DJIA contracts.

At ten o'clock that day Michael Townsend was ushered into Alexandra's office.

"Michael, its good to see you again," she greeted him with a dazzling smile as she shook his hand.

"Thank you for seeing me at such short notice," he said, taking the seat opposite her.

"When did you come to New York?"

"On Sunday. I'm following up on your meeting with Prince, ah King Tarik in Geneva."

"A lot has changed since then," she laughed.

"Yes. Believe me we didn't know anything either." Townsend smiled. "Anyway I'm here to tell you that Tarik did not forget his promise. He spoke with a number of his friends. This morning, UBS Geneva transferred two hundred and fifty million dollars to your account at Am Bank."

"That's wonderful." She gave him that warm smile again.

"It's for your hedge fund from ten Arab investors. By the way you mentioned in Geneva that the fund would be operational this week."

"Yes. We started on Monday."

"How's it going? It's a tough market to call."

"Very well. We all have to take our chances."

"Yes. I understand. You'll be getting the details on the investment from our old friend Doktor Siefert in Liechtenstein sometime today. If you have any problems please get in touch with my colleague here. His name is Bodger Afridi." He pulled a card from his wallet and handed it to her.

"Thanks. I don't think there'll be any problem."

"I spoke with Tarik last night. He sends his greetings and hopes to be in touch soon," Townsend got up from the chair to leave.

"I'm sure he's very busy. Please thank him on my behalf."

———

At 9.30 A.M. on Wednesday morning Alexandra picked up the phone in her office.

"Good morning. It's Victoria. I just wanted to see how you are faring."

"We're making some progress. Yesterday was better because of the market rally."

"You bought more contracts?" Victoria asked.

"Yes, a lot more. And the price held steady as well."

"Good. By the way Frank Harris tells me that your Saudi friend seems to be following a similar strategy. They have placed a very substantial order for puts through us. Frank believes they have done the same through some of the other banks."

"That explains the heavy volume we're seeing on the Options Exchange," Alexandra observed, feeling a great deal more confident about her strategy.

Fifteen minutes later there was another call.

"Alexandra?"

"Yes?"

"This is Jurgen Pohl."

"Oh hello, Jurgen. I didn't recognize your voice."

"I've been thinking about our conversation of last week."

She had phoned from Geneva and told him of her departure from B&P, her joint venture with Am Bank and most importantly about the new hedge fund.

"As you know our private bank puts money from time to time with outside managers. I've been able to persuade them to put a hundred and fifty million with your group." Pohl was impressed with Alexandra from their first meeting. She'd been his choice to run B&P if HypoVereinsbank had bought it. Besides he also felt guilty at the price she ended up paying for that document they had worked on together. He wanted to make up for that.

"Jurgen, that's extremely kind of you. I'm most thankful," she intoned warmly on the phone.

441

"Not at all. Paul Erhard will fax you the details later today."

There were divergent trends in the stock market on Wednesday. The Dow eked out a small gain but the S&P was in negative territory for most of the day and closed down two points. After a hectic day, Pericles' two traders succeeded in buying another 20,000 puts at a premium of 45 ¼.

Alexandra returned home early that Wednesday. She was in an ebullient mood at dinner with Phillip and the children. They talked about homework and the principal events at school that day. Phillip turned to Alexandra as they were having dessert.

"So how are you doing with the hedge fund investments?"

"It's going pretty well. We've bought the Treasuries and the euro notes."

"What about the currency positions?"

"You know the foreign exchange market is very liquid so that was very easy. We're long in euros now."

"How about the put options?" Phillip asked.

"It's a little slow. We've been able to buy only about a third of the contracts so far."

"How come?"

"The market can't absorb huge amounts without large price movements, so we have to be careful. A number of investors are also apparently buying put options in large quantities. But it will get done. We have some time. Oh, I forgot to mention I got four hundred million dollars in new investments in the hedge fund."

"That's great. Who from?"

"Tarik sent me some Arab investors who put two hundred and fifty million dollars in the fund and HypoVereinsbank gave me a hundred and fifty million dollars from their private bank," she said getting up and heading for the elevator at the back of the room.

"Where are you going?"

"I'll see the children for ten minutes. I promised to watch 'Buffy the Vampire Slayer' with them on TV."

Half an hour afterwards, Alexandra came into the bedroom and sat down on the bed where Phillip was lying reading a book.

"I need to talk with you."

"Yes?" He put the book down and looked at her.

"I want a divorce," she said without emotion. "You can talk with my lawyer."

Phillip was stunned. He got up from the bed and walked over to her. "Please don't do this," he begged.

"I no longer love you. I want a break from the past. I want to start a new life."

"Please don't break the family. We've had eighteen wonderful years together. I love you more than anyone else in the world."

"The past is history. I want to get on with my life."

A pained expression crossed his face. "Please Alexandra don't do this. It will hurt the kids terribly."

"My life is more important," she said icily. "The kids will be alright eventually."

"Please don't do this. I had no inkling of anything. You never said a word about being unhappy. Please give me a chance. I'll do anything you want," he pleaded.

"No. It's over. I can't wait any longer. I've met someone who is a very successful senior partner in a law firm. I'm in love with him. Don't worry. You'll be taken care of financially."

"Please, please, I beg you. Give me another chance. Let's see a marriage counselor."

"Sorry but I'm not going to change my mind. I have to go now. And I'm moving upstairs into one of the spare rooms."

With that she walked downstairs. Phillip heard the front door close behind her.

Fifteen minutes later she was in bed in the arms of Jack Carver.

In the morning session on Thursday the major stock indi-

443

3194-ISLA

ces edged lower. At one o'clock the Dow was down 30 points while the S&P 500 had lost 8 points. Then at 2.30 the surprise Fed announcement of a fifty basis point interest rate cut electrified the market. Investors rushed in. The bond market rallied in anticipation of a slowing economy and lower inflation with the Treasury long bond had gaining 1 ¼. That day the Dow gained 130 points and the S&P 500 moved up another 37 points.

The commentators on CNBC and CNN were in an expansive mood. The major television news networks carried the Federal Reserve's interest rate moves as their lead story that evening. Optimism pervaded the airwaves and investors sensed the beginning of another powerful rally.

CHAPTER 38

The presidential campaign was reaching its climax by mid October. The candidates criss-crossed the country in their ceaseless bid to persuade the voters. Their one-minute commercials filled the airwaves either praising themselves or attacking their opponent. Bob Kerrey had twenty five million dollars in his kitty at the start of the campaign. The Republican Party held over seventy five million dollars in so called soft money, which it used relentlessly on hundreds of thirty second television ads attacking the Democrat candidate and misrepresenting his position on social security, taxes, abortion and everything else. The Democrats were busy doing the same to their opponent.

Wake Forest University in Winston-Salem, North Carolina was the site of the second presidential debate on October eleven. It was the usual hackneyed sort of stuff that passes as a debate in the United States. In fact both candidates did little more than mouth two minute set speeches that barely responded directly to the questions that were asked and shed no new light on their positions on any given issue. After the debate the major television stations put on their instant analysis shows for the benefit of the audience. The pundits

445

on CNN's Larry King Live gave President Bush the edge in that night's proceedings as did CBC. Bob Kerrey was considered to have come out ahead by a different set of self-appointed experts, on the ABC, NBC and WNET networks. The final debate was scheduled for the following Tuesday in San Diego. To the surprise of most of the experts, the public viewed Bush as the clear winner in the first debate between the two men held eight days earlier in Boston.

The latest Gallup poll results released on October 14 showed Bush with an eight-point lead. In slightly more than two weeks during which the nation witnessed two presidential debates, the Republican nominee had made remarkable progress, pushing well ahead of the Democrat candidate from his very narrow earlier 44% to 42% margin. More and more of the undecided voters had made up their minds in favor of Bush. The momentum had clearly swung to the Republicans.

Most commentators attributed Bush's success to the excellent economic situation. The United States was in the midst of the longest economic expansion in its history. Not surprisingly the voters were attracted by Bush's "You've never had it so good" slogan that he repeated ad nauseum in every speech, at every opportunity, in every campaign appearance. The Democrats were furious at the interest rate reduction enacted by the Federal Reserve but there was little that they could do about it. The chairman of the Fed defended the action as necessary to prevent any further slowing down of economic activity. This had apparently been caused by the fifty basis point increase in interest rates earlier in the year. With Wall Street and the Republicans praising the Fed's timely action, the Democrats were left to fume in silence. They simply could not risk being attacked as the party that favored a recession.

The soaring equity market was playing a decisive role in the ongoing political struggle being waged by the two candidates. Driven by the raging "bull" more and more American's were opting for George Bush who appeared increasingly likely to win in November. The super-charged economy and the bubbling stock market were inextricably linked in the minds of most voters. They felt richer, much richer and they knew who was responsible for their riches. In the two weeks following the Fed's interest rate cut, the Dow Jones index advanced 7 ½ percent. On Friday the fifteenth of October it closed at an all time high of 19,176.65. The S&P 500 index performed even better during the same period, having gained 8.7 percent. It also closed at an all time high of 2,492.94.

"I love you too Jack," Alexandra said on the phone just as Anne Nicholson appeared at the door of her office and she waived her in.

"I've got to go now. I'll speak to you later." She put the phone down.

Anne came in to the office followed by Shah, Stewart and Watson.

"What's up?" Alexandra smiled.

"We've been talking among ourselves and need to discuss the matter with you," Anne said hesitantly.

"What's the problem?"

"It's the market." Shah was agitated. "We feel that the Fed's rate cut has changed the dynamics . . ."

"Equities will continue to go up. The bull's been given a new lease of life," Stewart said emphatically. "You can sense the change in sentiment on the street."

Shah spoke up again. "After the Fed's announcement last week the Dow gained 443 points. And the trend is continuing. In the first three days this week it increased by 385 points on Monday, 127 on Tuesday and today it closed with a gain of another 237 points. Given what's happening we need to change our strategy."

The smile vanished from Alexandra's face. "How many contracts have we bought so far?"

3194-ISLA

"All the hundred and sixty seven thousand, as of today," Shah confirmed.

"Just before we came here I priced all the contracts," Stewart said. "This week we increased the strike price as the market moved up. Our model shows that we have already lost one hundred and eighty million dollars on contracts purchased last week. The premium consists entirely of time value and it will decay fast as we move toward the expiration date. Now's the right time," he pleaded, "to get out and take our losses before they start ballooning."

Alexandra got up and walked to the window overlooking Park Avenue. For a moment she looked out at the scene outside, attempting to control her anger. Then she turned and faced them. "The interest rate move caught the market by surprise." Her voice was conciliatory. "Still it's not as bad as it looks. The rally in the bond market has raised the value of our fixed income portfolio. A big stock market correction is much more likely now after the OPEC meeting." She looked very confident but behind the mask uncertainty was beginning to nag her and her stomach churned with anxiety. "I'm certain of that. The fundamentals have not changed. Throughout this week the market has been extremely volatile. It's going to be even more volatile next week as fears of lower corporate earnings begin to predominate over the rate cut. Investors are very jittery."

The memory of that Cambridge day when she had first run into Annabel and her wealthy crowd floated through her mind just then. The dream of making money had driven her ever since. She had almost reached her goal and then lost it all. Right then she felt like a racing car, once bright and shiny, which over the years had tasted victory and defeat, but its body was now dented, the paint scratched and dull. This was her last shot at winning again and she had no intention of letting the opportunity slip away.

"But there is no guarantee," Shah said, acting as the

---

spokesman for the group. "Besides the rate reduction might be the more powerful impulse as far as the market is concerned."

Her green eyes glistened with anger. "I understand it is much easier to flow with the tide," she snapped. "But we have a strategy in place and I'm not going to change it in mid stream," she declared bluntly. Then glaring at them she added, "Is that clear."

The anger in her voice came through unmistakably.

They nodded. The former B&P portfolio managers felt humiliated. They thought their status had changed from employees to partners but apparently not in Alexandra's mind. At the first sign of questioning she had put them in their place.

Alexandra was shocked at the pusillanimity of her colleagues. The incident reminded her of the historian Trevor Roper's story of how Hitler's sheer will power had saved the German army in Russia from catastrophe that first winter in 1941 before the gates of Moscow when the defeatist German generals were all set to retreat. The portfolio managers were just like those weak kneed generals. They would be whip-lashed by the market without her steadying hand.

She switched her tactics to make her victory more palatable. "Didn't both of you tell me that demand for puts has increased significantly?" She asked demurely, looking at Shah and Stewart.

"That's correct."

"Well let me tell you who else is buying huge amount of puts. It's none other than Pegasus Investments. They are in the market in a very big way. And they are operating on actual inside information. After all the owner is also the author of the Saudi oil plan."

"How do you know they're in the market?" Shah asked.

"I have my sources. But you can check with your friends on the street. You're aware, of course, that they place orders through their private bank account officers."

The information assuaged some of their doubts. "She's

3194-ISLA

probably right," they thought. "After all she had met the prince recently in Paris. Perhaps he told her of his group's strategy."

She continued in a conciliatory voice, taking a different tack. "Anne, tell me how many accounts have we managed to win from B&P so far?"

"Four, of which one is Prince Tarik's and the other is the fund we managed for his bank. They total a billion. The other two are wealthy investors with fifty million dollars between them."

"Building the institutional money management business will be a slow grind as you can see. Despite our affiliation with Am Bank, customers have not rushed in." Alexandra pointed out. "Some of the consultants are talking of a two-to three-year period to assess our results. The hedge fund is our best bet."

She knew in her own mind that the process of creating a large institutional business would take years under normal circumstances. Unlike equity clients, fixed income customers did not follow their portfolio managers. And with the new situation in her life she wasn't sure she wanted to spend so much time traveling to countless unattractive cities pitching investment management products to pension fund consultants most of whom she despised. She was more certain than ever that the hedge fund gave them the best shot at speeding up the process. Good investment performance in the fund would lead to a rapid development of the rest of the business. She was trying to make her colleagues understand this.

The portfolio managers looked uncomfortably at each other. Then Brian Watson spoke up. "I don't know about you guys but may be we should wait a few days and then talk again."

Alexandra sensed an opening. She smiled sweetly and said, "Let's reassess the strategy after the OPEC meeting. I'll go along with the majority view if there is no change in the stock market after that."

With that the discussion came to an end. She had imposed her will on her unwilling colleagues once again.

"Anne can you stay back. I want to talk to you for a minute about something else."

When they were alone she continued, "I wonder if you overheard what I was saying on the phone when you came in?"

Anne grinned. "I couldn't help overhearing it."

"Between you and me I just want you to know that I'm divorcing Phillip."

"That's a surprise. I didn't know you two were having problems."

"Well, my old life ended with B&P. I want a change. It's as simple as that."

"So who is Jack?"

"That's the new man in my life. Jack Carver," Alexandra smiled. "He's a senior partner at Sherman & Sterling."

"How long have you known him?" Anne asked.

"I met him last month at the Council on Foreign Relations. It was love at first sight for both of us. Incidentally he is married and has four children. They're getting divorced as well."

"And how is Phillip taking it?"

"Not too well," Alexandra sighed. "He's had a nervous breakdown. He's in hospital."

"What about the children?"

"I love them but my life is more important. The younger ones don't understand. In any event they'll survive. What choice do they have in the matter," she shrugged. "Delphinia is upset but I know the way to her heart." She smiled that special winning smile of hers. "I've ordered her a Jaguar sports car. She'll love it and forget the rest."

Hillary Schuster was going over some papers in her office when a cheerful looking Sidney Rosenberg walked in.

"You're certainly in a very perky mood today Sidney."

That second Thursday in October it appeared that his

high stakes gamble had paid off. "Yes. Things are going very well. We're heading for a record year in earnings."

Hillary smiled. "By that I take it that the options we bought are doing well?"

"Yes. Very well." There was a big grin on his face. "Novak just told me that as of now we have close to eight hundred and twenty million dollars in profit on the options."

Rick Novak supervised the operations and accounting departments at B&P. He had come to the company with Rosenberg and was totally loyal to him.

"Shouldn't we cash in and be safe?" Hillary asked.

"Not yet. The market will go up higher, much higher. The bulls are roaring."

"So are you going to tell the partners about it?"

"No. I'm planning to wait until we reach our target number. Probably another couple of weeks."

"Isn't there a danger of the information leaking out?"

"No, there's no chance of that. Rick has booked the transactions in the name of two fictional institutional customers called Victor and Omnibus Investments."

"What about the loan?"

"That's been taken care of as well."

"How are we doing on the institutional equity portfolios?" she asked.

"According to Ronald the results have been excellent. We've outperformed the index by a wide margin so the numbers for the year are looking much better. In fact, we're ahead of the S&P 500 for the first time in years. By the way how's the performance in the fixed income area?"

"Also very good. We went over the numbers at our meeting yesterday. The bond rally during the past two weeks has been very helpful particularly as we had extended the duration on all the portfolios."

"Good. Let me have the numbers. I have a Management Committee meeting this afternoon so I also need to know how many customers have been lost as a result of our friend's departure from the firm."

Hillary took out a file from her draw. "As of yesterday we have lost twenty five accounts totaling two and a half billion dollars."

"Have you got the breakdowns?"

"Yes. We lost five high-net-worth individual accounts, the largest being that of King Tarik for five hundred million dollars. The total in this category is six hundred and twenty million."

"And the institutional accounts?"

"Twenty accounts. The largest client was Saudi National Bank with five hundred million and the Common Fund with three hundred million."

"Do we know how many went to Alexandra?"

"Yes. Three of the individual accounts and of course the Saudi National Bank."

"Let me have the list. The Management Committee will be pleased to hear this."

The stock market continued to move up in the second week of October but the gains were much smaller and volatility increased sharply. The Dow added only 138 points while the S&P advanced a more modest twenty three. The portfolio managers assembled once again in Alexandra's office on Friday, October 15. Stewart indicated that according to the Black-Scholes option pricing model their losses totaled three hundred and twenty five million dollars on the put option position. Yes, this was a lot less than the five hundred million number mentioned earlier but they were very concerned and worried. Alexandra did her best to put up a confident front but inside she too was filled with doubts and anxiety. For the first time she was beginning to fear that the interest rate inspired rally might be powerful enough to make investors ignore any reductions in crude oil production. It would be disastrous if that happened. After another lengthy discussion they agreed to wait until next Wednesday before making any sell decision.

That night, even the excitement of new love could not sweep away Alexandra's worries. She was unable to sleep.

"You seem worried? What's the matter, darling?" Carver asked solicitously.

"It's the stock market. I've taken a huge bet and the market is going in the other direction."

"It'll be alright." He tried to comfort her.

"I've gambled everything on this move. What if it doesn't work out?" She shivered in his arms.

It would be the end of her career. She did not know if she could cope with failure again. It would be a terrible way to exit the business as a loser.

Events were moving along nicely in Riyadh, six thousand miles away. In early October, Tarik announced the names of the new Saudi cabinet. It consisted almost entirely of young businessmen. No one was over fifty. Unlike the previous council of ministers, this one contained only two Saudi princes. The charming and well-connected Prince Bandar, former ambassador to the United States, occupied the all-important Defense Ministry. The Foreign Ministry was in the hands of the other princely cousin. This was duly noted in Washington and administration officials breathed a sigh of relief. Khalid Ashrawi replaced Ali Naimi as the new oil minister. On Sunday he flew to Geneva to attend the regular OPEC meeting scheduled for the following day.

Earlier that week the foreign and defense ministers of the member states signed the Gulf Treaty Organization pact. The formal signing of the Treaty by the heads of state was scheduled for Thursday, October twenty one at a secret ceremony at the Prince Sultan Air Base sixty miles from Riyadh. No Western nation had any inkling of this as yet.

Karl Lutz was not pleased. His Global Trading Group

had missed out on the action having been taken by surprise, like the rest of the market, by the unexpected Fed move on the interest rate front. He was determined to take advantage of the privileged information provided to him by Ralph Schuster. That week, the group took a very substantial position in Treasury bonds amounting to over twenty billion dollars. It was a matter of life and death. He was going for the kill.

Michael Townsend and Bodger Afridi finally completed their investment moves the Friday prior to the OPEC conference. All the put options had been bought at a cost of two point nine billion dollars. Through repurchase agreements, at a twenty percent haircut, Pegasus was able to parlay its seven billion dollars of funds into a thirty five billion dollar Treasuries portfolio with a duration of ten years. Treasuries were selected not only for their liquidity feature but also because their lower coupon–compared with higher yielding corporate bonds–made them more price sensitive. In addition, Townsend and Afridi controlled three point seven billion in short-term funds that could be utilized when necessary. Pegasus also liquidated its entire nine billion European equity portfolio in the first two weeks of October. Finally another four point five billion dollars, at a twenty percent haircut, gave Pegasus a further twenty two billion for future purchases of the euro in the foreign currency market.

The unexpected cut in interest rates and the subsequent stock market surge exposed the option position to enormous losses, estimated at some nine hundred and sixty million dollars. Neither Townsend nor Afridi were particularly concerned by these short-term movements. Their eyes were fixed on the big picture that was about to unfold in accordance with the scenario mapped out by their employer.

Bill Thompson and Victoria Spencer were in London that week. Am Bank had rented Blenheim Palace–a few miles outside the famous university city of Oxford–from its owner, the Duke of Marlborough. His Grace was in constant need of money and the rental of the opulent palace, which had been given as a gift by the crown to one of his ancestors, went a long way to meet this urgent need. On Friday, Bill Thomson hosted a magnificent party for the wealthy customers of Am Bank's private bank, many of who flew in especially for the event.

Later that night, a nervous Victoria, in the company of Tim Wilkinson, telephoned Alexandra from her room at "The Bear," an ancient hostelry located close to Blenheim.

"How is it going?" she asked Alexandra.

"Good. We finally completed our investments yesterday."

"It took quite a while."

"Yes. But you have to be patient and careful," Alexandra replied. "You don't want the competition to find out or you're at their mercy. That's what happened to Long Term Capital Management. They were taken to the cleaners on some of their short positions."

"By the way," Victoria informed her, "I learnt earlier to-day that your Saudi friend has invested three billion with Quantum. The money was transferred through us to several accounts which we have traced to Quantum."

Alexandra did not respond. Her mind was on Soros. He was probably working in tandem with the Saudi group. There had been rumors of Quantum buying put options but it was difficult to tell from the open interest statistics that were released by the CBOE.

"I was at a party at Blenheim tonight for our customers," Victoria continued. "A lot of them are worried about the stock market. Your presence would have been very helpful."

She heard Alexandra laugh. "Next time. It just happened to be at the wrong moment unfortunately."

After the phone call a worried looking Victoria put her arms around Wilkinson. "Oh darling, she plays her cards so close to the chest. But I sensed a bit of concern and doubt in her voice. I just hope it works out."

CHAPTER 39

The Organization of Petroleum Exporting Countries, commonly know by the acronym OPEC, came into being as a direct result of a provocative action taken by the United States Government. In 1959, the Eisenhower administration enacted the Mandatory Oil Import Quota Program restricting the amount of crude oil imports into the country. More importantly the measure also gave preferential treatment to oil imports from two neighboring nations: Canada and Mexico. This exclusion of other oil producers from the U.S. market had an unintended but immediate effect on the oil market. It depressed the price of oil. And this quite naturally decreased the income of these other countries. So in September 1960 representatives from Venezuela, Iran, Iraq, Saudi Arabia and Kuwait met in Baghdad and established OPEC. By 1973 eight other nations had joined the club.

The Organization's principal objective was simple: to coordinate and unify oil policies among the member states in order to secure fair and stable prices for oil producers. In other words price fixing through the manipulation of supplies. To make the group's goals appear more evenhanded, a number of other innocuous items were added such as ongoing and regular supply of petroleum to consuming countries and a fair return on capital to those investing in the oil industry. A permanent Secretariat, headquartered in Vienna, was set up to provide research and administrative support to the member countries. The formulation of the general policy of the body was put into the hands of the OPEC Conference of Ministers that ordinarily met twice a year–and more often in the event of an emergency–with each member country being represented at the Conference by its oil minister.

For the first thirteen years, the Organization had a negligible impact–indeed many people would say non-existent–on the price of oil. All this changed with the Arab-Israeli War of 1973. Then, by reducing crude oil production, OPEC managed to raise oil prices dramatically from around three dollars a barrel to more than eleven dollars.

This success brought OPEC on to the world stage for the first time.

Many observers credited the organization's rise to the decline of American influence and power. The 1970's were the era of Watergate, of weak Presidents and of the defeat in Vietnam which traumatized the nation and turned it into a helpless giant. Overseas, American prestige and credibility was in shreds. Domestically the country was mired in a deep recession.

So throughout the 1970's the cartel repeatedly flexed its muscle. The consuming countries stood helplessly by like inert drug addicts as oil prices escalated relentlessly, reaching their highest level of $35 per barrel in 1981. The Organization appeared to have the world at its mercy. Experts everywhere predicted higher and higher prices with some suggesting numbers like $200 per barrel. OPEC's power seemed total and absolute.

And then suddenly the powerhouse collapsed like a house of cards.

What happened?

Like Adam in the Garden of Eden, the cartel eventually

---

overreached itself. But there was something more that did not escape the shrewd eyes of the students of international politics, for the decline of OPEC coincided with the reemergence of America as a confident and mighty super power. The long reach of America's hand was once again felt everywhere. It kept the pot brewing, sowing dissent and animosity among the cartel's members, promoting rivalry among them and taking advantage of their weakness. The boastful arrogance of the Shah of Iran, the insecurity of the house of Saud, the susceptibility of the corrupt political elite of Venezuela and Mexico to American pressure, the rivalry between the Persians and the Arabs and most importantly, the element of greed all played a part in the fading of OPEC's power. Higher oil prices also created a self-correcting mechanism that led to the discovery of new sources of oil in the North Sea and elsewhere. Here again, America's cozy relationship with Britain and Norway eased the way. Non-OPEC countries supplanted OPEC as the major producers and suppliers of oil, making it more difficult, if not impossible, to fix prices.

As he planned future Saudi oil strategy Prince Tarik carefully reviewed the cartel's history, in an attempt to learn from the past, and concluded that the success of the organization contained the seeds of its destruction. It reminded him of a remark that Napoleon–probably the greatest military genius of all times–once made during the course of a remarkable career: "The most dangerous moment comes with victory." In the prince's view, OPEC member countries had failed to understand this simple truth. The group would have to keep this in mind in the future.

So through most of the eighties and nineties the cartel nearly crumbled. It was marginalized almost into oblivion having been reduced to a toothless body that no one took seriously, not even its own members. Increasingly, the Organization became more of a debating society, like the Oxford University Union, where fiery speeches were made

3194-ISLA

but agreements were either never reached or, just as often, never carried out.

Just when the obituary of the Organization was being written in newspapers around the world, the situation was dramatically reversed. By early 1999, oil prices had sunk to $10 per barrel and were heading south with oil production way out of balance with demand. There was even talk of prices going down to the $5 level. Many oil-producing countries faced social unrest and financial collapse. The terrifying economic disaster that overtook Russia came as a timely reminder to other states of what could happen to them. The fate of all oil producers, not just the cartel members, hung in the balance.

And that's when the state of affairs changed once again.

Help came from an unexpected source. From Mexico and its free-market oil minister, Luis Tellez. In a series of back-office deals he forged an alliance between Mexico, Venezuela and Saudi Arabia. Why did Mexico jump into bed with the cartel? For the simple reason that by early 1999 its economy was in chaos and it was on the brink of financial catastrophe. Oil revenues had fallen from thirty eight percent of total revenues to twenty eight percent in one year forcing a sharp slashing of its budget. Not once but three times!

It's a well-known fact in medical circles that extreme fear and desperation can make an individual perform incredible acts of self-preserving heroism. And so it did in this case. A series of production cuts combined with a remarkable return of discipline and compliance among oil producers brought about a resurgence in the price of oil. In the fall of 2000 it peaked at $37 per barrel and the oil producers were back, once again, in the driver's seat.

But the situation was not destined to last. The Americans, worried that higher oil prices would fuel inflation and damage their economy, did what they had done in the eighties. And once again the tactics worked. It was an election year and President Clinton, concerned about his legacy, felt particularly strongly on the matter. Massive pressure was exerted on Mexico. It succumbed to the arm-twisting. Dependent for over eighty percent of its trade on the United States, the Mexicans felt they had no choice but to cooperate with the Americans. The Saudis and the Kuwaitis caved in shortly thereafter. At the fall OPEC meeting they agreed to a production increase of 1.7 million barrels per day. And from there the situation slowly spun out of control.

Why?

The answer to that question was simple. Forecasting oil demand was a treacherously complex task and nudging down oil prices without causing a collapse was even trickier. And that's what they discovered. OPEC's newly found discipline cracked as its members resorted once again to massive cheating. Oil prices unraveled. By early 2001, the price of Brent crude was hovering at the $19 per barrel level, almost half the number prevailing a few months earlier. In the following years the price continued its downward spiral until it reached its current level of $10.

The 119th Ordinary Meeting of the OPEC Conference of Ministers got under way at the Intercontinental Hotel in Vienna on Monday, October 18, 2004 at 10.30 A.M. It began with a speech by His Excellency Youcef Yousfi, President of the OPEC Conference and the Oil Minister of Algeria.

"Excellencies, Ladies and Gentlemen. It is a great privilege and honor to welcome you to the 119th Meeting of the OPEC Conference," he began. "On behalf of all of you I would also like to welcome the ministers from two non-OPEC member countries that, like us, are concerned by the current state of the international oil market. They are Mr. Francisco Fuentes Carrera, Oil Minister of Mexico and Mr. Grigory Yavlinsky, Deputy Prime Minister of the Russian Federation.

"As you know, since January 2001 the oil market has been

461

plagued once again by an imbalance between supply and demand that has led to a drastic fall in oil prices . . ."

The speech went on for another fifty minutes ending with a warning that observers were once more forecasting the imminent demise of OPEC and appealed for a spirit of cohesion, solidarity and responsibility. He concluded by saying "I strongly believe that we can still act collectively to stabilize oil prices at a fair level."

Rilwanu Lukman, the Secretary General of the Organization was the next speaker. The dramatic collapse of oil prices in 1998 was compounded by an unfortunate OPEC miscalculation. Just as Asia's demand for oil was plummeting because of that continent's economic crises, the cartel had increased its oil production. The same mistake had been made in 2000. In the past the lesson had been ignored all too often. But not this time. Lukman very carefully went over the figures for projected world oil demand in the near term. In 2004, it was forecasted at 85 million barrels per day. At a projected growth rate of two percent, daily oil demand in the following year was expected to be around 87 million barrels. Total oil production was estimated to be running two million barrels above current demand.

After lunch, it was the turn of the oil ministers from Libya, Indonesia, Nigeria, Algeria and Qatar. They all cited the severe economic hardships that their countries were undergoing and how their national budgets were in a state of disarray. They pleaded for cooperation and solidarity and vowed to implement any cuts that the Conference agreed upon. Such was the measure of their desperation that each of them voluntarily offered to cut oil production by a minimum of a hundred thousand barrels per day.

It was at this stage that the carefully coordinated moves agreed upon in advance between Saudi Arabia, Iran, Venezuela and Kuwait took place.

"It is incumbent upon us to cooperate and agree upon

production reductions immediately," Bijan Zangeneh the Iranian oil minister said in the final moments of his speech. "The Islamic Republic of Iran is prepared play its part in this effort by reducing its daily production by one million barrels." He concluded with a thundering quote from a famous play, "The fault, dear Brutus, is not in our stars, but in ourselves, that we are underlings." Apparently the man had studied Shakespeare in his youth and was thoroughly familiar, as the audience now found out, with some of the works of the Bard of Avon!

The corpulent man sitting next to the Iranian was Sheikh Saud Nasser Al Sabah of Kuwait. Constant movement had kept his Bedouin ancestors physically fit in the not too distant past. But all that had changed with the advent of oil money. The only exercise Sheikh Nasser had undertaken in the last twenty five years was the short walk from his living room couch to his chauffeur-driven Rolls Royce. He now took up the Iranian challenge. "We agree with our Iranian colleagues that collective and concerted action must be taken now. Kuwait too is prepared to make sacrifices in a just cause. My government is willing to reduce Kuwait's daily oil production by six hundred and fifty thousand barrels immediately."

That was the cue for Carlos Rodriguez, the Venezuelan Oil Minister. He spoke at length about the suffering of the people of Venezuela and the urgent need to take action. He too volunteered that Venezuela, in a spirit of solidarity with other member countries, was willing to contribute to solve the problem. It was prepared to decrease its daily oil production by up to one million barrels.

By late afternoon all the ministers, except for Khalid Ashrawi, had given their speeches. All made the same point. Over and over. The Saudis just sat there listening and watching. It was then, at four o'clock, that Ashrawi finally took the floor. "We note the spirit of cooperation that has been in evidence today. During the past few weeks we have met with representatives of the governments of Mexico and the Rus-

3194-ISLA

sian Federation. I also held informal discussions with the Venezuelan and Iranian oil ministers yesterday and today. Saudi Arabia is convinced that we must have a credible and meaningful plan of action to deal with the grave situation that we are faced with."

There was a collective sigh of relief. Except for the Venezuelan and Mexican ministers, none of the others were privy to the discussions between their rulers and the Saudi Prince–now King–Tarik. So the same painful thought passed through their mind. What if Saudi Arabia took unilateral steps to decimate the price of oil? Their countries were already wounded economically. Any independent Saudi move would wreck them completely. And they too would be ruined.

"We have to get control over our economic destiny once and for all," Ashrawi continued. "At the very least for the next three to five years. The patient is on the verge of death so drastic remedies are needed." He paused for a moment for effect and then added, "We have come here today with a proposal."

A young man from the Saudi delegation got up at a nod from him and handed out green-colored folders to the assembled oil ministers.

Ashrawi spoke again. "We request that the Conference adjourn for a two-hour coffee break and then take up discussion of Saudi Arabia's proposals."

The Conference resumed at six o'clock and immediately took up the Saudi plan. Intense discussion and consultations had taken place among the delegates during the recess. At the request of the Conference President, the Saudis spent the next two hours making their pitch with the use of color slides containing charts, graphs, diagrams and other persuasive material.

Ashrawi concluded by noting that the plan represented a break from the past. "Our proposal calls for large production cuts. This is a difficult but not an impossible goal." Then he reminded the members, "We are picking up a significant piece of the action. Fully fifty percent of the OPEC production cuts are coming from Saudi Arabia. These temporary sacrifices have to be made by all our countries to achieve our common goal of fair oil prices. Saudi Arabia has demonstrated its willingness in this regard. We now ask other members to do the same."

The audience burst into spontaneous applause at the end of the speech. Severe financial pressures had created a mood that demanded action and sacrifice, compliance and a willingness to compromise. The stakes were high and rising by the day. The Saudi proposals responded to all these diverse emotions.

The Iranians, traditional opponents of the Saudis in OPEC, gave strong backing to the plan.

So did the Venezuelans. "The plan has been carefully crafted," Carlos Rodriguez, the Oil Minister of Venezuela, told the audience. "It takes into account the interest of all members. Venezuela strongly supports the proposals."

The representatives of the three Gulf states–Kuwait, Iraq and United Arab Emirates–followed. Their instructions were quite clear: back the Saudi position. And this is what they did. The remaining delegates also spoke in favor of the plan. They acknowledged that Saudi Arabia was bearing the brunt of the burden and were profuse in their praise of Saudi generosity.

For the first time the Mexican and Russian representatives addressed an OPEC meeting. They announced production cuts of eight hundred and fifty thousand and five hundred thousand barrels respectively that their governments were prepared to enforce immediately.

"Oil producers must have fair and equitable prices. For almost fifteen years now the price of oil has not kept pace with inflation and this has severely damaged the economies of the oil producing countries. This must be changed," said the Mexican Oil Minister, Francisco Fuentes Carrera, to the applause of the assembled delegates.

The euro-pricing mechanism was discussed at length. All countries favored the change. In the minds of many it represented a slap at America. They felt that the global financial system had been rigged for America's benefit. The reserve currency status of the dollar gave the United States a special advantage. It was the only country that could run huge trade deficits and meet the gap by simply issuing dollar-denominated bonds. If, as a result of this change, the dollar lost some of its advantage so much the better. After all, much of America's power was based on the strength of the almighty dollar and its economy.

As the last speaker, Libya's Energy Minister Abdulla Salem El Badri sat down, Saudi Arabia's Ashrawi got up and made another announcement. "I have been authorized by His Majesty King Tarik to advise you that Saudi Arabia has already taken steps to implement its proposals. Three days ago, the kingdom cut its daily oil production by two million barrels."

The announcement electrified the audience and galvanized it into action. Euphoria overtook the delegates. It took the Conference less than twenty minutes to unanimously adopt a resolution accepting the Saudi proposals and agreeing to take immediate collective action to cut back OPEC's daily oil production by seven million barrels. New quotas and the cuts to be made by each member country were approved by acclamation. Even more remarkably the Organization moved to maintain control over future oil prices. It established a secret upper and lower price band, which would trigger automatic oil supply changes when those levels were reached and it gave the Saudis the unusual power to require member states to increase or decrease their oil production.

Shortly after 10.00 P.M. the President of the Conference accompanied by the Secretary General of OPEC emerged to make the momentous announcement. The press had been

466

alerted an hour earlier that something significant was occurring at the OPEC meeting. The Secretary General answered the questions from the press. Was the decision unanimous? Yes that was required under Article 11. Was a price level discussed? What was it? OPEC was looking at a $38 price range. There were numerous questions relating to the euro-pricing mechanism. Lukman's answer to all of them was the same: in the ministers' view the euro was the best currency for this purpose. The press conference lasted an hour. Within minutes CNN flashed the news around the world. It was the lead evening news story on all the major television stations.

Analysts and commentators appearing on the CNBC and CNN business programs found the switch to the euro very troubling.

CHAPTER 40

Alexandra was just getting off the telephone with Carver when Colin Stewart rushed into her office. His face was flushed with excitement.

"Did you hear the news?" he asked breathlessly.

"What news?"

"It's on Bloomberg."

"Colin, calm down and tell me what it's all about." In the exhilaration surrounding her affair with Carver she had forgotten about the OPEC meeting.

"You were right. OPEC just made the announcement after their meeting in Geneva. They are reducing oil production by over eight million barrels."

She let out a subdued cry of joy.

Hearing the commotion, Anne Nicholson and Charles Bradley came running into the office. Ravi Shah and Brian Watson who were reading the newsflash on the Bloomberg screen joined them.

"But there is a real surprise," Brian remarked.

"What?" Several voices asked in unison.

"Oil is to be priced in euros."

"Oh my God, that's great," Alexandra said exuberantly.

They sat there talking for the next fifteen minutes. So now the big question was: will this prick the bubble in the stock market? It was a question that preoccupied the minds of everyone in that room. Their fate was riding on this one issue. The question "Is this a bubble and when will it burst" had been asked again and again for the past two years by many noted analysts, by respected newspapers and magazines such as the Economist and even by the recently-canonized Alan Greenspan, former chairman of the Federal Reserve. Many commentators worried that the speculative bubble might end badly. Only last month Barton Biggs, the Chairman of Morgan Stanley Dean Witter Investment Management, had reiterated his view that stocks were overvalued by at least fifty percent. Another skeptic, Charles Clough, chief investment strategist at Merrill Lynch had felt compelled to retire a few years earlier, unable to take the pressure any longer of the account representatives and through them of their customers. Legendary investor Leon Levy was quoted as saying, "this state of affairs cannot last more than a few months." But like John the Baptist they were voices in the wilderness. The market brushed off all such doubts and continued on its volatile upward streak. The prevailing view was that of analysts such as Abby Joseph Cohen of Goldman Sachs, the supreme commander of the bulls, who saw this happy state of affairs continuing forever. There were troubling similarities with the 1920's. Then too a similar mood had prevailed. On the eve of the Great Crash, one of America's most distinguished economists, Irving Fisher of Yale, had said with categorical certainty, "stock prices have reached a permanent high plateau. It is the dawn of a new era in the stock market."

"So what do you think? Is this the moment?" Brian finally asked Alexandra.

"No one knows for certain, but if my guess is right–and my gut tells me that I'm right–then we'll see a severe correction, perhaps even a market meltdown." She was thoughtful for a while and then continued, "I think the pressure will come from the currency market then spread to bonds and then in turn percolate to stocks."

"That's my view as well," Stewart acknowledged.

"And if I'm wrong, the market will simply ignore the 'noise' and continue on its upward course. It has happened in the past. You know what that would mean," Alexandra said.

Several of those present shuddered at the thought.

"I'm sure you're right," Anne smiled encouragingly. "And, in the words of Shakespeare, 'It's a consummation devoutly to be wished.'" The others laughed and nodded their heads vigorously. They felt the need to show a positive attitude. This was not the time to exhibit fear whatever their inner feelings. Hadn't she been right in predicting the oil price move?

"Ravi and I will be tracking the trading in Tokyo and I'll phone you later in the evening," Colin said to Alexandra.

He owned the latest Dell Inspiron laptop through which he could access Bloomberg and even trade if the situation demanded. The late breaking news was received in New York after regular trading hours, so what happened in Asia and then Europe would be the first real indicators of the likely impact on Wall Street.

After the close of the market that day, Intel and Yahoo announced that third quarter earnings would not meet analyst forecasts. Both companies also indicated weaker fourth quarter results in the face of slowing sales. In after hours trading their shares slumped by five percent.

Sidney Rosenberg left the office early that evening for a pre-theater dinner at Aquavit. Hillary Schuster was already there when he arrived. They chatted and talked about opera and music. Neither had heard the OPEC announcement. Later they went to Carnegie Hall to listen to the Russian piano prodigy Evgeny Kissin who was once again making a victorious tour of the United States thrilling adulating audiences everywhere. Tonight it was Chopin and Schubert. At five o'clock Treasury Secretary, Paul O'Neill was ushered into the Oval Office. He was accompanied by Patrick Blackwell, the acting chairman of the Federal Reserve. Bush waived them to the empty chairs on the other side of his desk. "As you know Mr. President," O'Neill began. "OPEC announced a new supply agreement half an hour ago in Vienna. This might eventually raise the price of oil . . ."

"Of course that will depend on whether they can stick together," Blackwell interrupted the secretary.

O'Neill nodded impatiently. "What's more important is the new policy of pricing oil in euros."

"What's the likely effect of this?" Bush asked.

"It will most likely put some pressure on the dollar," the Treasury Secretary responded as the Fed chairman shook his head in agreement. "Of course, the euro is an alternative reserve currency," O'Neill continued, "but to date it has not made much headway. This action will almost certainly help it become more important."

"Is it likely to roil the currency markets tomorrow?" the President inquired.

"It'll be a little rough but not much. I expect the euro will strengthen by three or four cents from its current level of 1.06 dollars per euro," Blackwell replied.

"Will you need to intervene in the currency market?"

Central banks periodically intervened in the foreign exchange markets, usually in the opposite direction of the ongoing speculation, either to strengthen the local currency or at the very least to maintain its existing level. Occasionally the action was undertaken to weaken the country's currency, as had been the case in Japan earlier in the year. But these attempts, almost invariably, failed. With daily trading volumes exceeding a trillion dollars the currency markets were much too large for the central banks to control.

3194-ISLA

"If we have to, but unfortunately intervention rarely works," Blackwell responded.

"Do we know who is leading OPEC in this move?" Bush asked the Treasury Secretary.

"Saudi Arabia as far as we can tell. But we have no idea, as yet, as to why they wanted the switch to euro pricing. It is clearly aimed at us."

"That's what I suspected. Unfortunately we know very little about the political views of the new Saudi King," Bush remarked.

O'Neill quickly briefed the President on the new arrangements put into place by OPEC, particularly those relating to the formation of a new council for monitoring compliance and the extraordinary powers given to Saudi Arabia to control oil prices.

"I believe we can still exercise considerable leverage on the Saudis. Bandar is the Defense Minister and is well-known to many of us. Mr. President, the Russians, the Venezuelans and the Mexicans have gone along with this move. If necessary you could put some pressure on the Mexicans, at least to get some information," O'Neill observed.

"Perhaps. But you have to remember that the new man in Mexico will be very sensitive to any pressure from us," Bush mused. "And Chavez and Putin are not going to help us. With the Saudis our real leverage is their fear of the Iranians and the Iraqis but unfortunately the situation has changed significantly on that front in the past several months. We were having difficulties even with Fahd, the previous king."

The conversation continued for several more minutes and then Bush indicated that the discussion was over. At least for the time being.

"Both the Treasury and the Fed will monitor the market situation carefully and we'll remain in close touch with the White House," O'Neill assured the President as he and Patrick Blackwell took their leave.

At about the same time as the White House meeting was

MARKET CRASH

taking place, Tim Wilkinson was dialing the direct number of
Victoria Spencer. She picked up the phone on the second ring.
"Victoria Spencer here."
"Vicki darling, it's Tim. Did you hear the announcement?"
Wilkinson asked.
"No. I just got back from a meeting. What
announcement?"
"From OPEC and it's almost exactly what I told you."
He was exultant. "They are reducing production by over
eight million barrels and oil is to be priced in euros effective
immediately."
"So now we wait and see what effect this has on the stock
market."
"I spoke with Michael Townsend a short while ago. He
said there would be a number of other announcements in the
next few days. In fact both he and Ashrawi sound very
confident that events will play out as planned."
"Let's hope so," she replied wistfully.
Jack Carver was on top of Alexandra. They had just started
to make love when the telephone rang. They continued, try-
ing to ignore the disturbance but the ringing was incessant
and Alexandra was forced to pick up the handset.
"Hello." Her voice was tentative.
"Sorry to bother you. It's Colin. All hell's broken out in
Tokyo."
"What's happening?"
"The currency market is going crazy. The yen's up in a
big way. From 105 to 99."
"What about the Nikkei?"
"Strangely enough it's up about two percent."
"May be the Japanese are selling their dollar assets and
switching to their own equity market."
"That's the only explanation."
"Let me know if anything major develops." She put the
phone down.

473

"What's happening?" Carver asked.

She quickly told him and they resumed their interrupted activity.

CHAPTER 41

The party came to an end at eleven o'clock Eastern Standard Time on Tuesday, October 19. And what a grand ball it had been. It had lasted twenty two years and had added fourteen trillion dollars to household wealth.

For it was on that date that the greatest crash ever witnessed on the American stock market finally began. It was sudden and it was unexpected. And on that Tuesday no one thought that it was the start of something momentous. So the key questions asked afterwards were: why now? And what caused it? After all, oil prices had been higher before. In fall 2000 they had even touched $37 a barrel and there was scarcely a ripple in the stock market. And the dollar had been weaker, much weaker, several times during the decade. So what was so special now?

The answers, of course, were discovered much, much later.

All sort of myths have flourished since then. The market's collapse has been blamed on the perfidy of the Arabs, the conspiracy of the oil-producing nations, the treachery of the Japanese and East Asians, the machinations of the Latinos, the jealousy of the Europeans and the hatred generally felt by the world at large for America.

———

475

But the truth was much simpler.

The disaster was brought about by the gullibility of ordinary investors. The allure of easy money had beckoned millions of Americans who saw in the market a way to get rich quickly, painlessly and without risk. For quite a while the stock market had turned into a lottery where everyone won all the time. It was like an ATM machine that dispensed cash at will. So foolishness, unscrupulousness, jealousy, fear, greed and myriad similar emotions had played the major role in the debacle.

Yet as everyone knows, events don't just happen. They need a cause. A trigger. In retrospect it is clear that the stock market was terribly overvalued. The symptoms were visible everywhere. But no one was willing to pay any attention. So in the end it was the American investors who brought the tragedy upon themselves like some modern-day Samson pulling down the temple. The irresponsibility of politicians and business people–stock analysts, financial consultants, money managers, market gurus and chief executives–fostered a disconnect from reality and a false sense of security among the investing public. Common sense, reason and judgment were banished and replaced by an over arching mood of self-perpetuating optimism and confidence. This attitude was at the heart of the problem.

At eight o'clock that morning, Ronald Shapiro sauntered into Sidney Rosenberg's office. He pulled a chair and sat down as Rosenberg peered across the Wall Street Journal to look at him.

"I've been looking at overnight developments in Tokyo and in the European markets." Shapiro's face reflected concern. The institutional equity portfolios that his group managed were fully invested. He felt uneasy and would have liked to reduce the exposure by fifteen or twenty percent by switching to cash but to make these moves he needed

Rosenberg's approval. That explained the reason for his presence there.

"And what's bothering you?" Rosenberg asked.

"The dollar took a beating in Tokyo and its down four cents in trading in London versus the euro. This weakness could easily spill over to stocks. I'm wondering if we shouldn't lighten up a little," Shapiro suggested. "Take some of our profits."

"You're just too nervous Ron. Two weeks ago you wanted to do the same thing and see what's happened since then. The Dow's up 1,338 points. This too will pass. Look, nothing fundamental has changed."

He paused for a minute to drink his coffee, and then continued, "Our economic growth continues to astonish the world. Its been going on for 164 months. That's the longest in our history. Just look at the growth rate. Over four percent in the fourth quarter of 2003, then three and a half percent in the first quarter and two and a half percent in the last quarter."

"I agree the economic expansion is awesome. But I'm looking at market technicals and the signals aren't good. So I'm thinking, maybe we should do something."

"Forget technical factors," Rosenberg remarked. "Let's just focus on fundamentals. The economy is strong and so are corporate profits. Inflation has all but disappeared. That's what counts. This confluence of events is truly incredible."

That was the impression throughout the world. America's economic performance was remarkable and, even more amazingly, it defied the laws of economics. The jobless rate was at 4.2 percent. For all practical purposes that constituted full employment and yet there were no inflationary pressures. In fact, inflation and interest rates were at the lowest levels in a generation. And still more surprisingly, even at this late stage in the economic cycle, worker productivity was actually increasing. A whole new school of thought had come into being, one to which Rosenberg subscribed whole-heartedly.

3194-ISLA

Technological advances, in this view, had created a 'new paradigm,' a new economy. One in which the business cycle had been abolished. Yet despite all this talk, the reasons for the strong economy remained a mystery. Innumerable opinions and theories were advanced but no one was absolutely certain.

"What about the OPEC moves?" Shapiro asked.

"It's been tried before. Oil prices in the first quarter were very much higher than today. Besides I don't expect them to pull this off collectively. It's a fractured coalition." Rosenberg dismissed the cartel contemptuously.

"You're probably right on that." He got up and left, satisfied with Rosenberg's explanations.

The point, however, was that the economic situation was not as sound as it appeared at first sight. True the economy had grown for over thirteen and a half years. But so what? Such longevity had been witnessed in other parts of the world. The economies of many East Asian nations had expanded for decades prior to the 1997 collapse. Japan's gross domestic product had barreled upwards for fifteen years before destructing in the early nineties following the stock market crash. To most observers, the U.S. economy looked quite healthy and well-balanced. Yet in many ways it was actually not very dissimilar to that of Japan in the nineteen eighties.

Beneath the smooth surface, this quiescent volcano was churning and bubbling deep inside. Newspapers and magazines had, on occasion, pointed out the fragility with headlines such as, "Living on Borrowed Time," and "America is Up to its Neck in Debt." But most investors paid no attention to the fault lines. Signs of excesses were evident in numerous areas. Households and corporations were on a borrowing binge encouraged by the enormous increase in wealth. Non-financial corporate debt was at a record five point seven trillion dollars, more than half the size of America's gross domestic product. It had increased by a staggering hundred percent in the past eight years. Last year these corporations had borrowed over three hundred billion dollars, but the funds were not utilized to increase productive capacity, as one would have expected. Instead, over half the amount was simply used by the companies to buyback their outstanding shares. It was a magical way of increasing earnings per share at the stroke of a pen. Credit quality was deteriorating, non-performing bank loans were rising and the default rate was at its highest level since the Mike Milken era of the early nineteen nineties.

American households were also doing their best to live up to their reputation as the world's champion spendthrifts. They refused to be outdone by their corporate brethren and their total debt, including mortgages, was now a massive 8.9 trillion dollars, having risen by one hundred and forty fifty percent in the past eight years. Credit write-offs at banks were at an all-time high and personal bankruptcies were at record levels.

All this did not matter in times of prosperity. But what if the economy stopped growing? Would they be able to repay these huge amounts? And if not, both corporate and household borrowers would be forced to readjust their finances. That's when the problem cropped up because, as everyone knows, debt does not shrink even when asset and equity prices decline sharply. In that event one simply became poorer. So massive defaults would be the only way out.

In fact this was exactly what happened in Japan. In the nineteen eighties they too had believed that rising share and property prices would continue forever. Alas it was not to be. Japanese banks were now burdened with over a trillion dollars of bad debts and the economy had been asleep, until fairly recently, for over a decade.

There was another even more serious problem. America's current account deficit was running at a staggering three hundred billion dollars. In each of the past three years a new record had been set. The increase last year was a hundred

479

billion dollars. The nation couldn't have enough of foreign cars, DVD's, electronic equipment, clothes, luxury goods and oil. Much of the country's manufacturing had shifted overseas. Labor costs were substantially lower there. The vast majority of Americans–almost eighty percent–employed in industry and business were in the service sector: trade, finance, insurance, real estate, data processing, e-commerce, transportation and a broad array of professional services such as accounting, law, medicine the legal profession and so on. Because of the current account deficit, the United States needed to borrow almost one billion dollars every day. The country was dependent on the willingness of foreigners to buy and hold dollar-denominated assets, and these foreigners now owned a staggering two trillion dollars. What would happen if the foreigners sold these assets? America was increasingly dependent–and therefore increasingly vulnerable–on foreigners for its raw materials, its manufactured goods, its oil and even for its finances. It was the world's biggest debtor.

Much of the talk of a new economic order was tied to the so-called productivity miracle. Even at this late stage of the boom, worker productivity, according to the statistics, was rising at an unmatched five percent rate. American workers were producing more and more per hour. That was what kept inflation in check and raised corporate profits which in turn were propelling the stock market to new heights. But doubts were beginning to surface. America by the year 2004 was a service economy and the largest category in the workforce consisted of "knowledge" workers whose work largely in-volved cerebral tasks such as developing computer programs, bond or equity trading, managing money, taking care of pa-tients and so on. The government's statistics for people in this category were seriously flawed. They showed that, on average, workers in the service industry worked about 33 hours per week. Unfortunately this simply wasn't true. Bank and brokerage house executives, for example, worked twelve-hour days. The official time may be 9 A.M. to 5 P.M. but as the executives knew, promotions were earned for work done before nine and after five and there were no overtime payments. If this was true elsewhere, then a large amount of time on work was not being picked up in the official statistics for the service sector.

The experts said "So what?" Once again they missed the point. Productivity had to do with producing more goods per hour not working longer hours. People could not work harder and harder forever. There's an absolute limit to it. What if the productivity miracle was really a mirage? In that case non-inflationary economic growth was simply not sustainable.

Another important development in America's economic miracle was the escalating government budget surpluses. The Congressional Budget Office estimated these at numbers as high as 1.9 trillion dollars over the next decade. But these too were largely fictional. Another illusion. They were based on estimates and assumptions that were as likely to occur as life on the planet Saturn. The numbers, just to give an example, assumed that the economy would grow at three percent per annum for the next ten years, that more and more Americans would be hit by the alternative minimum tax or that various expiring tax credits would not be renewed by a Congress beholden to special interest groups. Then there was the even more absurd projection that government spending as a percentage of GDP would decline by twenty percent over the decade, an occurrence that one Congressman said "was as unlikely to happen as the melting of the polar ice cap." So once again this was another mythical debate like so much else. The actual surplus numbers were probably in the 300 billion dollar range over ten years. Absolutely peanuts. Telling the truth, apparently, was now just another policy option in Washington just as fiscal deception and gimmickry had become a firm article of faith among politicians in the past twenty five years. Never mind that the large numbers mentioned had not yet materialized, but the talk of large surpluses created consumer and investor confidence. With the government no longer sucking funds from the market more would be available for the needs of business. And that was nirvana for the economy. And the stock market.

Signs of trouble were sprouting all over the economic landscape but the degree of vulnerability was not fully appreciated. Or understood.

At the same time as Ronald Shapiro was talking with Rosenberg, a similar meeting was taking place six blocks away. Alexandra and her portfolio managers were gathered together in her office where a wide and free ranging discussion ensued.

"So most of the action so far has been in the currency and fixed income markets?" Alexandra asked.

"That's right," Colin Stewart answered staring at the Reuters screen. "I see the dollar/euro rate has moved to 1.1025."

"Why do you think the European stock markets have not reacted sharply to the OPEC announcement?" Anne Nicholson looked at Alexandra.

The FTSE index in London was down about two percent, while the DAX was down a percent on the Frankfurt exchange. In Paris the CAC was down a shade over three percent. These declines were within the normal range of price movements witnessed on the exchanges in the past few years.

"For several reasons. Perhaps they don't give credence to the oil-producing countries being able to act in unison. Don't also forget that in Europe eighty percent of the high gasoline retail price consists of taxes, so even big changes in the price of crude have a muted effect on gas station prices."

"So it's very possible that the U.S. stock market might react very differently to the same news?" Anne asked.

"Yes," Alexandra responded. "In fact it happens quite often."

Ravi Shah who was very knowledgeable on the stock market now spoke up. "Look, we have a fourteen trillion dollar market consisting of thousands of stocks. Yet all it takes to send the indices soaring or sinking is big moves in a few dozen stocks. Do you know that last year just 16 out of Nasdaq's five thousand plus stocks accounted for forty percent of that index's total gains?"

"That's astonishing," Watson commented. "I had no idea that the rally is restricted to such few shares."

"It's the biggest narrow rally in Wall Street history. And while the indices are up, they mask a decline in 75 percent of the stocks that make up the indices. In fact more stocks are falling than rising each day."

Few people remembered the events of seventy five years ago but there were eerie parallels. John Brooks, tracing the story of that era in his book, 'Once in Golconda,' wrote, "The 1929 boom, was in fact, quite a narrow and selective one. It was a boom in a few stocks in the Dow index and a good part of the stock market had been depressed all through 1929."

"What makes the stock market so risky is that most of the gains have been concentrated in a very small part of the market as Ravi mentioned earlier," Alexandra remarked. "So a sharp reversal in these stocks could bring the whole edifice crashing down."

"And that's also one of the reasons for the tremendous stomach churning volatility," Shah explained.

In fact a basic shift had occurred in the way investors viewed the market that had made it even more volatile. Fundamental research and value investing were out of fashion. Momentum investing was the new game. Investors chased what went up and dumped what was cold. They went with the tide. So two hundred and three hundred point daily

3194-ISLA

moves were increasingly common. The Dow had its fourth largest loss one day and then was at an all-time high two days later. In one recent month, the technology-laden Nasdaq index fell from its all time high of 7,025 by ten percent over a one week period, recovered to set a new high of 7,102 fifteen days later, then tumbled six percent to 6,676 before recovering to close at an all-time high of 7,254 three days later.

The market had reached a point of extreme vulnerability. It was worth more than 162 percent of GDP by mid 2004, more than double the level in 1987. Even at its height the Japanese stock market never exceeded 140 percent of GDP. Did it make sense? Was it overvalued? No one knew for sure. Stock prices had long ago broken all historic valuation records compared to earnings, dividends or any other accepted benchmark. Analysts no longer even bothered to defend the stratospheric valuations of technology stocks, some of which were at numbers like 1,000 times earnings. In the 1970's investors balked at paying prices equal to eight times earnings. Now they were falling on top of each other to pay prices that were multiples of 700 times net income. None of these companies had any prospect of making such earnings in the foreseeable future. The S&P 500 was selling at 33 times earnings, nearly double its historic norm over the past fifty years. Shares of Cisco were worth more than the GDP of Iran; Oracle was worth more than Chile while Microsoft exceeded the gross domestic product of Spain. In good times there was a natural tendency to ignore traditional valuation measures. There was always the argument that the times were different. "This is a new era," the stock analysts loudly proclaimed as they went about promoting the shares of companies they covered. The whole business had become increasingly incestuous. Conflicts of interest permeated the system. Sell recommendations were almost unheard of. It meant the loss of underwriting business and a cut off from all contact with company management. Few analysts were willing or able to take such chances.

It was claimed that this was the era of technology, which was revolutionizing the way industries worked. Talk of new eras had prevailed in earlier speculative booms. In the 1920's in the United States, the 1980's in Japan. In the twenties the high fliers were electric utilities, cheap automobiles and television. Airlines and telephones had once changed the world too just as the internet was doing now. Technology had not suddenly been discovered in the nineties, as the bulls would have us believe. It had played a critical role in economic expansion throughout the twentieth century.

"There's one thing that bothers me," Ravi said looking at the others.

"What?" someone asked.

"Individual investors. Because the market has gone up for such a long period of time, they have begun to see stocks as riskless investments. And the Fed has buttressed this belief."

"How?"

"By its past actions, the Fed has created the impression that it will cut interest rates when share prices fall but will not raise rates when prices shoot up. This has encouraged investors to take greater risks. Big daddy is always there with a safety net," Ravi explained. "Commercial bankers have behaved in a very similar way during the past quarter century. The Fed was always there to rescue them. After all bank deposits were guaranteed. So the figured they didn't have any downside risk."

"That's true but even the Fed's actions won't help if investor confidence level suddenly changes and in the end that's what markets are all about," Stewart interjected.

"I think it's fair to say that we all agree that the market is teetering on the brink," Alexandra smiled. "The OPEC move, coming on top of yesterday's 362 point decline, may push it over the edge. The tech stocks are particularly sensitive. Yahoo has a price-earnings ratio of 750; America Online is at 186, Cisco at 190. Concentrated selling of a few dozen stocks could send the market spiraling down."

"Let's hope so," Ravi remarked.

"We're going to find it out in the next few days," Colin Stewart observed dryly.

So the market was a time bomb waiting to go off.

The question was when. In his farewell appearance in the Senate, shortly prior to his retirement, Alan Greenspan was quoted as saying, "History tells us that sharp reversals in confidence happen abruptly most often with little advance notice." But Greenspan, even under sharp questioning, was unprepared to specify any particular time. "Senator, none of us can answer that."

But bull markets, whether in tulips or stocks, don't simply end because of over valuations. They need a trigger like war, inflation, rising interest rates. None of these were in sight. Yet when the answer came, it came with terrifying speed. What most people had overlooked was that for eighteen years the market had been like a rocket hurtling at breakneck speed into the stratosphere. It was now coming closer and closer to the sun and the incredible heat of that bright star put it in severe danger of a meltdown. Now in hindsight it was clear that conditions were ripe for a fall. The nerves of the participants were frayed. All it needed was an excuse, a catalyst, and that was provided by the OPEC oil and currency moves. Fear, unendurably gripping fear, did the rest.

In the first two hours of trading in New York the action was confined mostly to the currency and fixed income markets. It had started in Tokyo, spread later to Europe and then moved to New York as investors, oil producers and central banks began switching some of their assets from dollars. After the Japanese it was the turn of Taiwan, Brunei, Thailand, Indonesia, Malaysia and Singapore. Then as the sun moved west, Kuwait, Saudi Arabia and the United Arab Emirates began dumping dollars for the euro. Simultaneously they liquidated their holdings of Treasury securities, which took a dive and suffered their worst one-day price drop in eight months. The bellwether 30-year bond fell 1 ⁷/₈ or $18.75 for a bond with a face value of $1,000.

The action soon spread to the commercial banks that are the really big players in the currency markets. Six hours before the market opened in New York, Jacques Junot gave the marching orders to his four currency traders at the headquarters of the Commercial Bank of Switzerland on the Bahnofstrasse in Zurich.

"We're going long euro against the dollar. Ten billion dollars. Spot."

He then assigned new limits to each of them. "Hans you have two billion; Fritz you have two and a half; Heinz and Pierre each of you have one and a half; I'll do the rest. Any questions?"

"How quickly do you want this done?" Heinz inquired.

"Immediately. But that may not be possible. We must try to do at least half today before the rates change substantially. The market's most liquid when both Europe and New York are open simultaneously beginning 3.00 P.M. our time. But we can't wait for that."

"What about customer orders?" Fritz asked.

"Execute the customer orders the usual way. But our positions take precedence. We take advantage of the market first. Get up to your assigned position limits as soon as the market opens. And hit London, Paris, and Frankfurt as well. Customer orders and inter-bank trading orders cannot come from your positions."

In other words fuck the customers. The bank came first. It wasn't the first time that this had happened in the world of finance. Customers all over the world would gladly corroborate that.

"So you think the dollar will weaken further?" Hans enquired.

3194-ISLA

"Yes. I think everyone and his brother will be selling today. This OPEC thing is going to worry a lot of people."

As soon as the European market opened, orders began to pile in. The Commercial Bank's traders rapidly began to build up their positions to the assigned limits. Subsequent customer trades put enormous pressure on the dollar, which weakened as a result. Similar scenes were taking place at banks all over Europe. UBS, Credit Suisse, Deutsche Bank, Commerzbank, HypoVereinsbank, the French banks, and the London branches of Citigroup, Morgan Chase were all in the currency market buying and selling, as were large numbers of multinational corporations. By late afternoon the action intensified as the scene shifted to New York where the big banks–Citigroup, Morgan Chase, Am Bank and Bank of America–got into the fray. Within the first two hours the dollar was down to 1.0805. It then recovered to 1.0702 as a result of temporary intervention by the Fed before sinking once again to 1.1025 by late afternoon.

The weakness of the dollar was transmitted to the fixed income market, which was already under pressure from the large sales orders placed by foreign investors. The currency markets added to the bond market's woes. In his office on Madison Avenue, Afridi cradled two telephones in his hands as he spoke with the private bank account officers at Am Bank and Chase who in turn were connected real time with their currency traders.

"What's the dollar/euro spot?"

"1.1004–1.1006."

"Okay. Sell a hundred million dollars for our account."

Almost simultaneously he was on the other line.

"What's the dollar/euro spot?"

"Good. Sell seventy five million dollars."

In the next two hours this conversation was repeated with many banks in New York, Frankfurt, London, Paris and Zurich.

At the end of that period he was short two billion dollars and long equivalent euros.

The selling soon took on a life of its own in the debt markets in New York. Rates began climbing across the entire yield curve as foreign investors shed their fixed income securities and headed for the exits in droves. It was later estimated that a fifth of the trillion dollars of interest bearing instruments that were held by foreign individuals, institutions and governments were liquidated that day.

Why this sudden liquidation? Smoldering anger at the United States was a factor but not the only factor, or even the most important one. They were driven by speculative greed and fear. And then things got out of control.

Looking back later, as events were reconstructed, it became evident that the explosion that ripped the stock market started a few minutes after eleven o'clock Eastern Standard Time. At about this time Bloomberg reported an unconfirmed rumor that a consortium of German banks and another consisting of the largest French banks had provided credit facilities totaling forty billion euros for use by a group of eight oil-exporting countries. Within minutes of this late breaking news another report was flashed on thousands of screens throughout the United States. The spokesman of Deutsche Bank in Frankfurt and Société Générale in Paris confirmed the existence of the facilities.

Within seconds of this news there was a sale order for a block of fifty thousand Yahoo shares. It was placed by a Japanese institutional investor. The Japanese were the first to run for cover. You couldn't blame them. After all they knew something about bubbles being the only surviving experts of that particular experience. The Tokyo stock market had gone up for twelve straight years peaking at 38,915 on the last day of 1989. Then–inexplicably–it went into a tailspin and lost 23 percent of its value in the first three months of the New

3194-ISLA

Year. Investors feeling that the worst was over started buying again. But the troubles were just beginning. By the end of the year it was down 39%. Eventually it slid to 14,309 in 1992, almost sixty five percent lower. Even this was not the low point. It moved fitfully up and down finally reaching an all time low of 12,880 in 1998. Since then the Nikkei had risen but was still below 20,000–just about half the level it was at fourteen years earlier!

"That was the trade that signaled the sale onslaught." A portfolio manager by the name of Lester Marks recounted several days later that Friday on Wall Street Week. He was referring to the sale order for the 50,000 Yahoo shares that had started the stampede.

"Then in rapid succession huge sale orders for Intel, Cisco, IBM, Microsoft and other technology stocks began piling in," added Frank Capiello, another participant in the popular Louis Rukeyser television program.

Through most of the morning Alexandra sat at her desk watching the screen in fascination as the market tumbled. "Christ," she said out aloud. "It's finally happening. The Dow is falling to pieces." The put options were at last gaining value. They had picked up some of the losses of the past two weeks. But nagging doubts still remained in her mind. Will the down blast continue in the next few days? For as long as she could remember the damned individual investors always charged in whenever the market fell sharply. The papers called it "buying at the dips." She desperately needed a break. Eighteen years of hard work and effort had gone up in smoke after her sacking by B&P. They had robbed her of her business. It was worth a small fortune. For the first time in years she silently prayed.

Six blocks away Ronald Shapiro was at his desk, his eyes darting back and forth between three screens. "Holy cow," he muttered to himself. All the indices were heading south. The Dow was down 438. What about the S&P? It had plummeted 82 points. And the Nasdaq was being blown away with the technology stocks. Then just as suddenly the Dow rallied ninety points off the lows as bullish investors began buying. Shapiro felt more comfortable. But then again there was nothing particularly unusual here. For the past two years the market had been on a roller coaster. Two hundred and three hundred point ups were followed closely by downs of similar amount. He went off for lunch.

An hour and a half later when Shapiro returned the market was down 725 and still falling. During the rest of the trading session there were one or two pauses. The Dow even picked up fifty or sixty points. But then the selling started again and at the close the industrial averages were down a whopping 1,447 points. It was the largest one-day drop in absolute amount in the market's history but only the thirteenth worst in percentage terms.

Shapiro telephoned Rosenberg. "So what do you think? Are we seeing something new here?"

"Ron, we've seen this happen before. Do you remember in October 1997 the Dow fell 554 points? That was the largest one-day drop until today. And what happened?"

"It recovered over the next three days."

"Right. It will be the same this time," Sidney reassured him.

As usual CNBC covered the market action throughout the day. After the close of trading several portfolio managers and investment strategists appeared on the Market Wrap and The Edge programs. Their words were meant to reassure. Mary Farrell, chief investment strategist at UBS PaineWebber was the first to appear.

"How would you characterize the action in the market today?" Ron Insana, the CNBC anchor asked.

"The market in the past month had gone ahead of itself," Farrell responded. "Today we saw a small correction."

"Tell us what you think is likely to happen next."

3194-ISLA

"I believe the fundamentals are strong. The economic expansion continues. Inflation remains low. So I feel the market will regain its footings."

Ed Kirschner followed her, an hour later. He was a long-time bull and his comments were even more positive. "All the signs point to another record year. I believe the Dow will finish the year with another 20 percent gain. Corporate earnings are still strong and will continue to fuel the stock market for several years."

On the following morning banner headlines, in large print, on the front page of the New York Times proclaimed:

STOCK MARKET IN STEEPEST DROP LOSES
1,447 POINTS

WORRIED INVESTORS FLEE AS INFLATION
FEARS IGNITE SELL OFF

The Wall Street Journal headlines informed its readers:

OIL PRICE FEARS SEND STOCK MARKET
PLUNGING

DOW DOWN 1,447 POINTS IN BIGGEST ONE
DAY DROP

The accompanying articles talked of the turmoil in the currency market following changes in the oil pricing mechanism and the inflationary fears it produced in investors. They noted the stunning size of the losses and alluded to previous drops in the Dow, all of which had proven temporary. According to the Journal, foreign investors had been the primary sellers as they fled from the weakening dollar. Both newspapers talked at length of the credit facilities that had been provided by the German and French banks to a group of oil producers led by Saudi Arabia. This, in the WSJ reporter's view, illustrated the strong competition among European and American banks in international finance and in this particular instance the Europeans had come out ahead. The New York Times noted the recent changes that had taken place in Saudi Arabia and opined that while little was known about the new kings political views the kingdom's actions indicated a strong nationalistic bent very different from the past when that country was closely allied to the United States. Both papers pointed out that in the past investors, particularly individuals, had bought stocks on each dip and that this drop made prices very attractive of a large number of companies. Technology stocks, which had previously operated according to a "different set of financial rules," were now beginning to look reasonable. The Wall Street Journal reminded its readers: "many technical analysts noted that the big volume accompanying Tuesday's session might mean better things ahead."

In overnight trading, prices of the S&P 500 stock index futures as well as large numbers of technology stocks began signaling that a big drop was in store when trading resumed on the exchanges on Wednesday morning. And that's more or less what took place. The selling that started in Europe spread to New York five hours later. Then it took a life of its own and everyone sold. This was the downside of momentum investing which had been the vogue on the street for some time. Its adherents bought stocks because they were going up. Now they were selling as prices were falling.

At 10.30 Alexandra returned from a meeting in Westport with Classic Pension Consultants. She sat down at the trading desk with Ravi Shah and Colin Stewart who were staring fixedly at the screen. Just then there was a news flash. President Chavez had confirmed that Venezuela had begun reducing oil production the previous week. Similar statements from the oil ministers of Kuwait and the United Arab Emirates had been reported at the market's opening.

493

"What's happening at NYMEX with oil futures?" Alexandra asked.

Crude oil futures were traded on several exchanges but the largest volume by far was on the New York Mercantile Exchange. As a result of the large trading volumes and the resulting liquidity this contract was extensively used as the main pricing benchmark for crude oil.

"They're going through the roof," Colin said looking at one of the screens. The price for November delivery is at 17.10."

The three sat in the trading room, watching the action, their eyes glued to the computer screen. At the opening bell the Dow had started to plunge. By 11.00 it was down 587 points and heading down big time. The bottom was falling out of the market.

"Holy shit," Shah exclaimed. "It's really going to hell."

Stewart was on the phone with a friend at Fidelity. Rumors were flying all over the street.

"Word's out that Soros and Marcus are selling big time. They're hitting the technology stocks," Stewart said putting the phone down.

"Look at Microsoft," Ravi pointed out. "It's down 10 ¼." IBM is down 8 ½."

"Cisco Systems is down 9 ½. Yahoo's down 15 ¼."

"The hedge funds have around six hundred billion. Even with a low leverage of three or four times capital they would have around two trillion dollars. That's an awful amount of firepower," Alexandra observed.

"Yes. And if they use it to hit a few key stocks they could wreak havoc. The markets rise was fueled by a very few stocks and the same ones now can bring about a big decline," Ravi responded excitedly.

"It's turning into a bloodbath," Stewart noted, looking at the action on the screen.

Having established their investment positions at the end of the previous week, Alexandra and her group had remained on the sidelines so far. Now they too joined the battle. For traders the action was simply irresistible.

"I think now's our opportunity to short five or six tech stocks," Alexandra said. "We'll never get a better chance in our life."

They had a hurried discussion. Ravi proposed America Online and Cisco. Alexandra and Colin went along. They quickly reviewed a list of twenty stocks and added Lucent, Microsoft and Intel to the list.

"I want to commit two hundred million dollars apiece to each of these names," Alexandra informed them. "Can you calculate the number of shares?"

"America Online is trading at 81 ¼ so that's 2.5 million shares," Ravi spoke looking at his calculator. "Cisco is at 101 ½ so that works out to 2.0 million shares."

"Lucent is at 101 ½," Stewart announced. "That gives 2.2 million shares. And 1.9 million for Microsoft. It's at 106 ¾."

"A million one for Intel. It's at 188," Ravi said.

"Okay boys, time to get into action."

They spent the next four hours on telephones selling the shares through Merrill, Goldman, Bear Stearns and Morgan Stanley. But they weren't the only ones. So were the Quantum funds, and Xenon and many of the other hedge funds. Many portfolio managers were playing the same game, as were some of the mutual funds that specialized in short sales. The pressure on prices was intense. It went crashing down.

Technology stocks which accounted for over thirty percent of the S&P 500's market value–and 25 percent of the Dow's weighting–had been responsible for all the indices' gains of the past two years. Now they led the decline.

Around noon time there was a pause. Then a bump up. In the next half hour the Dow rallied 195 points. Alexandra, Colin and Ravi got on the phone to do some checking. "Who's selling?" "Who's buying?" "What are the mutual funds doing?"

The selling resumed once again. By two o'clock the Dow

495

was down 1,165 points. There was almost total chaos. By now everyone had entered the fray. The behavior and actions of investors were usually driven by the two primary emotions of fear and greed. For eighteen years greed had prevailed as the driving force. Now suddenly at 2.00 P.M. on Wednesday, October 20 fear took over. The whole system was built on one thing: confidence. And now as this was blown away the floodgates opened with a vengeance. Once the level of euphoria was pricked the whole edifice came tumbling down. Many professionals had remained fully invested against their better judgment. They had been forced into this position by performance considerations. The big multi billion-dollar institutional investors who dominated the stock market were now in a selling frenzy having smelt blood. They behaved like hundreds of sharks battling for a solitary prey.

Portfolio managers of the seven trillion dollar mutual funds sold their huge holdings of blue chip and technology stocks. The herd mentality had always exerted a powerful influence on the street and now everyone from Fidelity to T. Rowe Price to Putnam to Janus to Dreyfus and the other seven thousand funds rushed in to unload buckets of shares before it was too late. No one wanted to be left holding the bag. Investment advisors like Alliance, Morgan Stanley, Prudential Insurance, Neuberger & Berman and Fayez Sarofim joined them.

Ron Shapiro sat at his desk and watched the horror unfold on the screen.

He groaned aloud, "What the fuck is happening. What the fuck is happening. This is unreal."

The market was crumbling before his eyes. It was sinking like the good ship Titanic. The rapidity of its fall left him dazed. He tried to get through to Rosenberg but he was out. Finally he could take it no longer. He picked up the direct line to the B&P trading room. "Sell," he barked in the telephone, "Sell. Just dump everything at the market. We can buy back later."

This frightful scene was being repeated at hundreds of investment advisor and mutual fund offices all over the United States.

Foreign investors were also busy. They held two trillion dollars in stocks and bonds and they were dumping in droves. The Japanese, the East Asians, the Arabs, the Latinos. Everyone was getting out as fast as they could. The virulent anti Americanism that lay just below the surface reared its head. America was disliked everywhere for being too pushy, for its unilateral actions, its economic imperialism, for its power and arrogance and for its wealth. Here was a chance to get even. It was time to bail out. And they did.

Foreign banks had also joined in the frenzied selling. UBS had almost a trillion dollars in its private bank from wealthy investors. Credit Suisse and the Commercial Bank of Switzerland held a trillion between them from similar investors. Large portions of these funds were in American stocks both because of the markets enormous size but also because the returns for the past decade had been so good. They too sold, just like everyone else. So did HypoVereinsbank and Deutsche Bank and the other German, French and British banks as they desperately tried to keep their performance records intact.

"The Treasury Secretary is on CNBC," Ravi yelled. Someone turned the TV on. Paul O'Neill was being interviewed. He tried to reassure investors that the stock market and the economy were sound. "Prospects for continued growth with low inflation and unemployment are excellent."

The market paid no attention.

"What's happening in foreign exchange?" Alexandra asked.

"The dollar is sinking fast," Stewart replied. "It closed in Europe at 1.1604. The rate's down to 1.2014."

Earlier in the day the European Central Bank had intervened half-heartedly at the Federal Reserve's request. The word among exchange traders was that the Central Bank did not believe that intervention would stem the tide. Its view was that the Fed should raise interest rates to make the dollar attractive for investors. Wasn't that what the IMF forced developing countries to do in 1997, 1998 and 2002? Indonesia, Thailand, South Korea, Brazil, Mexico and Venezuela. But the Fed was not prepared to take that medicine.

"The yield curve has become much steeper," Alexandra remarked looking at the computer screen. "Prices are down at the long end with foreign investors dumping securities. But the short end up to five years is rallying strongly."

Rumors were flying all over the street. Lehman was in trouble? Why? Something to do with call options. Goldman Sachs had lost a billion. A similar number was mentioned for Morgan Stanley. Omega Advisors a macro hedge fund, was reported to have dropped three quarters of a billion. But the biggest rumor of all was that Bear Stearns might go belly up.

Ravi was on the phone to a trader at Merrill. "Ravi. The little guys have thrown in the towel. And they're getting fucked. Many can't make the margin calls."

"What's your friend saying?" Alexandra asked.

"That the small investors have finally panicked. They're having difficulty meeting margin calls."

"I think the Fed will be compelled to throw open the Fed discount window. They did that in 1987. Then margin debt was only forty billion dollars and it played a big role in the market's fall. Now it's astronomical."

"What's the number?" Stewart asked.

"It's over 384 billion," Alexandra replied.

A few minutes later there was a news flash on the computer screen. The Fed had thrown open its discount window.

That day the market closed down 1,864 points. It was

the largest one-day loss, topping the loss of the day earlier. Trading volume exploded to over three and a half billion shares, the largest ever recorded on the exchange. The ticker tape seen on most screens was usually fifteen minutes behind. Today it was over twenty as the operations staff made desperate attempts to keep up with the share trading volume.

Victoria telephoned Alexandra shortly after the market closed.

"Quite a day."

"It was a hell of a day," Alexandra replied in a breathless voice.

"And I don't think it's reached bottom yet," Victoria said. "I spoke with Barton Biggs earlier. His group manages money for us. He was very pessimistic. Their valuation model indicates that the market was overvalued by fifty percent."

"So what does he think?"

"He feels it will drop at least another twenty percent. Oh by the way the Fed Chairman spoke in the afternoon to Henry Fielding–that's our chairman–and asked that we make margin loans available freely. The Fed is injecting liquidity into the system on a massive scale."

"Yes the rumor on the street is that the Fed's buying securities by the ton."

"Something else, confidentially between you and me," Victoria said in a whisper, "Our Trading group has made a killing in foreign exchange trading. Apparently to the tune of four hundred fifty or five hundred million, but they've taken a terrible beating on bonds. It seems they were heavily overbought at the long end."

In a nearby skyscraper, Hillary was closeted with Sidney Rosenberg.

"We took all our personal savings in bonds and money market funds and put them in stocks based on the plan that Ralph got from his friend. Now we're almost wiped out." She was in tears. "I don't know what we'll do. Our life savings are gone."

"You aren't the only one. All of us have taken a shellacking. Was Ralph able to get in touch with his friend in London?"

"You mean Wilkinson. Yes, Wilkinson says that his friend tricked him. He himself had never spoken to the Saudis. Only with his friend and former partner. He claims to have lost his shirt as well."

After a moment of silence while she contemplated her desolate financial condition she asked, "What's likely to happen?"

"The S&P is down around 17 percent from its highs. Technically we're in a severe correction. It's possible it'll go down a little more but my guess is there'll be a rebound."

"What about the calls? What are you going to do?"

"At the end of last week we had net profits of eight hundred and twenty million dollars," he smiled wistfully. At the close of business today the contracts were trading at 7 points. At that price we would get about thirty million out of our total cost of three hundred and twelve million excluding commissions. So it doesn't make sense to sell. We still have two months left."

That evening, the most renowned bull of them all, Abby Joseph Cohen appeared on CNBC. More than anyone else she had helped to spark the rally that had taken the market to new highs in the past five years. She had argued that the market was grossly undervalued when the Dow was at the six thousand level in 1996. In the next eight years it had more than tripled and at its height a week earlier had touched 19,176.65.

"Today the market had its largest one-day drop. Where do you think that leaves us?" Sue Herrera of CNBC asked.

"We were a bit surprised by the speed at which the market fell. I think we are close to the bottom if not at it. We'll see a rise soon. Technology and blue chip stocks are now very under-priced relative to earnings," Ms Cohen opined.

"The tech stocks took a real beating today?"

"Yes. Tech stocks are always hit hardest in a sell off. Between 1929 and 1932, RCA fell by 98 percent. During 1969-1970, ten computer stocks including IBM and Sperry Rand fell by 80% on average. Then in the short bear market in the mid-nineties Intel fell 46 percent and Oracle by 76 percent. But at today's closing prices tech stocks are very attractive."

"What will we see going forward?"

"From this point on we should see the market moving up. There's real value out there now," Abby Joseph Cohen replied enthusiastically.

But even her optimistic pronouncements failed to stem the tide. The market was caught by total surprise at the announcement of the Gulf Treaty Organization at a meeting in Riyadh on Wednesday evening of the rulers of Saudi Arabia, Kuwait, Iran, Iraq, Bahrain, Qatar and the United Arab Emirates. Simultaneously Saudi Arabia and the United Arab Emirates announced the cancellation of all existing defense purchase contracts with Boeing, Lockheed and other American manufacturers. On Thursday the market sell-off continued. Individual investors had had enough. They deserted the market en masse. The question posed by that day's New York Times, "Will the little guys come roaring in, as in the past, to snap stocks at what look like bargains or will they get cold feet?" was finally being answered. They were fleeing. Just as there had been a mad scramble to buy technology stocks at any price, there was now a desperate scramble to sell at any price. They could not get out fast enough.

Alexandra came over to the trading room to talk with Colin Stewart.

"How are our put contracts doing?"

Stewart grinned. "Just great."

"I know that," she laughed happily. "Tell me what the price is."

"Well we did them at four or five different strike prices. I'd say on average we did about half at around the 2,195 level and the remaining at about 2,250. The S&P is right now let me see," he looked at the screen, "at 1,969.46. So the puts are deep in the money by about 225 to 280 points. They're worth a fortune. But the expiration date is two months away."

Around 1.00 P.M. Bloomberg reported that many Blue chip companies that included IBM, General Motors, Coca-Cola, Wal-Mart and Merck among others were initiating big stock buyback programs. In 1987 this positive news had sent the blue chips soaring. On Thursday its impact on the market was muted. For a while the Dow was up. It even managed to gain 173 points from its lows. But under the weight of sell orders by institutional, individual and foreign investors the market slid precipitously once again. It was in the grip of total panic. All sectors were going down, some more than others–cyclicals, retail, consumer durables, technology, computer software, health care, banks, semiconductors, Internet, anything that represented a share. The slaughter continued. At the close the Dow was down a whopping 1,660 points to close at 13,843.18.

"The faithful have lost all faith," Alexandra cheerfully told her group that evening.

At 4.30 P.M. Paul O'Neill, the Secretary of the Treasury, Stuart Elliott, the Secretary of State, Floyd Norris, the Secretary of Defense and Patrick Blackwell, the acting Chairman of the Federal Reserve met with the President in the Oval Office.

"Gentlemen, markets don't just collapse," Bush began. "There has to be some catalyst that starts a run. That's what I don't understand. Corporate earnings are at a high level, the Fed recently cut interest rates which are at near historic lows, inflation is nonexistent, there are no wars on the horizon and America stands at the pinnacle of its power. So what's happening?" He looked inquiringly at the Secretary of the Treasury.

"What you say is absolutely correct," O'Neill explained in his most professorial manner. "But the market is driven by investor psychology which can change in seconds for no apparent reason. In retrospect it appears that investors were jolted by the OPEC moves particularly the switch to euro pricing."

"Yes, but oil prices were much higher earlier this year," Bush interjected.

"Again you're correct Mr. President, except then the dollar was very strong," the Treasury Secretary remarked patiently. "This time, however, the market perceived that the move would weaken the dollar and lead to inflation as well as declining corporate earnings as oil prices rose. No one knows what's the right price of any stock. And as we all know from our budget forecasts." He smiled, "No one can really forecast corporate earnings for ten or fifteen years or for that matter for the next six months. So in the end it all boils down to one single word: confidence. And this week, unfortunately, investor psychology suddenly turned bearish."

"Mr. President to back up what the Treasury Secretary just said. As you well know my revered predecessor, Alan Greenspan warned again and again about market exuberance. In the stock market when confidence is lost, all is lost."

"So what can we do to restore confidence?" the President asked.

"We must keep the economy on an even keel and take steps to prevent a recession," O'Neill replied.

"That's right, Mr. President. The Fed has opened the discount window and pumped enormous amounts of liquidity into the system. Sensible monetary and fiscal policy can prevent a decline from turning into a recession. We know that from the experience in 1987," Blackwell observed.

503

"Well ladies and gentlemen," Bush said looking rather dejected. "The Presidential election will take place in little over two weeks. This could blow the whole thing apart for us. We need to figure out what other counter measures can be taken. How about lowering the interest rate?" he asked looking at Blackwell.

"I polled the Open Market Committee prior to coming here and the Fed spokesman is announcing another fifty basis point reduction in the Fed funds target rate and in the discount rate as we speak," Patrick Blackwell said.

"What about intervening in the currency market?" Stuart Elliott asked.

"We did some but unfortunately it didn't work. The market is much too large and we simply do not have the firepower to match the speculators. The dollar will recover once investors realize that the economy is on a sound footing and is continuing to grow."

"The current account deficit is a real problem," O'Neill spoke up. "Three hundred or for that matter two hundred billion dollar deficits are simply not sustainable. We've had this problem for over a decade. Manufacturing has moved overseas and Americans have a love affair with foreign cars and DVD's and consumer products. We need to do something about this."

"Do you think we should keep the dollar weak? It will encourage exports and discourage imports."

"No, Mr. President. That was tried in the Reagan era. In 1987 and it backfired. As you know, foreign investors have pulled most of their financial assets out of the United States in the past two days. We need a strong dollar to encourage the flow of foreign funds to the country," O'Neill explained.

"Stuart is there anything we can do to pressure the Saudis, the Venezuelans or the Mexicans?" Bush asked his Secretary of State.

"I'm afraid that does not look possible, Mr. President. I've been trying to get in touch with the leaders of these nations. But none of the three was available."

"Do you want me to try?" the President asked.

"I'm not sure it's going to help. All three are very strongly nationalistic and they're under strong pressure from their people to be firm. On the oil front the Mexicans might wilt but they alone can't do much," replied Stuart.

"What about the Germans? I'm certain they're mixed up in this," the Treasury Secretary expressed his concern to the President. In Washington it was an open secret that the Treasury man was upset at the Germans. With the third largest economy in the world that country had finally come out of its shell and in recent years had become increasingly vociferous, refusing to take it cue from the United States any longer. More recently the Germans had forced America to accept their nominee as the head of the IMF to the intense dismay of Paul O'Neill who wanted a heavyweight Italian politician in that job.

"I spoke with Schroeder," George Bush told the Secretary. "He denied any prior knowledge of OPEC's plan. Claimed they were as surprised as we were."

"What about the role of the German and French banks?"

"He said that was a purely commercial transaction. The Government was not involved. American banks often made similar loans."

"Mr. President I would like to make one other important point here," O'Neill, generally regarded as one of the smartest economists of his generation, went on. "Too many stupid experts have been saying that oil doesn't matter any more in the internet economy. Unfortunately we have found out this week that it's still important given all our gas-guzzling vehicles and ever-larger monster houses. However, the price of oil as long as it's not above $38 in itself does not present a problem to the United States. All other nations who compete and trade with us have to pay the same price. What we have to guard against is not paying more than the others. That would happen if the dollar were weak against the euro. Strengthening the dollar must remain our key goal."

"I think you're right there, Paul," Bush observed thoughtfully.

"Isn't this the right time to tap into the strategic oil reserve," the Secretary of State asked.

"That's only for an emergency such as war or an embargo," Bush replied. "Price increases are not covered in my judgment. Besides I think the Saudis will respond very negatively to such an action. They have told us that in the past."

"What's the situation with the banks?"

"Their share price has fallen much more than some of the other sectors. That should not be the case given the low interest rates, so the market expects that banks will have a lot of bad debts and credit difficulties. That's very likely. In fact it's definite knowing from past experience. But its not a problem right now and we'll deal with it when the time comes," Patrick Blackwell replied reassuringly.

"What's happening in the Middle East," the President then asked, turning to look at his Secretary of Defense.

"Like so many other developments, the Gulf Treaty Organization announcement caught us by surprise. The CIA was totally in the dark."

"Well that Agency has been slipping for several years. We need to do something there," Bush observed with considerable pique.

"In any event Mr. President, we cannot oppose this move on the part of the Gulf nations. In the long run it's beneficial for us. The problem it poses is the closer cooperation that is taking place among them as a result, particularly when it comes to setting oil prices," Floyd Norris, the Secretary of Defense spoke for the first time.

"I agree with that assessment," the Secretary of State

responded. "But relations between Iran and Saudi Arabia have improved independent of this, largely as a result of the rise of the reformist group in Iran. So one way or the other closer cooperation would have taken place."

"What about the defense contract cancellations?" Bush asked.

"Under the contracts, Mr. President," the Secretary of Defense observed, "They have the right to cancel the contracts with the payment of a ten percent penalty. Both Saudi Arabia and the UAE have stated that this penalty will be paid."

Half an hour later President Bush appeared at the White House Press room and spoke at length with reporters. He informed them of the actions that the administration was taking to keep the momentum going on the economic front through significantly increased money supply and lower interest rates. He assured the country that the economy was on a sound footing, the state of the banks remained strong and that he was asking Congress for emergency spending totaling a hundred billion dollars to take up any slackening in consumer spending. This was precisely the time to increase government spending as all economists recognized. The Federal Reserve had already loosened monetary policy and these steps, the President reiterated, would keep the economy growing at a healthy pace.

On Friday the market was more restrained. Some institutional buyers began to trickle in. Congress promised quick action on the President's emergency expenditure proposals. The encouraging news sent the Dow in to positive territory where it remained for much of the day with gains of up to 258 points. Selling in the last hour reduced the gains and the DJIA ended the day up 24.06 points.

It had been the worst week on record. The Dow lost a shade over 5,309 points to close at 13,867.24. That was 28% lower than its all time high of 19,176.65 at the beginning of the week. The S&P 500 fared even worse closing at 1,745.32.

507

That was a record drop of 747.62 points or 30% from its all time high of 2,492.94. Over the next six days the market continued on its roller coaster course but the ups and downs were less pronounced. Nevertheless the overall slide continued and at the end of Monday, November 1, the Dow closed at 10,769.76 having lost a further 3,098 points. It was down 44% from its all time high. The S&P lost another 374 points, finishing at 1,371.58. That was 45% lower than it was on October 15, 2004. The dollar/euro rate settled in a new trading range of 1.3012 to 1.3218. Interest rates were sharply lower with fed funds trading at 4.25 percent and the ten-year treasury notes yielding 4.65 percent.

Inevitably the economy seemed to be heading for a sharp slowdown if not a recession. After all the carnage had produced vast rivers of red ink. Seven trillion dollars in stock value had vanished into thin air. Gone. Disappeared. Wiped out. That was larger than the gross domestic product of Japan the second richest nation on earth. Not surprisingly investor confidence dropped sharply. They felt poorer and in fact they were poorer. The carnage had been unbelievable. It was almost a repeat of the twenties with hundreds of suicides. The list included several managers of well-known mutual funds and quite a few portfolio managers. Large numbers of individual investors had been wiped out. They had lost their entire financial assets including their houses. Day trading on the internet, which had been a popular fad, was obliterated. Most of its freewheeling practitioners were now paupers.

The New York Times article on November 5, described the aftermath of the crash:

"Losers dominated every group of investors. Mutual funds that once numbered six trillion dollars in assets at the height of the great bull market are now down to only three point one trillion thanks to the expertise of their professional money managers." The article's author, Kenneth Gilpin, was scathing in his comments.

"Some did better than others but ninety five percent performed worse than the broad market," the article continued. "Last year by over weighting technology stocks the funds had beaten the S&P index. Now they paid the opposite price. The same was true for investment advisory firms. Proud old partnerships such as B&P that once managed thirty billion in equity assets are now investing just half that amount. The Magellan Fund is down to sixty five billion dollars from a hundred and one billion. Pension funds and foundations as well as universities have lost huge amounts of capital in the crash."

"But the biggest loser of all is the little guy. That's what happened in 1929 and that's what has happened now. The secretaries, the taxi drivers, the shoeshine boys, the waiters and shop assistants, and of course the mid-level business executives have lost most of their savings. These are the men and women who yearned and believed so fervently in the American dream. That was what brought them to the market in such big numbers. Their deep and abiding faith buttressed by self serving advice of thousands of financial consultants and securities analysts had pushed them deeper and deeper and so they were the last to get in and, as usual, the last to get out. They are the ones who really got creamed. As always, they were the ultimate suckers."

"Have you heard how some of the other hedge funds have performed?" Victoria asked Alexandra on the phone after reading the Times article.

"I heard at the party I was at yesterday that the big losers include Jeff Vinnik, Omega Advisors, Tudor Management and Louis Bacon of Moore Capital Management."

Many of the other hedge funds proved to be no exception either and according to stories making the round at the high society party circuit, even that legendary investor, Warren Buffet, got caught in the debacle. Very few professionals came out with burnished reputations. But then few had ever beaten the market in its golden years either. It was par for the course.

The bears had warned of a catastrophe for years but no one had taken them seriously. They finally had their day in the sun.

But it was not doom and gloom for everyone. As often happens, many wealthy investors did well. In fact phenomenally well.

"According to the rumors I've heard the income of Soros' Quantum Fund exceeded thirty billion dollars and the Xenon Fund, run by Louis Marcus, has done even better," Victoria said.

"I guess we'll never know with absolute certainty what the actual results were since these funds don't report their profits," Alexandra replied.

Then she asked, "What about Pegasus Investments?"

"Apparently they've made a bundle on their investment in the Quantum funds and in an oil futures joint venture with Exxon and Texaco. But the real pile has come from their own speculative activities in the United States. Their gains here are over 34 ½ billion dollars."

These results were never made public either.

The Swiss banks did well also. The Commercial Bank of Switzerland managed to make slightly more than three billion dollars in currency trading and short sale of stocks. Credit Suisse and UBS made money by simply following the moves made by Pegasus Investments through their private banking divisions. Theoretically there was a Chinese wall between the bank and its investment management arm but no one remembered this particular provision when the interests of the bank were at stake. It was the most profitable year for the foreign exchange operations of the Deutsche Bank and HypoVereinsbank as far as anyone could remember. Exxon oil traders did remarkably well on oil futures; their gains totaled twenty-seven and a half billion dollars. Of course a fifth of the profits went to Texaco and the remainder were shared equally with Pegasus. Since the income was booked in several Liechtenstein entities it could be kept secret, giving the two oil giants the ability to window dress their future earnings.

That dinner at the Carlyle Hotel when Alexandra had seen Prince Tarik in the company of two Latin ministers and her hunch on what was going on also paid off handsomely. When all the put contracts were sold at the end of November and the currency, oil futures and bond positions squared off, the gains for Pericles Asset Management–Am Bank's joint venture partner–came to a grand total of $10,723,234,162. Successful money management, it has often been said, has more to do with luck and having the balls to take big positions at certain points in time when the spirit moves you, than with great intellectual brain power. Guts and instinct had finally paid off for Alexandra Middleton.

Like a devastating tornado the Great Crash of 2004 suddenly appeared and left in its wake widespread financial destruction, havoc and ruin.

The Golden Age was over.

3194-ISLA

EPILOGUE

Senator Bob Kerrey won the election on November 2, by an overwhelming margin, as the 44th president of the United States. He lost only two states–Texas and Vermont. The Democrats had a majority of 10 in the Senate and thirty four in the House of Representatives and a large number of new faces would soon be walking in the corridors of power in the nation's capital. In the face of the great economic disaster that had befallen them, the American electorate had sent a clear and unequivocal message to the politicians. It wanted quick and decisive action.

Prior to the crash, saving social security was the number one issue in the campaign followed by education and health care reform. Tax reductions were a distant fourth. This was no longer the case. The latest Gallup poll showed voters overwhelmingly wanted tax cuts. They had selected the party that, more than anything else, stood for and was identified with tax cuts, for that subject now occupied the minds of the people as nothing else. Support for social security had fallen and it was no longer considered an urgent issue. At the moment only one thing counted–tax cuts. The clamor grew louder in December.

3194-ISLA

"Tax cuts will be the top priority of my administration," the President-elect declared in a meeting with reporters at the family house in Phoenix, Arizona. "We will send our proposals to Congress in my first week in office."

In early December, the Dow bottomed out at 10,436.12 and trading settled in a narrow range at this level. The old bulls had all disappeared from the scene. Their crown princess, Abby Joseph Cohen, had chosen early retirement, having suddenly discovered the joys of life on the golf courses of South Carolina. Their place in the spotlight was taken over by the former bears who were currently in great demand as guests on CNBC and CNN. They were now enthusiastic about the market's prospects. Barton Biggs, Chairman of Morgan Stanley Dean Witter Asset Management, appeared that second Friday of December on Wall Street Week.

"I believe the market is fairly priced now," he said in response to a question from Louis Rukeyser. "From now on we should see the S&P 500 moving up from its current level of 1,327.71."

"What sort of returns do you expect in the future?"

"Historically there's a powerful tendency for returns to move toward the long-term averages. Periods of very high returns tend to be followed by periods of lower returns. Over the past fifty years prior to this year, the S&P has averaged a 13 percent annual return. In the past ten years, however, this figure increased to 18.3 percent. So my guess is that in the next several years we'll see returns in the 8 percent to 10 percent range."

In the following week the market showed signs of improvement as institutional investors and wealthy individuals slowly drifted back.

The nation did not go into a recession. At least that's what appeared to be the case at this time. Quick action by the Federal Reserve and the priming of the fiscal pump played a big role in preventing an economic decline on top of the market calamity. The bureaucrats had learned their lessons well from the events of 1929 and 1987. The much lower value of the dollar also helped; it made exports much cheaper giving America an advantage over the Japanese and the Europeans. The United States was still unchallenged as the only military superpower but its confidence was sapped and there was increasing evidence that its people and politicians were turning their attention inwards to domestic issues.

According to an immutable law of nature, history moves in a circle. This axiom was reconfirmed as the old continent of Europe, till very recently written off by the experts as decadent and arthritic, moved out of the shadow of America and reemerged as the major economic power in the world, a century after it had lost its supremacy to the United States. A new confidence took hold and it began acting more boldly and aggressively. Both Jospin and Schroeder, showing signs of this newly discovered self-assurance, moved in the first week of December to dismantle some of the rigid laws that throttled economic growth in their countries. The euro now rivaled the dollar as one of the two main reserve currencies and in fact became the stronger of the two.

So the tables had been turned. The twenty-first century, it now appeared, would be the European century. It would not be an American one. The reversal was both sudden and unexpected but unlike many other reversals, this one was universally welcomed around the world. The French showed one aspect of this attitude when huge crowds marched on the Champs Elysées to express their joy that McDonald's was now most unlikely to destroy the wonders of the French culinary experience.

Oil prices rose rapidly due to the sudden supply restrictions and stabilized around $36 a barrel. The new agreements held up remarkably well, lubricated by the hundred million dollars that each of the four men in Mexico and Venezuela now had stashed in secret numbered accounts in

515

Liechtenstein. An extremely cold winter helped to preserve the demand and keep supply and demand in balance.

With the approaching end of the current accounting year Rosenberg was left with no choice but to confess his losses to the partners. He did so at the regular meeting of B&P's Management Committee on December sixteen: the bank borrowings, the amount invested in options, the profit objective and the eight hundred and twenty million in gains until the market suddenly fell apart.

He concluded by saying, "I was trying to make all of you rich and came to within a hare's breath of succeeding."

The shocking news of the enormous loss left the members dazed and speechless.

Then Rosenberg got up from his chair. "I am resigning from the firm effective immediately." He put the letter on the conference room table and shuffled out of the room.

Don Kramer's suggestions were accepted; Rosenberg's resignation was kept secret. The other partners were quietly informed early next morning and asked to keep the information confidential. Word of the losses had to be kept from getting out on the street at all costs. It would be extremely detrimental for the firm. That same day Kramer got in touch with David Fairfax at CSFB.

At a meeting of senior officers in the auditorium on December 16, Henry Fielding announced that the Board, at his recommendation, had at it meeting earlier in the day selected Ms. Victoria Spencer as the next chief executive of Am Bank and she would assume her new position at the beginning of the new year.

"This is a proud and historic day for the corporation," Fielding said in his booming voice. "Victoria is the first woman CEO of a major American bank."

Three days later, the announcement of Ms. Victoria Spencer's forthcoming marriage to Mr. Timothy Wilkinson appeared in the New York Times. The bridegroom, a partner of Townsend Associates, was moving from London to the United States to take over as the chairman of the management consulting firm.

That same week Alexandra telephoned to congratulate Victoria on her appointment.

"It wouldn't have been possible without you," Victoria told her.

Then she continued, "I got a call from a David Fairfax at CSFB. Your old firm is up for sale again and the price tag is only eight hundred million dollars. He wants us to look at it."

"I wonder what's happening there."

"We'll find out sooner or later. By the way they have an outstanding loan of two hundred and seventy five million from a consortium of banks led by us."

"That can only mean they were using the money to speculate in the market and it hasn't worked out," Alexandra theorized.

"Very likely. Anyway now is the time to buy some money management firms so we can build the business rapidly. I told Fairfax that you'd be in touch."

"I think you're right about the timing. I'll give him a call."

Alexandra Middleton's share of the income from the hedge fund came to 322 million dollars. She was now richer than she had ever dreamed of. Yes, she had finally achieved her all-consuming goal and knew she'd never be poor again. Like Victoria, she too was getting married in February, once her divorce came through next month. Her children were away in England for Christmas with their father at Lord Bixworth's estate, so Alexandra decided to take a weeklong trip with Jack Carver to Florence. They caught an Alitalia flight from Kennedy the day after Christmas. An hour into the flight, as the plane flew seventy five miles northeast of Boston, the pilot radioed for permission to make an emergency landing at Boston's Logan airport. Air traffic control gave him immediate approval. Five minutes later the plane disappeared from the radar screen. The coast guard and the U.S. navy arrived at the scene an hour later to look for survivors. None were found after an exhaustive twenty four hour search by ships and helicopters.

The market crash made Tarik the world's richest man with total assets of over ninety billion dollars. The same amount that Bill Gates once had. But wealth meant nothing to him now and he was indifferent to it. He donated eighty six billion dollars of this amount to the Saudi Pension Fund that was established at the outset of his reign. It was the largest gift ever made. Everyone he had touched seemed to have become wealthy. His advisors had done well; so had the men whom he had bribed or seduced with loans or valuable information.

His dream now made him march to the music of a distant. drummer. It aimed at the transformation of Saudi Arabia into a model democratic society within the confines of Islam. Such a goal had never been accomplished in the Muslim world and he wanted to go down in history as the greatest of Islamic rulers.

So he was busy working on this goal, recognizing that it could only be accomplished gradually and incrementally. On his direct orders, all the petty rules and regulations that made life difficult for ordinary people were either relaxed or abolished in early December. He was moving on the most heroic venture of his life. It was a worthy challenge but the road would be a long and hazardous one. They say that the journey of a thousand miles begins with a single step. On that December day Tarik took the first steps on that long arduous journey into the future.

On the Saturday before Christmas, Rosenberg arrived at his apartment in Deer Valley. His affairs were now in order. Two weeks earlier he had transferred eighteen million dollars, which was all that remained of his liquid assets, to a secret account in Liechtenstein through his private bank account officer at Am Bank. He also amended his will, naming Ronald Shapiro as the sole beneficiary. An explanation for this gift was provided in the document. On Sunday morning the maid discovered his body hanging from a hook in the ceiling. A suicide note was found on the coffee table.

In his last meeting with Hillary just prior to his departure, a tired and defeated Rosenberg provided the final epitaph of the now lost golden age, paraphrasing the memorable words uttered by the British Foreign Secretary, Lord Grey, on the eve of the Great War, "The lamps are going out all over America; we shall not see them lit again in our lifetime."

3194-ISLA

Printed in the United States
4602